ETERNITY'S BATTLESHIP

STARSHIP OMEGA BOOK 2

MIRTH PUBLISHING

HIGH RIVER

SCOTT BARTLETT AND JOSHUA JAMES

ETERNITY'S BATTLESHIP

Copyright © 2024 BY Scott Bartlett and Joshua James

Cover art by: Tom Edwards (tomedwardsdesign.com)

Library and Archives Canada Cataloguing in Publication

Bartlett, Scott and James, Joshua

Eternity's Battleship (Large Print Edition) / Scott Bartlett and Joshua James ; illustrations by Tom Edwards

ISBN 978-1-988380-63-6

Contents

Chapter One

Captain Bill Henderson

Primeval tech could do incredible things. It could simulate reality in ways that would baffle even the Imperium's most advanced technicians. It could mimic sentience so effectively that, at times, it seemed truly alive. Under the right circumstances, it could even bring people back from the dead.

It could not, however, mask the stink of the hundreds of thousands of frightened people crammed into the vast ship's winding corridors.

Splat covered his nose and mouth with one hand, swallowing an audible gag. "It smells like the Port-a-Johns from basic. What are they doing down here?"

Captain Bill Henderson kept his hands folded behind him. Nothing would be enough to block the smell, which by now had permeated the air filters on this deck. Besides, he preferred to meet peoples' eyes. What would people think if the one responsible for their safety flinched away from them in disgust?

Some aboard the ship now called him a hero, but Bill had never felt less like one. In fact, he felt nothing at all. He was numb. He'd been numb ever since Val, his contact with Omega, had shut him out. Many credited him with saving what was left of humanity, but that would feel a lot better if he had any real confidence that he'd be able to keep them alive for the foreseeable future. They'd picked up supplies on Callisto when they raided the internment camps, but they were forced to ration calories since they had so many mouths to feed and no idea when they'd get another chance to restock. As for the sanitation, the less said about that, the better. At least the Primevals' fairly humanoid biology meant that their waste facilities were useful, but they weren't designed to accommodate this many people.

"Has Captain Stone been able to keep up with security?" he asked.

Splat grimaced and lowered his hand. "As much as anyone could. He's designated civilian officers, but...."

He trailed off, and Bill understood without having to be told. It was the same problem, just viewed from a different angle: too many people, not enough training, not enough resources, and no vetting whatsoever. They hadn't screened the people they'd brought aboard. Any records they could have retrieved were long gone, along with the infrastructure of Earth itself.

He wasn't aware of how hard he'd been frowning until he caught the eye of a little kid, who grinned and waved. The boy didn't seem bothered by the smell. He didn't seem frightened at all. He was crouched amid a group of his friends. They were playing some kind of game with mismatched items. Bill couldn't begin to guess what the rules might be, only that it was something that served no purpose beyond a pleasant way to pass the time.

They were alive because of him. Safe enough, for now.

Which meant there was hope for tomorrow, even if he couldn't see beyond that.

* * *

Miriam Henderson opened the hatch of the tiny room where she and her husband lived. It was barely a closet—even if Bill had felt justified in giving his parents preferential treatment, it simply wasn't an option. The cramped storage room was the best he could offer them, but from the way his mother smiled at him, it might as well have been the Presidential Suite of a five-star hotel.

"Hey, baby." Miriam put her hand on the back of his head and guided him down so that she could kiss his forehead. Splat snickered, and Bill shot him a warning look. The laugh quickly faded into a cough.

"Hey, Mom." Even in the cramped, filthy corridors of the lower decks, Bill could feel himself stepping into the role of the 'good son'. Usually, it happened when he'd visited his childhood home. Stepping through the hatch somehow stripped away the layers of responsibility and stoicism that came with his rank, like a pair of shoes he could kick off or a coat left hanging on a peg.

There could be no disengaging from his role now, not with so many eyes on him—not with a guard at his side. He straightened up and fell back into his at-ease posture.

"How is he?" he asked.

Miriam's smile remained fixed in place, but he noted that the tension never left her shoulders. "He's good. Aren't you, Gordon? You're doing well, isn't that right?"

Gordon Henderson sat on the far side of the closet, his face turned away from the light, muttering to himself under his breath. Bill couldn't make out his words. It was troubling, but no worse than before. Things hadn't been right with Gordon since they'd recovered him on Callisto.

"He's doing well," Miriam reiterated, as if repetition would make it so. "He's gained a little weight, too."

Bill ground his teeth together. Given the shortage of rations, most people on the ship were losing weight. If the restricted diet was putting meat on Gordon's bones, how badly must the Crendelen guards have been feeding their prisoners?

A rhetorical question, of course. Bill tried not to think about it. It was one of the many topics his subconscious mind strayed to during the fretful moments before sleep. More than once, he'd spent his whole off-shift lying in the darkness, running through the ever-growing list of subjects he'd prefer to avoid indefinitely.

"How about you, darling?" Miriam's hand landed on his forearm and startled his grim train of thought off its tracks. "Do you know what you're going to do next?"

Perhaps it was Bill's imagination, but he could have sworn that the people nearby leaned closer, holding their breath, waiting to hear how the hero was going to pull his next impossible win out of thin air.

I wish I knew.

He couldn't say that—not to her, not to any of them. At best, it might break their spirits. At worst, it could incite a rebellion.

"There are plans in place," he assured her. "But you know I can't tell you the details. Security—"

"I know." Miriam held up one hand. "I just keep thinking...Callisto wasn't the Imperium's only forced labor camp. There are other people who haven't been rescued."

"Where do you want me to put them, Mom?" Bill tilted his head back toward the overcrowded corridor. "We can't take on another rescue mission right now."

"I understand that. Of course I do." Miriam rubbed the tight knot between her eyebrows. "I just don't understand what humanity did to deserve this."

Bill could think of a few things. Most of the people crammed aboard the Omega had spent their lives eating synthetic food, plugged into digital fantasy worlds. It wasn't as though the Ornu made a secret of their abuses. They'd televised executions. Dissidents were sent away to camps, dehumanized, brutalized, murdered. Bill's own kill switch had been flipped at the whim of an Ornu officer. Humanity could have risen up. Sought justice. But they never did. Their complacency had nearly cost them the future of the species.

So, yeah, he had some critiques about the road humanity had chosen for itself. Out of respect for his mother, he kept them to himself.

"I'll take care of it, Mom. Leave it to me."

Miriam looked over her shoulder at her husband. "Right."

Bill knew what she was thinking: that she'd already have her hands full. It was remarkable, really, how much could go unspoken in a conversation without having to utter the words out loud.

Chapter Two

Corporal Bob 'Splat' Oriel

Splat followed the captain all the way back to his quarters.

"You want me to stand guard, sir?" he asked.

Captain Henderson shook his head. "No need. I trust the locks, and I'll spend my downtime here. I promise I won't go running off. You can tell Captain Stone I said that." He winked, but it was a half-hearted gesture at best. With that, he stepped into his cabin and let the hatch slide shut behind him.

Splat sighed and ran a hand down one side of his face. With that, he turned to find Captain Stone.

The control deck of Omega was one of the few parts of the ship that wasn't cramped and reeking. They couldn't risk letting any unvetted civilians inside. Tull and the surviving Roughbacks had taken over that aspect of security duty. Between the bridge itself, the re-purposed rooms now packed with the contents of Omega's armory, and the safety of the crew, it was too much of a risk.

With the captain safe in his cabin, he was officially off-duty. All he had to do was find Stone and let him know that the captain was safely stowed away in the privacy of his rack.

Despite the size of the ship, there weren't all that many places Stone could be. Splat found him a few hatches down in one of the old mess halls, which now held a large portion of the ship's supplies. There was only enough room for a few tables near the hatch. Not that it was much of a problem, given how few crewmembers they had left.

He slipped through the hatch and stopped cold when he found the rest of the Marine team waiting for him. He still hadn't gotten used to the fact that there were only six of them now. The table looked lopsided and incomplete with only Termite, Guns, Tubes, Funny Bone, and Captain Stone. As he took a shuffling step toward the table, he counted the row of cups laid out before them.

Eight. One each for Porker and Newbie.

"Ah," he said aloud, although none of his somber compatriots had addressed him yet. "It's a wake, then. I hope you didn't start without me."

"Nah." Guns picked absently at one thumbnail, her eyes unfocused and blank. "Captain says we can only have one drink each. Doesn't want us getting hammered and blabbing all of our secrets to the unwashed masses."

"They wash," Tubes retorted. "We've got 'em on a water ration, but the moisture collectors are—"

"They don't smell like it," Splat interrupted. Some days, he could take Tubes' technobabble. Lately, everyone's patience had to be rationed as closely as their supplies. "And it's not like any of us are minty fresh, you know?"

Al produced a liquor bottle from beneath his chair. There was already an inch or so of air between the top of the liquid and the neck of the bottle. By the time he poured them each a drink, the contents were half gone.

I wonder if that will be the last Scotch ever poured. It was a somber thought, but likely enough, with Earth ravaged and abandoned.

They each took a glass, leaving two in the middle of the table, and raised them in a toast.

"Here's hoping they're in a better place," Termite said.

Tubes lowered his head and closed his eyes. "To Newbie finding something like peace at last."

"To the fall of the Imperium," Funny Bone spat.

Splat sighed. "To Private Jen Lambert and Private Kenny Yates."

Al didn't speak at all. He drained his glass. It would have been nice to have him say something, even if it was only to offer hollow words of comfort. But there was nothing to say, and as the names of their dead comrades echoed off the bulkheads, it occurred to Splat that they, too were relics of the past, just like Scotch. After tonight, nobody would say their names.

How much longer before the rest of them, like their friends, were swallowed by history? How long until every last one of them existed exclusively in the past tense?

Until humanity slipped into the rearview mirror, along with the Primevals.

Al sat his cup down with a thump, and the pressure in the room shifted. Their period of mourning was done. "Six of us and half a dozen Roughbacks won't be enough to keep the peace," he announced. "We need to fill our ranks. Funny Bone, I want you to come up with a list of candidates from the people we've brought aboard. I want to know who we can trust on our next mission, and we need to start training with them. Otherwise, they'll just get themselves killed." He got to his feet.

"Yes, sir." Funny Bone rose as well. "Tubes, you're with me."

Termite was already following Stone through the hatch. With a groan, Tubes got to his feet and followed their sergeant into the passageway. Only Guns and Splat were left behind.

"You're off-shift?" Splat added.

"Yeah." Guns shuddered. "Longfield wanted to take a look at the ship's Archive, try and figure out if there's another way to talk to Omega. She was hoping there might be some writing down there the commander missed, but no dice." She shook her head. "This group of guys was following us around while we were searching...they didn't try anything, fortunately. I'd probably have started a brawl, if I thought Longfield could hold her own."

"What do you think they wanted?" he asked.

"Maybe they saw a couple of ladies going off on their own and thought we'd be easy pickings." Guns smirked and flexed; it was hard to imagine that anyone would take her for an easy mark. "But I think they wanted my gun."

Splat frowned at the thought, wondering if the civilians had an actual plan, or just a vague notion that they needed more power. No wonder Stone insisted that the captain have a guard on him at all times. The man wasn't stupid, just...deliberately optimistic in the face of all the evidence.

Splat yawned hugely. "I need a shower. I smell like the lower decks."

"Get used to it." Guns reached for the last two cups. "Captain Stone wants to put us on water rations, too. We're still not sure how the filtration and capture systems work, and we have no idea how long they'll need to last."

"Do you ever think—" Splat bit off his question. "Never mind."

Guns snorted. "Do I ever think that we signed our own death warrants when we brought all these people aboard? For sure, I think about it. But I'm not dead yet, so I might as well keep hoping that Captain Henderson will pull a miracle out of thin air. It could happen, you know. Remember that time he died?"

Splat laughed as he took the cup she held out to him.

Guns lifted her glass. "To Val getting over his squabble with Henderson and doing what he's supposed to do."

Splat could happily drink to that.

Chapter Three

Commander Bina Chakravarti

"I was hoping to find something." Ensign Longfield raked one hand through her pale bob. She wore a weary expression, and her posture was slumped. "I'm sorry, Commander. I know you were hoping for more information."

Bina shook her head and sat back in the uncomfortable chair. It had been designed with the Primevals in mind, and not human proportions and anatomy. She crossed her arms and tried not to let her own exhaustion show. "Not your fault, Ensign. It was a long shot, anyway."

Longfield turned her attention to the rest of the officers gathered at the table.

"I'd like to keep checking around the ship; there might be some information. Maybe on the Engineering levels?"

They were grasping at straws, and they all knew it. Nobody except Bina was willing to meet Bill's eyes. They all had their own reasons. Some of them blamed him for the severity of their predicament, the ship's refusal to connect with them, and the sheer number of survivors they'd allowed aboard. Others respected his motives, but knew by now that there was no plan in place for what to do next. Resentment and fear drove a wedge between them—and if the Officers were this unsettled, what must the civilians think?

Then there were the greater issues, the galactic issues, that existed outside the ship. It wasn't just the question of where humanity would live now, and it wasn't just the threat of the Ornu. Bina couldn't help thinking about that first mysterious signal they found.

Omega has awoken and awaits the worthy. The soulless are coming.

Who were the soulless the message referenced, exactly? When would they show up? And would anyone know what do to when they did?

One thing she knew for sure: they were sitting on a powder keg—this ship and the galaxy both—and with each passing day the fuse burned shorter.

Bill dragged the pad of his thumb over his bottom lip and stared up at the overhead, lost in thought. Bina knew better, and still she found herself holding her breath, wondering what he would say next. Maybe he had a solution up his sleeve after all. Maybe Val had come to him in the night.

"Bina," he asked slowly, "what do you think?"

Or maybe not.

She didn't have a magic pill that would fix their predicament, but she had been thinking about next steps.

"I think we can't afford to wait and lie low indefinitely," she said. "And we can't count on Val or Omega to come back online and tell us what to do. I think we need to follow through with our plan: make sail for the Terraco shipyard and get the ship upgraded with the SRJ drive." They'd discussed it a hundred times by now, and they kept circling back to the logistics of this point. The SRJ—or "surge"—drive would enable the Omega to make short-range jumps, which would prove an invaluable weapon. All they had to do was…go deeper into Ornu territory, leave themselves vulnerable to attack while the ship was repaired, and keep everyone aboard from panicking. Assuming, of course, that the surge drive worked, and that they could find anyone willing and able to install it.

"People won't be thrilled about heading back into Ornu space," Commander Hans Norder pointed out.

"Who cares what the people think?" Lieutenant Keating demanded. She thumped her fist on the table. "They agreed to come with us. They practically begged. If they don't like the plan, they can find another ride."

Norder clicked his tongue. "That's all well and good, in theory, but think about it. We're horribly outnumbered. Even if we explain that we're doing this to help them, all it takes is one person getting it into their heads that we're selling them out...maybe still following orders from the Imperium...." He raised his eyebrows significantly and waited for the rest of them to connect the dots.

"There'd be a riot," Longfield murmured.

"There would be a rebellion," Norder countered. "And who could blame them? We're low on supplies, people are getting impatient, and we'd be circling back into territory controlled by the same people who blew up our planet in the first place."

"Don't call them people," Keating spat.

Norder smirked. "At least we can agree on that."

"We don't have to convince our new passengers," Al said. He spoke softly, but the rest were quick to turn his way. "If the information comes from us, people will leap to their own conclusions. Question our motives. But if the information comes from their heads of state…"

"Oh." Norder sucked in a breath and drummed his fingers on the table. "True, we do have their politicians to back us up."

Keating's chuckle lacked all humor. "I'm not sure they're on our side, exactly. They haven't been entirely cooperative."

"But they owe us." Bina nodded. "And even if they don't know us well, they have a better sense of how much we have to lose if the Ornu catch us again."

"Which does raise another question." Bill rubbed his knuckles across his jawline absently. "Without Val to help us, how do we avoid getting caught by the Ornu?" He waited a few seconds, and then said, "That's a rhetorical question, by the way. I have an idea."

Bina suppressed a sigh of relief. So he does have some answers.

"We've already made a deal with the Roughbacks," he continued, "so maybe it's time we call that in. If we're going to leave Omega as a sitting duck while the upgrades are installed, we'll need cover. Maybe there's something we can offer the Roughbacks as trade."

"We don't have a lot to trade with," Bina warned.

"Commander, please." Bill waved his hand at their surroundings. "We have the only known functioning Primeval ship at our disposal."

"But no Val," Al pointed out.

This time, there was an edge to Bill's reply. "And who else knows that, exactly?"

That made everyone sit up a little straighter.

"I'm not suggesting that we lie to the Roughbacks," Bill went on. "But we've shown the Imperium what this ship can do. Right now, I'm sure they're scrambling to secure Lindinis against a retaliatory attack. Seems like the perfect time to find our footing and get out. Even without Val's assistance, we can hold our own in a fight. We should press our advantage."

"It's a big risk," Al said. "But you're right; the longer we sit, the more we'll burn through supplies. The Roughbacks might be able to help on that front as well."

"Are we in agreement, then?" Bill asked the table.

Keating and Longfield nodded enthusiastically. Bina caught Norder's eye, and he gave a silent, expressionless thumbs-up.

"Wonderful." Bill clapped his hands together. "Keating, Norder, I want the two of you on the bridge. See what intel you can gather from the databases about space traffic around our target shipyard. If you see any cause for concern, whatever you do, don't sound the alarm. We don't need a stampede on our hands. Bina, I want you and Longfield to start talking to the politicians. Don't tell them what the plan is, just that we have one, and that we'll pass it on when we feel that it's safe to do so. You know the drill."

Longfield nodded. "Understood, Captain."

"Al, you're with me." Bill rose, smoothly from the table. "Let's see what Tull can tell us."

They dispersed, with Bina and Longfield in the lead. Norder and Keating were already squabbling about something. Bina told herself not to worry, that the two of them would sort it out without intervention—but in reality, she simply didn't have the energy to involve herself in yet another spat.

"We should plan what we're going to say." Longfield sounded almost cheerful. Probably because she was back in her element of communications, with a clear directive and the beginnings of a plan in place. "Do you think we should call a conference, or…"

"One-on-one," Bina said. "We'll tell them to expect an announcement once plans are finalized. If we call them all together now, they'll want to know why we aren't telling them more. They'll gang up on us. For now, let them wonder if we've told other people more than we're telling them. Let them be just a little bit more suspicious of their allies. That way, they'll be more likely to look to Captain Henderson for answers, rather than working together to undermine him."

Longfield whistled. "Okay, now I see why the captain wanted you to handle this. No offense to Bill, but he doesn't exactly...you know...politics and diplomacy aren't quite his...." She grimaced. "You know what I mean."

"I think he'll fare better with Tull than with the heads of state," Bina agreed. "Roughbacks seem to be a bit more direct."

Longfield waited until they were long out of earshot before laying a hand on Bina's arm. "Speaking of being direct, there's something I wanted to ask you. Ridding's alive, but the captain hasn't invited him back into the fold. Any idea why?"

A chill raced over Bina's skin, and her knees locked. "I...think he's worried about Ridding's health. You've seen how shaken the survivors were by their time in the camps."

"I've talked to Ridding a few times. I know he had a hard time, but we could use all the help we can get, and we know he's opposed to the Imperium. Besides, he might know something that could help us."

Or something that could hurt us. Hurt me. Bina hadn't been able to ask Ridding how much he knew about his arrest, or who had sold him out to the Imperium. If he ever learned that she'd been re-sponsible, and he let it slip, it wouldn't be just the civilians out for blood. She'd promised to tell the crew what she'd done, but to do it now seemed...ill-ad-vised.

There were no easy answers, and no telling what spark would light the fuse and blow their whole mission—the future of humanity—into ruin.

Chapter Four

Former Signifier Nonus

Nonus was slumped in the corner of his cell, reading one of the books he'd been permitted and trying to think about anything, anything, outside of his current circumstances. It didn't help that the book in his hands was about the history of the Imperium, the glorious ascendance of Lindinis, and the Emperor's abrupt climb to power over the majority of known space.

Not so long ago, he would have devoured a book like this one. After all, he had been part of that legacy. He had been on the front lines of the Emperor's army, overseeing one of the most difficult captains, and subsequently one of the most important missions.

Until, that was, Pertinax stabbed him in the back and stole his glory. Now he was imprisoned, stripped of his rank, languishing in a small cell in the city for which he'd risked it all. The universe wasn't fair sometimes.

At least he was still being treated as an Ornu. The cell was small but private, the meals bland but edible, and he was allowed to keep books in the room with him, so long as they were titles cleared by the Imperium. Sharing a cell with a vassal species would have been humiliating. And if he'd been told to bunk with a human? Nonus might very well have started plucking off his own scales and stuffing them down his throat. He'd rather choke on his own hide than spend time near a filthy, smooth-skinned, hairy human ever again.

He was flipping distractedly through the pages of the book, not really seeing the words in front of him, when the door to his cell rattled. Nonus closed the book and set it on the table just as his mother swept in.

Another privilege reserved exclusively for Ornu prisoners: visitation rights. Of course, not all of his visitors were friendly, but at least this one was on his side.

"Nonus!" Livia reached out all four of her arms, placing two on his shoulders and cradling his face in the other pair. "My poor darling, what have they done to you?"

His cell didn't have a mirror—there were too many dangerous things one could do with broken glass—but as she prodded his damaged cheek with her thumb, he knew exactly what she was talking about. His last visitor had asked a lot of questions that Nonus couldn't answer, and when he'd protested the indignity of his treatment, the other Signifier had been...rough with him.

Nonus didn't like thinking about it. Each time he prodded that painful memory, he felt his head hitting the table all over again while his interrogator slammed him against the sturdy surface. He'd caught a glimpse of himself reflected in one of the windows as he was returned to his cell. Bruises were already blooming on his face, and the blood vessels in his right eye had burst, turning his usually golden eye an angry, sickening brown.

"It was nothing," he said. "An accident. I got up in the night and...fell."

Livia frowned. "How?"

"Too dark," he hedged. "Didn't see the table."

Livia gave him a long, searching look. It was still disorienting to make eye contact so freely. In the military, at least for those of lower rank who served off-world, Ornu invariably wore a standard-issue pair of reflective goggles. The goggles served several functions, but the one everyone talked about was that the Ornu hated looking vassal species in the eye. From behind their lenses, they could observe their lessers without being observed in turn.

Livia, however, could see right through him. The goggles wouldn't have helped. She was always the one pulling strings, issuing orders, earning him promotions and favors that even Nonus knew he hadn't earned. Usually, at the first sign of trouble, he complained to her.

Not this time. Even Livia couldn't make this disappear. His mess was too big to be scrubbed away with a well-placed word in the right ear.

"If you say so, darling." Livia settled into the only seat in the room. She folded one pair of arms over her belly and gestured with the other pair as she spoke. Her long ultramarine tail curled beneath her. Even in private, his mother tried to emulate the casual power exuded by someone well above her station.

Every time they spoke in person, Nonus was glad she was on his side.

"You know, if anyone lays their hands on you, I'll have their skin." Her eyes searched his, looking for something that he apparently didn't provide. "Maybe I could have your guard made into a coat of some kind. Or a wall hanging." She shot a nasty look at the locked door.

Her bravado soothed his nerves, but he knew it was mostly for show. The Emperor was personally invested in his fate now, and not in a flattering way. One need only flip through the pages of the book he'd been reading to see what had become of anyone else who'd failed to uphold the ideals of the Imperium.

"As I said," Nonus informed her, "I fell."

Livia hummed. "Philo will get this all sorted out soon. Clearly you cannot be held responsible for a disaster on this scale. The Council wants someone to blame, and they have chosen you. Justice will be restored in time. You will be given a chance to redeem yourself. Philo promised that you would be made an Imperator, and I will see it done."

"Of course." He bowed his head. "Thank you for your words of comfort, Mother. I look forward to proving my loyalty." Even as the words left his lips, he wasn't sure he meant them. He should have. The Imperium was everything, and Emperor Albus had once been his idol: a god and ruler wrapped into one. In the last few weeks, however, Nonus had seen that the Emperor was fallible, and that no matter how earnestly he served the will of the Council, everything could be snatched from him at a moment's notice.

Philo had tried to warn him about the nature of the game, but Nonus hadn't listened. Trapped in his little cell, he had nothing to do but think, and he didn't like his conclusions.

The door was yanked open from the outside, and a guard beckoned to Livia. "Time's up," he barked.

Livia's lips curled upward to reveal sharp teeth. "Already?"

"Visiting hours are over." The guard's bulk filled the door.

She flicked one hand at him. "Very well. We were done talking, anyway." She rose up and adjusted the fall of her elegant garments, made from green and gold beetleweave and ultra-thin material that was all the rage in Lindinis fashion circles. Of course she'd dressed well for a visit to a prison. Livia would, he suspected, rather die than bow her head to anyone but Emperor Albus himself.

She waved goodbye and winked as she departed. Nonus flinched at the unnecessary force with which the door was slammed behind her.

He was still standing there a few minutes later when the door was opened again. Another guard—a female this time—thrust a tray of food inside. Instead of placing it on the table, she left it on the floor, and dropped it with such force that the drink spilled and two of the dishes overturned and sent their contents skittering across the concrete.

"You dropped it," he said, as if she might not have noticed. As if it hadn't been intentional.

"Then eat off the floor," she sneered. "You can always get your revenge in the future, Imperator Nonus." She howled with laughter as she slammed the door again.

He didn't bother getting up to salvage what little remained of the meal. After

Livia's visit, he wasn't hungry anyway. Either he'd gotten better at reading his mother's emotions, or she was more anxious than she'd ever been before. For all her posturing, he'd seen the fear in her eyes. She was smart enough to know that he was likely beyond saving.

If she couldn't get him out of this mess, who could?

He dropped onto the little bunk, curled up into a tight ball, and closed his eyes. If he was lucky, he could at least dream of revenge. His dreams were the only thing the Imperium couldn't control.

His last conscious thought was of Bill Henderson's smug, pink, hairy face. Out of everyone in the universe, why did he have to be the one to cheat death?

Chapter Five

Captain Bill Henderson

Bill had thought the humans' sanitation problems on the lower decks were bad, which just went to show how little he knew about Roughback behavior. Things could have been so much worse.

In exchange for their guard services, the Roughbacks had taken over one of the passageways near the bridge, which had once been a bland and unassuming corridor lined with individual rooms. Omega's design was simple and smooth, and Bill had marveled over its beautiful simplicity more than once.

"What did they do?" Al asked as he eyed the corridor in dismay.

"Caves," Bill croaked. "They built caves."

It was probably best not to ask what exactly they'd used to do the building. The material that lined the bulkheads was hard-packed and moist, and suspiciously like dirt...although, how they'd managed to get dirt without leaving Omega ruled out the less disturbing possibilities.

At least it didn't stink. In fact, there was an almost pleasant, earthy aroma in the air, reminiscent of petrichor and moss.

Tull lumbered out of a nearby room and lifted a hand in greeting. "In here, Captain Henderson. We'll have some privacy."

Bill and Al picked their way across the earthen floor. At one point, Bill stumbled and pinwheeled his arm, saving himself from a fall by grabbing a protrusion on the wall. When it moved, he realized what it was: another Roughback, burrowed in the muck, with only its shell-like covering visible. All of its softer, more vulnerable appendages were safely tucked out of sight.

He spent the rest of the walk trying to decide whether he should be irritated that the Roughbacks had converted one of Omega's corridors into an alien ecosystem without telling him. In the name of diplomacy, he decided to let it slide.

"Is this typical of Roughback homes?" he asked, trying to sound more interested than disgusted.

Tull shrugged. "Not really, but it's the closest we could get without more resources."

"Supplies are stretched thin for everyone," Al said diplomatically.

"I wasn't complaining. We make do."

Bill fixed his eyes on Tull's broad, armored back. He had a feeling that if he met Al's gaze, one or both of them would start laughing like schoolboys, and they could kiss their diplomatic efforts goodbye.

"Have you remained in touch with the Roughback government?" Bill asked once they were seated. He would have sat in the muck, if he had to, but fortunately there were storage crates in the room Tull led them to that had escaped the fate of the bulkheads. They were just about the right height to serve as chairs.

"Some." Tull squatted on the floor in front of them and rested his elbows on his knees. "We've been careful, since Omega is more of a priority for the Imperium than ever. I'm sure they're trying to intercept every communication we send and receive."

"The Ornu engineers aren't the brightest," Al pointed out.

Tull turned his black eyes toward the Marine captain and cocked his head. "They don't need to be. They have all the other engineers under their thumbs. Every vassal species will do exactly what they're told—especially now, when the Ornu have made it clear that they will not tolerate dissent. Between your world and Armon..." The Roughback shook his head.

"But the Roughbacks will still help us, right?" Bill leaned forward on the edge of the crate. "Our agreement stands."

There were times when Tull's slow, steady movements and inhuman physique reminded Bill of the immense Galapagos tortoises he'd seen at the zoo when he was little. It was like he saved up all his rage and precision and speed for when he was in combat. He was moving even slower than usual, though, and he stared at Bill for a long time.

"Are you all right, Tull?" he asked, pitching his voice low in case the Roughback leader was ill and hadn't told his crew.

"I've lowered my metabolism," Tull explained.

Al frowned. "What does that mean? Are you malnourished? If you need more supplies, we can try to make them stretch."

And where exactly are those supplies going to come from? Bill wondered. The heat and ferocity of his momentary anger startled him. It wasn't Al's fault that they were in this position, after all, and if the Roughbacks needed a higher caloric ration in order to function, they'd find a way to make it work. They'd have to.

But Tull shook his head. "No. For the time being, we've all gone into...what's a good word...." He sighed and stretched his neck. "Not hibernation, but something like it. I don't know a better word in your language."

"Oh." Bill eyed the Roughback with renewed interest. He'd taken their similarities for granted, and put the issue of their differences aside, but he was starting to see that there was a lot he didn't understand about his unlikely allies.

"As for the alliance." Tull bobbed his head from side to side at the speed of cold molasses. "That prospect has inevitably become a lot less attractive, now that most of humanity has been destroyed."

Even Al winced at this blunt assessment of their circumstances.

"We still have Omega," Bill reminded him.

"True." Tull considered this for a long moment. "It probably is worth visiting them to ask directly. It will be harder for our leaders to refuse a request made in person."

And easier for them to try to steal Omega, if they decide to take a shot at acquiring a Primeval ship.

Bill took a page out of Tull's book and turned this problem over in his mind before answering. The Roughbacks could sell them out to the Imperium, of course, but given the ferocity with which they'd resisted Ornu rule, he thought it much more likely that they might attempt to lay claim to the ship for their own purposes. That was a risk, but there were always risks in any mission. Nothing ventured, nothing gained. Besides, they were short on alternatives.

"Any chance they'd be able to help us with supplies, too?" Al asked.

"We'd have to talk to them," Tull said. It was obvious that he wasn't going to make any more promises without consulting the Roughback leaders.

"And how would we go about that?" Bill asked. "Should we hail them directly, or wait for you to contact—"

"Captain!" Norder's voice echoed through the passage outside, somewhat muffled by the makeshift cave system. "Captain Henderson! Captain Stone, are you there?"

Bill and Al leapt to their feet as one and rushed into the passage. Norder had stopped at the mouth of the cavern and stared at the modifications in bewilderment. As Bill approached, the weapons officer poked the mud with one finger, sniffed it, and shuddered.

"What's the matter, Commander?" Al barked.

Norder dropped his hand to his side. "You said not to sound the alarm, Captain, but we have an emergency."

Bill's whole body tensed in anticipation of whatever bad news he was about to receive. "Has the Imperium caught up with us?" That was his worst fear, in part because he had no idea if their skeleton crew would be able to cover all of the controls without Val's help.

"No, sir, it's the civilians. They started a riot on Deck 3, and now we've got a group of angry people trying to break into the food stores—"

Bill didn't wait for him to finish. He was already racing down the corridor toward the bridge and cursing under his breath the whole way.

Chapter Six

Sergeant Shawn 'Funny Bone' Piker

Funny Bone and Tubes sat on the deck of the otherwise empty dining hall. They'd started at the table, but there simply wasn't enough room to sort through all of the notes they'd managed to gather in the last thirty-some hours. It had been Tubes' idea to move to the deck, and Funny Bone found it oddly comforting to be intentionally messy for once.

They had laid out a variety of small objects to recreate a passable model of the ship's lowest level—hence their transition to the larger surface area—and were planning out a possible training route through the ship. The Marines would need to do more than lift weights to stay in fighting shape, and they didn't exactly have a gym setup for maintenance workouts. On top of that, if they were going to train replacement crewmembers, they'd need space to work as a unit.

"What about..." Tubes scratched his chin. "Remember the Engineering room where Porker got stabbed?"

"Where we fought the Jackals." Funny Bone nodded. "Of course I remember." A little bubble of emotion rose in his chest at the mention of Porker, but he quickly smothered it.

"That area has been blocked off for security reasons, but we could train in there. Use the vertical space...."

Funny Bone nodded slowly. "We could. If we felt comfortable bringing new people into the Engineering levels."

"If they're training with us, we'll have to trust them with our lives."

"True." Funny Bone rested one elbow on his knee and propped his chin in his right hand.

"I get it—I'm not looking forward to training new guys any more than you are." Tubes had the grace to look sympathetic, even though Funny Bone would likely be the one to take on the majority of their training. In theory, that role should fall to Captain Stone, but he'd had his hands full lately. They were all stretched far too thin.

"It's not just the training." Funny Bone abandoned their makeshift layout of the ship and reached for his notes. "I'm not even sure who to recommend."

"Seriously?" Tubes peered over his shoulder at the chicken scratch he'd written out in his notebook; his tablet had died ages ago. Omega had a lot of fancy alien tech, but it lacked universal charging ports. "You don't have a single candidate?"

"Oh, I do." Funny Bone frowned at the paper. "But most of the people on this list have either served in the military or have loyalties with an existing government. How can I trust any of them to put aside their national interests and serve everyone on the ship? But if we don't recruit someone with armed service experience, they might not be up to par. Then again, I can train a recruit's body more easily than his mind, so...." He looked over his notes again.

"I hate the idea of starting over with green recruits. Especially in the middle of a mission." Tubes scowled at the paperwork.

"There's another problem." Funny Bone flipped a page. "Newbie will be easier to replace—"

Tubes jerked back.

"No disrespect meant." Funny Bone held up a calming hand. "I meant in terms of training. Porker was our medic, and we'll need to find someone else with medical training. Most of us can bandage a wound all right, but it's stupid to go on a mission without a corpsman."

The other man nodded in understanding. "Ideally, they both would have triage experience. We split into two fire teams often enough."

Funny Bone snorted. "I wonder if eight Marines is even sufficient anymore. We can't take on the Imperium with only eight people."

"We have the captain," Tubes reminded him. "And a Primeval ship."

"A ship that can't break atmo to go planetside. Even with Omega, how many times have we been the ones deployed to do the actual combat? We infiltrated the embassy, rescued the world's leaders...we're the ones who took Omega in the first place. And now we're expected to keep peace on board this ship? How are we meant to be in two places at once? On top of all that, we lost two of our exosuits, and have no replacements. If we only have two new recruits, they won't be able to keep up with us."

Tubes slumped beside him. "You paint a pretty bleak picture, Sarge."

"Look, I can sit here and whine all day, but the point is that we've got problems, and I can't just dump all of them in Captain Stone's lap. I want to be able to go to him with solutions, but any advice I give him is going to be reluctant at best." Funny Bone turned another page. "One way or another, we're going to have to break protocol. Sometimes I think all that Imperium brainwashing really did get to me. I'm so used to being told what to do. Used to a routine. But everything's changing, and it's happening so fast." He lifted one hand to pinch the bridge of his nose. A headache was building, the pressure sharp and hot behind his eyes. He needed a break. He needed enough sleep to leave him feeling fully rested. He needed a meal that filled him up, for once.

He wasn't going to get any of that in the foreseeable future. As always, he had to power through, but that was getting harder by the minute.

"We need more than a list," Tubes said. "And we won't be able to decide just by looking at them on paper."

The words rattled something loose in Funny Bone's brain. Captain Stone had asked for a pool of applicants to choose from. People lied on applications all the time—oversold their better qualities and undersold their flaws.

"You're right. We won't be able to get a sense of their temperaments without seeing them in action." He felt like the world had shifted slightly, and the beginnings of a solution had come into focus. "If we bring in a large pool of candidates for a physical test...get 'em trained up..."

"Whoever meshes with the team can fill our ranks," Tubes prompted.

"And the runners-up can be trained as peacekeepers on the ship." Funny Bone tapped his finger on the page. "We could assign them to patrol units, and make sure there are conflicting national interests represented in each unit, so they can't be controlled by the whims of a single state. Yeah, that could work."

Their mapping session quickly became a brainstorming session. For the first time in days, Funny Bone let his crushing worry slide away. He could see how it would all work.

So long as the world didn't go all to pot in the next few days, things might just turn out all right.

Chapter Seven

Captain Alden Stone

Al was in excellent shape, and he still couldn't keep pace with Bill. In all fairness, part of the problem sprang from the crush of people who filled the passages, screaming incoherently and fighting with one another as they pushed toward the entrance to the supply vaults. Bill was able to slip between them with relative ease, but Al's bulky suit made it difficult to squeeze through the crowd.

He considered pulling a weapon and demanding that they let him through, but he didn't like his odds. He'd rather face a team of Jackals alone in the jungle than try to fight this many unarmed human civilians at once. All the training in the quadrant couldn't make up for their sheer numbers, their unbridled fury, and most of all their recklessness. If he pulled a weapon, he'd better be prepared to use it.

But he'd be surrounded. He'd end up crushed in a dogpile if he turned the crowd against him. For now, they were disorganized. If they turned on him with single-minded intent, he'd be a dead man.

He let the weapon dangle at his side and took the slower but less deadly route. People didn't pay him much mind as he wormed his way through the crowd, fighting down a surge of something akin to claustrophobia.

And then, quite suddenly, he emerged into an open pocket near the hatch leading to the supplies. Guns, Termite, and a group of civilian police forces were holding the rioters off. The people at the front of the group were chanting and pumping their fists in the air, but despite the tense atmosphere, things hadn't turned ugly.

Yet.

He could tell it was only a matter of time before someone snapped and the whole situation went sideways.

"What's going on here?" Bill demanded.

Guns scowled at the crowd. "Isn't it obvious, Captain? People have organized to go after the supply chambers."

Al lifted one eyebrow and kept his back to the civilians when he said, "They don't look that organized to me."

"Maybe not." She jerked her chin at a small group of people near the front who seemed to be conferring amongst themselves. "But this was planned, sir. They've hit a couple of the supply rooms at the same time. Longfield and the commander have a group of vigilantes guarding another one, and Splat is consulting with the third group. We're lucky we held our ground. If we'd moved all our units to one place, we'd have lost the others."

Bill whistled. "But nobody's escalated to outright violence?"

"Not yet, but I think they're testing us." Guns didn't take her eyes off the little group, which seemed to be growing by the minute. "I get that people are hungry and desperate, but I don't like this. It feels...calculated."

Civilians wouldn't plan something like this on their own. For one thing, a tactical strike required some level of strategizing, which required someone to lay a foundation.

A crowd of thousands with no one at its head would be impulsive and direct. Instead, these people seemed to have staked out the leadership and barricaded the guards in a stalemate. It was as if they were waiting for something to happen, or for a new set of instructions to arrive.

They're waiting us out, Al realized. And it's going to work. I don't have enough men to replace the current defenders, but the crowd can just keep coming. If they get tired, they can rotate out. We don't have that luxury.

Once again, he was struck by the precariousness of their situation. The Ornu were hunting them from without, and now their own people were turning on them from within. Everything Al and his team were fighting to protect was on board Omega. The people were the mission, and now they were trying to sabotage their only hope of survival.

That realization enraged him like nothing else. What business did these people have, in pulling a stunt of this magnitude? Didn't they realize the crew was on their side? He was overcome by the urge to walk up to every man and woman in that corridor and shake them, one by one, until they came to their senses.

We are doing this for you! he wanted to scream. We've given everything we have for you. If you don't like it, why don't you try your luck in deep space? Or back on Earth, which the Ornu bombed into oblivion?

"Al?" Bill asked. His tone suggested that he'd tried to get his attention once already.

"Yeah?" He shook off his burst of anger and pulled himself back into focus. They were all on edge, and he wouldn't do their cause any favors if he snapped.

"I want to talk to Bina. Come on." Bill nodded his head in the direction of the next supply room. Between the winding layout of Omega's corridors, the concentric rings that made up its structure, and the press of the crowd, their destination was well out of sight. After so much time on the ship, however, Al knew where he was headed. He'd understood Omega on a fundamental level the first time he came aboard, and since his initial conversation with him, the ship had come to feel like home. He understood its layout in the same way he'd understood the back alleys and criss-crossing streets of the neighborhood where he'd grown up: deeply, intimately, and with a familiarity born of affection.

Omega was part of him, and these people were messing it up.

"Right. I'll go first this time. Stick close to me." Al took a step forward. "Bill, are you armed?"

The captain nodded once and made a subtle gesture toward an unseen object that bulged beneath the jacket of his uniform.

"Right. Come on, then." Al plunged into the crowd once more.

They seemed more reluctant to let him through this time, but nobody would meet his eye as he shouldered his way through the crush of bodies. They weren't ready to risk getting shot or arrested. Not yet. But eventually, the Marines' luck would run out. Something had to give.

If the crowd managed to take the food stores, then the team would withdraw to the bridge and bar everyone else from entry. They had enough supplies there to last them for months, at least. The civilians would likely run through their rations in a few weeks before turning on the crew once more. If they did...when they did...Al could ensure they held the bridge at all costs.

It was an ugly thought, but he couldn't stop himself from imagining the confrontation in gruesome, vivid detail. Omega would become a tomb. Humanity's last stand, defeated from within by its own hand.

The Imperium would get a kick out of that. Ornu poets would write songs about it.

His expression must have been frightening, because people were quicker to let him through when they saw his face. It only took him a few minutes to lead Bill to their destination.

Bina and Longfield had more company than he expected. In addition to civilian authorities, a group of people in military fatigues surrounded a man that Al vaguely recognized. He was one of the heads of state that they'd rescued from the Imperium prison, although Al didn't know his name. His light brown hair was close-cropped; he managed to remain well-groomed despite being stranded in space with limited supplies.

"Captain Henderson!" Longfield waved them both closer. "Perfect timing. This is

Prime Minister Oto Sever. He came here to make an offer."

Bill slipped past Al, but kept his hand behind his back rather than offering his palm to the man. "Is that so?"

The PM dipped his head in greeting. When he spoke, his English was heavily accented. He sounded Eastern European, but Al couldn't narrow it down beyond that.

"We have some equipment with us," he intoned. "We had the foresight to include some crowd control tools with our supplies. I am aware that you have weapons with which to arm your crew, but rather than opening fire, perhaps you might like to dispel the crowd without loss of life?"

Bill lifted his chin. "And you have a way to do that?"

"I do." The PM's smile was a touch too self-satisfied for Al's liking. "We had the foresight to bring some...less lethal methods aboard with us. This situation benefits no one. Perhaps these will help."

Sure, it'll help you ingratiate yourself to us and buy our trust, Al thought bitterly. All the same, he would rather be indebted to this stranger than deal with an outright riot.

Bill took a moment to answer. His eyes swept over Oto Sever before he inclined his head slightly to meet Bina's gaze. They did that thing they did, where neither of them said a word, but an understanding passed between them.

The captain nodded. "Al, Longfield, you're with me. Let's see what the Prime Minister has to offer."

Chapter Eight

Ensign Sally Longfield

The three of them stood before the Slovenian arsenal in stunned silence. Longfield bit the inside of her cheek to keep from saying something she might regret. Captain Henderson, standing to her left, had gone very quiet. He was as still as a rock.

Al, however, was vibrating with rage. He was trying to hide it, but it matched the fire that burned in Longfield's own chest. This was a monstrous amount of equipment, and it must have taken a great deal of effort to bring it all along. How much space had all of it taken on the shuttle? How many more people could have been rescued in the last moments before the Imperium scourged the face of the Earth?

Al cursed under his breath. "They ran for supplies, and they chose this?"

Longfield flinched. His words echoed her thoughts to some degree, but as always, Al was practical. If the PM and his party had brought MREs instead of crowd control....

"This is off." Al turned to Bill, who was taller enough than Longfield that the two men could make eye contact over her head. "It's not just me, right? There's something fishy here."

"I agree," Bill murmured. "But they're offering to let us use it, rather than turning it against us. And we don't have a lot of options at the moment."

Al shook his head, but he made no argument.

Not for the first time, Longfield was tempted to pinch herself, just to see if this was all a bad dream. Things had gone downhill so quickly, and so drastically, that she could hardly wrap her head around it all.

There truly was a staggering amount of equipment in the Slovenian cache. Sponge grenades, pepper balls, tear gas, dazzle guns, even some sort of shoulder-mounted cannon that bore a remarkable resemblance to the M234s favored by Marine teams, although they appeared to be made of lightweight plastics and had no ammo can to go with them.

"What are those?" she murmured, nodding to the latter.

Al glowered. "DEWs, I think. Directed energy weapons. If I'm not mistaken, this model was outlawed due to its known harmful effects on kids and the elderly. They're nonlethal, but...."

"I don't like the idea of using them on the people who are supposed to be under our protection," Bill added.

Before Longfield could ask anything else, the tramp of boots sounded from the corridor outside, and a swarm of civilians charged through the hatch. They were blocked by the Slovenian guards, but one of their leaders shouted, "We're police! We've got to talk to the captain. Now."

Bill turned to them, but it was Al who stepped forward and approached the rough-and-tumble militia. "What's going on?" he asked.

"The mob made a move on one of the supply chambers," the leader panted. He elbowed aside a Slovenian guard who had tried to physically restrain him. This time, the guard let him go. "It looks like they were trying to decide which one to hit."

Al cursed again. He spun toward the PM. "We'll take your equipment," he barked. "And we'll remember who provided it."

Oto Sever inclined his head with a polite, if somewhat stiff, smile. "We are, of course, happy to loan it to you." His emphasis on the word loan left no room for misunderstanding.

Longfield found herself shuffled out of the way as the civilian police swarmed forward, directed by Al to grab equipment seemingly at random. Longfield had been in a firefight before, but as the civilians streamed past her, she experienced a new flavor of fear. When the Tennyson had been deployed on a mission, even a mission that she found morally abhorrent, there had at least been a plan. She had known what she was supposed to do, and similarly understood the consequences of failure.

In this new world, following Captain Henderson's lead, there was no such order.

The rules were ill-defined. In many ways, that freedom was a good thing—something she'd longed for all her life. In the face of imminent violence between two factions of what should have been a unified front, however, Longfield trembled. Their enemy could be in their midst. There was, in fact, almost nothing that would help to differentiate friend from foe.

The goals of the opposition, too, were bewildering. If the civilians dug into their rations, they would temporarily alleviate their hunger, yes. But they'd also cut down the timeline before a dangerous emergency resupply run became necessary. Even worse, this riot could set a precedent and establish an ongoing conflict between the rescuers and the rescued. How much blood would have to be spilled to reestablish even a fragile sense of peace?

Suddenly Bill was at her side again, pressing a dazzle gun into her hand. "Come on, Ensign," he urged. "You're with us. We need all hands on deck."

She stumbled after him, swept along in the midst of the civilian police force as they surged down the passageways in a disorganized mass, shouting as they went.

Why should civilians trust us? she wondered. They put blind faith in the Imperium, too, and look how that turned out. She glanced down at her jacket just for a moment, painfully aware of the insignia still stitched to the breast.

At the earliest opportunity, she was going to tear the thing off.

Chapter Nine

Lance Corporal Rhonda 'Guns' Penney

Guns dug in her heels and roared as the crowd pushed forward. They'd procured metal sheets from somewhere—she hoped they hadn't stripped them from Omega itself, although she thought it more likely they'd been scavenged from a transport ship.

Tactics and strategy weren't her strong suit, but she was pretty sure that whoever had mobilized these rioters had been thinking of Greek hoplites when they came up with this plan. They'd formed a wall of the metal sheets and were using them as shields as they pushed forward.

Guns had her feet braced against the metal deck and was pushing right back.

At her side, Termite was doing the same. She wished she could say likewise for the civilian police at their side. They seemed disinclined to resist.

"Guns," Termite moaned. The soles of his boots left black streaks on the deck as he lost ground.

"Hold on," she grunted back. "Captain Stone will think of something, and—"

"Guns," he said again, more urgently, and she realized that he wasn't saying her name or referring to her arm muscles. His eyes were fixed behind her. When she turned, she saw one of the civilian police lift his rifle to his shoulder.

"Put that down!" she snarled. She stopped trying to push back against the makeshift shields and lunged forward to swipe the weapon out of the man's hand.

He tried to snatch it back. "If they keep this up, they'll crush us against the wall!" he snapped.

She glanced back. Sure enough, there were only a few feet between the crowd before them and the outer bulkhead of the storage bay behind them.

"And what do you think is going to happen if you start shooting?" she demanded. "If you kill someone, we'll be trampled in the aftermath."

Never mind that they were on a ship in deep space. Never mind that any damage to the life support systems or the hull's integrity would be a disaster. The moment blood was spilled, everything would change...not just for the moment, but forever.

She yanked the weapon fully out of his gasp and raised her voice. "These are our people, idiot!" She pointed to the wall of sheet metal. "I don't know if you got the memo, but Earth is done. We're on the same team, and I'm not going to stand here and watch the only survivors of our species shoot each other!"

Maybe it was her imagination, but Guns thought there was a new hesitation on the far side of the metal barrier. The crowd hadn't stepped back, but they'd made no progress, and nobody was in any more danger of being crushed than they'd been a few moments ago.

The man didn't reach for his gun again, but he didn't seem convinced. "If they dig through our supplies, we'll all end up dead."

"I get that," she told him, still keeping her voice raised. "But if we start shooting, someone's going to die, too. And good luck claiming the moral high ground if we draw first blood."

No, she definitely wasn't imagining it...the line of aggressors had begun to retreat. Judging by the sounds echoing out of the corridors, though, she wasn't sure she could take credit for the mob's withdrawal. The metal sheets wavered and wobbled, and were eventually cast aside as the crowd turned to face a new onslaught from behind.

She smelled the sting of the pepper bombs first. It was accompanied by a periodic thrum, like the basso beat of a subwoofer, but without the accompanying sound. It moved through her chest like a second heartbeat.

The mob had begun to scatter, and Guns rushed to pick up one of the sheet-metal panels, using it the same way the crowd had, except that now she was pushing them back. Termite saw what she was doing and rushed to help. Soon, their ragtag police force joined in. She saw the man she'd squabbled with flinch when he cut his hand on the knife-sharp edge of one panel, but he lifted it on the second try and followed her lead, despite the blood that ran down his wrist.

Good, she thought. They can be taught.

Maybe it would be a good thing after all to have some new blood on the Marine team—who hadn't been subjected to the brainwashing of Ornu bootcamps. Of course, everyone had been brainwashed to some extent, but the Imperium dedicated its greatest cruelty to its vassal soldiers when it taught them to override every moral instinct that would have driven them to resist. New recruits would have a lot less to unlearn.

Maybe now, they could find a new way of doing things.

Her sense of hope and satisfaction was shattered by a scream. She twisted to one side, breaking the line just for a moment, to see a man lying curled up on the ground in the corner of the passage. Three people, two men and a woman, were standing over him, striking him with their fists and boots.

She couldn't tell who was who. Was he with the volunteer militia? Were they? Or were all of them members of the mob, fighting over something else entirely?

It didn't matter. Whichever 'side' the man was on was her side, too. They were all supposed to be working together. If he'd known that the crowd would be this much trouble, maybe Captain Henderson would have been a bit more discerning when he brought these people aboard.

And those he turned away would be already dead. That knowledge sat like a cold stone in her belly, and suddenly, she discovered that she was angry. No, she was furious. Maybe the Ornu had been right about their species after all, when they claimed humans were little more than feral animals.

With a roar, she charged forward and put herself—and her shield—between the man and his attackers. She pushed them back until he was able to scramble to his feet, one arm wrapped across his chest as he tried to catch his breath.

"Get out of here!" she snarled. She didn't care where he went, so long as he wasn't her problem anymore. He nodded once, sending a lock of lank, unwashed hair into his eyes, and fled.

Something popped against the far side of her shield. Were those idiots trying to punch her through the metal?

Two more sharp pops convinced her that something else was going on. She looked to Termite, uncertain what to make of the impacts, and unwilling to expose herself to an attack in the name of finding out. To her relief, he grinned and gave her a thumbs-up, then pointed to what looked like a tennis ball that rolled past her feet. It was small, like the ones people bought for their silly little dogs that couldn't open their pint-sized jaws enough to grab the real thing.

She peeked around her shield and breathed a sigh of relief when she saw Al, Bill, and a few dozen members of the civilian militia dispersing the crowd. Al was holding something that looked like a NERF gun, but the grown-up version. As she watched, he fired on a member of the crowd who was trying to hold his ground. The man grunted and stumbled back as one of the rubber balls caught him in the shoulder. Judging by the distress in his expression, that was going to leave a bruise, especially given the close quarters, but it would be better than getting hit with a bullet.

The crowd, which had been assembled for over an hour, took less than five minutes to disperse. Soon, the only people left in their immediate vicinity were the Marines, the crew, the militia...and the casualties.

Guns rushed to the side of a woman, who was lying limp-limbed with her head twisted to one side. She was bleeding from somewhere on her back, and Guns was afraid to turn her over in case something was broken. To her relief, the woman was still breathing, but she couldn't be left to fend for herself.

Al's knee hit the deck beside hers. Together, they rolled the woman onto her side, and Al hissed.

"She got hit with a pepper bomb," he said. "I told them not to fire directly into the crowd."

There was plastic shrapnel embedded in the woman's back, and a nasty rash covered the area around her open wounds. That was going to hurt when she woke up...if she woke up. Whatever was in those bombs wasn't designed to enter peoples' bloodstreams.

Guns curled her hands into fists. "Is she...?"

"We'll take her to the medbay," Al barked. He didn't say what she was thinking: that Omega was no longer helping them in the way that it had before, and that even though Primeval tech was powerful enough to bring a man back from the dead, there was no guarantee that they could operate it without help from Val.

"I'll carry her," Guns told him.

She phrased it like an offer, but it was a coward's move. She wanted to get out of there, to be somewhere else. Anywhere else. The militias might have handled the crowd in the short term, but she could feel in her bones that it was far from over. Every step they'd taken in the last few weeks seemed to get them further and further down the wrong path.

Mercifully, Al let her go. She scooped the woman into her arms and set off for the medbay, hoping fervently that nobody from the dispersed crowd got it into their heads to jump her along the way.

Chapter Ten

Captain Bill Henderson

The hatch to the little closet where his parents had taken up residence was closed when Bill arrived. For one terrible, heart-stopping moment, he was convinced that they'd been attacked. When he thumped his fist against the hatch, the sound was muffled, as if a body lay slumped against the other side.

"Mom?" he called. Please, let them be okay. Please....

If that hatch opened and his parents weren't on the other side, he was going to crack in two.

There was a thump on the other side. "Billy?" his mother's voice asked.

He slumped sideways and caught himself against the bulkhead. Thank you. "Yes, Mom. It's me."

The hatch opened, and Bill nearly gagged on the smell that wafted out. It wasn't just sweat and unwashed bodies this time. There was something worse, low and foul and rotten, mixed with the sour smell of old urine.

Miriam pulled him into a hug, but he couldn't make his arms work enough to hug her back. He was too busy staring in open-mouthed horror at the scene behind her.

Perhaps twenty people were wedged into that tiny space, most of them men, all of them sallow and thin. He was used to seeing people with prominent cheekbones and bags beneath their eyes; everyone aboard Omega was feeling the effects of short rations these days. There was something different about these people, though, an emptiness that spoke of more than simple hunger.

"Who are they?" he asked.

"Oh." Miriam pulled away and turned back toward the hatch. "It's some of the other prisoners. From Callisto, you remember. Some people came around and were telling the rest what to do, and everyone went off. These were left behind. And they were scared, Billy, so scared, it was horrible. The worst part is—" She pressed a hand to her mouth and dropped her voice to a low, horrified whisper. "The worst part was the fits. I don't know what happened, but one of them started screaming. I thought it was just a panic attack, but it was so much worse." She leaned against him, and even though he'd been on the brink of collapse only moments before, he stayed strong for her. She pressed her cheek to his shoulder and closed her eyes. "I tried to help him, but it was too late."

"Too late?" Bill asked. "For what? What do you mean?"

"He died," Miriam whispered. "A few of the others began to panic then. I tried to get them calmed down, but they were convinced that the Ornu had flipped his switch, and they started sobbing. Like little children, Billy. Sobbing and clawing at the walls, at each other, at their own flesh, just here." She pointed to her own collarbone, where the kill switches were implanted in military personnel and any other humans who worked closely with the Ornu.

"But—"

"I know it isn't possible." Miriam let out a long sigh. "I know the switches are gone. I tried to tell them that—that it was something else. Malnutrition, maybe. Or an injury he'd sustained in the camps that went untreated. It took them a long time, but they settled. As for the other one, I don't know what happened. She was quiet. Didn't make a sound. One minute she was sitting in the corner, and the next she was...."

"Two people died?" Bill said. "In here?"

"We moved her out." Miriam gestured vaguely to the passage. "Your father and me. I don't know what's become of her, but she weighed nothing, Billy. Nothing at all."

"I'm sorry, Mom." He wrapped her in a hug and breathed deeply. For most of his life, she had smelled the same: the synthetic floral aroma of her old shampoo mixed with the bright lemon of her favorite dish soap, along with some lingering sweetness of whatever she'd last baked. After being stuck in that cramped little room, though, that familiar smell was gone. She smelled like close quarters and too many days spent in deep space, under artificial lights, away from the sun.

A sun they'd long since left behind. It struck him afresh that nothing would ever be as it had been. He had to believe that things would get better, but even if they did, some things could never be reclaimed. One of these days, he would knock on this hatch and find her, bird-boned and hollowed out, having passed as silently as the woman who'd died here only hours before.

Unless they could get their hands on the SRJ drive.

He'd been a fool to go against Val's advice. At the time, he'd been so sure he was right, but as usual he'd underestimated the complexity of the situation. He was built for tactical combat, and had grown too complacent with taking risks and counting on his good fortune to see him through. He'd thought himself invincible, especially after cheating death. Now, the last remnants of humanity were counting on him. He was wasting time they didn't have.

Bill released his mother, and was about to take his newfound resolve up to the bridge so that he could contact Tull's superiors, when a reedy voice called, "Billy? Is that you?"

Gordon was still crouched in the claustrophobic little room, but he'd lifted his head and was staring at the pair of them with unclouded eyes. He reached out a trembling hand, and Bill knelt beside him to grasp it.

"There you are, Billy." Gordon's fingers were nearly skeletal, but he clutched Bill's fingers with astonishing strength. "There you are. I was looking for you."

Bill squeezed back. "I'm right here, Dad. I'm right here."

Gordon opened his mouth, as if he was going to say something more, but nothing came. He stared for a long moment, searching Bill's face as the light left his eyes. He let out a choked sob and yanked his hand away.

"Oh, Gordon." Miriam, too, dropped to her knees. The rest of the Callisto survivors watched with vacant interest as she stroked his thin, matted hair with loving fingers. "It's okay, Gordon. Billy's here. I'm here, too."

Gordon curled his knees even tighter to his chest and buried his face in his hands. He sobbed uncontrollably, but when Bill tried to touch his shoulder he flinched away with a yelp, as if he'd been burned.

He was still crying when Bill left. It made him feel like dirt to depart with his father in that state, but there was work to be done, and no comfort he could offer would make things right. He told himself that it was for the best. That his best move was to find them someplace safe, where the danger of starvation would no longer weigh on them with each passing day. A world with clean air and abundant water and enough room for them all.

And he hoped with all his heart that such a place existed, because otherwise, all of this suffering would be for nothing.

Chapter Eleven

Sergeant Shawn 'Funny Bone' Piker

He should have been relieved to get so many applicants. He should have been delighted at how smoothly the first day of training had gone.

In reality, he was neither. Any relief was diluted by the specter of the riots. If people had swarmed them at random, Funny Bone could have passed off the whole incident as an impulse decision fueled by hunger and despair.

But the organized nature of the events was what truly disturbed him. It spoke of planning and consideration. It spoke, in other words, of an organized attempt to undermine Captain Henderson.

He had to wonder where it was coming from, given that humanity had languished under the thumb of the Imperium for the better part of three generations. How come the survivors had finally grown a spine?

Because they're not afraid of Captain Henderson. They think him weaker than the Ornu.

The frustrating part was, they were probably right.

He watched with a critical eye as Tubes and Termite led the hopeful recruits in a series of drills. Termite had his team drilling on the stairs, running at a steady pace up the right side and down the left in a perpetual loop. Tubes was making his team run laps around the Engineering deck, weaving through the walkways and stopping every two minutes to do burpees.

"Does anyone stand out to you?" Bina technically wasn't part of this exercise, but she'd been lingering at Funny Bone's elbow for ten minutes or so, watching the proceedings with undisguised interest.

"Her." He pointed to a woman whose long black hair was tied up from her neck. The group was taking the stairs at a fixed pace, but he could tell from her posture that she had no trouble keeping up, unlike some of the others who were red-faced and sweating. She had a startlingly pretty face, but she was light on her feet, and she'd done well during target practice the day before. They'd used the crowd control guns that fired rubber rounds, of course. He wasn't ready to trust any of them with real ammunition. "Jana Nemec. She's...Czech, I think?"

Bina hummed. "She's small."

Funny Bone arched an eyebrow at her.

The XO smirked. "And young."

Funny Bone couldn't resist a laugh. "Since when is that a bad thing?"

"Never said it was. But how much experience can she have?"

"I've got bad news for you." He gestured to the crowd. "They all look young. For one thing, we're old. And for the other…all our peers are dead. The Ornu saw to that." Between the kill switches and the self-destruct mechanisms built into Imperium warships manned by human crews, anyone they might have known from their old academy days was long since gone.

Bina's smile faded. She cupped her hands around her mouth and closed her eyes. "Yeah," she murmured. "Yeah, of course."

He should probably have tried to soften the blow, but it was too late now. "So, let's see. There's Nemec, and then those two fellows there. Waleed Awad and Kan Song-Jin. Except, Awad's Egyptian, and

Kan's Korean, and I don't know if they'll be willing to work together after that shipping issue a few years back...maybe they don't care, but their governments might. At least, what's left of them. And that fellow there, Angelo Christiano, he's an excellent marksman but he's never worked with a cohesive team."

Funny Bone groaned and dropped his head into his hands, trying to smooth away the tension from the muscles of his face. Unsurprisingly, it didn't work. "And Nemec's not a medic," he continued, "so if we take her, I'll probably have to take at least four of them to keep our numbers even, since Al wants two corpsmen, and Awad's the only one with field training. But the most experienced doctor who applied is that fellow there with the shaved head, and...." He made a helpless gesture at the man in question, who at that very moment tripped on his way down the steps and took two other trainees with him to the deck below.

"Huh." Bina rubbed her jaw, watching as others rushed to help. "Well, if you can't use him on missions, I'm sure we can find another place for him. So long as his clearances check out."

"And how am I supposed to check those, exactly?" Funny Bone demanded.

Bina didn't have an answer, because there wasn't one.

Termite and Tubes both signaled to him. He nodded and strode forward, bellowing as he went. "All right, that's enough for the morning. Grab your things and line up against the far bulkhead. We're going to conduct in-person interviews before you leave."

The doctor who'd tripped sighed gloomily and hobbled after the others. Most of them looked relieved to be done for the moment, except for Nemec, who was already joking with one of the other women who'd applied.

They'd piled their things by the hatch to the Engineering bay: water bottles, rucksacks, and whatever other possessions they'd brought along with them. The amount of things they toted around had puzzled Funny Bone the day before, until he realized that for many of them, everything they owned was in those bags. Their belongings could hardly be left unattended for hours on end, or they'd surely be taken by the other refugees.

"At least you have a few worth keeping around," Bina said. "It's better to have options, isn't it?"

Not if I make the wrong choice.

It was a bleak thought, but it weighed heavily on him, and there was no way to know for sure until it was too late. If he welcomed a traitor into their midst, he might as well shoot his team in the back with his own rifle.

The recruits seemed to be thinking the same thing. As they dug out the bottles they used to hold their water rations, most of them were silent. Surly looks passed between them, but very few words were exchanged. Nemec was the only one smiling as she took her first swig.

"If you can narrow down your list to ideal candidates, I can ask Longfield to take a look," Bina suggested. "She might be able to tap into whatever records are left, at least on the Ornu's end."

"Excellent." Funny Bone waved Tubes and Termite over to him, producing the list of candidates as they drew near. "We'll split up for now," he told them. "Interview the candidates one at a time and see who we can weed out today. Bina, can you think of anything specific we ought to ask beyond this?" He showed her the list of questions he and Tubes had mocked up earlier. They spent a few minutes looking things over while the candidates cooled down.

"Do you want my help?" Bina asked. "I could talk to a few, at least, unless you'd prefer to keep this process within your team."

"No, that would be helpful. At this stage—"

A scream made all four of them whip around. The woman Nemec had been chatting with only a few minutes earlier was shrieking at the top of her lungs in a language Funny Bone didn't know. It didn't take a genius, however, to see what had set her off.

Jana Nemec had fallen to the ground. Her half-empty water bottle lay at her side, the contents spreading in a pool beneath her as her body twitched and spasmed. Her eyes rolled back in her head, bulging from their sockets, and her face was a dark purple. Nemec's heels drummed against the deck, and a terrible, guttural sound was wrenched from her throat.

Funny Bone rushed to her, but the doctor who'd fallen got there first.

"What's going on?" Funny Bone snapped.

"I don't know for sure." The man looked up at him with a panic-stricken expression. What was his name, anyway? Avilay? Avilos? He was Puerto Rican, Funny Bone remembered that much. "But if I had to guess...."

"Well?" Funny Bone resisted the urge to grab the man by the shoulders and shake him. "What is it? Help her!"

Nemec gasped again. Her twitching grew more frantic.

"I can't. Not without taking her to the medbay." The doctor sucked in a breath. "I think she's been poisoned."

Chapter Twelve

Petty Officer Mike 'Tubes' Lamprey

Dr. Aviles hovered over Nemec's pod. The young woman lay prostrate with her eyes closed. Her chest still rose and fell; except for that, Tubes would have thought she was dead. Her pale skin, formerly flushed with exertion from their training exercises, was almost gray.

"These pods are remarkable," Aviles observed to nobody in particular. "I've never encountered diagnostic systems like these." There was no joy in his voice, just a matter-of-factness that made Tubes look him over again.

"You have field training, right?" he said.

Aviles shook himself slightly and lifted his chin. "Me? Oh, yes. With a volunteer corps."

Tubes did a double-take. "Really?" He didn't bother trying to hide his surprise. Medical volunteers had never had it easy, but under the rule of the Imperium, it was an even greater risk. They tended to operate in remote or troubled areas, especially in places where the Ornu saw no benefit to keeping people alive...or, in some cases, actively wished them harm.

Aviles was soft, and had trouble keeping up with the younger recruits. Tubes had assumed he'd spent most of his time working a cushy, well-paid hospital posting for the majority of his career. But with experience like his, he must be tougher than he looked.

"Why would you want to serve with us?" Funny Bone eyed the medic up and down mistrustfully. "I would think you've seen more than your fair share of danger."

"I've seen suffering you can't even imagine." As before, Aviles' voice was cool and direct. "I want to make things better for as many people as I can. If all of us did that, we'd be much better off as a species."

Funny Bone arched one eyebrow and caught Tubes' eye. Of course they could imagine the kind of horrors Aviles was referencing. More than once, they'd been the cause of them.

"Ah, look." Aviles bustled over to the side of the pod, where a new readout glowed. The message appeared to be in English, but when Tubes squinted at it, the letters swam and blurred into an absence of meaning. Primevals wouldn't have used English, so either the readout had some sort of universal translator function, or the AIs hadn't abandoned them completely.

The thought sparked a little flame of hope in Tubes' chest, which was instantly smothered by Aviles' next words.

"I was right. She was poisoned." The medic tapped the readout. "Strychnine."

"What?" Funny Bone surged forward. "How?"

Aviles ran his hands through his short hair, making it stand up in every direction. "She must have ingested it. Strychnine is relatively fast-acting. We were exercising, so it couldn't have been with breakfast."

"Her water bottle." Funny Bone punched his fist against his open palm. "They were all guzzling from their water bottles throughout the entire training session."

Aviles pressed a hand to his chest, and his warm complexion turned ashen.

Tubes was about to ask how she could have failed to notice something wrong with her water, but that answer, at least, was obvious. The recycled water already had a strange taste, and once it had been dispensed into canisters, then poured into bottles, it always tasted at least a little off.

Funny Bone had a better question. "How come she was the only one affected? Could she be more sensitive to it than the rest of us?"

Aviles shook his head. "There's too much in her system for it to have been a trace contaminant in the water supply."

"So she was targeted," Funny Bone said. "And whoever did it either put rat poison in her water bottle before she arrived for training, or they did it while we were all in the same room."

Tubes felt his knees turn to jelly. Aviles, who was quickly proving just how unflappable a medic could be, only nodded. "Exactly."

Funny Bone closed his eyes, wincing.

"There's one bit of good news." Aviles laid a hand over the top of Nemec's medical pod. "This equipment is astonishing. Without it, she would surely be dead by now. There seems to be a distinct possibility she'll pull through. In what condition, I can't say. She did sustain serious neurological damage with that poisoning."

Tubes had seen for himself just how miraculous the Omega's medical equipment could be, but without the ship's help, he didn't know what Nemec's odds of recovery were.

"Thank you, Aviles." Funny Bone turned to look down through the pod's covering, where Nemec's chest rose and fell in slow, shallow breaths. "Any chance you'd be willing to stay with her?"

Aviles cocked his head. "You trust me?"

"If you were the one who wanted her dead, all you'd need to do was wait. But you didn't, did you?"

Aviles hummed. "Maybe I wanted to get in your good graces by saving her life."

To Tubes' surprise, Funny Bone laughed. "Maybe. I can't help her, and I can't stay here, so I'm hoping that I'm right about you. I'm not sure you're right for our team, but there are plenty of people on this ship who need medical care. And like you said, Omega has some incredible equipment."

"Are you asking me to put together a medical task force?" Aviles' eyes widened. "I would be honored."

"We should run it by Al," Tubes murmured.

Funny Bone shook his head. "I'm making an executive decision. Al's got his hands full, and we need this." He held out a hand, and Aviles shook it.

Tubes kept quiet until they were in the passage, out of Aviles' hearing. He didn't like undermining the sergeant, but he had misgivings about this whole situation. "Are you sure about him?"

"Sure? No. Confident? Enough." Funny Bone lowered his voice. "I'm more concerned about how someone managed to dose one of our top candidates with poison. Whoever did it must have done so right under our noses...and they did it in a way that would send a message. If they'd wanted Nemec dead, they could have gotten to her in private. But they waited. That was a calculated move, and I don't like the math."

Tubes scratched the back of his neck. It itched, the way his skin sometimes prickled when he felt eyes on him. He was used to that sensation on the battlefield, and he'd spent years under Ornu surveillance. At least then, he'd under-stood the danger. This was worse, be-cause he didn't know who he was look-ing for. Anyone could be the enemy.

Anyone. After all, someone on the crew had sold out James Ridding to the Im-perium. They'd never really settled that issue, had they?

"How'd they even get strychnine?" he asked.

Funny Bone huffed. "They must have brought it with them."

"What, like in their luggage?" His voice echoed down the passage, and he quickly lowered it again. "The world was ending, and people brought poison in their carry-on?"

"Poison, and who knows what else." Funny Bone scanned the corridor. "If Val and company weren't MIA, they could scan this place in a heartbeat."

Only, Val was missing. The winding and intersecting corridors of Omega, which had once seemed unimaginably vast, had begun to remind Tubes of a warren. The ship was powerful, its weaponry unmatched by modern engineers, but what was the good of all that armor and artillery when the danger was trapped inside with them?

There were millions of people aboard the ship, but Tubes had never felt more isolated.

Chapter Thirteen

Sergeant Shawn 'Funny Bone' Piker

Funny Bone leaned back and looked down his nose at Angelo Christiano and Hugo Garnier. The two men sat across the table from him, eyeing each other up.

"I thought these interviews were supposed to be private." Garnier sniffed. "What's he doing here?"

"These are a bit different from our regular interviews," Funny Bone informed them. "As I understand it, you two were sitting on either side of Jana Nemec in the mess hall this morning."

"The Czech?" Garnier asked.

Christiano pressed one hand to the side of his face. "The one who collapsed."

Funny Bone wished with all his heart that Val or Tobias could weigh in. They'd know who poisoned Nemec. There were no video feeds onboard, and no central security system, but as Funny Bone understood it, Val had eyes everywhere.

Alas, instead he had to rely on his gut and his powers of observation alone.

Garnier sat with his knees spread and eyes narrowed. Christiano's posture was slightly less open, with one arm crossed over his chest and the other lifted to touch his face. It could be a tell, or he could be on edge after watching one of his peers suffer convulsions that nearly killed her.

"Nemec was with you this morning, correct?"

"Not really." Garnier waved a hand. "Yes, she was there, but so was everyone else."

"You didn't talk to her?"

The Frenchman shrugged. "Why would I?"

A counter-question, not an answer. Funny Bone tapped the heel of his boot against the deck.

"I did." Christiano's voice was softer, but he met Funny Bone's eyes when he spoke. "Or at least, she talked. She was chatty. Friendly. She was telling me about her family."

"But you didn't speak?" Funny Bone asked.

"A little, to answer her questions. I told her I had a younger sister. So did she."

The use of the past tense made Funny Bone whip his head up from his notes. "Nemec is alive."

"Is she?" Christiano's surprise was obvious. "I'm glad to hear it. I assumed that was not the case, since you are speaking to us, and not to her."

Garnier yawned extravagantly. "I still haven't had lunch. Can we move this along?"

"Did you see what she ate this morning?" Funny Bone asked.

"How should I know?" Garnier asked, at the same time that Christiano said, "Nothing."

Funny Bone pointed to Garnier. "Let's try that again. You first."

"I wasn't paying attention. I mind my own business. Things work out better that way."

Christiano sighed. "None of us ate anything, Sergeant. Nemec was talking about it with the man across from us. They were joking that they didn't want to waste rations if they exercised so hard they threw up. They agreed it was better to wait and eat after the session, when we would be hungrier anyway."

"Did she drink from her water bottle while you were there?" He didn't bother looking to Garnier for an answer this time.

Christiano pursed his lips. "I don't think so. She was drinking coffee, though, like the rest of us."

"Did you see her or anyone else add anything? Sugar, perhaps?"

Garnier let out a bark of laughter. It was so loud that it made Christiano jump. "Sugar? Sugar! Pouvez-vous le croire? Do you see a sugar bowl anywhere?" He shielded his eyes with one hand and peered around. "If Nemec had been offering sugar, I would have noticed for sure!"

Christiano's lips twitched into the ghost of a smile. He shot an apologetic glance in Funny Bone's direction. "There was no sugar, Sergeant."

Funny Bone tapped his pen on the notepad and glowered at Garnier. "Point taken. The two of you are free to go."

Garnier shot to his feet and stomped toward the hatch. Christiano watched his departure, then turned his attention back to Funny Bone. "Will you be calling us back for another interview? I can stay close by, if it would help."

"No need for that," Funny Bone assured him. "We'll be in touch."

The man's regretful expression almost changed his mind. Garnier had been too quick to claim total ignorance, but Christiano's precise answers awakened another kind of skepticism. Attention to detail might be a good thing, but if he accepted either man onto the team, he would always wonder if they were culpable. It wasn't worth the risk.

As Christiano left, Splat and Tubes skirted around him. They nodded in acknowledgment and waited until the hatch closed before turning to Funny Bone.

"Garnier's clean, as far as I can tell," Splat announced. "I searched his sleeping area and his belongings. The strychnine could have been passed to him, of course, but I couldn't find anything like proof."

"Same with Christiano." Tubes flopped down into one of the chairs across the table. "I've got nothing either way."

"Then he's out. They both are." Funny Bone dropped the pen to the table with a groan. "Out of the team, I mean. We can't allow either of them to join."

Splat rested his hands on the back of the other chair. "What happened to the concept of innocent until proven guilty?"

"I'm not accusing them of what happened to Nemec. But do you want either of them at your back in the field, knowing that we can't prove their innocence?"

Splat grimaced, and Tubes shook his head.

"Exactly. In the meantime, we've just lost our top candidate and disqualified one of the runners-up." It was too bad. He disliked Garnier's dismissive attitude, and in order to run with their small team, their group had to be somewhat cohesive. He would have been happy to consider Christiano, though. It was a shame.

"We do have a medic," Tubes pointed out.

That was true. Aviles could prove a valuable asset. And there were two other top candidates to consider as well.

What an awful way to narrow down the pool of applicants.

Chapter Fourteen

Commander Bina Chakravarti

James Ridding lay in his pod in the medical bay, breathing but comatose. Sometimes, if Bina watched very closely, she could see his eyes moving beneath those paper-thin lids. She thought he might be dreaming, although aside from the occasional twitch of his hands and the rise and fall of his chest, he gave no other indication of life.

Fortunately, the pods had been designed to shift slightly beneath the weight of their patients, so as to adjust their center of gravity from time to time and stop bed sores from forming. Waste was cleared away by a mechanism she didn't fully understand.

Why are you here? she asked herself, in an inner voice that sounded surprisingly like Bill. *What are you hoping to gain by it?*

Not that she had to want anything. Couldn't an XO simply be concerned over the wellbeing of her crewman? If anyone asked, that's what she would have insisted.

In her heart, though, she knew the ugly reason for her presence. The Crendelen had done something horrible to Ridding, something that he was still suffering from, and he might never be the same.

And it was her fault.

Did he know that? When he woke, would he tell everyone the terrible thing she'd done to him? If word spread that she'd betrayed him to the Ornu, the passengers would demand blood. Her blood. As for the crew...would they stand by her? Or would they despise her as a traitor?

She deserved it, she knew. All their hatred, all their disgust, and whatever punishment they saw fit to dole out. But not yet. She needed them to trust her now, until they could get somewhere safe. Until then, she could be of use.

Was it monstrous of her to hope Ridding stayed like this, resting and recovering until they were outside of the Imperium's reach? Then she could tell everyone the truth in her own words, and she would be absolved—not of her betrayal of Ridding, but of her subsequent betrayal of the crew.

She turned her back on his pod when Dr. Aviles cleared his throat. "Commander, I didn't hear you come in."

She cocked her head. "Are you stationed here, now?"

"At the sergeant's request." Aviles ran a hand through his hair. Like hers, it was black, shot through with generous quantities of early gray. His hairline receded at the temples: a sign of stress, almost certainly.

She wondered if he'd ever had a kill switch. In her experience, the constant threat of erasure wore people down, while those who could keep their heads down and their vision tunneled were more content.

Aviles clearly wasn't military, but he didn't seem like the sort of person who kept blinders on.

"We should get you some help." Bina rubbed her temples. While Funny Bone, Tubes, and Aviles had brought Nemec to the medbay earlier, she and Termite had stayed to make sure that none of the recruits left, or fell into similar spasms. She'd managed to get a few hours of sleep, but Nemec had gotten her thinking about Ridding, and the guilt had been weighing on her shoulders like a training rucksack. She hadn't poisoned Ridding, but what she had done was arguably far worse. The attack on Nemec had been anonymous and impersonal, and likely had more to do with politics than any personal grudge.

Bina, however, had sold out a friend. When people found out, they would never forgive her.

"I don't need help." Aviles cocked his head to one side, studying her without obvious judgment. "To be honest, other than acting as a sort of bodyguard, I'm not much use here. There are people on the lower decks who have much more serious concerns and who need immediate help."

"Hungry people," Bina said. Her headache mounted. She hadn't eaten anything after her last sleep cycle—she hadn't been hungry, even though she knew she needed fuel. Withholding food seemed a suitable punishment for her transgressions, anyway.

Aviles hummed. "Food is certainly a concern, as is sanitation. The real concern, though, in my opinion, is despair."

She let out a sharp huff of mirthless laughter. Despair had lodged itself inside her long ago, and with each passing day it worked its way deeper into her chest. "I don't know how to treat that, Doctor. Don't suppose you have a remedy."

His brows pulled together. "Do you have an interest in history, Commander?"

"Medical history?"

"Wartime history, although yes, the two overlap." His ensuing chuckle was grim. "Which, I'm afraid, is the only history most of us remember, given the state of the world—" He stopped abruptly and sucked in a breath.

No more world, she thought. The last surviving remnants of human history are contained on this ship. Not unlike the Primevals, come to think of it.

"I know some history," she murmured. "As taught by the Ornu."

"Yes, they do have a tendency to rewrite things when it suits them, don't they? But I was going to say, there are all sorts of stories from our earlier wars...and perhaps from your own experience, although I won't presume to guess. There are tales of men and women braving impossible situations: fires, floods, frostbite, grievous wounds, things that should kill a person twice over. And yet they hung on."

"While others slipped away." Bina glanced back at Ridding. "Believe it or not, the Ornu didn't offer history lessons on the triumph of the human spirit at the academy. But I've seen it for myself."

"People need something to live for."

"Something like hope." She kept her back to Ridding this time. Or something like revenge.

"Exactly. And I know it's in short supply, but—"

There was a loud noise from the corridor, and the hatch to the medbay flew open. Al plunged through, breathing hard, a sheen of sweat gleaming on his brow.

"What is it?" Bina forgot her exhaustion as her pulse spiked. "Another riot?"

Al raced over to the supplies. "No, nothing like that. I was doing rounds, keeping an eye on supply distribution. Did you know Miriam Henderson has been taking care of people?"

"Bill's mother?"

"Yeah. It seems like she knows people. Like she's keeping track of what's going on. Who needs care." He scooped up supplies seemingly at random. He was jittery enough that she would have thought he was on something, if that hadn't been practically impossible. Sleep deprivation and delirium could be the culprit, but at least he was excited. If he didn't present a danger to himself or anyone else, she could hardly begrudge his enthusiasm.

A pile of gauze bandages toppled over, and Al swore. She rushed to help him.

"Sorry. Guess I'm a little wound up." He smiled at her. Al smiled. She'd almost forgotten what it looked like. "I need to get back out there. Maybe I should grab a cart or something?"

Bina caught Dr. Aviles' gaze and sighed. "I'll come with you."

Al paused, still crouched on the deck of the medical bay, and looked up at her. "Really? You have time?"

"Well, no...." She should be in the Archive, searching for clues. But what did it matter, really? She and Longfellow hadn't found anything, and even if they did, Omega's systems were ignoring them by choice. She didn't really expect to uncover some magic solution that would make Val talk to them again. Besides, they had a plan: get the surge drive and get out of Dodge.

In the meantime, she might as well be useful.

"I can make time," she decided. If she was going to give people hope, like Dr. Aviles had suggested, this seemed like a good place to start.

* * *

Bina had, on some level, understood how dire the situation was, but she'd never really let herself fully absorb the plight of the passengers.

Miriam Henderson led the pair of them around, pointing out people who needed antibiotics and bandages as she went. People were wary of the crewmembers at first, but Miriam smoothed the way, and soon people were approaching them by the dozen, sometimes with specific requests, other times out of simple interest.

It didn't take Bina long to realize that Aviles was right. Gauze could only help external wounds, but the biggest problems were harder to see and harder still to heal.

"My husband was at home," a woman said while Bina examined her arm. There was a long, deep cut across her forearm, as well as smaller cuts on her hands. Bina had the uncomfortable feeling the woman might have gotten them from handling a large and unwieldy piece of metal, much like the ones the rioters had used as shields. She kept the thought to herself for the time being.

"What do you mean?" Bina asked as she dug through her supplies in search of disinfectant. She was only half-listening while the woman talked.

"When we evacuated." The woman cleared her throat. "He took the day off. He'd decided to visit his parents for the day, to celebrate their fortieth anniversary." Her hands were shaking, and her voice was increasingly hoarse.

"I'm sorry for your loss." Bina cleaned the wound and began to wrap it. It wasn't the prettiest job, but it would hold—she'd dressed enough wounds in the past to know how it was done. "I wish we'd had more warning. If it's any consolation, he didn't suffer." Not for long, anyway. The destruction meted out by the Ornu had been swift and absolute.

The woman began to cry. "Maybe he didn't. But what about me? I wish..." She rocked back and forth, doing her best to hold her arm still while she used the other hand to hide her face. "I wish I'd gone with him."

Not I wish he was here. Bina couldn't blame her for that. Who would wish this situation on their worst enemy, much less someone they loved?

The woman sobbed harder. "Better to be wiped out in an instant, surrounded by his loved ones, than to be trapped on a ship and hunted like beasts until we starve to death."

"That's not going to happen," Bina told her.

The woman shot her a dirty glare. "How would you know?"

Bina was keenly aware there were eyes and ears all around them, and that her answer would likely spread throughout the deck long after she spoke. "Because the captain wouldn't let that happen."

"It's happening now!" the woman snapped.

"No." Bina released her patient's bandaged arm. "It isn't. Right now, we're working on a plan. We have a solution, but it's going to take some time to implement. Believe me, if the captain had given up, he wouldn't be so insistent about rationing what we have."

She looked around to make eye contact with everyone in her vicinity. "If he thought we were doomed, he'd open the stores, declare a feast, and fly us toward Lindinis so that we could use this ship to take down as many Ornu warships as possible. To diminish their ability to do to other species what they did to us."

A few people in the crowd smiled grimly or nodded their approval, but Bina held up a hand.

"Like I said, that's not happening. Because there is a plan. It's a long shot, and it's dangerous, but if it works, we'll be free. Not like we were before, under Imperium rule. Not vassals fed the same old lies about being elevated and enlightened. We'll be truly free."

People were staring at her in wonder. With each word, Bina felt herself sitting a little straighter. Everything she was saying was true, and yes, their plan was mad and dangerous and very possibly doomed, but they had one.

The woman she'd helped cradled her arm against her chest. "Is that really possible?"

Bina nodded and collected her supplies. "That's the plan. But we'll have to work together to make it happen...the escape plan and the rebuilding efforts."

The woman ran one thumb over her bandage.

One of the onlookers, a man who had been watching their exchange in silence, spat at his feet. "Captain Henderson worked for them. For the Ornu. We were safe under their rule, and now he's ruined everything."

"Who dropped the bombs?" Bina kept her voice steady as she gathered up her armload of supplies. "Not Captain Henderson. If it weren't for him, you'd all be dead at the hands of the Imperium. We could be long gone, with all the supplies we need to survive, but he came back. He took you in." She straightened up and looked down at the stranger, frowning. "Someone viewed your life as disposable. But it wasn't Captain Henderson."

With that, she turned on her heel and left. Any more arguing, and she might say something she couldn't take back, or start a brawl she was ill-equipped to win. She could hear the people speaking behind her, probably debating the truth of her words. She ignored them and kept moving. It seemed like the best course of action.

She was looking for her next patient when a girl appeared at her elbow and tapped her arm twice.

"Hey, Commander," the girl whispered. On second glance, it was obvious that she was in her teens; hardly a child, especially under the circumstances in which they all found themselves.

"Hello." Bina came to a stop and examined her new companion. "Do you know someone who needs help?"

The girl looked around furtively. Her hair was cut short, and it hung in lank black curls around her face. Her clothes were torn and shabby, and she reminded Bina oddly of a Victorian street urchin from one of the old British novels, despite the fact that her accent was more Eastern European than Cockney.

"Do you believe the things you said?" The girl tipped her head back in the direction from which Bina had come. "About the future? And about working together?"

"Yes." She didn't have to think about it, now that she'd expressed the thoughts out loud.

"And the captain, you believe he can make this happen?" The girl squinted up at Bina.

"I believe he'll do everything he can to ensure our success."

The girl sucked her teeth. She crossed her arms and stepped back, eyeing Bina up and down with the same intensity as one of the automated scanners one had to pass through on the way to the deployment shuttles.

"I believe you," the girl said. She gestured to the medical supplies. "Lose those, and come with me."

Bina looked around in search of Al and Miriam, but saw no sign of them. They'd been pulled apart as they worked.

"Now!" the girl snapped. "We don't have much time."

Full of misgivings, Bina tucked the medical supplies against a bulkhead. If someone took them before she came back, there were plenty more in the medbay, and they might still be put to use.

"What's your name?" she asked the girl.

"Nadija." The girl was already moving, and Bina had to jog to keep up.

It was probably unwise to let this stranger lead her away from witnesses and aid, but somehow Bina trusted the girl.

Besides, I'm armed. Not well, and she couldn't take on a group of opponents, but she knew the ship. She could find a way out.

"You must be very quiet, Commander," Nadija warned her as they progressed into emptier and emptier corridors. "For both our sakes. I will be in trouble if anyone finds out that I've told you."

"Told me what?" Bina whispered. "You haven't told me anything yet."

Nadija paused near the bulkhead and grinned over her shoulder. "You're right. And I won't tell you...I will show you." She knelt down and pulled on one of the panels. It came free in her hands, and she set it carefully aside before dropping to her knees and climbing into the cavity behind the bulkhead.

If Bina was going to turn back, now was the time. Instead, she squatted by the hole and peered through. The bulkhead here wasn't thick, and Nadija was already out the other side, standing in one of the storerooms.

When she'd first wandered the corridors of Omega, Bina had felt that she was being led along by a kindly hand. She'd understood the ship in ways that shouldn't have been possible. As she crouched there now, trying to make sense of the strange shapes on the other side, her training instincts told her to run.

And then—with such clarity that she was certain she'd been touched—she felt the pressure of a hand upon her shoulder, and a voice in her ear that whispered, Go.

She jumped and looked around, but she was the only one in the corridor. The sound had come from the sigh of the ship's air systems kicking on. That touch, though...she couldn't explain that.

She dropped to all fours and scrambled through the hole before she could think better of it.

The storage bay on the far side of the bulkhead was dim. She almost bumped into Nadija when she emerged into the packed room.

"What's all this?" she whispered. "Supplies?" If one of the governments was hoarding food, she was going to lose it.

Nadija held one finger up to her lips. She reached into the pocket of her ratty coat.

The pen light was small, and the beam it cast was dim and yellow, as if the power was fading. Still, it was enough for Bina to make out the symbols on the sides of the boxes.

She crawled forward and dragged her fingers over an unfamiliar word on the side of a box, printed in what she thought might be the Russian alphabet. Longfield would have known, but Bina had to ask, "What does it say?"

"Strelivo," Nadija whispered back.

"I don't—" Bina began. Her fingers stopped tracing when they reached the boldly printed silhouette of a firearm.

"Ammunition," Nadija explained.

Bina's blood ran cold. Weapons. The whole bay was full of weapons. Not the low-impact crowd control weapons that Prime Minister Sever had lent them, either. This was enough ammo to kill everyone onboard.

And whoever had brought it onto Omega was keeping it a secret.

Chapter Fifteen

Consul Philo

Philo had understood since he was small that politics required a light touch. Yes, Emperor Albus was at the very top, and wielded unimaginable power, but great progress could be made by currying favor with the right Imperator, or planting a thought in the mind of an ally, or spreading a nasty rumor about a rival that would bring him low.

The most effective methods of influence were almost impossible to trace, because they relied on secrecy and subtlety.

There was nothing subtle, however, about the Emperor's summons. The four guards who had been sent to collect Philo were stone-faced, indifferent, and cold. If they'd been cruel or taunting, he could have given as good as he got. But no—these young Ornu treated him with the kind of indifference that was usually reserved for vassal species.

Philo stood facing the glass wall of the shuttle as he was conveyed to the Emperor's private residence. He kept all four of his hands folded behind him, fingers interlaced and back upright.

He sought out the eyes of the nearest guard in the reflection. "Did the Emperor say what he wants with me?"

The guard's expression never changed. "Your presence."

Insolent little broodling. If they were back on Earth, Philo could have reduced the guard to a cowering mess with a single threat. Well-bred children respected their betters.

Best not to consider that this insolent youth might not see him in that light. What if he knew something Philo didn't?

What if Philo had been deemed Defunct?

He kept staring out the window and hoped that the guard couldn't sense the change in his heart rate, or the flood of adrenaline that accompanied his fear. It was a pitiful response, suitable for members of vassal species, but not elevated biology such as his.

Philo had visited Emperor Albus several times before, although his long deployment on Earth meant that he had not had the pleasure in some time. The meeting hall of his memories was elegant and lavish, the table laden with tasty morsels, the air filled with soft music and stimulating conversation.

This time, when he entered, it was as quiet as a tomb.

Albus was waiting at the head of the table, his pale tail draped over the reclining stand. The table was empty, and there was no one else in the room, not a single Imperator or Consul or even a Signifier. There were only the guards who had accompanied Philo on the shuttle.

"Emperor Albus." Philo bowed low. The usual ornaments and decorations had been removed from the walls, and his voice echoed strangely in the barren room. This chamber was often used in propaganda broadcasts, and to have it sumptuously appointed at a time when outer Ornu worlds felt abandoned would have been...unproductive.

The crisis with the Perseids, along with the loss of Earth, had created a certain amount of instability for the Imperium. It was a time for stepping lightly and for messaging things delicately. Albus had ever been the nimble political creature, even if his power was supposedly absolute.

Philo found that his Ornu was rusty—had he really grown so used to speaking with humans that he'd lost his grasp on his native tongue? It took him a few seconds to recall the appropriate words, and he kept his head down while he thought, so that he would not have to see the guards smirking at him. "I have missed the pleasure of your company. I am so glad to be back in this beautiful city, and I await any orders that you might—"

"Leave us." Albus waved one clawed hand toward the guards. He didn't bother to acknowledge Philo's greeting.

"Alone, sire?" The guard who had been curt with Philo on the shuttle seemed surprised.

"Yes." Albus bared his teeth in a cold smile and looked to Philo for the first time. "Philo poses no threat to me. Do you?"

"No, sire." Philo dipped into another lengthy bow, although his heart was pounding within him. He had never been alone with the Emperor before. In another time, he might have seen this as an opportunity, but it did not feel like an honor this time. If anyone posed a threat, it was Albus, and without witnesses, he might do anything.

The guards withdrew from the room. The door closed behind them with a final click that made Philo's scales itch, the way they did before a molt.

"Emperor Albus—" he began.

Once again, Albus cut him short. "Why do you think you're here, Philo?" His voice was soft, almost kindly.

Perhaps it won't be as bad as I've assumed, Philo mused. Perhaps he's called me here to discuss how we might destroy Captain Henderson. Together. Who, after all, knew humans better than the Consul who'd been stationed among them for years?

"Because of what happened on Earth."

"What happened on Earth," Albus repeated. He interlaced the fingers of his upper arms, leaving the lower pair folded over his stomach. "What a neutral way of putting it, Consul. Your nephew lost the only Primeval ship we've ever recovered, failed to subdue the captain he was assigned to monitor, and forced my hand into destroying a valuable asset at the cost of an entire vassal species." He made a faintly amused sound. "I suppose, if I were you, I'd want to downplay the scale of the disaster, too."

Philo swallowed his words, and his hope along with them.

"The Empire is in turmoil," Albus went on, in an exquisitely conversational tone that made Philo want to sink through the floor. "After our attack on their home-world, the Perseids have launched an attack on our border colonies. And some of our vassal species may well be getting ideas of their own. There are signs of that. Perhaps they think us weak after our losses."

There was nothing Philo could say to any of that. His brain wasn't working as it should. He felt slow and cornered, and painfully aware that he must say something, and equally aware that there was no right thing to say.

"Well, Philo?" Albus watched him with pale, unblinking eyes. "Surely you have some sort of rebuttal to that?"

"No, sire," Philo rasped. "Your judgments are correct. I can only hope they will be merciful as well." It was a gamble...if he tried to distance himself from his idiot nephew now, Albus might find his loyalty lacking. As the matter stood, there was some small sliver of hope that his good name might yet be redeemed.

"Why should I be merciful? You promoted Nonus." Albus drew himself upright, and Philo sank lower on his tail in deference to his ruler. "You elevated an individual who is, at best, an incompetent. At worst, he is a traitor."

Philo flicked his suddenly dry tongue between his lips and regretted it at once. He could taste Albus' anger, potent as wine in the air. The Emperor's scales whispered over the floor as he approached.

"This blatant nepotism has far-reaching consequences," Albus said.

Philo uttered a strangled groan. "The empire runs on nepotism, sire."

Albus chuckled. He was almost within arm's reach. "True. And if he'd performed well, I would have called you here to reward you. But the blade cuts both ways, I'm afraid. You cannot lift your bloodline into positions of power without risking that, if they fail, you will follow their rapid descent."

Philo flicked his tongue again. "Yes, sire. I understand."

"Do you?" A clawed finger hooked under Philo's chin and forced his head up. "I'm not sure I believe you. You know, I could gut you right now, and nobody could stop me. I doubt anyone would say a word against me when they learned of it. I could display your head here in the solarium until the flesh melted from your bones, and then I could have your ashes shipped back to the ruined world that your antics cost me."

Philo knew the Emperor well enough to recognize that this was not an idle threat.

"The Perseids are testing me, Philo. Perhaps I should send that nephew of yours to them as a peace offering. Tell them that he acted on his own, and that they can do what they like with him. I don't think they've ever had a live Ornu in their cells before. What do you think they would do to him?"

Philo held his breath. That might not be the worst outcome, actually. So long as it spared him from being disemboweled.

"But you have been loyal. And we cannot treat Ornu lives as disposable things, or the people will lose faith in me. They will think that I am weak, Philo."

"No," he hissed. "Never. I live to serve you, Emperor."

"You live to serve yourself." Albus released his chin. "And for now, you live for both. You are surprisingly good at what the humans called public relations. If you can make Nonus seem like anything other than the sniveling worm he is, imagine what you can do with real material." He returned to his seat and draped his tail over the resting bar, resuming his original posture as if the last few minutes had never happened. As if he hadn't had his claws only inches from the delicate veins in Philo's throat. "Restore the people's faith in me, Philo. You will be my eyes and ears in Lindinis. As for the boy, he will remain in my care until I decide what to do with him."

"Yes, sire. I am pleased to do whatever I can in your service." Philo bowed.

Albus summoned the guards. "Philo will be given quarters in the central fort," he told them. "He is a guest, for now. He is to be treated as such. Orders will be forthcoming, Philo. Don't get too comfortable."

As he was led away, Philo kept his head deferentially lowered until they were sealed in the shuttle once again. There was no danger of him getting comfortable, and even less concern that he would stick his neck out in his nephew's service again.

Nonus had spent the last of his social currency—in fact, his account was overdrawn. Philo has done what he could for him, but the boy had squandered every opportunity placed before him.

Philo would no longer pay the price for his nephew's mistakes. Let his mother fret over his future.

As of this meeting, Nonus was on his own.

Chapter Sixteen

Commander Bina Chakravarti

Bina stared up at the weapons cache in horror.

"Who does this belong to?" Her voice was harsh in her throat; it sounded more like a stranger's voice than her own. "How did you find it?"

"My boyfriend's companions." Nadija turned off the flashlight, plunging the room back into darkness, except for the light that spilled through the gap in the bulkhead. "One of his friends is part of the militia. They were talking the other night, and I overheard them. My boyfriend is a good man, but his friend...." She trailed off with a hum that, while nonverbal, made her feelings on the matter pretty clear.

"Did he explain how they got all of this here?" Bina remembered how stressful and disorganized the evacuation had been, but to think they'd missed a ship-ment of such magnitude was horrifying.

Nadija clicked her tongue in disapproval. "When the evacuation began, the militia took over one of the shuttles—the ones our politicians were meant to use. They killed everyone who was supposed to be in charge and took over their ship. They smuggled all this with them." She gestured into the bay.

"And we just let them in." Bina shivered. Of course they hadn't checked everyone. They'd been pressed for time, their sys-tems were down, and they couldn't ex-actly run fingerprints. Even if the militia hadn't taken a government vessel, they would have been subjected to the same cursory security checks.

"Where are you from, Nadija?" she asked.

"Hold ten-thirty-three." The girl's harsh laugh echoed through the otherwise quiet space. "At least, I am now. But if you're asking who all this belongs to, it's the Slovenian militia."

"Slovenia?" Bina nearly choked on her next breath. "But then why would...."

Oto Sever—who, for all she knew, could be anyone—had come to them to offer use of the crowd control supplies. Why would he do that if his intentions were malicious?

"The militia organized the riots," Nadija said frankly. "They're going to do it again. Soon. Apparently, the first round went better than they expected. People got hurt, and so they will get angrier next time."

She could see it now, the shape of Oto Sever's plan, even if she couldn't be sure what he was after. Did he want control? Was he working for the Imperium? Or had he simply been conditioned to believe that power was the end goal, and decided that he wanted it all to himself?

Nadija wouldn't be able to answer those questions, but she could answer something that had been bothering Bina ever since she saw the clipart of the Kalashnikov printed on the side of the crate.

"Why are you telling me this? If you have an in with the Slovenian military, wouldn't it benefit you if they took control?"

The girl snorted. "In the short term, maybe. But this friend of my boyfriend's, he is not the sort of person I trust. He reminds me of my father. He, too, was military. He thought...oh, there is an English phrase for this..." She fell still for a moment, then snapped her fingers. "Might makes right. He did not have faith in any religion, but violence was his god. He found many ways to worship."

Bina grimaced. She'd known men like that. She'd known women like that. For some people, the presence of family was the only relief from their suffering under Ornu control. For others, like Nadija's father, their homes were the one place they could exercise control, and they did so with little regard for the wellbeing of their dependents. A man's home was his empire, and that type became little Imperators of their private lives.

"But this captain of yours," Nadija went on. "You believe that he can make things better. To me, there is no benefit to leaving the Imperium, only to end up under the rule of asps in human form."

"I understand that," Bina murmured.

She could also, at least to some degree, understand Sever's mindset. Humanity had been powerless for so long that violence had been pressed into them. Even

Bina believed that violence was necessary in a certain time and place. She knew a thing or two about survival.

"Thank you for telling me, Nadija," she said at length. "I can't imagine this was an easy decision, but I'm glad you made it."

"What will you do now?"

"I'll tell the captain." Bina turned back toward the hole. "He'll decide what to do, but I'll make sure that you're...hey!" She caught a flash of movement from the corridor and a confusing glimpse of a boy's startled face, and then a blur of moving boots.

She lunged through the opening and scrambled to her feet. The boy had a good head start on them, and her legs had gone partly numb from crouching next to Nadija for so long. Pins and needles prickled up and down her legs as the girl followed her into the corridor, shouting something in, presumably, Slovenian. Bina took a few stumbling steps in the boy's wake, then stopped.

"He's getting away!" Nadija cried.

"I know." Bina weighed her options, then turned in the opposite direction. "I bet you anything he's going to tell the militia members that someone knows their secret. He might not have recognized us, but I can't take the risk."

Nadija had gone deathly pale. "Your uniform's hard to miss. It's how I recognized you."

"All the more reason to go back to the bridge." Bina took a few steps backward. "Find someplace safe, Nadija. If you hear anything, come to me, and I'll find a way to keep you safe. And your boyfriend," she added, seeing the girl's stricken expression. "In the meantime, lay low. I'll sort this out the best I can."

"Do you need me to lead you back?" the girl asked.

"No." Bina turned on her heel. "I know the way."

Once before, she'd run through the passageways, driven by something like a premonition of things to come. Back then, she'd had Omega on her side, and they'd managed to face down their enemies despite being horribly outnumbered.

Without Omega, she couldn't be sure what would happen next. Who were their enemies, anyway? She didn't want to see the Slovenians punished. She had no desire to turn their weapons against them. If it came down to it, though, she'd do whatever was necessary to secure the safety of their passengers.

As she pelted through the corridors of the ship, the vents sighed encouragement: go, go, go.

Chapter Seventeen

Captain Bill Henderson

Oto Sever leaned across the table, steepled his fingers, and smiled. It was not a particularly warm smile. The man's teeth were less pointed than those of the Ornu, but his posture was just as predatory.

"So, Captain," he intoned, "we finally have a chance to speak, now that things are under control."

"For the time being." Bill hoped his smile was more pleasant. "We are most grateful for your assistance with crowd control."

Guns, Splat, Tubes, and Hans Norder stood behind him; Longfield was seated to his left. When the Slovenian PM suggested the meeting, Bill had tried to track down Al, to no avail. And where was Funny Bone? At least he'd been able to send Keating to talk to Tull. Everything would have been so much easier with Val around.

If Val was still around, we wouldn't be in this mess to begin with.

Whose fault was that?

Sever had four of his people with him, too. They were a surly bunch. Supposedly they were unarmed, but Bill didn't trust that they'd been fully honest on that front. They certainly didn't seem relaxed in his presence.

"Now that we have some breathing room, it is time to make plans." Sever gestured between them. "You and I are alike, I think, Captain. We both believe in the Latin phrase, Carpe diem. We are men of action. So, what is our next move?"

"I believe Longfield has already explained our plans," Bill said amiably.

"She has told us nothing more than what she tells the others." Sever wrinkled his nose. "But I think you and I have reached another level of understanding."

There it was: the reminder of his debt, such as it was. Slovenia had lent him weapons, and now they had come to collect.

"I think there's been a misunderstanding." Bill folded his hands in front of him and plastered a smile across his features. It was the same smile he'd always used in the presence of Nonus, the one that was halfway between friendly and bemused. "What more were you expecting?"

"Greater insight." Sever tilted his head to one side. "Not just the party line. The real information."

Longfield bristled. Under the table, Bill nudged her foot with his. When her gaze flicked toward him, he gave the tiniest shake of his head.

"There is no real information," Bill said. "Or rather, the only information I can offer is the same I'd offer anyone else."

Sever slapped his palm down on the table so sharply that Longfield jumped. "I helped you, Captain. I will not be left in the dark!"

"You misunderstand me. I can only tell you what I've told the others because that's all there is. You know the plan." Bill kept his posture open, his tone cordial. It grated on him, but it was no worse than every time he'd been forced to play nice with the Ornu.

Even so...he was too tired for this. There were more important things to do than smooth this man's ego.

A vein pulsed at Sever's temple. For a politician, he had very little patience for diplomacy. "I can't accept—"

The hatch to the meeting room opened, and Bina slipped through.

"What is this?" Sever sat back, his eyes darting to Bina and then to Bill again. "Another member of the command crew? Why wasn't she here earlier?"

In his peripheral vision, Bill became aware of the Marines shifting their body weight into more prepared stances. Longfield leaned forward in her seat.

"Is something the matter, Commander?" Bill asked.

Bina, whose face glistened with sweat, moved her gaze toward Sever. Her hands moved in a familiar gesture—one of the signals they'd developed aboard the Tennyson that allowed them to communicate in front of the Ornu without drawing their attention.

Danger, the movement said.

Bill's hand dropped below the edge of the table in answer.

When Bina spoke, her tone was calm. "I'm sorry to interrupt, Captain. Captain Stone is on the lower decks, accompanying your mother. There's been an incident."

"Is she hurt?" Bill asked.

"No." Bina glanced at the Slovenian PM again. "But we should talk. In private."

Sever's lip curled. "I'm sorry to hear your mother is in trouble, Captain, but surely this meeting takes precedence if she isn't in immediate danger."

"I'm sure we'll only be a moment," Bill said, although he made no move to get up from his chair. Val, on behalf of Omega, had been able to make complicated split-second calculations regarding angle of attack, range, distance, and relative threat. Bill wasn't up to par with

Primeval tech, but he had plenty of experience when it came to combat strategies. If he moved now, he lost his only advantage, but he had no good way to communicate his concerns to the Marines waiting behind him.

A soft beep made the Prime Minister glance over his shoulder toward one of his guards, who immediately checked her comm. He asked her something, and received a terse reply.

Longfield cleared her throat. "Who is Nino?"

Sever froze. "What?"

"She said something about Nino." Longfield leaned forward. "Are you talking about Nino Rupnik?"

Feeling that he'd lost the thread of the conversation, Bill looked to Bina, who only shrugged.

"What do you know," Sever asked in a thin, crisp voice, "about Nino Rupnik?"

Longfield cocked her head. "He was the head of the Slovenian militia, wasn't he? I've been reviewing the backlog of messages we received around the time of the evacuation. I was under the impression that Nino Rupnik was killed on Earth, and that he and his team never made it to the transport."

Sever's lip twitched toward a sneer. "How odd, to remember such a specific detail. Many people died on Earth. Surely you don't know all of them by name."

"True." Longfield, to her credit, maintained her facade of perfect composure. "But only one country smuggled crowd control resources onto Omega without telling us. I've taken a special interest in Slovenian politics ever since."

Sever sighed. He addressed Bill. "Your commander has found the other weapons cache. Your comms officer has learned my real name. I hoped this would end differently, but here we are."

He made a sharp gesture to the guards behind him, all of who drew their concealed pistols.

They were supposed to be unarmed, Bill thought wearily. Once, just once, he'd like to catch a break.

Evidently, he shouldn't hold his breath.

He heard the Marines move behind him, and Norder's soft curse, but it was already too late. Bill had four pistols aimed at his head, and Sever—no, Rupnik—was leering at him.

"Any last words, Captain?" Rupnik asked.

Bill considered the other man for a moment.

"You first," he said.

He pulled the trigger on the pistol he'd been holding under the table ever since Bina arrived.

Rupnik screamed, and Bill pitched sideways with such force that he knocked over his chair and Longfield's, too.

It wasn't a smooth exit, but at least the rounds fired by the Slovenians missed both him and the ensign. Once they'd hit the deck, it took Bill a few precious seconds to extricate himself from the tangle of limbs and chairs. The Marines were shooting, and Bina had swung around behind the nearest Slovenian guard. She grabbed the back of the man's head, slammed his face into the table, and took his gun. The guard beside her made a move, but Norder's first shot hit the man in the neck, and the next one dropped him.

Bill, meanwhile, focused his attention on Rupnik, who had slid off his chair and was bleeding profusely from his thigh onto the deck.

But the Slovenian wasn't done yet. His right hand rose, shaking, but clutching a pistol trending toward Bill's chest.

There was no time to think—there was only time to kill or be killed.

He aimed and fired. This time, his bullet found Rupnik's sternum, and he slumped against a table leg to breathe his last.

Chapter Eighteen

Lance Corporal Rhonda 'Guns' Penney

Thank God the captain didn't get hit, Guns thought, right before the bullet slipped between her ribs.

That was how it felt, at first: a sudden, confusing pain, like a bee sting, except that it punched a bloody red hole through her shirt on its way in and took a chunk of her flesh and a chip of bone on the way out.

She wasn't used to getting shot in anything but her exosuit. Bullets didn't rip through the meat of a person when the suits were involved. Sure, they stung, and they could still kill you, but it was a different sensation altogether.

This made her mad. What business did these fools have shooting her, on her own ship, in a diplomatic meeting? She'd been so nice!

Time to switch it up and try being definitively not-nice instead.

The left half of her body was a mass of agony, but at least she'd gotten shot in her non-dominant side. She fired off a round at the goon who shot her. Her bullet hit at the same time Termite's did, and he dropped like a stone.

That left one of the Slovenians in action, and it took Guns a second to find him. When she realized where he'd gone, she bit back a curse. He had Longfield by the throat and the barrel of his pistol pressed to her temple as he retreated toward the hatch, using her as a human shield.

He hissed something in the comms officer's ear. Longfield gritted her teeth. "He says...he says he'll shoot me if you try to bar his way."

"I gathered that," Bill spat. He lowered his weapon and gestured for the others to do the same. There were too few of the old crew left, and they were all too close to risk losing anyone else. Guns stumbled and caught herself on the edge of the table; her palm was so slick with her own blood, it almost slipped out from under her.

"Don't move!" the guard spat. He withdrew toward the hatch, which opened automatically as he approached.

Guns closed her eyes for a moment and tried to catch her breath. Surely she hadn't been hit in the lung? It didn't hurt to breathe, although she was definitely hurting. How was it fair that one bullet could make two holes in a person?

She forced her eyes open, and understood a few things better. There was quite a lot of blood on her outsides, which by rights should be on her insides.

Ah, she thought, with disorienting clarity, I'm going into shock.

Her legs gave out, and she fell with a bone-jarring thump.

There was a burst of gunfire, and Longfield screamed. When Guns lifted her head, she saw that she wasn't the only one whose red blood cells had made an abrupt exodus from their usual environs. Al had appeared through the hatch as if by magic, and the Slovenian guard lay dead at his feet. Longfield stood with her back to the bulkhead.

"Great timing, Captain," Guns slurred. She tried to give him a thumbs up with her good arm and discovered, to her chagrin, that even that one wasn't feeling particularly cooperative.

Termite dropped down beside her and tried to apply pressure to the wound on her back. Guns laughed deliriously and poked the hole in her front with an exploratory finger. Termite slapped her hand away.

"How did you know what was happening?" Bill asked.

"I didn't." Al looked around at the remains of the Slovenian representatives. "I came to tell you there was trouble on the lower decks. Another riot...and this time, I'm positive there are organizers."

"Probably the other Slovenians," Bina said. Guns mouthed the word to herself. Slovenian. It sounded funny, and Bina was being so serious. "There's a massive weapons cache in one of the cargo bays," the commander added.

"More like the ones they gave us?" someone asked—Norder, maybe. Everybody's voice sounded very far away, as if she was lying in a bathtub with her head submerged. She was warm, too. Better still, the pain was receding.

"No." Bina's voice again. "Live rounds."

Somebody cursed.

Guns tried to echo the sentiment, but her tongue had a mind of its own.

Al's head snapped toward her. "Termite, get her off the deck. Take her to the medical bay now, and then suit up with the rest of us. I'm done screwing around. This ends now."

"We'll cover you—" Bill began.

"You certainly won't. You and the other officers are going to lie low until this ends, one way or another. I don't trust the civilian peacekeepers to keep it together, and without an exosuit, you're too vulnerable."

"My parents are out there!" That must be Bill. He sounded mad. Or scared, maybe. Likely both.

Al's voice dropped to a growl. "Captain Henderson, get out of my way and let me do my job, or so help me, I will make you. If Val and Tobias were still here with us, things wouldn't have escalated to this point. We've seen what happens when you make impulse decisions, and I'm too tired to keep cleaning up your messes. We're doing things my way this time."

An awkward silence followed, into which Guns slurred, "Brutal, sir."

"Get her out of here," Al said, and turned toward the hatch.

Walking to the hatch was like being dragged through cold butter. The pain came back when she leaned against Termite's side.

"You're too skinny," she told him, with all the eloquence of a woman who'd just downed a fifth of bourbon on an empty stomach. "Lookit your little arms. You gotta do more presses, Gonzalez."

"You can come up with a routine for me," Termite grunted, "but only if you promise not to die."

She braced her free arm, the one that wasn't clinging to him for dear life, against the bulkhead of the corridor. "Don't wanna die. Not like Newbie. Or Porker. I should stick with you." She could probably pilot her exosuit, at least for a little while. The joints would keep her upright. "Should be fighting together."

"Yeah." Termite's voice was strained. What idiot, she wondered, had built the medbay so far away? It was downright irresponsible. "That would be a great plan, Guns. I'm sure you'd be really—oof!—effective."

"Five's unlucky," she told him. "There's s'posed to be eight."

"Don't die," he repeated, "and we'll be back to six in no time."

The next time she had to pause and close her eyes, she thought of Porker's final moments engulfed in flame. She was still thinking of him when her legs gave out for good, and the gathering darkness at the edges of her vision rose to claim her.

Chapter Nineteen

Captain Alden Stone

Three years. Al had gone three years without losing a Marine in combat, and in the last few weeks, his team had been reduced by nearly half. He hoped Guns would be able to make a full recovery in record time with the help of Omega's machines...if she survived her trip to the medbay.

His worry over Guns' wellbeing, and the inevitable fallout with Bill over the last words they'd exchanged, soon took a back seat to his new concerns. Namely, the mob rampaging through the corridors of the lower decks.

An hour ago, he'd been moving among the people, convinced he was building bridges. Whatever PR strides he might have made hadn't lasted the afternoon. Now, he was leading an ill-trained swarm of volunteer police into a sea of malcontent.

"Marines to the front!" he bellowed. "No live rounds unless someone shoots at you first, is that understood? This is crowd control, not a war zone."

His team nodded, and he trusted that they understood, but the volunteers were another matter. At least they didn't have guns, to his knowledge. Still, they'd already proven how much damage they could do with equipment they didn't know how to use. If any of them managed to take a firearm from someone in the crowd, they would almost certainly put it to use.

At least the civilians seemed to be afraid of the exosuits. That was just fine by him, at least for the time being. As long as people got out of his way, he was happy.

They made for the cargo bays where the supplies were stored. At the first bay, they found that the volunteers had been surrounded and were being forced to retreat. They were almost overwhelmed by the time Al and his crew arrived, but at the sight of the suits, the rioters scattered.

"Splat!" Al barked. "You're in charge here. Tubes, Termite, get to the other two bays. Don't hurt anyone if you can help it, but if you have to use force, choose your targets wisely. Funny Bone, you're with me."

The team lurched into action. The suits made them slower, but they could easily crush bones with a single blow, and they could take a fair bit of damage without compromising the Marines inside.

"Where are we going, Captain?" Funny Bone asked.

"We're going on patrol" he said, turning his exosuit toward a passageway he knew led deeper into the civilian corridors.

Before long, they encountered a crowd that had gathered around a group of sickly looking people. As Al approached, three of the ones that appeared malnourished were dragged free from the rest of the group, and the crowd fell upon them with cries and blows.

"Waste of food!"

"Extra mouths!"

"I'm not giving up my rations for you!"

Al caught one of the assailants by the back of his shirt and lifted him clear off his feet. "What are you doing?" he barked.

The man's eyes widened, and he went limp in the exosuit's grip.

Coward, Al thought. He imagined throwing the man across the corridor and against the bulkhead. Let him see how he liked being hurt, just because someone stronger came along.

Al held tight and turned to the rest of the savage crowd. They abandoned their victims and withdrew, although Al could tell they were weighing their options. There were dozens of them, and only two Marines.

Try me, Al thought, and his fury must have shown on his face, because the crowd withdrew.

Funny Bone bent to help the three injured exiles up, but they cowered before his suit. Which was fair enough, given their recent experiences with authority. Al gave the man in his grip a vigorous shake.

"Who gave you orders?" he demanded.

"No one!" Now that he'd lost the upper hand, the assailant looked petrified. "People talk, that's all. We're sick of going hungry, sick of letting these freeloaders use up supplies better given to people who stand a chance of surviving,"

Al stared at the man coldly.

Funny Bone strolled to his side and glared at their captive. "Not to tell you how to do your job, Captain, but I don't think these people are organized. This isn't a coup. Based on what Commander Chakravarti said, I'd bet money the Slovenians have collaborators all across the ship. People here and there, causing trouble. Riling up folks like this."

Al released his grip, and the man he was holding dropped to the ground with a grunt. Within seconds, he was on his feet and running. Al let him go—the man clearly didn't know anything.

"I don't get it." Al frowned at the man's retreating back. "If the Slovenians really are up to their eyeballs in weapons, why haven't we seen any?"

Funny Bone's eyes widened. "You think Bina's wrong?"

"No. I think there's another plan in the works, and we need to figure out what it is."

They'd cut the head off the enemy army when Bill killed their leader, but if there was already a plot in place, they'd need to act fast, or the corridors would end up flooded with contraband weaponry. Al didn't trust his volunteer police force, but he despised the idea of the crowd returning to kill off the band of exiles with live rounds. Morons with weapons were as bad as the Ornu, and a lot less predictable. He waffled for a moment, reluctant to leave, but knowing full well they couldn't stay. Too many lives de-pended on them.

The answer came to him, but not in the way he'd expected. From one intersecting corridor came a high-pitched cry of, "Captain Stone!" At the same time, from the other, a man's voice called, "Sergeant Piker!"

The former proved to be a young woman, dragging a boy in her wake. They were teenagers, and both of them looked absolutely petrified. The pair reached Al first, and the girl dropped to her knees at his feet, breathing so hard her slender body shook with the effort. Her companion stood behind her, panting, although he was in no great rush to step closer.

"Captain Stone," the girl gasped, "my name is Nadija. I showed the commander the cache."

"They're going to kill us," the young man said. He reached up to run a hand through his hair and froze, trembling, with wide and terrified eyes.

"They aren't," the girl snapped. "Bina promised. She said she'd keep us safe."

From the other corridor, three men approached. They were a mismatched group, but Funny Bone seemed to know them.

"Awad, Kan, Christiano." Funny Bone pointed to each of the men in turn by way of introduction. "Three of the top candidates from the applicant pool."

"We want to help," Christiano said. "Whether you take us or not, we want to help. I tried to convince Garnier to come too, but—"

"He's a clown," Funny Bone said. "Not surprising. Glad to see you. I bet we can put you three to use, right, Captain?"

Al knelt down beside Nadija. "Do you know what the plan is? Where the rest of Rupnik's crew have gone?"

"There are some at the weapons cache," Nadija said at once. "The rest are trying to take the Engineering decks. And...and the bridge." She sat back on her heels.

"If they take the bridge, they'll kill the officers."

"They've already tried that once," Al said. He considered his options, such as they were. "If Bill took my advice, the bridge is secure enough for the time being. We need to secure the weapons first, or we'll end up with an even bigger disaster on our hands. Nadija, can you show us where to go?"

"No!" the boy exclaimed. "We can't go back there, they'll kill—"

"Enough, Cveto." Nadija struggled to her feet and glared at him. "I'll help. Our lives are worth nothing if they take the ship."

Al turned to Funny Bone and his three new recruits. "Think of this as your test," he told them. "I don't have weapons for you, but we're going to fix that." One thing in particular haunted him, though. His earlier choice of words kept repeating in his ears on loop.

If Bill took my advice.

What, realistically, were the odds of that?

Chapter Twenty

Commander Hans Norder

Norder had shed his military coat before slipping off the bridge. Captain Henderson was going to kill him later—he'd openly defied the orders of his superior officer and the Marine captain. Technically, he wasn't beholden to the latter, but that wouldn't stop Al from being mad.

There wasn't much he could do about his uniform trousers, but nobody was paying that much attention to him anyway. The closely-packed crowd was in a frenzy. People were packed so densely that if he fell, there was a very real possibility he'd be trampled beneath the feet of the men and women on either side of him.

The thought had just crossed his mind when someone shoved him—not deliberately; the man had hardly glanced his way—but it was enough to make Norder stumble sideways.

Before he hit the ground, another man caught his arm and steadied him.

"Careful," the stranger warned. "I hear people near the front have passed out from being pressed too close together."

Norder eyed his rescuer. At a glance, the man didn't strike him as Slovenian. People moved all over the globe, of course, back when there was a globe to traverse, but his richly melanated skin and lilting accent were more in keeping with residents of the Caribbean than with Eastern Europe.

"Thanks." Norder didn't have to fake his enthusiasm. "I was this close to being crushed."

The newcomer frowned. "You wouldn't be the first."

Norder glanced toward the deck and gulped.

"Marcus," the man said.

It took him a moment to process the meaning, and another moment to decide between a fake name or his real one. "Hans," he said, after a beat. His first name was suitably innocuous, and since Marcus hadn't offered a last name, there was probably no harm in it. If the man didn't know his face, he likely wouldn't recognize his given name. Unlike Bill, Norder didn't spend his free time traipsing around the civilian decks.

"I'm German," Norder added, just in case. "And you're from...?"

"Grand Cayman." Marcus flashed a rueful smile. "I thought you might be Slovenian, actually."

Of the two, Norder certainly looked more the part. He looked around and saw the crowd had thinned a little as people forced their way onward toward the store rooms, but there was still a high chance of being overheard. The last thing he needed was to attract the attention of the Slovenian militia.

Although, if Marcus wasn't with them, he might be able to provide some insight. That was why Norder had left the bridge, after all. He hated the thought of sitting around and waiting for the mob to come and trap him in his quarters, or worse. Hence his dubious decision to approach the mob on his own terms.

"If you're not with the Slovenians," he asked, "then why are you here?"

Marcus tilted his head to one side, studying Norder with renewed interest. "I'm not Slovenian, but I can respect the cause."

"The...cause?" Get with it, Hans, he told himself. He was going to get in serious trouble if he didn't learn to think on his feet. Personal interactions had never been his strong suit. He was a man of action, not debate.

"Against these men at the top." Marcus huffed in anger, although fortunately his rage seemed to be aimed at the crew and not at Norder directly. Sure, he was part of the crew, but Marcus didn't know that.

Yet.

"I worked at a restaurant back in Cayman. Spent the last fifteen years serving dignitaries and Ornu better food and drink than I could ever afford. Now this crew 'saves' us, and what do we get? You and me, we go hungry, while they keep the best for themselves."

Norder opened his mouth to protest, then thought better of it. Marcus had a point about the way Ornu had treated people, which was something they had indeed both experienced firsthand. But that wasn't the case with Bill and the bridge crew, not by a long way. How had that story taken shape?

Assumption, perhaps. Although, given what Bina had uncovered about the Slovenians, people's assumptions had almost certainly been fed by rumor.

Anger crashed over him in a wave. The Ornu had primed humans to hate one another, and to distrust those in power. If the crew was larger, they might have been able to get ahead of the rumors like Bill had hoped, but they had been spread too thin, with too much to do.

As the silence stretched on, Marcus raised an eyebrow. "Are you a sympathizer?"

"With the crew?" Norder licked his lips. "I don't know about that." There were times, certainly, when he wanted to throttle the captain.

Marcus raised an eyebrow. "But?"

"But I don't know that I trust the Slovenians. Do you really think they're looking out for...for you and me? What are they going to do if they're in charge?"

"Feed us," Marcus said at once.

"And then what?"

The other man's mouth opened, but he seemed to have trouble formulating a reply.

"The Slovenians smuggled weapons onboard with them," Norder added.

"And loaned them to the crew," Marcus retorted.

He was in no position to delve deeper on the subject, so he only nodded. If there was one flaw in the Slovenian plan, it was that: they'd allied themselves with Bill in order to win his trust, and thereby undermined the storyline that they were humanity's saviors. How many people were going to make that logical leap, though? And even if they did, they might turn against the Slovenians, but they'd still blame the crew.

What a mess.

"I'm going this way," he told Marcus. "Thanks again for the help." He loped off down the corridor, away from the crowd. If nothing else, he'd succeeded in one part of his self-imposed mission. He'd worked out why someone who wasn't Slovenian would be willing to fight for them.

He turned a corner and came face to face with a trio of young blond men bearing guns. Real guns, not the ones the civilian police force carried. There was no time to decide how to react—the nearest youth was already on him, kicking his legs out from under him. His friends asked him something that Norder couldn't understand, and his attacker drove a knee into his side before barking his response.

Only one word was clear:

Norder.

"Get off me!" Norder protested. In response, something hard and cold pressed between his shoulder blades, right against his spine. He immediately went limp. This was a fight he had no hope of winning, but if he went quietly, they might not shoot.

The other two youths crouched down beside him. One of them yanked his hair, forcing his head back at a painful angle. The other held up a small device so that the screen was pressed against his cheek. A phone, perhaps? Although what good would a phone be on Omega?

"Norder," one of them said with a self-satisfied nod. They must have gotten their hands on photographs of the crew.

His hands were tied behind him, and only then were the knee, and the gun, removed from his back. Norder groaned as he was dragged upright.

"Don't resist," one of the men growled in accented English.

"What did you say?" Norder asked in German, just because he could.

The young man slapped him so hard that his head snapped sideways. "We know who you are," he said. "Don't play games. We're taking you hostage."

Norder put up a fight, although not a serious one. They'd be suspicious if he went too quietly, but they had him outnumbered and incapacitated. They were unlikely to shoot him under those conditions, and as a hostage, they needed him alive.

He hadn't lost, he decided. The mission had simply changed. He'd hoped to go undercover, after all.

Maybe he could learn more about the Slovenians' plans...straight from the mouth of the enemy.

Chapter Twenty-One

Sergeant Shawn 'Funny Bone' Piker

"Should we call in the rest of the team?" Funny Bone asked as they loped after Nadija.

Al shook his head. "I don't like the idea of pulling forces away from the bays of rations. If people get into them, they're going to devour them, and then we'll really be screwed."

Let them eat, Funny Bone thought bitterly. We've got more rations on the bridge, enough to get us through. It was a nasty, mean sort of thought, one he would never have indulged before this mess started. Hunger and exhaustion had worn his patience thin. He'd survived so many battles fought on behalf of the Imperium. Was he really going to let himself starve on this ship just because the civilians couldn't keep it together?

He pushed his anger aside, well aware it would come back to bite him eventually, and waved to their companions. "We can't take a bay of weapons by ourselves."

"You're not on your own," Awad said in clipped, precise English.

"You're not armed," Funny Bone pointed out.

Kan and Awad exchanged a look. Kan shrugged. "He's right."

Ahead of them, Nadija stopped short and held up a hand. She pressed herself to the bulkhead of the corridor and peered around the corner, then dipped back. Her boyfriend, Cveto, hovered behind.

Talk about useless. Funny Bone didn't trust the kid to keep quiet. He'd made it pretty clear that he was only interested in saving his own hide. Might even turn in his girlfriend, if the opportunity arose.

Nadija retraced her steps and whispered, "There are four guards in the next corridor, just around the corner. I don't know them, but they're wearing militia colors."

"Four?" Christiano frowned. "That's convenient."

"Con—?" Funny Bone began.

Christiano bolted past them and slipped around the corner of the passageway. Awad's eyes widened, and he moved to follow, but Kan caught the back of the other man's shirt and shook his head.

"Piker," Al grumbled, "you sure know how to pick 'em. I thought you said we could trust these guys?"

Funny Bone's next words were cut off by a cry and a burst of gunfire, which died almost instantly.

"Now they'll know we're coming." Al bared his teeth. "No one else run off, got it? That'll bring more of them down on us, and at this point, we're sitting ducks."

Around the corner, a radio chirped. Footsteps followed, and then Christiano was back, four rifles slung over one shoulder and a handheld radio clutched in his fist. There was blood on his forehead and his hands, but none of it appeared to be his.

Without a word, he thrust the radio into Cveto's hand. The boy almost dropped it in surprise, but Nadija caught it before it hit the deck.

"What do you want me to do with that?" Cveto hissed.

Nadija grabbed his arm and forced the radio into his hand. She said something in Slovenian, and Cveto's already ashen face turned green. This time, he took the radio and answered. There was a brief back and forth before he switched it off again. Nadija kissed his cheek and took his free hand in hers, interlacing their fingers.

"He told them it is nothing to worry about," she said, looking pleased with herself. "That a civilian approached and we panicked. Well." She shook her head. "That the guards panicked. They think this corridor is secure."

"And look." Christiano shrugged the straps off of his shoulder and held up the guns. "Now we're armed." His grin was decidedly smug, but Funny Bone reckoned he couldn't begrudge the fellow that.

Christiano passed weapons to Awad, Kan, and Nadija. He gave Cveto only an apologetic shrug. The boy clutched the radio to his chest and clung to Nadija's hand like his life depended on it.

"I take it we're going that way?" Al tipped his chin toward the cross-corridor.

Nadija nodded and led the way.

Funny Bone almost felt sorry for the four kids in the corridor. They had all been in their teens, probably the same age he'd been when he started boot camp. Two of them, mercifully, lay face-down, but one was curled up on the deck, clutching a bullet wound, and the other had fallen against the bulkhead at an awkward angle.

Funny Bone averted his eyes. This was the enemy? They'd traded the Imperium for a handful of wayward children.

Cveto whimpered at the sight. For all Funny Bone knew, they had been his friends.

"They would have shot us," Christiano said softly.

"Yeah." Funny Bone kept moving. "Yeah, they would. You did what you had to."

Al's upper lip curled back in a disgusted snarl. "If Emperor Albus heard about this, he'd be thrilled. We're doing his dirty work for him by killing each other off. Humanity, I mean," he clarified, but Funny Bone knew his captain well enough to understand that he, too, was feeling guilty over the teens' deaths.

The radio chirped again. Cveto, who'd been hanging back as they walked, cried out and lunged forward. He caught Nadija's shoulder and yanked her back so hard that she fell.

Almost at the same time, the end of the corridor exploded in flames.

"What the?" Funny Bone said, but his words were lost in the din. Whoever had fired on them was stationed on a cross-corridor, thankfully. As flames licked the air, Funny Bone's limbs locked up. It had been years since he'd panicked in the field, but the fire reminded him of Porker and Newbie. He could swear he saw the outline of a man's body in the flames.

Nadija scrambled to her feet just as they sputtered out. "We'll go another way. Come on!" She grabbed Cveto's arm and hauled him back the way they'd come, running faster than Funny Bone would have thought possible.

"Go!" Al told the trainees. "The suits will slow us down, but we have more protection. Don't wait for us. Follow Nadija, see if you can find a back way."

The new recruits nodded, and if this had been a planned training session, Funny Bone's heart would have grown three sizes at their precision and willingness to follow orders. Al and Funny Bone lumbered along in their wake. The exosuits were always slow, but after seeing the gouts of fire, he felt like he was in a bad dream, the kind where he kept trying and failing to outrun something that was chasing him while his legs refused to carry him away from certain disaster.

He glanced back over his shoulder and saw the shadow move across the passageway. In seconds, their pursuers would be on them. His suit could take a shot or two, even at close range, but he'd seen with his own eyes what fire could do. The exoskeleton would likely survive, given how hot the temperature would have to be to melt metal.

Alas, human flesh was a lot less resilient.

Without waiting for instructions from Al, he dug in his heels and turned back. If he could hit their enemy first, they might stand a chance. He needed to get that flamethrower, or whatever it was, out of the picture.

Then Nadija screamed, and there were two sharp reports behind him. He didn't need to turn to understand what had happened.

The Slovenians had come from both directions. They hadn't bought Cveto's reply after all.

The little group of Marines, trainees, and defectors was surrounded.

Chapter Twenty-Two

Captain Bill Henderson

Bina remarked on the lack of any sign of Tull or the other Roughbacks as she, Bill, Longfield, and Keating made their way as stealthily as possible toward the bridge.

Together, they'd arrived at the decision to use the shipwide intercom to try to swing events to their side. The ship and her infrastructure were one of the few things they had any control over, now.

We need to use everything we have at our disposal. If I can manage to talk some sense into people, reason with them....

He wasn't feeling as confident in the plan as he would have liked, but they had to try something.

Do you think we should reach out to the Roughbacks?" Bina asked in a stage whisper. "Ask them for help?"

As good as backup would have been, Bill shook his head. "Tull's already expressed some hesitation to keep his promises as a diplomat. I don't think he'd be interested in getting more involved in human affairs. On top of that, asking an alien race to help us fight other humans feels too...."

"Imperial?" Bina suggested.

"Exactly. It could hurt our cause, and suggest to Tull that we see him as a vassal, just like the Ornu did."

Diplomacy had always pushed the limits of Bill's abilities. He knew a fair bit about Ornu thinking after spending so many years in their focused education systems. He could rally a fighting force and, not to brag, but he could give a pretty good speech. Politics, however, required a level of thinking and scheming and lying that was anathema to him.

At least the Roughbacks were straightforward and blunt. Bill appreciated that.

They were three corridors away from the bridge when Keating darted toward the bulkhead, crouched low, and tapped one finger against her ear. The rest of them followed suit, and sure enough, Bill could make out the lilt of voices.

Longfield's brow furrowed as she listened. The voices drew nearer.

"Slovenian," she whispered. "I think...I think they don't know that Rupnik's dead. It sounds like they expected him to meet them here so that they could take the bridge."

Of course Rupnik planned to be here. He thought he'd either win the crew over or kill them all. Maybe both.

That presented a new problem, though. Al had assumed that, with Rupnik gone, the Slovenians would fall into turmoil. Instead, they were still following orders, assuming that their fearless leader would end up in control of Omega.

All the more reason to set the record straight with a shipwide announcement.

Bina reached for her pistol and raised an eyebrow. Bill nodded. He tried to count steps, to identify voices—how many of them were there? Six, maybe? Almost certainly more than four.

He leaned in close to Longfield's ear and whispered, "As soon as you can, make a break for the bridge. If I don't make it there to broadcast, it'll be up to you." He tapped Keating's shoulder and gestured to indicate that she should go with Longfield. He hated sending the two of them off alone. What if there were already Slovenians on the bridge, waiting for them?

He had to trust his crew, though. Their instincts were good; as much as Keating clowned around in private, she was an excellent soldier.

He was still giving himself a little pep talk when the first of the Slovenians stepped into view.

He wasn't sure who fired first, but he'd have put money on Bina. Both shots hit the Slovenian forerunner point blank, one in the gut, one in the chest. Bina maintained her position so that she could use the bulkhead as cover, but Bill wasn't sure how well-trained the militia was. If even one of them had enough time to get away and summon help, it would only make their situation worse.

So instead of hiding from the action, he lunged into the corridor. He grabbed the injured man around the middle and pulled him close, with his back to Bill's chest.

"Go!" he bellowed, although he had no time to confirm that Longfield and Keating were obeying his command. He pressed forward, aiming before each shot. With limited ammunition, he needed to make sure each round was put to good use. Somehow, he didn't think the Slovenians would let him pause to reload mid-firefight.

He'd guessed wrong: there were eight militiamen in total. By the time they were able to react to Bill's attack, four of them were already down. The other four, unfortunately, were good shots, and Bill winced when a bullet clipped his ear. He paid the man back with a shot in the neck.

The last three Slovenians fell back, barking commands to one another. Only then did Bill release his grip on the corpse he'd been dragging along for the last few paces. Bina finally emerged from her protected corner. One of the Slovenians tripped over a fallen comrade, and Bina shot him as he fell.

The last two tried to make a run for it. Bill aimed between one fellow's shoulder blades and pulled the trigger, only to realize he was out of ammo. Bina dropped the other, but she, too, had used up her last shot.

Bill cursed, kneeling to retrieve one of the dead men's weapons, but it was too late. Their target was gone. He was tempted to give chase, but the real mission was behind him. Keating and Longfield needed backup, and he had a broadcast to send out. He let the lone survivor go, but he could feel in his gut that this wasn't going to end well.

"The bridge," Bina reminded him.

"I know." They scooped up a rifle each, and as they headed toward their goal, Bill reloaded his pistol.

They met no further resistance along the way, and in less than thirty seconds, they had both plunged through the hatch to the bridge.

It was empty.

Bina stopped in her tracks and lifted her weapon, spinning in a circle as she surveyed the chamber. "Longfield?" she called. "Keating?"

There was no blood. No sign of struggle. Nothing was present to indicate what had become of the two officers.

"I don't like this. Do you think they were waylaid?" Bill asked.

"No." Bina was still turning on the spot. "They were here."

"What makes you say that?"

His XO pointed to the comms station. The screen was lit up, displaying a button below the words, Shipwide Communications System Activated, Press To Begin Transmission.

"She got it up and running for us," Bill said quietly.

"Or Val did." Bina closed the bridge hatch behind them.

That was a disconcerting idea, but he had no time to dwell on it.

He approached the comms station and dropped into the chair. He'd worry about Longfield and Keating later. First, he had a transmission to send out.

Chapter Twenty-Three

Petty Officer Mike 'Tubes' Lamprey

If he was being honest with himself, his first concern should have been the swarm of civilians milling around the storage bay. When he'd arrived, they'd been chanting and pushing forward, demanding the supplies be handed over. In the last half hour or so, their vitriol had begun to peter out, and they seemed reluctant to press their luck with an exosuited Marine hanging around.

Barring that, Tubes should have at least been paying attention to the civilian police at his back. They were just as dangerous as anyone in the crowd, and if one of them went off, the whole situation could deteriorate quickly.

Unfortunately, he was much too distracted by his screen to pay much attention to either of them.

Funny Bone and Captain Stone had been standing in the same corridor for an awfully long time. It made sense that the other two dots—Splat and Termite—would be lingering in roughly the same position, but if the captain had stopped moving, there must have been an incident.

Tubes didn't like it. They'd trained as a team. Even when they broke off into pairs, they were still a unit. They were still watching each other's backs. Standing alone in a corridor didn't sit right with him.

On the other hand, he was following orders.

On the other other hand, Al could only give orders based on his understanding of the situation, and this scenario with the Slovenians was unfolding in real time.

He typed out a quick internal message on the Marines' private channel. Everyone good?

Termite responded immediately. Good here.

Splat's message took a little longer, presumably due to its length. These idiots keep getting out of hand, and I'm sick of it.

Termite: The rioters?

Splat: Them, too. But I meant the civvies we armed.

Tubes suppressed a smirk and sneaked a sidelong peek at the men and women behind him. They were clearly champing at the bit to shoot someone. Splat's words weren't the nicest, but as far as

Tubes could tell, they were pretty accurate.

He waited, hoping for some reply from the captain or the sergeant. Perhaps there was some form of interference. If they were in the middle of something, they might not respond right away.

On his screen, the two dots began to move.

There was no way to tell their exact location. Tubes could see their relative distance, but his device couldn't provide the ship's layout or any information regarding the surroundings. There could be three thousand people between himself and his superior officers, or only a few hundred. There was no way to know, and the deeper into the ship they went, the harder it would be for anyone to assist them if something did go wrong. Which, in Tubes' opinion, was inevitable.

He pursed his lips, hummed, and made an executive decision. Sitting on his hands was doing no one any good.

"All right, folks!" He raised his voice to maximum volume. While he was at it, he switched on the mic built into his exo-suit that amplified his voice. The people standing closest to him flinched.

Served them right.

"We're done here," he said. "Clear this space. If you're not moving within the next two minutes, you will be forcibly removed. Anyone who relocates of their own volition will be allowed to retreat without penalty or reprisal. Two minutes, starting now."

He glared out at the assembly, whose surly frowns suggested they were disinclined to follow his command.

Then, above them—with almost miraculous timing—Captain Henderson's voice issued from unseen speakers. "Passengers of the Omega, this is Captain Bill Henderson speaking. Earlier today, an attempt was made on the lives of the ship's officers. A man calling himself the Sl ovenian Prime Minister was revealed to be a traitor, who had killed his countrymen and taken their identities in an at tempted power grab. The traitor in qu estion, Nino Rupnik, is dead..."

Bill kept talking, but his words were lost in the ensuing noise from the crowd. Most of them seemed confused, but a handful at the front looked stricken and began to whisper to each other. They were, Tubes assumed, Slovenians themselves, agents of Rupnik's who'd been sent to rile up the crowd.

He lumbered over to them and glowered into their faces from only inches away. "That's right, your boss is dead. Clear out. This little insurrection of yours is over." He'd forgotten that his speaker was still on and that his voice would carry, but it worked out in his favor by drawing attention to the Slovenians. They stumbled away and slipped off into the crowd. With their leaders gone, other people began to withdraw as well.

He switched off his auxiliary speaker and turned back to the civilian police. "Hold the line," he said. "I'll be back as soon as I can. Defend the bay, but don't start anything. Got it?"

They nodded. He wasn't convinced they'd follow orders, but his gut was telling him to move. He plowed through the crowd, urging people to pick up the pace. All while Bill's voice came from the speakers, repeating the information about the Slovenian militia, and how miserable everyone would be under their command.

Tubes met up with Termite and Splat, who gave similar orders to their police forces.

"I don't like this," Splat admitted. "Some of these folks want to play at being the hero, and some of them just want an excuse to fight."

"Can I be honest?" Termite frowned at the civilians milling around them. The corridors were crowded, but people were careful to give the exosuits a wide berth. "I don't really care if they start a brawl. The Slovenians really started this. You didn't see Guns when I left her at the medbay. She looked rough. I'm not sure she's going to make it, and I'm tired of losing friends."

"If it was just us against the militia, I'd be all for pulling out the stops." Splat arched an eyebrow. "But there's well over a million people on this ship who have nothing to do with this conflict."

"Then they should stay out of it," Termite grumbled. He pushed on ahead, following the dots that represented Al and the sergeant.

"I think the kid's losing it," Splat confided.

Tubes snorted. "You think? I'm pretty sure we all lost it a long time ago."

Ahead of them, Termite stopped. "Uh, guys? Am I hearing things?"

The sound of the deck was deafening: people arguing, boots striking the deck, Bill's voice detailing the crimes of Nino Rupnik, and the unmistakable pop of weapons fire.

Not crowd control. Real ammo.

From the same direction as the two dots on his map.

Tubes snarled. "I hear it, all right."

The three of them broke into something approximating a run.

Chapter Twenty-Four

Captain Alden Stone

Nadija crouched over Cveto's body. The kid was still breathing, but it was an ugly, shuddering breath that forced a bloody foam from his lips with each exhalation.

"Why?" she wailed. "Why? He was no threat."

Al assumed the question was rhetorical, until the young man at the head of the Slovenian soldiers laughed. He made a careless signal with one hand, and the soldiers at his back held their fire.

Al's finger was on the trigger, but he kept it slack. His three potential recruits shift-ed nervously from foot to foot. There were too many enemies, and nowhere to go. Once the shooting resumed, they would almost certainly be killed, no matter how many members of the militia they eliminated in the process.

"Because he's a traitor," the soldier said in perfect English. Like Nadija, he was young. He couldn't possibly be twenty, although his eyes held a cruelty that made him seem much older. There was something vaguely familiar about his features. Al had seen him before, during the last round of rioting, though they hadn't talked.

"He was your friend," Nadija blubbered.

"Maybe." The young man laughed again. "That's what I thought. Too bad he was hanging around a traitorous little wretch like you. I think we both know whose fault this is."

Nadija lifted Cveto's head into her lap.

The kid's in charge here, Al realized. And she's got him distracted. If I shoot him first, then maybe—

The young man lifted his head and met Al's eyes. "Captain Stone," he said coolly, "I don't think we've met. I understand that Nadija's the reason you're here. Bad intel, I'm afraid, although it works in my favor. You've come to me, which makes this so much easier."

"And who are you, exactly?" Al asked.

The kid bared his teeth. "Maks Rupnik. Pleasure to meet you."

Well then. Another Rupnik.

"You know what I just learned?" Rupnik knelt in front of Nadija. "I just heard, over the ship's comms, that these officers killed my father. And if you think your life was worth a fraction of his, you're dead wrong." He reached for his pistol.

A rifle report echoed through the passageway. Rupnik looked up in alarm.

"This way!" Funny Bone bellowed.

He must have used the distraction to take out the guy with the flamethrower. Things were still dicey, but at least they weren't surrounded now.

"Behind me!" Al told the recruits. Rupnik's people were already firing, and they'd be safer if they put the exosuit between themselves and their attackers.

Nadija, however, didn't stand a chance. In the seconds it took for Al to understand what had happened, Rupnik had already drawn his pistol and fired from less than two feet away.

As usual, the exosuit was both a help and a hindrance. It absorbed and diffused most of the impact of the bullets, but it took time to move the bulky arms, and Rupnik had no such limitations. He disappeared into the swarm of militiamen and vanished from view. Al had to be content with firing on his subordinates.

Funny Bone was trying to lead every-one away down the other end of the corridor, but Al couldn't aim and walk backwards and serve as a moving blind for three fighters with any kind of haste. He was shot a few times, but the suit held firm, though the impacts stung like crazy every time.

At least the three men behind him were able to hold the Slovenians at bay. Christiano in particular was an excel-lent shot, and from what Al could tell, every bullet the man fired hit its target.

He'd almost reached the cross-corri-dor, and paused in his retreat just long enough to stomp on the flamethrower, which had slipped from the limp hands of its former owner. He didn't want an-other member of the militia picking it up and giving chase, and he certainly wasn't going to risk using it again in an enclosed space running artificial atmo.

As Awad, Christiano, and Kan darted around the corner and out of range of their pursuers, a cry went up from the rear of the Slovenian forces. They withdrew in haste, leaving their wounded behind.

To Al's immense relief, three bulky silhouettes appeared at the other end of the corridor.

"Looks like we ran 'em off!" Tubes called cheerfully.

"Good timing," Funny Bone replied.

"Captain, you really gotta check your messages—" Tubes began.

Al's hands, usually steady as a rock, shook as he made toward the remainder of his team. "What are you doing here?"

"Saving you," Tubes informed him. "The words you're looking for are, Thank you, boys..."

"I gave you a direct order. You're supposed to be with the supply bays. You were supposed to stay there! I'd have you court-martialed if I could. The supplies take priority."

Tubes stood his ground. "People dispersed when they found out Rupnik was dead. We left the volunteers in charge, but the tides are turning, sir. Did you hear Bill's announcement? Nobody's going to support the Slovenians now."

All of them seemed confident they'd come out on top this time around, but Al could feel in his gut that it wasn't that simple.

He strode past his team, moving as quickly as he could. Between the suit, his exhaustion, and the battering he'd just taken in the firefight, every step cost him. He had to know, though. He had to see for himself. He'd believed wholeheartedly that, with Rupnik dead, the

Slovenian militia would collapse under the weight of its own deception.

You got so used to winning that you forgot you could lose. The voice in his head sounded a little too much like Nonus for comfort.

Even before they reached the nearest storage bay, he noticed people running past, arms laden with supplies. He heard his subordinates curse behind him, and Awad uttered something under his breath in what sounded like Arabic.

Still, until they reached the supply bay, Al told himself that there was still a chance, however slim, that his instincts were wrong.

Then the bay came into sight, with its hatch blasted inward and torn from its hinges. It was packed with people, many of whom were trapped inside, their arms full of rations but unable to escape with them as the frantic mob kept them from fleeing. It was a total disaster.

"Captain...." Tubes' voice shuddered and cracked. "I thought they could handle it..."

"Take Awad and get back to your post. Splat, Christiano's with you. Go. Kan, Termite, Splat...we're going to try and salvage this. Without killing anyone."

It would be easy to blame the volunteers for this failure, and easier still to blame the men who'd left their posts. Rupnik, too. It was easy to find fault with all their choices.

As he waded into the screaming, sobbing mass of people, Al found that there was one man he blamed more than anyone else.

Himself.

Chapter Twenty-Five

Imperator Pertinax

The humans had a saying: the apple doesn't fall far from the tree. There were no apple trees on Lindinis, but the sentiment made a certain amount of sense. A direct translation into Ornu might be something like, the bloodberry drops its fruit in the shadow of the elder bush.

Not that he'd ever heard a phrase like that uttered in Ornu. There was a line of poetry in the Forbearance Archives that Pertinax much preferred.

The flesh of glassbacks shapes the appetites of their young.

Glassbacks were a common sight out in the marshlands. They were ferocious beasts, truly nature's perfect predator, with six swift-moving legs, a venomous bite, and teeth as sharp as knives. Earth's Komodo dragons could have taken lessons from the glassbacks, and the only time they showed anything but brutality was after their young hatched. Mated pairs kept watch over their eggs in tandem until then, and cared for their young until the juveniles were large enough, and strong enough, to kill and eat their parents.

They only got one chance. Once battle was initiated, glassback parents had no reservations about fighting back and devouring their own offspring if the opportunity arose.

Privately, Pertinax wished Ornu society was more like that. Weaklings like Nonus would die off while they were still young.

Then again, without Nonus, who could he have sacrificed as a scapegoat?

Across the table from him, Consul Philo was watching a hologram in silence. The fingers of both his pairs of hands were interlaced, with the lower pair resting on the table and the upper pair supporting Philo's chin. So far, he had been very quiet. Whether he was as weak as his nephew, or made of sterner stuff, remained to be seen.

Secundus, too, was watching Philo intently. The two of them had worked together to destroy Nonus' reputation and save their own skins. The sniveling little worm had deserved it, but Philo might take issue with the course of events. Presumably Nonus had already blubbered to him what had actually happened aboard the Omega.

If the Consul tried to stand up to them, it could be an inconvenience, but not an insurmountable one.

Emperor Albus would ask questions if the Consul went missing under their care. Probably not too many questions, though. And glassbacks were marvelous at destroying evidence, so long as that evidence still had flesh on its bones.

Philo muted the projection. "This is quite disturbing," he said. "I knew the Perseids were slandering the Emperor, and I expect nothing less from Defunct species. But it seems that even Ornu settlers in the border colonies are questioning his fitness to rule."

"Indeed." Pertinax flicked the end of his tail back and forth, but gave no other outward sign of his curiosity.

Speak one word against Emperor Albus. I dare you. Give me a reason to hurt you. How satisfying it would be to visit Nonus in his dreary little cell and announce the unfortunate death of his favorite uncle.

"We cannot be divided at a time like this." Philo frowned at the pair of them. "Surely you understand that to be divided at this moment would reflect poorly not only on Albus, but on the Imperium itself."

"Emperor Albusss," Secundus spat.

Philo shot him a tepid glance. "I meant no offense, of course. I care deeply for the Emperor, and respect his values. He has been an excellent ruler...and, in my case, a generous one."

Pertinax couldn't resist a jab. "He's been generous with your nephew, as well."

"My nephew." Philo's lip curled to reveal his fangs. "Don't speak of him in my presence. He manipulated me, and his foolishness nearly cost me everything." His eyes narrowed. "Just as he did with you."

In spite of himself, Pertinax leaned forward. Was the fool trying to blackmail him? He must either know, or have guessed, what Pertinax and Secundus did to discredit the young Signifier.

There was, however, no threat in Philo's tone.

"You were a victim of your nephew's...machinations?" Pertinax asked.

"Of course, Imperator. For a long time I believed him to be a fool, but a harmless one. And even those who have shed many skins find that our scales remain soft when it comes to family. I had hoped that he would be a credit to my bloodline one day, that he would rise above me and make a name for himself. That he would care for me, and for my sister, in our old age."

Secundus' tongue flicked between his lips. "I know what you mean, about his foolishness. Nonus is...impulsive."

"No," Philo countered, "it is more than that. I could forgive him for being hasty and reckless. If that were the case, as I once believed, then he could be taught. After the terrible orders he gave you at

Armon, however, I see that it is more than that. I believe that he meant to frame you. More than that, I am beginning to suspect that this was his intention all along. Dissent in the ranks. Division in the empire." Philo nodded to the projection. "He wanted to destroy the Ornu, from the inside out."

Ah, so that was the game. Philo wasn't blackmailing them at all—he was offering them a way out. Pin the blame on Nonus. And why not? It had worked so beautifully before.

Nobody on Lindinis suspected Pertinax of being responsible for the current political climate. Nonus was disliked, and friendless, and too stupid to defend himself credibly. His one advantage had been his familial connection with Philo, and evidently that had soured.

"Why would he do that?" Pertinax added. "Wouldn't he stand to lose as much as the rest of us, if the Imperium toppled?"

Philo's tongue tasted the air. Evidently he was pleased by what he sensed, because the tension in his tail eased visibly. "I see that his wily plans are still a step ahead of you, Imperator. It is no fault of yours, of course. My nephew is a true deviant. Consider this: who, at the moment, presents the greatest physical threat to the safety of our beloved homeworld?"

Secundus didn't miss a beat. "Captain Bill Henderssson."

"Precisely." Philo nodded his approval. "And who would be in the best position to come to an arrangement with Henderson?"

Pertinax's tongue darted in excitement. "Nonus."

"Correct again." Philo leaned forward conspiratorially. "We know that Bill Henderson is a corrupting force. We know that Nonus has always felt... inadequate. Is it such a stretch to believe that Nonus would betray his people not to ensure our destruction, but to ensure his ascendance to the highest position in the known universe? The seat of power?" Philo gestured upward, toward Emperor Albus' ship floating in the sky above.

"It's not a stretch at all," Pertinax said. "In fact, it sounds very believable. What do you suggest that we do about it?"

"The Ornu in the outer settlements want proof of Albus' strength. The Perseids want revenge for what was done to Armon. Those who fear the intentions of a Defunct species crave assurance that their leaders will do whatever is necessary to secure the future of our people. And—this is a small thing, but I think it worth mentioning—the three of us wish to prove to Albus that we are loyal to a fault. My apologies: Emperor Albus." He nodded solemnly to Secundus.

Pertinax inclined his head in agreement, although he was tempted to laugh aloud. He had most certainly underestimated Philo. Like the glassbacks, he had nurtured his nephew until it no longer suited him.

And like the glassbacks, he would not risk being tested twice.

Chapter Twenty-Six

Commander Bina Chakravarti

Two laps of the bridge revealed no clues as to the whereabouts of Long-field and Keating. Norder, too, was conspicuously absent.

Ever since Ridding had been arrested, Bina had felt as if there was a weight on her chest that made it hard to breathe. Guilt was a terrible burden, but at least she knew who to blame for Ridding's disappearance. As awful as it was to see him lying comatose in the medbay, at least she knew what had become of him.

Keating, Longfield, and Norder were a big blank. A mystery. Out of six officers, only she and Bill were left standing.

Bill finally took his finger off the comm's button and turned away. "I can't think of anything else to say. At least people know what's going on now. That has to count for something."

"Mm." Bina strode back over to him. Whatever rules had governed humanity before the scourge no longer applied. Did people care about the truth, or only about filling their empty bellies?

There was no point in challenging him, though. If being upbeat and painfully optimistic helped him maintain his sanity, so be it.

Something on the console chimed, and Bill swiveled back toward it. He frowned at the flashing button. "Someone's...hailing us." He wrinkled his nose. "Can they do that?"

"I suppose they must be able to." Although, she admitted inwardly, strange things were happening aboard Omega lately. She hadn't mentioned the nudge she'd felt when following Nadija through the bulkhead, or the way the ship had seemed to guide her to Al, and then to Bill, just in time to alert him to Rupnik's plan.

It was all so vague, so intangible, so wishy-washy. Besides, she'd experienced strange bouts of intuition long before she'd set foot on Omega. Battlefield intuition. Following your gut. There were all kinds of names for the knowing-without-proof described by experienced personnel.

"Well?" she asked. "Are you going to take it?"

Bill extended one wary finger, as if he thought the screen might explode on contact, and accepted the call. "Hello?" he croaked.

"Ah, Captain. I'm glad we get this chance to speak man to man. I thought you were going to ignore me." There was some interference on the call, but the voice was eerily familiar. Bill rocked back in surprise, and Bina's legs wobbled. No, surely Omega hadn't resurrected Rupnik; she'd seen his corpse with her own eyes, and Val wouldn't back him over the crew.

"Who is this?" Bill demanded.

"The future captain of the Omega." The man laughed. "Haven't you heard? We've already taken one of the supply bays. Your reign is coming to an end."

"My reign?" Bill snorted, although he looked as shaken as Bina felt. "You make me sound like a king. I'm just the captain...and I'm afraid I'm keeping the title, which might put a damper on your future career plans."

"What good is a captain with no crew? Because I have three of your officers right here. I will kill one of them every hour, on the hour, that you delay handing over control of this ship."

Bina's tongue felt as though it had swollen to fill her own mouth, and her gorge rose. No wonder they couldn't locate Keating and Longfield. The two officers must have been ambushed on their way here.

Bill licked his lips. "You're bluffing," he said.

"Maybe. But maybe not. You'll find out in a n hour, I suppose, when I get in touch t o tell you about... what was your first na me, lepotica?"

There were muted sounds of rustling, a sharp crack! and a low groan. "S-Sally...."

"Ensign Sally Longfield, is that right?" the man's voice asked.

"Yes."

An iron band closed around Bina's chest, so tight she could barely breathe. She had spent years protecting the crew. After joining the Tennyson, she had found her people—for the first time in years, she'd cared about what happened to her subordinates. In hindsight, she hadn't always made the right choices, but she'd done her best to care for the men and women under her command. Betraying Ridding had cost her, but she'd consoled herself that at least she'd given the rest of the crew a fighting chance.

But for what? Now, Ridding might never recover, and the rest of the crew was in the clutches of a bloodthirsty madman who would risk the future of humanity for power.

Bill, too, appeared to be in shock. He swallowed a few times, Adam's apple bobbing harshly with every gulp. "You still haven't told me who you are," he said at last.

"Maks Rupnik. I believe you knew my father." The man spat the words. "Speaking of which...aren't your parents somewhere onboard? Perhaps I will pay them

a visit if you haven't come to your senses by the time I'm finished with your c
rew."

The com died.

Bill leaned forward and rested his elbows on the console, cradling his head
in his hands.

She knew exactly how he must be
feeling. They were made of different
stuff, and any empathy she'd learned
in recent years could be attributed to
him. His sense of justice had revital-
ized hers, and he had risked everything—not just his life, not just his
reputation, but everything—to save as
many people as possible. Now, those
people had turned on him.

And worse, they'd turned on his crew.

"Bill," she whispered. "What do we do?"
He would have an answer. He always
did.

The question seemed to galvanize the captain. He sat up straight, rolled his shoulders, and took a deep breath.

"He said that they've taken one of the store rooms. We need to make sure the other two are defended. If possible, we need to find a way to shift the supplies to more secure locations. And then, we need to find a way to get to Rupnik before he harms a single member of our crew."

Chapter Twenty-Seven

Captain Bill Henderson

Until he could see with his own eyes that Rupnik had been telling the truth, Bill held onto the faint hope that the young man had lied. Maybe he was trying to pressure Bill into making a stupid and foolhardy decision.

Then he reached the compromised supply bay, and the truth could no longer be denied. Termite, Al, Splat, and some recruit Bill had never seen before stood guard in the corridor, although there was precious little left to guard. Civilians had cleared the area by the time Bill arrived, and they had taken everything but their trash with them.

"What did they do with it all?" he asked Al.

The Marine captain squeezed his eyes shut. "If you're asking about the Slovenians, they aren't responsible. This wasn't an organized hit. It was hungry people, fueled by anger and desperation, taking what they could get." He bowed his head, hiding his red-rimmed eyes. Bill had never seen Al in such a state. In every challenge they'd faced together, Al had been able to separate his emotions from what needed to be done. They'd come through some terrible times together.

The man before him was on the verge of breaking.

"This is my fault," Al murmured. "I left the team to defend the supplies and went off to look for weapons—"

"I thought it was my fault?" Bill crossed his arms. "Based on what you said earlier."

Bina sighed and rubbed her temples. "Is this really the most productive use of our time?" she asked. "We're more than halfway through Rupnik's allotted hour." They'd had to take back routes through the ship in an effort to evade Rupnik's men, and with every second that passed, Bill was painfully aware that protecting his own life might cost one of his crew their own.

"No, and that's my point." Bill laid a hand on the shoulder of Al's exosuit. The cold material felt like a promise of things to come. "We've both taken calculated risks, and not all of them have paid off. That's nothing to be ashamed of, Al. What we need to do is figure out what happens next."

Al passed one hand over his eyes and looked around the empty chamber. All that remained were broken crates, empty wrappers, and crumpled trash. Bill followed his line of sight. Judging by the number of discarded packets and wrappers scattered around, some people had been desperate enough to tear into their rations even before leaving the scene.

"I don't know," he murmured.

Bill tried to be cheerful. "It's only a third of our supplies, and if anything, it'll placate people for a while. They'll be more motivated to protect whatever supplies they took than to risk their lives for more. And maybe we can convince someone to help us get the jump on Rupnik."

Bina snapped her fingers. "That girl, Nadija—"

"Dead," Al grunted.

Bina rocked back on her heels. "What?"

"We were ambushed in the corridors. Rupnik shot her." Al ran a hand absentmindedly over his weapon, his eyes glazed. "I don't know what our options are, Bill. We can't fight them head-on. With Omega, sure. If the ship was empty, maybe, but if they open fire on us with everything they have...a lot of innocent people are going to die."

Bill's ears rang as if he'd been struck in the head. "No," he whispered. "You're thinking of surrendering?"

"What are we doing here?" Al's hands stopped their slow movement, and he lifted his face toward Bill's. There was no fight left in him, only the blunt matter-of-factness that Bill had always respected. "What, exactly, is the mission?"

Bill looked over his shoulder. He could make out the silhouettes of the Marines standing in the passageway. He'd always been better at seeing nuance than Al had; the Marine captain's thinking could be painfully black and white.

Maybe it wouldn't hurt to try thinking that way, just for a moment.

"The mission," he said slowly, "is to save as many lives as we can."

Al nodded. "And what's the best thing we can do for the mission right now?"

Bill closed his eyes and cursed.

"It doesn't have to be a complete surrender," Bina reminded him. He'd expected her to argue, but she, too, seemed resigned. "We stand a better chance of defeating Rupnik if we can get him to let his guard down. Let him think he's won."

"We need rest," Al added. "And we need as many of our crew alive as possible."

Everything in Bill wanted to argue, but the last time he'd done that, he'd lost Val, and control of Omega. He couldn't take much more before he'd start to crack, and then he'd be no good to anyone at all.

He was still looking for another alternative when the com at his hip chirped.

"We've got a few more minutes, Rupnik," he said into his com.

"You have as much time as I decide to give you," the Slovenian snapped. "And I'm done waiting. It seems you need a push in the right direction." The timbre of his voice changed, as if he'd turned away from the speaker. "Tell him whatever you want to tell him, Sally. Let the former captain hear your last words."

"Rupnik, stop." Bill clutched the com in his sweating hand. "Let's talk."

There was a broken sob, and then Longfield's voice warbled from the mic. "Captain, I'm so sorry, please—"

And then there was a sound so horrible, he couldn't begin to describe it. A wet thud that didn't come from a gun.

He could only imagine what Rupnik had done to the ensign. He didn't want to know. He didn't want to hear Longfield's scream, or the way her voice cracked when the next blow came.

Back when the Ornu had taken him away to the Academy, Bill had taught himself how to sit still and look alert without really being present. While his instructors droned on and on about their version of humanity's pathetic history and the glory of the Empire, he had let his mind wander off to another room, far away, and occupy itself with distracted thoughts: daydreams, song lyrics, the plots of old book and shows, anything to keep his mind free of the poison his professors were intent on dribbling into his ears.

He managed it again, and he stayed in that faraway, dissociative place until Longfield went quiet, and Maks Rupnik laughed into the speaker.

"Was that message clear enough, Henderson? Or shall I send you another? Sally was a clever woman, but I think the other two are tougher. Shall we find o ut? Or will you hand over control of this s hip to someone who won't dither and f uss the way you do?"

His ears could hear the message. His eyes could see the horror on Al's and Bina's features. Yet still, his mind was safe in that faraway place where nothing could reach him when he said, "You've made your point, Rupnik. I surrender. The ship is yours."

Chapter Twenty-Eight

Captain Maks Rupnik

Commander Norder sat, stiff as a board, at the navigation controls of Omega. His hands were folded in his lap, his eyes fixed on some point in the middle distance, his posture rigid and brittle.

Maks leaned over and rested a hand on the man's shoulder. He smiled to himself when he flinched at his touch. It was only a tiny gesture, but it was proof that he had been paying attention, and that he knew enough to be afraid.

Good. Fear was better than loyalty. Honorable intentions served men well enough in times of peace, but under duress, their better natures could be eroded with carefully placed pressure. Just look at Bill Henderson, so proud and upright only hours before. He'd been easy enough to break: one dead crewmate, and the work was done. Pathetic.

If he'd still been alive, his father would have agreed.

Maks patted Norder's shoulder a few times, making the commander twitch with each fresh contact. "I'm surprised at you," he drawled. "I thought you would have figured out how to fly this thing by now. And yet you sit there, useless as a brick, and do nothing."

Norder ignored him.

He closed his eyes and took a deep breath. Apparently, Henderson's XO, Chakravarti, had taken over Nav duties after they'd lost the officer formerly in that role for some reason.

But Chakravarti had somehow managed to vanish between the time he'd killed Longfield and taken control of the bridge. Her colleagues claimed to have no idea where she'd gone, and that was probably true—otherwise, he could have tortured the information out of them. As it stood, his men were scouring the ship for her.

I doubt she can cause much trouble on her own, anyway.

"Didn't you see what I did to your compatriot?" he asked Norder. "I could have sworn that you were paying attention."

The man's head swiveled toward him in slow motion. "Can't," he grunted.

"Can't remember?" Maks reached for the knife at his belt. "Perhaps I should remind you."

Norder rolled his eyes. It was an impressive display of indifference, to be sure. Maks could use more men like him.

Too bad stubbornness meant that he couldn't trust this fellow. If he welcomed Norder into the fold, he would have to spend the rest of his life watching his back.

"I can't," Norder enunciated, "pilot the ship on my own." He spoke deliberately, as if Maks might not be able to understand him. "This isn't a Mark XI, or some little puddle-jumper. This is Primeval tech. A ship the size of a city. Flying it is not a one-man job."

"Maybe I should kill you," Maks suggested, "and find a man who can handle it."

Norder's eyes flashed, and he leaned forward with a leer. "Good thinking, Maks. Kill the only people who know what they're doing and put one of your toadies in control. With thinking like that, it's a wonder you and your father couldn't get elected into office for real."

Maks let out a bark of laughter. He squeezed Norder's shoulder. "You're a tool, Norder. I like that about you. Perhaps you'll be kind enough to explain to me what we should do?"

"Or perhaps," Norder intoned, "you could walk out an airlock."

With a surge of anger, Maks yanked the knife free of its sheath and gripped the back of his neck.

"Norder," Bill Henderson interrupted, "don't be an idiot. The man's in charge now. Do as he says."

Maks noted the question in Norder's expression, and the subtle nod Henderson gave him in response. This crew was up to something. He'd expected nothing less, although he still found their camaraderie irksome. His father had warned him to keep his short temper on an even shorter leash, but without Nino's presence and guidance, Maks was lost at sea.

At least he knew what his father would have wanted him to do. They'd discussed their plans in detail ever since they set foot on Omega and got the first inkling of its potential.

He lowered his knife, but kept his grip on the back of the officer's neck. "Are you going to enlighten me, Henderson?"

"I'm happy to." Henderson pointed to the char at the center of the bridge. "I need to be in the command chair. Right now, the ship's running on minimal power; we've been holding steady while we formulate our plans, and I'll need to engage the systems before we can alter our course. Would you like me to take over?"

Maks considered the offer. Henderson and his people were outnumbered, but they were an overconfident lot, and he didn't trust them to do as they were told. The Marines had been shut out of the bridge, leaving only Norder and the deposed captain in their old positions. The other one, Keating, was being kept as collateral on the lower decks.

"I think not," Maks announced. He pointed his knife to one of his militia recruits. "You," he said, this time in Slovenian. "Get in the seat." If the command chair really could control the whole ship, he didn't want Henderson to get any ideas. Then again, it might be a trap. Perhaps the chair was rigged, and whoever sat there would be killed as soon as they were in position. He wouldn't put anything past this lot.

The recruit did as he was told. Maks held his breath as the man sank into the seat, but nothing happened.

"I think you're lying to me, Henderson," he growled.

The former captain shook his head. He stood at ease, his hands clasped behind him, his chin lifted. He didn't look like a broken man, and his courteous tone belied no sorrow or deceit. "I'm not. Omega chose me as its captain."

"In the past," Maks sneered. "But I'm the captain now." He strode over to the command chair and shoved the recruit out of his way.

Still, nothing happened.

His neck burned with humiliation. Omega would have reacted to Nino. His presence had always been so commanding that surely even a Primeval ship would have submitted to his will.

"Get over here," he commanded.

With his hands still folded behind his back, Henderson strode over and sank into the chair. Was there, perhaps, just a touch of uncertainty in his stance? Perhaps it was all part of a joke designed to make Maks look like a fool. Well, if that were the case, they would soon learn that he would not tolerate such behavior.

Henderson dropped into the seat. Instantly, a hologram display came to life around him.

Maks took a few deep breaths. This was what he wanted, after all. It wasn't ideal that only Henderson could make it happen, but the man had complied so far. All those years in service to the Ornu must have made him malleable and complacent. Yes, that must be it.

"Where are we headed, Captain?" Henderson asked without a trace of irony.

"To Vale," Maks said at once.

"Vale, Captain?" Henderson studied him sidelong. "The vassal world of the Awn?"

"Are you questioning me?"

"No, sir. Just making sure I understood. I wasn't aware that there was anything worth our time on Vale. Goes to show what I know." He moved his hands about and swiveled in the chair, interacting with the hologram as he moved.

Maks would have to be careful with him. Norder's brand of defiance made him easy to goad, but Bill Henderson was almost guaranteed to get under his skin. Even worse, he might sow dissent among the other members of the militia.

Still, he was a tool, and Maks would wield him until his usefulness ran out. The moment he became disposable, Maks would find a way to make him pay.

Chapter Twenty-Nine

Lance Corporal Rhonda 'Guns' Penney

"You look terrible," Termite grunted.

Guns dragged herself along through the corridor and kept her eyes averted. "You think so? Because I'm still prettier than you are."

Usually Termite would have had a retort, and soon they'd have been insulting each other's mothers, but it seemed neither of them could muster the energy for it.

She didn't know what Termite's problem was, but she felt like death incarnate. Fortunately, her exosuit did most of the heavy lifting. Even so, every muscle in her body protested her movements. Dr. Aviles had insisted that she needed more recovery time, but she refused to sit around twiddling her thumbs, waiting for that Rupnik to descend on her and kill her in her bed.

When she'd struggled out of med bay, Al had assigned the two of them to guard one of the surviving food stores. In the meantime, he and Funny Bone had taken most of the civilian police and a handful of potential recruits into the more settled areas to try and put down the ongoing riot.

As miserable as Guns felt, the captain had looked worse. She wasn't sure what kind of deal he'd made with Rupnik, but she could guess how it had gone:

Test me, and I'll kill Keating.

Or Norder.

Or Bill's parents.

Or everyone on Deck 3.

Into the awkward lull between her and Termite, she blurted, "I heard about Longfield. Can't believe it."

"I can," Termite said. "I was on the cleanup crew."

Guns whipped her head toward him, despite the protestations of her spine. "Really? They didn't do it themselves?"

Termite shook his head. "They wanted us to see."

That made a sick kind of sense. Daddy Rupnik had been a monster, but giving a kid like Maks access to an arsenal? That was nightmare fuel.

Termite lifted his chin. "Look alive," he said.

A small cluster of people were making their way toward the storage bay. Guns' hackles went up at once, although she didn't recognize anyone in the crowd. They were mostly men, and all of them carried weapons. Crowd control weapons, she realized—probably stripped from the civilian police during the last riot. They wouldn't do much good against the exosuits, but it wasn't a good start to whatever conversation they were about to have.

She whistled, and the small group of civilian police left under the Marines' command shot to their feet and reached for their weapons.

Guns sighed. "Wait for my order. Don't get too trigger happy with those dazzlers."

A few of the men exchanged sullen glances. They didn't like this any more than she did, and she wondered how long they'd stick around. Technically, they followed Maks' lead now. The chain of command was messed up, and they didn't like being told to hold their fire.

Termite took a step toward the newcomers. "What can we do for you folks?"

The small crowd shifted, and one man stepped forward, urged by his companions. "We need food," he said. His accent was thick, English-by-way-of-India, perhaps. Guns didn't much care, so long as he wasn't part of the Slovenian militia.

"I'm not opening that hatch," Termite replied. "You civvies stripped a whole cargo bay."

"You civvies?" The man's eyebrows pulled together. "Who, exactly? Show me this food that I supposedly carried away. I have none. There is nothing left. We did not join the riots!"

"Your weapons say otherwise," Guns drawled.

The man lifted the gun he was holding. "This? A weapon? It makes bright lights! These were left behind, and we took them to defend ourselves from the troublemakers. I am not a thief. We trusted Captain Henderson, and we told the rioters that we would not join them. Still, we need to eat! Where is our share?"

"My family is hungry!" one of his companions added.

Termite looked over his shoulder, and Guns shrugged. If the man was lying—and she really hoped he was—then he didn't deserve anything. But if he was telling the truth....

There really was no winning, was there? With the storage bays locked down, offering him food could incur Maks' wrath. Turning him away would mean turning him against the crew, and they needed all the allies they could get.

Maybe they could offer just one box of MREs to hold this group over until things got sorted out.

"Don't move—" she began.

Gunfire erupted from the cross-corridor. She wheeled toward the police behind her, thinking they had opened fire. Then the men who'd come to beg for supplies began to scream. Whoever was shooting had real weapons, not just dazzlers and rubber-coated bullets.

"Stop!" Guns bellowed, but nobody heeded her.

The men who'd come to ask for supplies tried to flee, but it was too late. A handful of militiamen emerged into the corridor, and they didn't stop shooting until every one of the supplicants was dead.

Guns gripped her own weapon with trembling hands. She couldn't bring herself to look at Termite. This isn't right. None of this should be happening.

The leader of the band of militiamen nudged one of the dead with his toe, then turned to her. "That's what they get for disobeying! We gave you orders, soldiers. Next time, you follow them."

We're not soldiers, we're Marines. But somehow, Guns doubted the Slovenian would care about the distinction.

He strode right up to Termite and prodded a finger against his chest plate. "No talking. There are rules. Keep them away with these...." He flicked one finger against the smoke grenade launcher clutched in the Marine's gloved fist. "Otherwise, we kill them. Understand?"

Termite nodded. Guns stayed immobile. If she let herself so much as breathe, she was going to do something reckless. Like tackle the man in front of her. Break his neck, maybe.

But their enemies were like a hydra, with more heads than she could fight alone. Brute force wasn't the solution to this mess with Rupnik, and she wouldn't risk more lives for the sake of temporary satisfaction. So she just stood there as the Slovenians and the civilian police dragged the bodies out of sight.

There were people, she decided, who had less humanity in their hearts than the Ornu did. The very notion made her sick.

If the last of humanity could be this ruthless to one another, who and what exactly were they trying to save?

Chapter Thirty

Commander Bina Chakravarti

She'd done it.

She'd managed to escape the Slovenians' grasp, early enough to run to her quarters and grab some clippers and tweezers, a pocket mirror, and a set of old civilian clothes she never wore around the ship.

After that, she'd run to a secluded corner in Power Cell Storage to shave her head and pluck her eyebrows down to little slivers. Changed into the civvies, she looked like a completely different person.

At least, she thought she did. And if she managed to walk different, and talk different, she thought there was a very good chance she'd be able to escape the notice of the militia that had taken over the ship by slipping in with the millions teeming aboard Omega.

She wasn't sure where she was going as she plodded through the passageways. Screams and shots echoed through the corridors, mingling with the memory that had been replaying in her head ever since she'd fled the bridge before Rupnik's arrival:

Longfield, screaming as she died.

She soon found her way blocked. People were fighting over scraps, raking at each other tooth and nail for a mouthful of expired rations. Bina had to back away. The sight was too much to bear.

Still, she wandered, immersing herself in the horrible reality of life aboard Omega. A little boy and his sister were sharing what looked like the remains of a rat. How had rats gotten aboard? If they got into the supplies, it would be yet another disaster.

As if two children sharing morsels of rat flesh for dinner wasn't a disaster in its own right.

Eventually, her feet carried her to the same place that always called her: the Archive. It was the last place she had communed with Omega, and the first place where she'd made contact with the ship. In a way, each journey here had come to feel like a pilgrimage. The hatch, unlike most of the others, was closed when she arrived, but it opened to her touch.

Inside, the chamber was just as it had been that first day. Even the cries and weeping fell away when the hatch closed behind her.

She flung herself into one of the strange chairs and closed her eyes. Only then, in that utter solitude, did she let herself think of Longfield.

They had been friends, of a sort. Norder was always standoffish, and Keating was loud and brash. Bina had never been particularly close with either of them, nor with Ridding, who had always struck her as reckless. Longfield, though, had been quiet and reserved. Like Bina, she had kept her past private. Whether that was out of some private shame, or merely the result of her nature, Bina had never asked.

Now, she wished she had. Even if it meant she had to reveal her own secrets. She'd never gotten the chance to tell Longfield the truth about how she'd betrayed their fellow officer.

And she never would.

Her throat closed, and her eyes burned with unshed tears. "It's not fair," she muttered. Nothing was. Nothing had been, since the Ornu arrived. In her mind, Bina had built up the time before the Imperium's conquest as a sort of golden age, an era of glorious human triumph that had been destroyed by the war. If Maks and his father were anything to go by, though, she couldn't blame all of humanity's problems on the asps.

She rubbed the pad of her palm below one eye. "I don't know what to do," she whispered. "If Longfield...if Sally was right, then you can still hear us. Why didn't you help her? Why won't you do anything? She deserved better. If it had to be one of us, it should have been me."

A weight settled on her shoulder, as light as the touch she'd felt outside the weapons cache with Nadija. There was no warmth to it, only a faint sensation of pressure.

She lifted her head, knowing that there would be no one there.

A familiar figure stared down at her, his blue eyes cold and brilliant.

Bina screamed and pulled away. The figure watched her impassively. His unnaturally long neck bent to one side as he studied her. She'd encountered the Kanami before, when Val first taught her the history of the Primevals. In fact, he had shown her this one specifically. This was Hyx, the unmodified child who had urged his people to give up their lust for technological self-augmentation. In the simulation, Val had described Hyx's rise to fame.

The Kanami was there on his own. When she looked around, there was no sign of Val. Only Hyx stood beside her in the familiar chamber.

"Are you...." She took a moment to compose herself and order her thoughts. "Are you a simulation?"

Hyx stared at her. He seemed to wait a very long time between blinks. That, coupled with his bizarre proportions and immense height, made her squirm in her seat.

"It was I who discovered the sleeper disease," he said. His voice had an unnatural cadence, reminiscent of a recording in the old holo-museums, and it sounded like three voices rolled into one. Everything about his posture was stiff. Even the motion of his arm seemed rehearsed.

Bina held up a hand. "Val, I know that's you. Hyx has been dead for... centuries? Millennia? There's no way he's here, which means this is a simulation."

Hyx blinked. He made the same expansive gesture with his arm as before. "It was I who—"

"Val, talk to me!" Bina reached out to grab the alien by his shirtfront, but her hands passed through him. Hyx did not seem to notice this discrepancy. He simply started over.

"It was I who discovered the sleeper disease."

"Ugh." Bina stomped her foot against the deck. "All right, I'll listen. But you'll have to talk to one of us eventually."

She played along, turning to look in the direction Hyx had indicated. When she did so, the Archive fell away, to be replaced with a vast, midnight space, populated here and there with distant stars.

"Thanks to the advanced technology of my people, most diseases were easily discovered and cured. Generally, they popped up on a single world, which made them easier to contain and, eventually, to treat. This one was different." Hyx flicked his fingers, and one of the faraway stars rushed up to greet them. He cupped his hands around one of its habitable planets.

"I had many reasons to think that this one was unique. For one, it did not appear on one isolated world." He flicked his fingers again, and the star receded, although it remained visible. Several others grew in size, each orbited by planets that began to pulse with a sickly red glow. "It appeared simultaneously on a dozen of them."

Bina shivered and wrapped her arms around herself. "What did it do?" she asked.

As before, Hyx ignored her. "There were other reasons, too. It mutated quickly, but it often took time to manifest. Between the delayed symptoms and the many points of origin, it was able to spread faster than we could mobilize against it. Truth be told, this was not the first lab-grown disease that had plagued our people, but it was the most virulent. Its outcomes were strange and varied. Some patients died. Others were left infertile, or with gaps in their memory, or with an aversion to food. Each new strain manifested differently, which made it hard to diagnose, and it ravaged our people. Before long, it had spread through Kanami civilization."

Another gesture brought hundreds of worlds into focus, all pulsing red. As he continued to speak, some of the lights faded, and the planets went dark, swallowed by the void around them.

"I was sure it was an attack, designed by some faction within our society. Who created it? I can only speculate. Some member of the disenfranchised masses? A terrorist organization with a bone to pick? The head of a particular planet hoping to bring rival economies to their knees? In the end, it doesn't really matter. Whoever created it may have thought themselves invulnerable, but they fell victim to the collapse it brought about, just as the rest of us did. If it weren't for the voidservants, ever doing all our work for us, our economy probably would have fallen apart then and there."

"This plague...." Bina looked around at the worlds. Some had, evidently, died out, but there were so many of them. It was unthinkable that a single disease would wipe them all out. "Is that how your people became extinct?"

She might as well not have spoken.

"While others looked for a cure, I continued to search inward. This crack in our collective façade was the beginning of what I'd predicted: our civilization's downfall to its blind pursuit of novel tech. Medicine and science were needed to treat the disease, but the ailment was a symptom of a larger rot at the core of our collective consciousness. We did not care for one another. Along the way, we had forgotten that life had value, and begun to value tech and power over one another. But no one would listen to me."

"Wonder why," Bina said, assuming that Hyx would ignore her as he had every other time she spoke.

The Kanami turned to her. He reached out to lay his hands on each of her shoulders. His glowing eyes seemed to bore into her.

"Because to admit that they were wrong would have required them to change, and they were unwilling."

Chills raced up Bina's spine.

"There was only one solution that I could foresee." Hyx released her and turned back to the image of open space. He extended one long arm to point out a specific planet. "I decided to set out for Azure, the Kanami planet of origin. I wanted to see if any answers could be found in the place where everything began."

Chapter Thirty-One

Sergeant Shawn 'Funny Bone' Piker

"I don't need to rest," Jana Nemec insisted. "I'm ready to train. I want to serve, sir." She was sitting on the edge of the medbay pod, still wearing the cargo pants and black tank she'd been wearing when she collapsed.

Al and Funny Bone exchanged a glance. Al raised an eyebrow, and Funny Bone nodded: Nemec was good. As long as Dr. Aviles cleared her, she would be an excellent addition to the team.

Unfortunately, Nemec wasn't addressing them. She was looking up into the face of Captain Rupnik as she spoke.

"Excellent." Rupnik laid a hand on her shoulder and turned to Al and Funny Bone. "This right here is the kind of enthusiasm we need from a new recruit, don't you think, Captain Stone?"

Al inclined his head in the slightest of nods. "Indeed."

Rupnik's eyes remained fixed on the captain's face. Funny Bone knew better than to let his emotions show, but Rupnik's expression made his skin crawl.

"We are in agreement, then." Rupnik bared his teeth in a ghastly smile. "You will commence with training the new recruits."

A tense silence settled over the room. Dr. Aviles hung back, his eyes bouncing between Rupnik and Al. Nemec seemed unaffected by the tension, although she watched Rupnik with interest.

Funny Bone cleared his throat. "The thing is, Captain, we haven't decided who to bring onto the team. We were only looking for two recruits, and now we're looking at three, maybe four people..." And the three I trust to have our backs were the ones who shot your soldiers. He'd been impressed by Nemec during training, but she seemed indifferent about the identity and actions of the person in charge.

"You'll be training all of us," Rupnik said.

Funny Bone did a double-take. "I'm sorry?"

"You'll be training all of us." The Slovenian militiaman sneered at him. "Clearly, my own forces need improvement, too. And who better to train us than the Imperium's finest?"

Funny Bone bit back a groan. Of course. He should have known that the Slovenians wouldn't let them run around unsupervised with weapons. It was too much to hope that Rupnik would leave them to their own devices.

They might not be confined to quarters, but he and the crew were prisoners all the same.

* * *

"If we're all here," Guns asked in a low voice, "then who is guarding the storage bays?"

"Rupnik said it's taken care of," Funny Bone muttered back.

Guns grimaced and ran a hand through her hair. It was short by most standards, but Funny Bone had never seen hers so unruly. As the situation on Omega escalated, personal care had long since fallen by the wayside. All of them were increasingly thin and unkempt, and it made him sick to admit that, in some ways, they had been better off under Ornu control.

Only because we're in a real state of war. That's a first. We've always lived in the heart of the empire, sent out on temporary missions into deep space. Until now, w

e've always had a home base to return t
o on leave.

Funny Bone had hated life under the Imperium's thumb, but he couldn't deny that, given the chance, he would murder a synthetic burger and a heaping pile of starchfries.

Oh...and a beer. His fantasies had never been simpler, or more enticing.

"I don't trust Rupnik's brand of caretaking," Guns said.

Funny Bone swallowed the saliva pooling in his mouth and wiped his lips on the back of his sleeve. "Uh, yeah."

She cocked her head. "You okay, Sergeant?"

"Fine, fine. Hey...where do you think we should start with training?" he asked. "I'm going to be in charge of running drills, but Captain Stone wants to see what our trainees are made of."

"'Captain Stone,' huh?" Guns said. "Are we getting all formal now?"

"I don't want to be too…familiar with him, all things considered. Don't want to give anyone ideas."

Guns grimaced. "Makes sense, I guess."

She hadn't complained about her injuries, at least not where he could hear, but she was still moving gingerly. There was no way she'd forgotten who gave her those injuries in the first place, and training alongside the culprits must be a challenge. It wouldn't take much for a fight to break out, and Rupnik's men outnumbered them significantly. The team hadn't worn their exosuits to the training session, and even though they were better trained, he didn't want to risk an incident.

Rupnik hadn't tried to take their exosuits yet, but that was probably only a matter of time. For now, he was likely letting them keep the suits to avoid upsetting them enough that they would refuse to train his men.

They left the smaller chamber they were using as a locker room and went out into the training area, where the other Marines were waiting for him to start.

Funny Bone sucked in a breath and clapped his hands together. "All right, folks! Line up. I'll be dividing everyone into two teams. One of you will be doing some sparring with the crowd control weapons provided by the Slovenians; the rest will be working on your target practice. No live ammo—we're going to need it later. We'll be working on form using rubber rounds. Just don't shoot each other. If I see anyone acting irresponsibly with any weapon, you're out."

The recruits fell into line, and Funny Bone divided them into seemingly random groups, although in truth he was paying special attention to who was shuffled into each team. Guns and Tubes were with the target practice team, partly to give Guns a bit of a respite while she finished healing, while Termite and Splat were on sparring duty. He put Kan and Awad in one group, and Nemec and Christiano in another, dividing up his top candidates... and the three recruits he actually trusted. The others, he sorted based on known strengths; if he put all of the best fighters in one group, the others would never get a chance to improve.

And, of course, he split up the Slovenian trainees.

While the Marines assigned to each team led the drills, Stone and Funny Bone walked among them, observing their strategies and offering insight when they could.

To Funny Bone's surprise, Stone stopped alongside Nemec while she sighted in on a target.

"Think about your stance," he said. "You're focused on your upper body, but in real combat, you'll have to be prepared to move at a moment's notice." He stayed with her while she fired off three shots, offering pointers in between each. When he was satisfied, he moved on.

Nemec waited until he was several rows away before turning her attention to Funny Bone. "The captain is very precise, isn't he?"

"He's seen a lot of good Marines come and go," Funny Bone explained. "He hates losing people, and proper training can mean the difference between life and death."

Nemec nodded thoughtfully. "When I was younger, I went elk hunting with a friend. We were young. Didn't know what we were doing. I wish we'd been better prepared."

Funny Bone cocked his head. "Yeah?"

"Maybe if we'd had someone like Captain Stone to train us, my friend would still be alive." Nemec raised her practice rifle and peered through the scope, incrementally adjusting her stance. "Poor Hubert. His aim was never very good."

There was something about her tone, and her expression, that set Funny Bone on edge. A small smile turned up the corners of Nemec's lips.

The next time she fired, she hit her target dead on-center.

"Precision is everything," Nemec said.

On her lips, the words had the timbre of a threat.

Chapter Thirty-Two

Commander Bina Chakravarti

"I was familiar with Azure's history," Hyx said. "I had long since come to the conclusion that in order to shape our future, we must understand our past. How else could we avoid making the same mistakes? How else could we re-chart our course? But much of my reading revolved around the philosophy of earlier eras, the writings of our great minds, the records of our most success-ful leaders. By returning to the archae-ological sites of our homeworld, I hoped to learn more about our technology." He smiled wryly. "I was coming to think of tech as my enemy...and until you understand your enemy, you cannot know how to fight it."

Azure, the Kanami homeworld, expanded as he spoke. What had begun as the size of a ball bearing was now a globe. Gradually their perspective shifted, until Bina and Hyx stood over the planet with a satellite's-eye view over the landscape.

"I envy you that," she murmured. "When the time comes for humanity to reflect on what brought us this, we'll have no archaeological record for reference. Any books and archives that were left behind are gone."

"Omega is the archive," Hyx said.

Bina swiveled to face him. "What?"

Hyx was looking back at her, his glowing blue eyes fixed on her face. Without thinking, she reached up to trace the X-shaped scar over her nose. His attention made her shift uncomfortably. He was so intense. She was starting to understand why some of his people were so drawn to him.

And why others feared him.

"Omega is the archive," Hyx repeated. "Time only moves in one direction, but those who remember carry the past with them."

Bina's heart beat double-time. "But—"

He turned back to the planet. "Based on my reputation, I was able to gain access to the site with relative ease."

The planet spun up toward him, telling Bina's senses that she was falling. She had to close her eyes to ward off the wave of nausea unfolding in her belly. As soon as she did, the sensation faded. None of this was real. Or at least, it wasn't really happening to her. Hyx had been dead for a long time, and the thing beside her was nothing but a simulation—a technological record of an era long passed.

When she opened her eyes again, she was standing in the middle of an archaeological dig. The site itself looked typical—all ruins shared a certain bittersweet appearance—but the skyline was alien, the weeds growing in between the old footprints of buildings were unfamiliar, and the sky above them was such a brilliant sapphire shade that looked photo-edited.

No wonder Hyx had translated the name of his homeworld into a word for blue. Instead of the clouds Bina recalled from her days on Earth, wisps of meandering white streaked across the heavens in winding ribbons. She could make out distant solar condensers and metal towers on the plain between the dig site and the stone spires along the horizon.

Hyx still stood beside her, but he was dressed differently than before, in a fitted green jumpsuit and work boots. The Kanami woman standing across from him was dressed in the same way, but Bina's eyebrows shot up as she examined this newcomer: she was dripping in tech, some of which she wore like jewelry, some of which was embedded deeply into her body. Likely, there was more that Bina couldn't see. Implants. Modifications.

Both of the figures stood frozen, as if they'd been paused mid-conversation. Bina was still looking around when they sprang, simultaneously, to life.

"—so excited to have you here," the woman said. "I'm familiar with your work, of course. What's really fascinating to me is that you've chosen to live in essentially the same way our ancestors did. Like the people who would have lived here, back when the site was still a thriving metropolis." She waved her hands to encompass the ruins. "You're like living history! You've chosen to deny the advantages our modern world has to offer, and to eschew upgrades."

Hyx gave the woman a small smile. "I appreciate your enthusiasm, Kalykk, but I am not a historical relic. I live in the present."

Kalykk pressed her hands to her face. A soft blue glow emanated from her skin. "My apologies. Of course, of course. I spoke without thinking."

"You spoke the same way many of our fellows think. I am not offended." Hyx made a strange gesture with his hands, which Kalykk appeared to find comforting. "I hear you have made a recent discovery...?"

Evidently relieved by the change of subject, Kalykk turned toward Bina. Before the commander could jump aside, the alien was walking right through her to get to a covered table at Bina's back. She hadn't noticed it before. In fact, she was pretty sure it hadn't been there when she was looking around earlier. A corruption of memory? Or an intentional omission, for the sake of dramatic effect?

"Yes," Kalykk said, "we've found these." She gestured to a cloth, atop which rested little fragments of metal. They were small, and many of them were crusted in mineral deposits. The two Kanami leaned over them, and Bina did the same, although she was careful not to touch either of the aliens as she did. The world around her looked so real that passing through it was an unsettling prospect.

Hyx reached toward a fragment of metal, but stopped before his fingers brushed it. "May I?" he asked.

Kalykk produced a pair of gloves from a pocket of her jumpsuit. "Put these on first, please. The oils from our fingers could damage the artifacts and cause issues with any samples we may take later."

Hyx dutifully pulled on the gloves, then lifted the object closer to his face for inspection. Each of the little pieces was different from the next, with some smooth, regular elements that were obviously manufactured, while other sections were rough and jagged from where they'd been damaged or broken.

"What are these?" he asked.

"That's the thing. We don't know." Rather than appearing dismayed by her lack of insight, Kalykk was positively bursting with excitement. "I've never encountered anything like them, at any dig. None of my colleagues have either. In fact, they appear to be unique in our records. Several of them are made from metals not found on Azure."

Hyx, still holding the object, turned to face her. "Really? But I was under the impression there was no extraplanetary mining capacity at the time."

"That's the thing. There wasn't." Kalykk could barely contain her excitement, and even though the Kanami herself was long gone, her enthusiasm was infectious. Bina leaned closer, trying to make sense of the artifacts herself. "And before you ask, yes, I'm sure that they're from the right era."

"Can you tell where this mineral came from?" Hyx asked.

Kalykk hesitated. "Well, it's not just one mineral. There are several of them, and they aren't found together. Can't you tell?"

Hyx set the object back on the cloth and reached for another. "I assume you have an implant that recognizes the object ID tag," he said.

Kalykk pressed her hands to her face again and uttered a sound that meant nothing to Bina. Presumably, it was a Kanami curse that either Hyx or Omega hadn't bothered to translate. "I'm sorry, I forgot again! I can provide a hard copy of the data this afternoon, if you like. Actually, I can have a voidling run and collect it right now."

"No," Hyx said sharply.

The other Kanami just looked at him, eyes widening.

"Sorry, I—I didn't mean to speak so harshly. I would just prefer that the data not pass through the hands of a void-servant. If I can trouble you, would you mind pulling it and giving it to me your-self?"

"Of course."

"Thank you. Anything you can tell me would be much appreciated."

Kalykk made a series of nervous ges-tures. Bina didn't know much about Kanami biology, but she was beginning to suspect Kalykk was quite young. She'd also begun to pick up on the physical gestures made by both aliens. Hyx's movements, like the rest of his demeanor, were muted and reserved, but they bore a resemblance to Kalykk's that had to be more than coincidental. They seemed to add another layer of nuance to their communication that was lost on Bina.

"I don't mean to pry," Kalykk said, "but do you mind if I ask...why the interest in this old tech?"

Hyx bobbed his head back and forth. "Where does yours come from?"

"Like I said, I'm fascinated by the way people used to live." Kalykk cast a longing glance at the site. "In some ways, I think I would have liked to live back then...but I'm not sure how I'd go about it now. I wouldn't be able to do my job without my upgrades. And I would lose contact with people I love. You, though, you already know what it's like."

Hyx hummed. "Believe it or not, I don't hate technology. I simply believe in moderation, and believe that we've long since passed that point. As a species, I mean. And yes, I know what it's like to live without upgrades, as you call them, but I am still navigating life in a time and place where these things are ubiquitous. I cannot imagine a reality in which someone like me is considered normal any more than you can."

Kalykk made a soft noise of dismay. "I've said the wrong thing again."

"I would prefer that you speak frankly, so that we may be honest with each other. Please, don't censor yourself on my account." He gestured to the table of artifacts. "May I spend some time with these?"

Kalykk twined her fingers together. "Well...."

"I won't harm them, I promise. I hold great reverence for the past." Hyx straightened up. "As do many of my associates, who might be willing to put in a good word for your efforts here."

Kalykk's eyes widened. "You think you could get the project more funding?"

"I certainly hope so."

"That would be wonderful. Our grants have been limited. Even the universities would rather invest in the future than the past."

A door opened beyond Kalykk, and a small figure no more than two feet came in bearing a tray bearing a metal canister and two cups. Its skin was a smooth, shifting tapestry of reds, greens, and blacks. Bina found her gaze drawn to it, mesmerized by its appearance.

When it reached the pair of aliens, Hyx drew back suddenly.

"Oh...what is it?" Kalykk asked. "What's the matter?"

"That...I'm sorry, I don't make use of void-servants. I'm not used to them."

"I see. Well, would you like some madi?"

"No. No thank you."

Both figures froze again, and the second Hyx, the older Hyx, reappeared at Bina's side.

"Kalykk was most cooperative. I admit that I liked her...we did not always see eye to eye, but I respected her insights, and her implants helped me gather information that I could not have accessed on my own. After that initial meeting, we worked together for many months."

Hyx waved a hand, and the scene blurred back into motion, but at great speed. Night and day chased each other across the sky. The plants around them grew taller, then bloomed, then withered.

"For more than half a solar cycle, I stayed there, learning all that I could from the records, and from the site, and from Ka-lykk herself. Until one evening, in the darkest part of the year...."

The spinning wheel of the year stopped abruptly. The younger Hyx, now wearing a scarlet jumpsuit, sat on the floor of a small structure. Around him lay a growing array of tech, including larger pieces than the site manager had shown him in the field. A bound catalog of the objects lay open beside him, and the Hyx was poring over it. Bina couldn't read the writing on the pages, but the images were recognizable enough.

Hyx flipped another page. He reached for the matching object when a sudden sound, like a pop of static, echoed through the quiet room. He froze.

The sound intensified. Young Hyx and Bina looked around, but the Kanami's older counterpart was already pointing to an object near the edge of the room. It was a small box, less damaged than the metal fragments, but also less distinctive. With shaking hands, Hyx reached for it. When his gloved fingers brushed its surface, he recoiled momentarily. It must have given him a static shock, or been vibrating in a way he hadn't anticipated.

Gingerly, with both hands, he lifted the box from the floor.

"What is this?" he murmured to himself. Shifting his grip so that it sat in one hand, he reached for the booklet and began flipping through the pages in search of a matching entry.

The static shifted, and instead of white noise, Bina became convinced she could hear something more...distinct.

A voice. A word. A message.

"Hyx," the box said. "Hyx?"

The young Kanami stopped cold. He was so still, for so long, that Bina wondered if something had happened to him.

Only when a full ten seconds had elapsed did she realize that, once again, he'd been paused.

"Well?" She turned to her guide. "What happened then?"

The older Hyx stared at his younger self. Gradually, he turned his face toward her. His blue eyes were so brilliant, she couldn't look away. Everything was saturated in blue as his eyes expanded into the skies of Azure, marbled with pale clouds, and then—

She sat up from the deck, scrabbling at the metal plates beneath her. At some point, she had slipped or stumbled away from the chair where she'd been sitting when Hyx first appeared.

The Archive was empty once again, and when Bina finally raised herself to her knees, she found no indication that anyone or anything had visited her. She hadn't really expected to, since she'd known it was all a sim. Still, she pounded her fist against the deck in frustration.

"Why stop there?" she cried. "Why tell me that much, and then send me away again? What am I supposed to do about any of this?"

Her words echoed through the room, and died away, leaving only silence in their wake. Bina's head was killing her, and her anger made her temples throb with every heartbeat.

Whoever had visited her was gone.

Bina checked her watch and groaned when she saw the time.

I can't stay here for so long! Rupnik and his goons were no doubt occupied, but if they caught her here, she'd surely be found out.

Chapter Thirty-Three

Petty Officer Mike 'Tubes' Lamprey

"W on't Funny Bone need us in training today?" Tubes asked.

Stone kept his back toward the petty officer. "Wish I knew why you were asking questions, Lamprey. I gave you an order, and I expect you to follow it this time."

Tubes ground his teeth together. He respected his commanding officer a lot, he really did, but when was the captain going to let that go? Yes, he'd messed up...but he'd also saved Stone's life. Baby Rupnik had proven that he was more than happy to kill anyone who didn't play nice. If Tubes hadn't acted when he did, five more people would be dead, and Rupnik would be in an even stronger position. Yes, he'd defied an order. Given the choice, he'd make the same call again.

Somehow, he didn't think that admitting it aloud would go over well.

Termite cast him a sympathetic glance. "I'm just surprised they're letting us patrol," he said. "We've only been at this a couple of days. Are Rupnik's forces spread that thin, or is he just that cocky?"

"It's a test," Stone said. "Everything's a test. And even if it's not, treat it like it is. We don't know who's on his side and who's on ours. But there's one thing we can all agree on: another riot would be bad for everyone."

The three Marines set off through the ship on patrol. They passed clusters of civilian police as they went, many of whom lifted their hands in greeting. Tubes still wasn't sure where they stood with most of the volunteers, but he doubted they could count on them for backup. Rupnik's rumor mill was always churning, and he had his fingers in far too many pies.

"Are we going somewhere specific?" Termite asked.

"Officially, no." Stone turned left down a corridor. Some of the civilians ahead of them scattered, but others watched them intently with varying degrees of distrust. "Unofficially? I want to check in on Bill's parents. He hasn't been asking about them, because he doesn't want to remind Rupnik about them. After what happened to Longfield...."

He didn't need to say anything more. Longfield's absence was an ongoing weight on all their shoulders, and nobody had seen Keating since she was taken. At least they knew for sure that Norder was alive, since he spent his shifts on the bridge.

It soon became apparent that the lower decks had descended into an unprecedented level of chaos. Civilians looked much worse for wear, and factions were more clearly delineated. While Bill and the ship's officers had done their best to encourage people to work together, Rupnik's regime had taken the concept of divide and conquer to heart.

Abruptly, someone started screaming. It was a woman's voice, and her wailing was quickly joined by the cries of children, and then more adults. Whatever was happening, it was close by, and it was escalating quickly.

Tubes lurched into action, hampered as always by the limited mobility of the exosuit. Nearby civilians, usually deterred by the presence of suited-up Marines, swirled past him as they, too, tried to get closer to the source of the noise.

"Tubes!" Termite called after him. When he glanced back, he saw the crowd had come between them, and that short of trampling people to get ahead, the captain and Gonzales would find it difficult to catch up.

At last, the crowd broke, and Tubes stumbled into the disruption at its core. Two men were fighting a woman, who lay on the ground clutching something in her arms. Three children watched, wailing in dismay, holding each other, their skinny faces streaked with dirt and tears.

At first, Tubes thought the woman was holding a fourth child in her arms. The bundle pressed against her chest was swaddled in fabric, and might easily have been a baby, given its size.

"What's going on?" he asked the spectators. The whole experience was strangely reminiscent of a playground squabble, although the stakes were clearly much higher.

"She stole from them," a nearby woman said. Her eyes were fixed on the bundle. "She tried to snatch some food for her children."

Even as she spoke, the fabric around the bundle unspooled, and MREs scattered across the deck. The woman dove for them, as did her assailants, along with the rest of the crowd.

Tubes left them to it. There was no way he'd be able to stop the ravenous refugees from taking whatever they could grab, and no point in trying. Instead, he reached for the woman, with some vague notion that he should separate her and her children from the men she'd tried to rob.

As he did, something stabbed him in the armpit. The exosuits had layered seams, weak points where the joints met, and he realized that one of these seams had been breached almost before he realized that he'd been attacked. For a moment, his arm locked up, and he tried to move it a few times, more confused than alarmed.

Then the pain came, blinding and hot, accompanied by a warm trickle of blood that ran beneath his suit, clinging to his skin and soaking his clothes. He had to crane his neck at an unlikely angle until the shard of rough-edged metal came into view. Someone had jammed it up through the armpit of his suit right into his skin, not only stabbing him, but effectively locking his shoulder joint forward so that he couldn't reach the metal to remove it.

He stood there for a moment, unsure of what to do while white-hot pain radiated outward from the wound. He couldn't even wield his weapon effectively, which severely hampered his ability to respond to the threat.

Termite dove through the crowd, weapon raised. Tubes hadn't seen the man who'd attacked him, but evidently Termite had. He was on him in a flash. He drove his gloved fist into the assailant's chest with such force he was thrown to the ground. Before the man could regain his footing, Termite drove the barrel of his gun into the man's chest. If Termite pulled the trigger, the civilian would be obliterated.

"No!" Tubes yelped.

His response, however, was lost in the cry of wordless rage that echoed through their helmet speakers. Termite was hauled back, lifted off his target by the only person on the ship strong enough to lift a Marine in a several-hundred-pound exosuit: another member of their team.

"We don't execute civilians!" Stone snarled. He set Termite down to one side and yanked the M234 out of his grasp.

"Why not?" Termite demanded. "That man could have killed Tubes. You want him to end up like Longfield?"

"Tubes isn't dead." Stone shoved the younger private away. "And even if he was, it's not our job to execute civilians, Gonzales. We turn them over to the civil authorities."

Termite was shaking so badly that even the exosuit couldn't hide it. "What civil authorities? Rupnik?"

Stone glared at him. "Get your fellow Marine to medical."

"Captain—"

"Get him to medical. That's an order." Stone turned his back on them.

Termite huffed and turned to face Tubes. "Should I pull that out?" he asked, nodding to the metal wedged into Tubes' joint.

The crowd was already dispersing, cowed by the fight between the Marines. No doubt word of their argument would get back to Rupnik soon enough.

"No," Tubes said, after a moment's consideration. "I think we should leave that to a medic." Already, he could feel blood pooling in his left boot, trickling all the way down his back from the site of the injury.

"Can you walk?" Termite asked.

"In this suit?" Tubes managed a weak smile. "It'll be slow going."

They left Captain Stone to subdue his attacker. As the only one injured, despite his best intentions, Tubes was left with the feeling that he had screwed up the mission significantly.

Again.

Chapter Thirty-Four

Captain Bill Henderson

The surface of Vale lay below them, filling the screens of the bridge. It was a surprisingly lovely planet that didn't at all match his experience of the Awn, or even his expectations for a world within the bounds of the Imperium's grasp. Earth—and, indeed, most of the other inhabited worlds Bill had visited—had been polluted and deforested for decades. Only the smaller planetesimals, like one from which Omega had been recovered, were still brilliant and beautiful.

Vale was mostly blue, although its coastlines were almost violet in hue, while the deepest reaches of its oceans were a bruised blue-black in places. Small volcanic islands peppered its shallows, but there was only one true continent—an amalgam of tectonic plates divided by three rivers so wide they could be seen from space. There wasn't a single fleck of green on the land, at least that he could make out: instead, its forests were predominantly purple in tone. It made Vale look less like a habitable planet and more like an enormous jeweled orb, its globe colored in by a child who had chosen from the box of crayons more or less at random.

At his side, Norder shook his head. "How did such a beautiful planet produce such an ugly dominant species?"

Bill snorted. "I was wondering the same thing." He folded his arms over his chest and turned his attention back to the planet before them. Not for the first time, he wondered what game Rupnik was playing. Surely they hadn't come all this way and risked so much for wealth? Awn was known for its mineral deposits and deep-sea mining, but what was the point of money if you were an outlaw?

Maybe he plans to approach the Perseids. Try to strike a deal with them. Either way, they needed food and supplies aboard the Omega, and the Awn would have those in abundance.

The hatch behind them opened, and Maks Rupnik strode through. He was wearing the same cocky smile he seemed to wear when he was convinced he had the upper hand.

"You lied to me, Captain," he announced. "I just had a very illuminating chat with your Weapons officer, Keating. She informed me that Omega has also listened to Captain Stone. All it took to find this out was threatening to kill your old Nav officer, Ridding, who I understand is in a coma in the medbay."

"Hm," Bill said.

"But isn't this interesting? Here I was, laboring under the impression that Omega would listen to you and only you, while all this time it's been willing to work with the Marine captain, too."

Bill dipped his head. "I've got to hand it to you, Rupnik, your English is getting better by the day."

"Thank you for noticing." Rupnik arched an eyebrow. "Is Keating telling the truth?"

"She is," Bill said. There was no point in lying, and telling the truth might spare Keating any physical harm.

"I find it interesting that you failed to mention this, but I'm sure it merely... slipped your mind. You've been under so much stress lately." Rupnik patted his shoulder, and Bill fought the urge to recoil from the contact.

"Omega decided that it would prefer to work with me," he said. "I can't guarantee that it will work for Captain Stone, now that it's become... attuned to me." There was no way he was going to explain the full complexity of the situation with the Primeval tech to this little rat.

"Let's test it, shall we?" Rupnik turned back to his men and said something in Slovenian. Two soldiers moved forward to grab Norder.

"Now, hold on—" Bill began.

Rupnik held up a hand in warning. "Careful, Henderson. I've decided to be understanding for now, but I don't like surprises, and my temper is running short."

Bill quietly seethed, but Rupnik never so much as blinked. The soldiers dragged Norder away, and eventually they returned, this time with Al in tow. At least they hadn't tried to lay hands on him. He appeared to have come quietly.

"It's time for Mr. Norder to stay away for a little while, I think," Rupnik said. "If you behave, Henderson, perhaps you will meet him again someday. As for you, Captain Stone...congratulations!" Rupnik spread his arms wide. "You're in temporary command of the Omega. Please, have a seat." He ushered Al toward the command chair.

As soon as Al sank into the chair, the console came to life. Rupnik clapped his hands like a toddler who'd just received a shiny new toy.

"Wonderful! Captain Stone and I will stay here and...get to know each other better." Rupnik pointed to the jeweled planet on the massive screens. "Henderson, you will be going to Vale. By now you must have quite a reputation with the Ornu vassal species, and you're the most likely to be taken seriously. I'm sure you can convince the Awn government to ship up as many resources and supplies as they have on hand. Especially when you inform them that if they don't, I will have to use the Omega to bombard their cities into rubble."

Bill did his best to keep his expression neutral. He saw a few problems with Rupnik's plan, not the least of which be-ing that he doubted Al would cooperate with it.

"Keep in mind, Henderson," Rupnik went on. "A lot depends on your success. Not the least of which is your crew's well-being, as well as that of your mother and father. Two hours." He held up two fingers, in case there was any chance of misunderstanding. "After that, we will start firing on their cities if there is no deal. Do I make myself clear?"

"Crystal," Bill spat. He turned on his heel and marched off toward the landing bay. A pair of Slovenian militiamen followed behind.

* * *

Splat flew Bill down to Vale, taking the Can through the atmosphere and over an amethyst jungle. As they got closer, the Marine began to broadcast a generic greeting and assurance they meant no harm.

If Longfield was here, we could broadcast a n Awn-specific greeting, Bill reflected. He still couldn't believe Longfield was gone. These last few days, he could almost still feel her presence aboard the ship...judging him for everything he'd failed to do, most likely.

"We're coming in for a landing," Splat said. "Looks like we're being met by a welcoming party."

Bill leaned forward to study the nearest screen, dreading what he was about to do.

Chapter Thirty-Five

Captain Bill Henderson

Don't judge a book by its cover was an old pre-Ornu adage, but Bill had learned the same sentiment applied to alien species. Take the Roughbacks, for example... they were hardly paragons of beauty, but they were loyal and steadfast creatures who would fight to the death for their kin. The Ornu, by comparison, were far more regal and mesmerizing, but they hid their cruelty behind a guise of refinement.

The Awn, however, were exactly what you'd expect based on their appearance. Their enormous eyes, roughly the size of dinner plates, pointed out from their heads in opposite directions, and had a tendency to turn independently of one another. Their bodies were soft, with slime-covered skin that sagged when they sat still for too long. Their mouths hinged open right in the middle of their faces. If a toad and a blobfish had a baby, and that baby grew to the size of a German shepherd, it would probably look something like the Awn.

No, scratch that—the Awn were uglier than that.

All of which would have been fine if it was possible to have a normal conversation with them, since nothing would ever be as disturbing as the sight of Crendelen. Unfortunately, Awn communication was...unique, at least by human standards.

Three of the aliens stood closest to him, arranged in a little crescent, watching him with their strange, rotating eyes. They had introduced themselves, but

Bill found their names incomprehensible...not just difficult to pronounce, but difficult to hear, since their vocal range ran both lower and higher than his.

The rest hung back, evidently divided into three factions, although Bill could make out no unifying characteristics that would distinguish them. The Awn were a variety of colors, ranging from bright pastel tones of yellow and pink to a dark, mottled gray. They wore no uniforms or emblems. Perhaps they differentiated one another by other means. Scent, maybe, or something that could not be perceived by human senses.

A bit of the muck on which they stood had begun to seep into Bill's boots, and he shifted his stance. The movements were accompanied by a sucking sound; he was already sinking into the soggy landmass upon which they stood. The shoreline was only a few dozen yards away, and rather than being made of sand, this beach consisted of soil that reminded Bill of old videos of Earth's peat marshes.

"Greetings, honored delegates." Bill bowed to the Awn, specifically the three that stood before him. Rather than loom over them, he got down on one knee, resting his hands on his leg for stability. Within seconds, the thick muck began to leach through the knee of his already well-worn trousers.

"Greetings, Captain Bill Henderson," said the middle delegate, and her words—his words? Who could tell?—were echoed back by the assembly in chorus, reminiscent of the cries of spring peepers.

"Greetings.

"Greetings!"

"Greetings...."

Bill was relieved to learn that the delegates understood English. He missed Longfield on a personal level, but her absence in this sort of meeting left more than a sentimental wound. He would need to be understood, and without someone versed in Awn customs to guide him, it would be all too easy to commit an offense that would sour relations.

"Thank you for accepting our request to meet." Bill cleared his throat. "I understand that doing so could compromise your standing with the Imperium."

One of the leftmost delegate's eyes rolled skyward. "We have been Empowered," she rumbled, "as the Ornu call it. But this only means that they strip our supplies from us. We ravage our world in service of their greed."

"Greed.

"Greed!"

"Greed...."

The right-hand delegate narrowed her eyes; her eyelids folded in from the sides, but the expression was familiar enough. "Why are you here, Captain?"

"We're here to request aid. We've left our world behind, as I'm sure you know by now, and we're running short on supplies. We've come to request that you send us back with as much human-consumable food as you can spare."

The three Awn delegates turned to face each other, their eyes splaying uncannily so that all three of them could make eye contact at the same time. They did not speak aloud, but Bill quickly became aware of a slight buzzing in the air, a hum like that of a distant engine. He'd spent so long aboard Omega that he'd gotten used to certain types of background noise, but amid the ambient birdsong and the rustle of leaves, the sound was unnatural. He thought it might be coming from the Awn themselves.

From the back of the crowd, one of the Awn said, "Dip."

"Dip!"

"Dip!"

The cry was immediately taken up in chorus, and the Awn turned as one, hopping away toward the waterline. Soon, the entire delegation—at least two hundred in total, he was sure—were submerged in the water, with only their bulbous eyes still visible.

After a few moments of soaking, they re-emerged from the water. Bill noted that many of them had changed color, so that they now fell into two distinct categories: pale, bright colors, and dark tones approaching black. Their skin had changed texture as well. The brightly colored Awn were smooth, while those who had darkened their pigment were now bumpy and ridged. Perhaps he had underestimated their species' complexity after all.

"We need to maintain our moisture," the central primary delegate said. She was among those who had darkened her pigmentation. Her two associates, however, were lighter than before. Did that mean that they were more sympathetic to the humans' cause? Or was he reading too much into it?

"Too much dry air is not good for our pores."

"Pores!

"Pores...."

"Now, as to the matter of your request...." She extended one damp finger in Bill's direction. "We understand the depth of your need. We are all sympathetic. However, some of us are concerned over the possible repercussions for helping you. This is a tumultuous time, and while the Perseid's invasion of Imperium space may afford an opportunity to—"

"Hold up," Bill said. "The Perseids are invading the Imperium?"

"Yes. In retaliation for the brutalizing of Armon."

Bill raised his eyebrows. "I see."

"At any rate, I cannot speak for all of our people."

"I understand, but if you're their leader, then—"

The Awn delegate let out a loud burp. It seemed to go on for an interminable length of time, and she trembled during it. Eventually, Bill realized she was laughing.

"The three of us are co-senators," the alien explained. "We represent the three arms of the Magnetic North. At present, only I am moved to cede to your request. My co-senators are, I'm afraid, more reluctant." She bobbed her head toward the other two.

So Bill had gotten it wrong, then. The brighter colors represented dissent. He supposed that, in nature, brighter colors were frequently associated with poison—a clear warning to predators to stay away. A quick survey of the Awn suggested that more than half of them were against the idea of helping.

"I am willing to speak on your behalf," the Awn delegate went on. "But before I can offer up any aid, we will need to discuss the matter with the co-senators of the other regions."

Bill grimaced. "How many of you are there?"

She considered this. "There are forty-three districts, although a two-thirds majority should be enough to secure—"

"We're on a bit of a time crunch," Bill said through gritted teeth.

The delegate frowned. "Surely you understand the significance of your request? If we agree to help you, we will risk the wrath of the Imperium. We could be deemed Defunct."

And if you don't, the madman who took control of our ship will wipe this place off the map.

"And I will not subject my people to the same fate as yours," the Awn added. "Not without discussing the matter with my peers. Vale is not Earth."

"Earth," the chorus around them echoed, but somberly, as at a funeral.

Bill worried his bottom lip between his teeth. At last, he rose to his feet. "I need to radio back to my ship," he said. "May I have a moment?"

The Awn inclined her head. "Of course. In the meantime, we will take a refreshing dip."

"Dip.

"Dip!"

"Dip...."

The Awn hopped one way, and Bill went the other, back up the slope to the Can where he could radio Rupnik in private. He was certain that the Awn, too, were deep in discussion regarding their next move.

He sank into the pilot's chair without explaining anything to Splat and reached for the com. He powered it on and waited, in silence, until Rupnik answered.

"I hope you have good news for me, Henderson."

"I'm afraid we've underestimated the complexity of Awn society. There's no centralized global body. We need time to meet with more of them."

Rupnik was silent for a long moment. "You know the problem?" he asked at last. His voice was low and dangerous. "I don't think you're taking me seriously."

"I am," Bill said evenly. "And we're making progress."

"Maybe a display of our might would help grease the wheels," Rupnik suggested. His voice became muffled for a moment; he was clearly speaking to someone else. "You can target from there, can't you? Aim right at one of the cities. Not the one where your beloved former captain is...but close enough to make them sweat."

There was a pause. Someone else spoke.

Rupnik's answering growl made the speakers pop and crackle. "Henderson, tell Captain Stone to do as I've said, or I'll shoot him."

Bill's mouth opened, but no sound came out. I won't risk my crew. In a choice between the Awn and his own people, it was no contest.

But Al would refuse. His morals wouldn't allow him to fire on one of the aliens' cities. And then Bill would have to listen to him die, just like he'd listened to Longfield.

"Rupnik," he said, surprised at how level he kept his voice. "We need supplies. The people need food. We don't know Awn territory, and we surely don't know how to navigate their cities, which are almost certainly underwater, given their particular biology. We can either start another war and waste time we don't have, or we can make a deal with the Awn like civilized adults. If word gets out that we're bombarding every planet we approach, we'll make everything harder on ourselves. We'll be fighting a war on all fronts. Just give us more time, will you?"

A long silence came over the com.

"And how long do you think is reasonable, Henderson?"

"Two days. Or whatever passes for days on this world. It'll give us time to get the information we need, and either convince the Awn to help us, or determine your best target."

"Two days," Rupnik said. "If I find that you're going behind my back...."

With that, the line went dead.

Chapter Thirty-Six

Former Signifier Nonus

Nonus was leafing through another book on the rise and might of the Ornu Imperium. This one seemed to be written for hatchlings, and followed the childhood of Emperor Albus, who—according to the literature—had been a prodigy since he first crawled out of the shell. The literature was littered with cheerful phrases, promising the reader a bright future if only they followed the clear-cut ideals of the empire.

Nonus snorted and tossed the book aside. It was ridiculous. The sort of thing only a child would believe. The sort of thing he had believed until recently, fortified by the lies he'd been spoonfed by his mother and uncle.

In hindsight, he could see the lie for what it was: a false promise, told to make neonates fall in line. Contrary to the book's promises, the Imperium did not offer him the chance to thrive, much less to recover from his mistakes. He had been cast aside at the first opportunity, after dedicating his life to the cause.

Unfortunately, there was precious little to do with his time, so he found himself sitting in idle silence, musing over his misfortune.

And, on occasion, plotting elaborate and implausible schemes for revenge.

He had lost track of the passage of time, down here in the prison where the only light he ever saw was artificial. When the door to his cell rattled, he thought it must be time for another meal. The door swung open to reveal, not a guard, but a familiar sympathetic face.

"Uncle Philo?" He lurched upright, nearly toppling the resting bar where he'd been sitting.

"Nephew." Philo inclined his head in greeting, and Nonus stopped short of throwing himself into his uncle's arms, the way he had as a neonate. Instead, he bowed and let out the breath he'd been holding.

Philo turned and shot a pointed look at the guard, who locked the door behind him and withdrew.

Nonus couldn't think of what to say, so he held his peace as Philo glanced around the room, taking in the details. Nonus curled his hands into fists: it was humiliating to live like this, but far worse for his uncle to see the depths to which he'd been sunk.

"It's good to see you, Nonus." Philo's perusal of the room ended, and he turned the full force of his attention on his nephew. "These are most unfortunate circumstances, I'm afraid, but I have hope that wrongs will be righted in due course."

The familiar authority of his uncle's demeanor soothed Nonus' worries. Already, his earlier anger had begun to cool. Perhaps he'd judged the system too harshly. If Philo was here, his future must be looking up.

"I know that you've been waiting here a long time, nephew, but I have not been idle." Philo approached the table and braced all four of his palms against its surface. The usually rickety table did not so much as wobble, as if it, too, respected Philo's authority. "I have the ear of Emperor Albus, and we have come to...an agreement regarding your future. I will speak on your behalf, but there is something I must know if I am to defend you properly."

Nonus closed his eyes. He knew what was coming, and did not want to see the expression on his uncle's face when he asked the inevitable question.

"What really happened at Armon?"

Nonus breathed through his nose. It is an understandable question, he thought. And after all, this was Philo. His uncle. His best ally, and greatest defender. His own flesh and blood.

"Was Pertinax truly responsible?" Philo pressed.

Nonus considered lying...but instead, he bowed his head. "No, Uncle. I thought I was doing the best thing for the Imperium."

Philo sucked in a breath. "Against the Emperor's wishes?"

"We were at war. I followed my training, and thought it prudent to prove the might of the Ornu—to bring the treacherous Perseids to heel with our new-found tech. Emperor Albus wasn't there, of course, so we were the ones making the decisions. Yes, I gave the order. But Pertinax—"

Philo held up a hand. "Enough. There is no need to defend yourself. You are not on trial today."

Nonus fought to keep his breathing even. It would not do to show unnecessary weakness now, when he'd just spoken about the might of his people. "I swear, I did it for the good of the empire," he whispered.

"What's done is done, but I think it best that you tell me everything."

Nonus' head whipped toward the door. "But the guard—"

"The guard knows his place. As I said, I have the emperor's ear."

Nonus sank back onto the resting bar, coiling and recoiling his tail in a vain attempt to calm his nerves. At last, he began to tell his story—not the one he'd told before, but the truth.

Chapter Thirty-Seven

Private Jorge 'Termite' Gonzalez

"This is freaky, right?" Guns looked around. She was jumpier than usual—understandable, given everything they'd been through, but still disconcerting. Tubes had seen his fellow Marine pull off some pretty tricky maneuvers in the past, risking life and limb and laughing at death as she did it. Seeing her so twitchy made him twitchy.

Not good, especially in light of the recent dressing-down he'd gotten from their captain.

"Which part?" Termite asked. As far as he was concerned, 'freaky' didn't begin to cover it.

"Being all...split up." Guns paused to frown at a cluster of children who hurried by. They didn't so much as glance at the Marines. Most likely, they were scared. It was certainly an understandable response.

"We've been split up before."

"Yeah, for missions. Where we had a plan." Guns counted out their fates on her fingers. "But Porker and Newbie are gone, Splat's had the Can out for days, Tubes is still in the medbay—with a busted exosuit, don't ask me how we're going to repair that. And now Rupnik has the captain on the bridge, and he's basically taken Funny Bone hostage to keep Captain Stone in line." She smirked at Termite. "Plus, you're an idiot. So it's really just me."

Termite shoved her. "Takes one to know one," he said. "Respectfully."

Guns smiled, but it faded quickly. "Seriously, though, it's like watching my family fall apart. I miss the Tennyson."

Now that was a feeling Termite understood. Her emphasis on that word in particular, family, was like a punch to the chest.

"Did any of them escape?" he asked. "Your...family?"

Guns shook her head. "Not that I know of. I didn't have much left to speak of, anyway. You?"

"I've got a few cousins who were deemed Defunct—three, maybe four years ago. They're probably mining minerals on some asteroid, if they're even still alive."

Guns nodded. "I'm glad we found the Hendersons. And who knows? Maybe we can bust your cousins out of jail, like we did with Bill's dad."

"Yeah. Maybe."

The corridors were astonishingly quiet. Suspiciously so. It was that, more than anything, that made Termite come to a halt and throw out his arm to stop Guns' progress.

"What?" she asked.

"Just a…feeling." He looked around. "Have you seen anyone come through here since those kids?"

"No. Gonzales, what's going on?"

"Turn back. Now."

"But what—?" She was already turning to do as he said, but it was too late. More than a dozen people were already spilling into the passage behind them.

As far as he could tell, they weren't trained. Nothing about their posture or the way they handled their weapons suggested they had even a cursory knowledge of combat. They clustered together, shoulders hunched and postures sullen.

"Oh, come on." Termite shot them a disgusted glance. "Not this again."

"Jorge," Guns hissed. "Behind us."

Termite spun in place, and cursed. There were even more people behind, hemming them in, like the Slovenians had tried to do with Al and Funny Bone. But these folks didn't look like militiamen, and why would Rupnik waste time with a distraction like this when he'd proven he could easily kill them?

Not that Termite was going to ask. He'd focus on surviving first and worry about the rest later. He reached for his belt, and he heard Al's voice in his ear, as clearly as if the captain were truly standing next to him:

We don't execute civilians!

Fortunately, he had multiple weapons with him this time.

"Close your air filter!" he bellowed to Guns. He didn't have time to check and see if she'd done as he asked before he hurled a grenade at the feet of the smaller cluster moving in behind them.

A plume of dark smoke burst across the corridor, and their would-be assailants began to cough and cover their mouths. Guns and Termite immediately lunged into the smoke. Their suits kept the tear-inducing gas out of their systems, but their assailants weren't so lucky, and the group behind them would have to think twice before giving chase.

The smaller group scattered as the two heavy exosuits lumbered through. Once he was in the clear again, Termite turned back to face them. He reached for the gun on his left hip, rather than his right, and took aim.

The man on the other side of his scope rubbed his watering eyes and opened his mouth. It looked as though he might be begging for mercy, but Termite had already made up his mind.

He pulled the trigger.

A shock of scarlet exploded against the man's chest, and he stumbled back. Termite chose his next target, and fired again. This time, a splash of blue hit one man in the shoulder and splattered across the fellow behind him.

On a ship with water rations and limited supplies, the saboteurs would find it difficult to wash away the evidence of their involvement. Between the splatters—and bruises—left by his paint gun, and the irritation caused by the emissions from the smoke bomb, they stood a decent chance of being able to track down members of this group for questioning, once they were able to call in backup.

Guns reached for her own paintball rifle and fired shots into the crowd more or less at random.

They were halfway down the corridor when their shared channel was hailed by Funny Bone. "Get back here," he said. "We need you."

"Our hands are kinda full at the moment, Sarge," Guns replied. It was, perhaps, an exaggeration by that point. They were wildly outnumbered, but far from outmatched, and the coughing, puffy-eyed civilians had elected not to give chase.

Still, the attack felt coordinated. Termite thought of the man who'd stabbed Tubes only two days before.

This could have ended badly—and the attack had been too purposeful for his liking. Why would hungry civilians target them?

"I don't care what you're dealing with down there," Funny Bone said. "Captain Henderson is still dealing with the situation down on Vale, the XO's still missing...and a handful of Crendelen warships just entered the system."

Chapter Thirty-Eight

Captain Bill Henderson

Bill sank to one knee before the quorum of Awn senators and bowed his head. "We are grateful for your assistance, honored elders."

Some of the Awn were still pigmented in brilliant colors, a clear mark of their distrust and dissent. Over the last two days, however, Bill had managed to persuade enough of the senators to allow the effort to move forward to ship supplies and minerals. Unfortunately, he'd had to mention Rupnik's intentions to bombard their planet several times to accomplish it—as much he'd hated doing that.

I'm not the one threatening to bomb them. I'm just relaying the threat. Even so, it felt dirty.

But amazingly, the Awn seemed to understand, and even to like him despite of the grim tidings he bore.

"It has been a pleasure." The first Awn he'd met, the co-senator of the Magnetic North, reached out a three-toed hand toward him. "I hope we can meet again some day, under more auspicious circumstances. Let us shake on this deal, as is the way of your people."

Bill tried not to squirm as the Awn's slimy palm settled against his own. He meant to be gentle—did the Awn even have bones?—but the senator gave his fingers a rough squeeze that left the nerves in his fingers tingling.

"And now we will dip together," she announced, "as is the way of our people."

Two days of observing Awn customs had led him to suspect that this would be the case. As the Awn senators hopped down to the shoreline, Bill followed, striding into Vale's sea.

The water was warm, at least, and it lacked the briny sting of Earth's oceans. Bill let himself sink into the surf, even letting his head slide below the shallow waves. The chemical makeup of Vale's seas made him buoyant, and he floated there for a moment as the strange vibration that accompanied the Awn's private communication thrummed through the water.

Rupnik aside, Longfield aside, Bill knew he had done something he could be proud of. He'd bought humanity a little more time—and, perhaps, a bit more credibility with the other vassal species of the Ornu.

If they could somehow find a way to unite enough of the vassal species against the Ornu, they might well stand a chance of taking Emperor Albus down once and for all.

But he couldn't do that without regaining control of Omega. So that came first.

Even if he had no idea what the first step toward it might be.

* * *

Half an hour later, back aboard the Can, Bill was still wringing the water from his uniform. Something was crystallizing in his hair, too. He needed a shower and a fresh set of clothes, and even before Splat started talking, he knew he was unlikely to get either anytime soon.

"We've got bad news, Captain," Splat announced, breaking the last of Bill's fragile, exhausted peace.

"I'm not the captain anymore," Bill said wryly.

Splat took his eyes off of the controls long enough to glare at him. "I'm not calling that brat captain, Captain. Besides, I have a feeling you're about to be put back in command, at least temporarily. I just got word from Funny Bone. There are Crendelen warships on the way."

Bill dropped his soggy boot to the deck and leapt to his feet. "Are they on our scanners yet?"

"They're well out of the Can's range, and we've got some time before they come into firing range, but Funny Bone sent this along with the message." Splat tapped a few buttons, and one of the Can's screens switched over to a grainy rendition of a system scan.

We really need to get this thing upgraded. "Twenty warships," he muttered. He rubbed a thumb over his bottom lip, already lost in thought. "Looks like they've modified their strategy, too." The warships had fanned out, rather than clustering together so that Hailstorm missiles could take several of them out with a single shot.

He noticed other blips, rising from the planet's surface—the Can's onboard scanners had picked up the small transport ships bearing the rations and mineral resources offered up by the Awn.

They should rendezvous with Omega well before the Crendelen are within range.

Omega's fleet of drones was still relaying mineral deposits from Vale when the Can reached Omega, and they had to wait onboard before the docking bay could be closed and they could safely make their way into Omega's main decks.

Battle was upon them again. But considering what he'd been dealing with these past weeks, it almost felt like a relief.

Chapter Thirty-Nine

Former Waiter Marcus Powery

Marcus had been mulling over his run-in with the crewmember of the Omega ever since they'd parted ways. He had recognized the man when he dragged the fellow to his feet, although he hadn't realized why his features were familiar. Twice now, he'd seen the officer being dragged around by the Slovenians.

Norder, his name was. He'd learned that, since.

In the intervening days, he'd seen a lot of things he'd rather forget. Slovenians shooting dissenters. Militiamen placing bets on survivors, as if they were watching a horse race or a cockfight rather than two desperate people fighting over scraps, sometimes to the death.

He'd seen even more suffering among the people since that kid, Rupnik, took power.

So much for the cause he'd put his life on the line for. Rupnik and his ilk were even worse than the crew, and Marcus was beginning to wonder if he and his compatriots had been right to back the uprising.

"Of course we were," his friend Dorsey insisted. He'd formed a shaky alliance with three young Jamaicans, predicated mostly on their shared work history, and cemented by the recent horrors aboard the cruise ship they'd worked on.

Dorsey, Trinica, and Regis had worked together on a luxury cruise liner that just so happened to be hosting a private wedding for the children of two influential American families when the world fell apart.

The whole liner had been evacuated, along with the staff—like Marcus, the three of them had heard no word from their families, and had come to the conclusion they never would again.

They had taken to splitting MREs four ways at mealtimes, and while it wasn't enough to leave them satisfied, they were faring better than many loners.

"I don't know." Trinica nibbled the edge of a stale biscuit. "The Slovenians are awful, but was the crew any better?"

"They saved our lives," Regis reminded her. He was soft-spoken, and his words were almost lost in the constant noise of the lower decks.

Dorsey scoffed. "They saved the lives of the cruise ship's passengers. We just got... lucky."

Luck. That was one word for it. Marcus wasn't sure it was the right one.

"I heard that this man Rupnik wanted to target civilians on that frog planet," Marcus said. "And that the captain didn't."

"Oh, so we're sparing frogs now, when we could be getting more supplies?" Trinica hunched her shoulders.

Marcus shook his head. "No. I hear he sent the captain down to make threats...but the captain found a way to get what we needed without anyone getting hurt. The supplies are coming, but without bloodshed." He finished half of his portion of the MRE, and tucked the rest into an inner pocket of his coat for later.

"Really?" Dorsey frowned. She was always frowning, and Marcus could hardly blame her. She was nineteen, and scared, and the world had ended. Was she supposed to be happy about it?

"Where'd you hear that?" Trinica pressed.

Marcus shrugged. "Rumor," he admitted.

"So it might not be true." Dorsey brushed crumbs from her shirt.

"I believe it," Regis said. All three of them turned to him, and the shy young man dipped his head self-consciously. "I know his mother. Miriam Henderson? She's the lady who goes around helping people."

"Miriam is his mother?" Trinica's eyebrows rose. "You sure? She's so nice."

Regis nodded. "She and a couple of the officers were going around with medical supplies to help people before Rupnik took over."

"More rumors?" Dorsey asked, with obvious skepticism.

Regis shook his head. "I saw them my-self."

The others considered this, and Marcus saw the familiar uncertainty in their ex-pressions. When nobody else spoke, he took it upon himself, as the oldest, to get to his feet. "Let's go ask her. You know where to find her, Regis?"

It didn't take much urging to get the oth-ers to follow; there were few enough ways to pass the time, and having a purpose was a true relief. They set off through the ship, asking if anyone had seen Miriam. Some people were clue-less, and others were openly hostile, but they were eventually directed to an old supply closet.

Marcus was the one who knocked on the hatch, which opened to reveal an old couple. The woman looked horribly exhausted and distressingly gaunt, al-though the appearance of the man be-hind her was even worse. Then again, it had been well over a month since Marcus had seen his own reflection, and he doubted it would match his memory.

Miriam managed a weak smile. "Can I help you?"

It was Regis who stepped forward. "You're Miriam Henderson, yes? The captain's mother?"

She bit her lip, and real fear flashed in her eyes. "Are you...with Rupnik?"

Marcus shook his head. "No. We're not with anyone. We're just curious. About the captain. We don't mean you any harm. Here." On impulse, he pulled the remains of his meal from his pocket and handed them to Miriam, who took one look at it and immediately knelt beside her husband.

"Come in," she said. "It's cramped, I know. Close the hatch behind you and we can talk about anything you want."

The four of them stepped inside the tiny chamber, crowding to one side to give the older couple enough space. Marcus crouched so that he could be eye-to-eye with the pair of them.

"What do you want to know?" Miriam asked as she painstakingly fed bite-sized pieces of the MRE to her husband. The old man had yet to say a word. His eyes were unfocused, his movements jerky and erratic.

"We heard some rumors about the captain. We want to know if they're true. Is he truly as good a man as they say?"

"That certainly sounds like my Billy." The affection in her voice was raw and sincere.

Marcus hadn't expected to feel sympathy for the captain, but he couldn't imagine what it would be like to watch his family waste away before his eyes. When Miriam spoke about her son, the hard lines of her face softened. That, more than anything, convinced him that Henderson and Rupnik were of two very different varieties. If Henderson and his family were this close, he wouldn't leave them to starve while he stockpiled resources for himself.

"Why are you asking about this?" Miriam folded the now-empty MRE wrapper and tucked it into her pocket.

Marcus glanced over his shoulder and caught the gazes of his friends one by one. Each of them nodded, even Dorsey, who was always a skeptic. "Because we want to help," he said.

Miriam seemed surprised. "How? I don't mean to offend you, but you're young and unarmed. What can you hope to do against Rupnik?"

He didn't have an answer, but he was saved from admitting as much.

"The same thing he did to us." Dorsey lifted her chin. "Rupnik and his father sent out spies to spread lies about the crew and turn us against them. We've seen how much power people have, and we all heard that message the captain sent out right before Rupnik took over. We're going to do the same thing. We can spread rumors as well as the Slovenians can...except, we're going to tell the truth."

Chapter Forty

Captain Bill Henderson

Bill stood inside the command sim and studied the tactical situation. The Crendelen had presented him with something of a puzzle. Their ships had spread out enough to all but neutralize the advantage conferred by his Hailstorm missiles. But they hadn't spread out far enough for him to be able to engage one or two ships at a time, without bringing Omega into the firing range of their neighbors.

If they'd had the surge capabilities he'd hoped to upgrade Omega with, it would be a different story—he could see a way to winning this engagement handily, with the ability to jump instantly to any point in the battlespace. But as things stood, the risk seemed too great, especially with how many civilians were on board Omega.

He stepped out of the simulation and back into Rupnik's presence.

Al and Funny Bone were still waiting on the bridge, surrounded by Rupnik and his men. The vein pulsing in the Slovenian's forehead suggested he was not to be trifled with.

"I've studied the array," he said, trying to modulate his voice so that he sounded both humble and wise in the same breath. He was more than a little skeptical of the result. "My advice would be to abandon this battle before it begins."

"You want to run away?" Rupnik snapped.

"No." Bill paused a beat to smother his mounting anger. "I want to buy an advantage. If the Crendelen are forced to give chase, we might be able to catch them off-guard."

"The situation is too dire," Rupnik said.

If this was about Vale's riches, Bill was going to snap. "We just brought more supplies aboard, and we can hardly requisition more from Vale if we're in the middle of a firefight. The transport ships wouldn't be able to keep up, and they'd be too easy for the Crendelen missiles to pick off if they tried."

"I'm not talking about that." Rupnik stepped forward and glowered into Bill's face. They were close to the same height, and Maks' posture suggested he was looking for a fight. If Bill took the bait, the kid wouldn't play fair. His men would be on Bill in an instant. They'd love an excuse to make an example of him, especially now that they knew AI could also access the command sims.

"I'm talking," Rupnik spat, "about the people. I have you and your crew well outnumbered, and your Marine trainees answer to me, but if the civilians get wind of this battle and panic? They could easily overrun the bridge, and there's nothing to stop them from costing us this battle. We need a quick, decisive win. Thankfully, Hendersons are known for that. Are they not?"

"Got it." Feeling as he did right now, Bill didn't trust himself to say any more than that. Besides, Rupnik did have a point.

Before the kid could respond, he dropped back into the command chair and slipped seamlessly into the sim.

It was a good thing he did. The sensors were going haywire as they registered a barrage of S-590 guided missiles launched from the Crendelen ships.

Bill swore. The S-590s were known for their large fuel capacity and therefore their long range.

But the S-590s were Perseus munitions. Given the Imperium and the Confederation were at war, Bill could only imagine how the Imperium had gotten their hands on a supply, but it hardly mattered. Without Val to help him or Tobias to offer advice, he would have to single-handedly deal with the incoming barrage before he had a chance to engage the ships that fired them.

A spark of excitement shot through him, much to his chagrin. This was important and dangerous work, and if he failed, the result would be catastrophic.

But he'd always loved a challenge, and the higher the stakes, the more satisfying the victory.

Rupnik was right. Hendersons played to win.

Chapter Forty-One

Imperial Citizen Livia

Livia reclined on her resting bar and picked through the sumptuous meal she'd laid out in anticipation of her brother's arrival. Philo seemed to have no trouble eating, and her mate, Hadrian, was chattering merrily away about the most recent developments of the war. True, Nonus was not his son, but couldn't he at least show some respect?

Her children by Hadrian sat on the far side of the table. Aquila occasionally chimed in with rumors he'd overheard in training. Soon, Aquila would be assigned a posting of his own—he was too young, she thought, but the war with the Perseids had accelerated everything.

Aquila's sisters, Canula and Cispia, listened with varying degrees of interest. Cispia, too, was in training, although she served with the Embassy rather than the military. She had a sharp mind, and Livia occasionally caught glimpses of her younger self in Cispia's sharp gaze.

None of them acknowledged Nonus' absence. He had, of course, been away for years by now, and the younger children didn't know him well. They didn't mention him much, but in recent weeks, his absence had taken on a new flavor. His name was never mentioned in idle conversation, and at times it was intentionally avoided. Her concern was their shame, and she'd even caught Cispia looking at her with sympathy, as if her attachment to her eldest was a foolish lost cause.

When she could stand it no longer, she lifted a hand, and the party's chatter fell away into silence.

"Leave us," she said. "Philo and I have business to discuss."

Aquila, ever the willing soldier, rose at once. Canula followed his lead, but their sister remained sitting.

"Perhaps you should let me stay," she suggested. "I am well-versed in diplomacy, after all."

Livia narrowed her eyes. "I said, go."

With a sullen hiss, Cispia followed her broodmates from the room. Hadrian lingered, reaching for Livia's hand, but she slapped it away. Her husband had his uses, but he was no great tactician. With a hurt look, he too withdrew.

Livia waited until the door closed behind him before demanding, "I hope you have some explanation for why your eldest nephew is still locked in a cell?"

Philo had been charming and amusing all through dinner, but in his sister's presence, his amusement died away. He shoved his empty plate aside. "Nonus is finished," he announced.

Livia sat bolt upright. "How dare you s-s-say such things-s-s, brother!"

Philo let out a mirthless laugh. "I know your ambition, Livia. You love to be told no, if only because it inspires you to try harder. For once, you must listen to me. This has become far bigger than you realize. There's no saving Nonus, and the sooner you accept that, the better."

Livia rose to her full height and braced her palms on the table. She briefly considered flipping it sideways, if only for the spectacle. If they'd still had company, she would have done it—but Philo would not be impressed by a display of petulance. She would do better to reason with him.

"Pertinax should be the one to pay!" she cried instead. "He betrayed the Imperium! He's the reason my poor boy is behind bars—"

"Your poor boy is a traitor to the Emperor," Philo hissed.

"You believe Pertinax?" She could hardly believe what she was hearing.

"I believe Nonus." Philo reached into his sumptuous dinner jacket and produced a small recording device. He held it up so that its glossy case flashed in the light that spilled through the high windows behind them. "He admitted it on his own. I have the recording."

Livia lunged toward him. She meant to make a grab for the device, but stopped cold when she saw the thin, jeweled blade clutched in one of Philo's other hands.

"You wouldn't," she hissed.

Philo shook his head slowly, as though disappointed. "I obviously have a back-up of the recording in a safe location. I need you to think, Livia." His wheedling tone made her skin itch, the way it did before a molt. "If you continue to support Nonus through this, you will sacrifice everything."

"Gladly," she said, with all the righteous conviction she could muster. "He is my flesh and blood, Philo. As he is yours."

"Yes, he is." Philo tucked the recorder away. "As are Aquila, and Cispia, and Canula. Would you sacrifice their futures, too? And what of Hadrian? He may not have been your first choice, but he is a dutiful father and a willing pawn. He trusts you. There is no saving Nonus now, but you may still save them. Or would you rather see them slithering through the streets of Lindinis, begging for scraps?"

Livia shrank away from him. "But—"

"Believe me, it may come to that." Philo rubbed his temples with two hands and gestured around her home with a third. His fourth hand was out of sight, likely still holding the dagger he'd aimed at her only moments before. "Aquila will be sent to fight a war his half-brother started. Do you understand that? Think for a moment: Nonus is not your only child. If you cut ties now, if you prove that you are loyal to the Emperor, you may have another chance. Perhaps with one of your more observant broodlings." He nodded to the high windows behind them.

Livia turned to face the garden, which lay on the far side of the reinforced glass. The construction of the room was enough to ward off most threats, and was sound-proofed. Still, the windows were transparent, so that diners lingering over a rich meal could enjoy the view over the city. Her villa sat on a hill, and the windows offered an unmatched vista of the carefully-tended gardens and the city beyond.

Cispia was outside, seated on one of the benches, pretending to read; but Livia had no doubt that her daughter was watching them from the corner of her eye. Her chest constricted with pride. It was exactly what she would have done if she'd been sent away from an important meeting.

Perhaps Philo was right. She was Nonus' only mother, but he was not her only child, and if her brother was telling the truth, she stood to lose everything.

"You're sure?" she asked. "About Nonus'...actions?"

"I could play it for you, if you wanted."

Livia took a deep breath. The sun was setting, turning the skies of Lindinis the color of freshly-spilled human blood. "Play it," she commanded.

Philo did. The sound of Nonus' voice took her breath away, but what he had to say was even worse. Livia clung to the edge of the table for support. Perhaps it was a good thing she hadn't overturned it after all.

It was a long recording, and by the time it finished, the sky had darkened to the color of an old bruise. Livia passed a hand across her face, wiping away any evidence of the tears that threatened to spill over.

"I believe you," she whispered. "On the Emperor's life, I believe you."

"And?" Philo prodded.

She looked around the room. She thought of her family, and her future, and all the promises she'd made over the years. She had promised her son that she would do anything for him. Anything. But was that true? And what did Nonus owe her in return? If he was innocent, she would have spilled her own blood to protect him. She would have slit Aquila's throat in sacrifice and let him bleed out while she begged the Emperor, far above the surface of their shining city, for clemency.

Nonus was not innocent, though, by his own admission. She knew propaganda when she heard it, and a recording played by the Emperor himself would not have convinced her, but Philo wouldn't lie. Not to her. Not about something so terrible as this.

Her brother must have sensed her uncertainty. "If you help me expose him, we will be spared. We can try again, with Cispia. All is not lost, sister. We have time to make this right."

The night sky was clear enough that she could see Emperor Albus' ship above them, shining as brightly as a star.

"Tell me what to do," she said.

Chapter Forty-Two

Commander Bina Chakravarti

Bina knelt on the deck of the Archive, trying to summon help through sheer force of will.

"I need you, Hyx!" she insisted. "We're in trouble. Please, send Val. Send Tobias. Let me talk to Omega!" She ran a hand across the deck in agitation. "We're running out of time, and I can't believe we've come so far just to die here. Longfield didn't believe it, and I don't either. How much do we have to lose before you'll help?" Angry tears stung her eyes, and she dashed them away with her still-damp sleeve.

When her vision cleared, she was no longer in the Archive. Instead, she knelt by the younger version of Hyx, who sat holding the box that he'd been speaking to when she had seen him last.

"Hyx," the box whispered.

Bina sat back on her heels. She looked around in hopes of seeing the older version of Hyx, the one who'd been her guide through this ancient history, but there was no sign of him. Amid the damaged artifacts, she and the memory of a curious young revolutionary were the only signs of life.

Hyx studied the box. "What are you?" he asked.

"I am here to warn you," the box said.

"Warn me?" Hyx's glowing eyes widened. "About our obsession with tech?"

"Kanami society is on the verge of collapse. But it is not your collective obsession with technology and self-enhancement that will cause it. Those are only the symptoms of a larger disease."

"I knew it." Hyx scrambled to his feet, still holding the box, and began to restlessly pace the periphery of the room, careful to avoid stepping on the other artifacts. Rather than spin in circles to watch him, Bina followed, although she was able to sidestep the items that littered the floor much more easily than the Kanami could.

All the while, the box kept talking. "The problem is that your people have lost all sense of the good. It's not that they don't have the right priorities—it's that they don't even know what a priority is anymore. They are perfect existentialists, and they've done away with ordering goods, or distinguishing them from the bad. Everything is acceptable to them based on emotions, on personal preferences, even on whims. Everyone is permitted to do anything, provided it doesn't hinder anyone else from doing what they want. That's the principle this new galaxy-spanning society is built on...and yet that principle is constantly violated."

Hyx nodded his agreement. "Yes, yes! We're often jailed unfairly, or pressured into changing our bodies and senses to conform to social expectations. We're told to do what we want...but we're supposed to want to be just like everyone else."

"Indeed. And violence has become widespread, in spite of what your society claims as its golden rule. Kanami are maimed and killed en masse, at all ages, at all stages of your development. And it is called enlightened."

Bina tripped over the simulation of an artifact. There was nothing actually in her way, but the box's words, coupled with Hyx's enthusiasm, reminded her of Bill. Before the Crendelen had rendered humanity Defunct, people had also thought themselves enlightened. They'd been so easy to subjugate, their loyalty so cheaply bought. Tech and comforts and entertainment had been enough to make them forget the cost of the Ornu's leadership.

Perhaps the troubles had started even before that. Had humanity really fought tooth and nail to avoid being subjugated by the Ornu? That was how she'd always imagined it, but lately she was less convinced. What percentage of humanity had actually been willing to make sacrifices for the greater good, and how many of them had been complacent, even eager, to benefit from the wealth of the Imperium?

Given the corruption Bina had witnessed firsthand among the political leaders they'd rescued from imprisonment, how many people had even known the difference between their old

human overlords and their alien conquerors?

Hyx's question cut into her musings. "But what can we do?" he asked.

"Your people have lost their inner com-pass. But you have the ability to pre-serve something, if you stay the course. Remember yourself. Remember the old ways. If you truly commit yourself to this, then I will help you."

Hyx was trembling with excitement. "I can. I swear it. But I still don't under-stand who, or what, you are."

There was a brief moment of silence. And then:

"I am Omega."

Bina let out a cry of disbelief. Sure-ly she'd misunderstood. How could the box be Omega? Was it the same Omega that powered the ship? The Primevals were supposed to be the most advanced civilization in history. If Omega predated them, then who had made him?

She had so many questions, and every time the Archive doled out answers, she found herself with a hundred more.

"How is that possible?" she demanded.

The young Hyx jumped, startled so badly that he almost dropped the box. When he recovered it, he clutched it to his chest and glared at Bina. "Who are you?" he demanded. "How did you get here?" His lip curled as he looked her up and down.

Bina looked behind her, just in case he was talking to some other part of the sim, but the two of them were still alone. She pointed to her own chest. "Are you talking to me?"

"Of course." Hyx bristled. "You just appeared out of nowhere."

Bina licked her lips. "I think...I think Omega brought me here."

Hyx's frown deepened, and he held up the box. "Hold on. You're with Omega? What...is it, then? What are you? What is happening?"

That, Bina thought, was a pertinent question indeed.

Chapter Forty-Three

Captain Alden Stone

On the scanners, the first of the S-590s exploded. Presumably Bill was targeting them—Omega's laser array was certainly operating at full capacity, so unless Val had made a surprise reappearance, Bill was the one responsible.

Al watched the display in silence. He was exhausted, but at least his hunger had faded to a dull ache. Perhaps, with the Awn's fresh supplies, he could eat a real meal sometime in the foreseeable future.

But in order to eat, he'd have to be alive, and Bill was just one man. He couldn't take out the missile barrage alone. He'd need help.

Al fidgeted as the laser array took out missiles that came ever-closer to the ship. Beside him, Funny Bone shifted from foot to foot. "I don't think he can do it on his own," the sergeant whispered. "That's a lot for just one man to coordinate."

Rupnik seemed to be in no hurry, probably because he didn't know the first thing about missiles, laser defenses, or how to command a crew. He was watching the display with open-mouthed awe, like a child watching a particularly riveting vid.

Al managed to maintain his calm until the first missile streaked past the array and struck Omega's hull. Their enormous ship tremored under the impact. Omega could take some hits, but each roll of the ship would be like shaking a can whose contents were under pressure. Eventually, the people aboard would be moved to riot, just as Rupnik had suggested. And too many missile strikes would eventually lead to an occupied compartment being breached—or something critical getting destroyed.

Someone had to help, and if Rupnik wasn't going to step up, Al would have to take charge.

"Enough of this," he bellowed. He pointed to Funny Bone. "Get the others...Guns, Termite, Tubes if he's on his feet. Gather up your trainees, too. I want legitimate crowd control in the lower decks right now. We're not killing people, we're maintaining the peace. Got it?"

Funny Bone nodded and barged toward the hatch. Nobody tried to stop him. The militiamen had been happy to play soldier when they were up against civilians, but the arrival of the Crendelen made it clear that this was no longer a game.

Only Rupnik took offense. He got up in Al's face and jabbed a finger into his chest. "What do you think you're doing?"

Al wished he was wearing his exosuit, and that he could settle the matter right then and there. He could break Rupnik over his knee like an old broom handle and either restrain or eliminate the cowed militia in a matter of minutes. Al didn't believe in killing civilians, but his enemies were another matter entirely.

He bared his teeth at Rupnik. "I'm doing what you can't, Captain." He shoved past the boy and took his place at the station that should have been manned by Hans Norder. Fortunately, Rupnik didn't try to stop him. Perhaps even he could admit that he had no idea what to do next.

Al was a bit rusty, especially since he hadn't had much chance to become truly familiar with Omega's interface. At least the controls were intuitive, and they seemed to adapt as he went.

He wasn't sure exactly what instructions Bill was giving within the command sim, but the weapons display provided him with predictive data that allowed him to issue secondary, interim commands.

"Show me what you've got," he whispered. Whether it was a pep talk for himself or a quiet plea to Omega, it worked. A small symbol on the controls flashed, and when he pressed it, it opened an interface for launching Peregrine missiles. Just below, it read, Ideal for missile defense, the Peregrine missile is able to be launched rapidly in large numbers, with sophisticated instructions based on engagement objectives...

Bill had been the one to name those missiles Peregrines, Al knew, and the ship had apparently integrated his nomenclature readily enough.

As the captain was occupied with laser defense, Al set about intercepting the incoming missiles Bill was missing with the

Peregrines. The smaller missiles lanced out, zipping toward their targets and neutralizing them one by one.

A private screen pinged with a text message from within the command sim:

Thank you, Al.

Al had no idea how to respond, and he didn't want to draw Rupnik's attention, but he found himself relaxing more into his seat. Things were always better when he and Bill were on the same side, and they both did better with a clear mission—such as stopping the Crendelen attack.

Still, the missiles kept coming, with the warships drawing ever closer. As soon as they were within laser range, they'd start firing secondary weapons, guaranteeing them more hits on Omega's hull.

He and Bill needed an opportunity to start targeting the ships, thereby reduce the quantity of enemy fire.

And if they couldn't find an opportunity, they'd have to make one.

Chapter Forty-Four

Sergeant Shawn 'Funny Bone' Piker

As far as Funny Bone could tell, the civilians were no longer rioting. Riots had a purpose, a mission. Riots had intent.

What he and the crew encountered belowdecks was nothing short of chaos.

The trainees—if they still counted as trainees, given how sporadic anything that might reasonably be called training had been—were armed with sponge rounds. They'd circled up around the two remaining supply bays, and were doing their best to keep the civilians back. Jana Nemec was firing with such precision that he was forced to admit she was his best marksman, despite his growing misgivings about her character.

It was not the time to offer praise, however. A few of the civilians were still trying to rush the supply bay, but they were increasingly inclined to turn on each other. The trainees could protect the bay, and protect themselves, but the bloody fights breaking out between civilians seemed destined to end badly.

Without warning, Guns tried to break away from the line of defense. Funny Bone grabbed her shoulder.

"Back in formation!" he bellowed.

Much to his indignation, Guns shook her head and pulled away. After the stunts Termite and Tubes had pulled recently, Funny Bone was convinced they were all losing their minds. Why couldn't they stick to their training? It was going to get someone killed.

He followed her into the crowd, hoping to bring her to her senses. When he realized what she'd spotted, however, his priorities shifted. One of their volunteer policemen had a man pinned to the ground. Another volunteer stood beside him, boot raised. Funny Bone cried out as the volunteer brought his boot down on the civilian's face. He raised the boot again, leaving behind a smear of dirt and blood across his victim's face, right over his eye.

They're aiming to kill that man, aren't they?

Guns, meanwhile, had kept her wits about her. She fired a sponge round at the man with the bloody boot and sent him sprawling. Two paces later, she lifted the other volunteer by the back of his shirt. He swung, trying to kick his way out of her grip. She flung him aside.

Funny Bone finally caught up with her, and the two of them helped the downed man to his feet. He swayed between them and held his sleeve to his bruised and bloody cheek, but to Funny Bone's shock, he managed a grin.

"For Captain Henderson!" he cried. "For the crew of the Tennyson!" He saluted them both, then plunged back into the fray.

Funny Bone watched him go. "What is going on?"

"Beats me." Guns cocked her head. "You hear that?"

Now that he knew what he was listening for, he could hear familiar names being chanted by members of the mob.

"Remember Rupnik!" some people chanted.

As if in answer, they were met with cries of, "Henderson means hope!"

"Well, would you listen to that," Guns drawled. "Looks like we've got some actual support."

"Great to know. Now, get back in formation!"

By the time the two of them straggled back, something was becoming increasingly clear to Funny Bone. Rather than stamping out the violence, the trainees' attempts at crowd control only drove the mob into a greater frenzy. Funny Bone could no longer tell who was on their side and who was against them. Several of the volunteer police opened fire on each other, while civilians used makeshift weapons, or even their own fists, to strike their fellows. Those who fell to the deck were trampled underfoot.

At least the bays seemed secure. Since it seemed he no longer had to worry about the safety of the supplies, he was able to turn his attention to figuring out his next move. His thought process was further hampered by the occasional shuddering boom! that reverberated through the ship when a missile strike slipped through their defenses.

Funny Bone paused to enjoy the luxury of a single grounding breath. You are a Marine. You are not going to panic. You can handle this.

"Sergeant Piker!" The voice was faint, and it came from one of the connecting corridors, in the rough direction of the other supply bay, where Termite and Tubes were stationed. Since his crew rarely called him by that name, he assumed it to be one of the trainees.

"Stay here," he told Splat and Guns. "That's an order."

Guns snorted. "What happened to holding the line?"

He ignored her, wading once again into the fray. The fighting thinned out slightly when he reached the corridor the voice had come from, and unless he was very much mistaken, the civilians he passed seemed to actively make way for him, blocking those in the crowd who would have tried to give chase.

Eventually, he found the trainees Kan and Awad standing with a group of civilians. Two of them in particular seemed to be in charge: a woman who couldn't have been more than twenty years old and a man a few years her senior. They were both black, but a quick survey of their associates suggested that the rather ragtag group that accompanied them was united over something other than national interest. The only common denominator was their age; like Rupnik's men, many of them were young.

When Funny Bone finally reached them, Awad stood to attention. "Sergeant, these people want to speak with you.

They say they've been going around the ship, drumming up support for the captain."

"Captain Henderson," the young woman clarified. "We want nothing to do with Rupnik."

"Henderson means hope," the group chanted, more or less in unison.

"Ah." Funny Bone looked them over again, more intently this time. "I…see. Well, I'm glad to hear it. I happen to believe that Captain Henderson is the only thing keeping this whole mission from falling apart."

The young man nodded his agreement. "Dorsey and I have talked to Miriam Henderson. We don't know the captain personally, but he sounds like a better option than Rupnik, from what we've learned."

"Nice to meet you." Funny Bone held out a tentative hand. "That doesn't explain why you're here, though..."

"Marcus." The young man shook his hand. "Nice to meet you, too, Sergeant Piker. We didn't just come here to chat, though. Dorsey and I learned something you should know. Your man, Hans Norder. He's an officer, right?"

Funny Bone nodded. "Yes, if he's still alive. Rupnik took him."

"I know." Marcus' mouth curled up at one corner. "And he is alive. That's what we want to tell you. Or show you, I guess. Dorsey and I? We found him, and we want to help you get him back."

Chapter Forty-Five

Commander Bina Chakravarti

Hyx gawked at her. It was such a human expression on such inhuman features that she almost laughed in astonishment.

"Are you...?" He swallowed, and tried again. "Are you an alien? Are you from the past?"

She shook her head. "No. From the future, I think. You've been dead for a long time."

Hyx patted himself as if to confirm this fact. Finding himself very much alive, at least by his own reckoning, he looked up at her again. "Are you sure about that?"

"Yes," she said. "Although we've met before. Kind of."

"Even though I'm supposedly long dead?" His voice dripped with skepticism.

"You are, though. I grew up hearing legends about Primevals, and I bet you've never even heard of humans before."

Hyx's eyebrows pulled together. "What's Primeval?"

"It's what we call the Kanami, where—when I'm from."

Hyx didn't seem convinced. "But I found this in an archaeological dig."

Bina crossed her arms. "Technically, Kalykk found it."

"You know Kalykk?" Hyx raised an eyebrow. "Does she somehow survive for—what, a few thousand years? You're not really selling this."

Bina sucked her teeth. "I liked you better when you pretended you couldn't see me."

"When did I—"

"Omega brought me here." She pointed to the box. "I don't understand how any more than you do. I don't even know what it is. I thought Omega was a ship."

"A ship." Hyx held up the box. "So you're not only from the future, but you're tiny. Am I getting this right?"

"She is not tiny," Omega said. "If you succeed in the task I have laid out for you, Bina will be the beneficiary of your handiwork. Indeed, if it were not for what you will do, Bina would probably have died by now."

She held up both hands. "I'm not following this. Verb tenses are part of the problem, but I have a lot of questions. And I think Hyx does, too. Or the simulation of Hyx. Or whatever he is."

"I'm not a simulation!" Hyx cried. His cheeks were flushed, and he waved the box madly between them. "If anything, you're a simulation. We're still at the dig site, see?"

"Which is being projected inside the Archive of Omega," Bina retorted.

"You are both more than that," Omega explained. "You have been observing Hyx's life exactly as it unfolded, because you have truly observed it unfolding. Yes, a simulation guided you here, but only so I could ensure you would understand what I am trying to tell you, and I only have one chance. Time is short, Bina, so I folded time in order for you to bear witness, because I consider you worthy of it. Until now, you have only had the capacity to observe. And now, for the first and last time, I will afford you the opportunity to affect the ancient past, and to change it."

"What?" Bina took a stumbling step away from Hyx. "I'm really in the past?"

"For the time being, you are both in the present...but that present is occurring long before the era of your birth."

"How?" she croaked.

"You are bound by time, and must be. I am not. Because your intentions are pure, I am allowing you to intercede for your people in this way—once. It is not for you to understand how. All time is valuable, Bina, but this time is particularly hard-won. I advise you to ask a question that will be of more immediate use to your current mission."

"Why?" she croaked at last.

This seemed to be the right question. "Because I see how the conditions aboard your ship have deteriorated. And if extraordinary action is not taken, even the small remnant of humanity that exists aboard her will be diminished further, and drastically."

"Can I get some clarification?" Hyx interrupted. "Who are you? Who is she? Did you really bring her here?" He turned his attention to Bina. "Did you come from that box? And if so, why does the box continue to speak to me in that deep male voice?"

"I'm a human from the future, who traveled back to the present in order to help you help me save the future." Bina snapped her fingers a couple times. "Try to keep up, Hyx. I thought you were a genius."

Hyx blinked. "And you're going to help me...help you...by doing...what, exactly?"

"You will build the ship," Omega said. "It is your life's most important work."

"I will?" Hyx didn't seem all that impressed with his life's calling. "I'm going to be a glorified mechanic?"

"You are going to save a species from certain destruction."

"But not my species," Hyx clarified. Bina had to give credit where it was due: he was taking all this in stride.

"Your species has chosen destruction, and the time they have now is a mercy. But that does not mean the Kanami will perish for ever. I will preserve your seed, Hyx, in a place far removed from here, so that to this galaxy the Kanami will appear gone forever. As a Kanami who has rejected the corrupted will of your people, you have unique insight into something that will plague Bina's species in the future."

"Hm." Hyx turned the box over, studying it from several angles. "And you know this because...?"

"Because I am at all times."

Hyx met Bina's eye, and they both shrugged. It made her feel a bit better to know he was clueless, too.

"Bina, I brought you here to save your kind," Omega continued. "If you tell Hyx to include it, your starship will have it. What would you ask of him?"

Bina's heart leapt. Longfield had been right—she hadn't lived long enough to experience it, but her hypothesis was correct. Omega hadn't abandoned them. And she didn't think he ever would.

She bit her lip and tried to think. "Right now, what we need most is food. I don't know of any food that will keep for thousands of years, though...."

Hyx spoke slowly. "I think I understand that I'm to finance the construction of a starship. But if that's the case, shouldn't I include Nourishers on it regardless?"

"Nourishers," Bina echoed. "What are they?"

"They can reconstitute a great number of materials as food," Hyx explained. "Not very good food, but it will keep you alive. Am I to understand I go on to build a starship that doesn't include Nourishers?" He appeared personally offended by the suggestion.

"You left them until last," Omega said. "And you ran out of time."

"That sounds...ominous." The Kanami shook his head. "If I did run out of time before I could install them...then if I prioritize them now, surely I'll leave something else until last, and there will be no time to include that."

Val had sung Hyx's praises before he abandoned them, so Bina was already aware he was supposed to be quite intelligent. Even so, she was surprised by how quickly he'd accepted his new mission, and how quickly he'd come to the next conclusion.

"If you're going to leave something else out, make sure it's not important, please." She folded her hands in front of her.

Hyx narrowed his eyes, "Well, I can't see myself including anything unimportant on purpose. But apparently I'm going to be strapped for time."

"The destabilizer field," Omega suggested. "They haven't discovered that yet, and they can't miss what they don't know about. Leave that till last."

"That sounds like it could...come in handy?" Bina said hesitantly. If she really was influencing the past, though, she didn't want to tell Hyx to leave out something that they'd already used. Then she might double-impact the future, or something. Anyway, more changes could be bad. Unless they worked out in her favor...but how would she know which one would? She could feel a headache coming on.

"The field can be reinstalled using your era's technology," Omega said.

"Hang on. If you can fold and unfold time, do you already know my future? Humanity's future? Do you know what happens next?"

But the voice had fallen silent.

She expected the vision—or whatever she should call this, now—to end. When it didn't, she folded her hands in front of her and dipped into a bow. "I'm glad I got to meet you, Hyx. I gather we won't meet again, though maybe I'll get a chance to observe you some more. Thank you for your work on the ship you'll build. It leads to a lot of trouble, but ultimately it saves my species from slavery, and from total destruction."

"You're welcome," Hyx said, still seeming somewhat mystified.

"You know," she mused, "it's possible I'm not actually here. For all I know, this is just a drama Omega cooked up. A little simulation to clue me into some tech that has always existed on the ship."

Hyx gave her a lopsided smile. "By the same token, maybe you're just something I hallucinated so that aliens could brainwash me into building a ship. You could be a...."

"High-tech guilt trip?" she suggested. "Now, you'll feel obligated to do the bidding of your alien overlords because you promised you'd save my life?"

Hyx nodded. "Something like that."

Bina snorted. "Not a chance. Take it from someone who's done the bidding of alien overlords...the evil ones don't profit from altruism. I'm real, all right."

Hyx's eyes bulged. He opened his mouth, presumably to ask another question, but when she blinked, Bina was back in the Archive, standing a few paces away from where she'd knelt before.

She let out a shaky breath. "Well, that was weird."

"Oh, you have no idea." The woman's voice came from behind her, and for a breathless moment Bina thought it was Longfield's voice. She turned around and found herself face to face with a being made of pure light.

Like a ghost.

Like an angel.

"Sally?" Bina reached out to touch the woman.

Omega was capable of miracles. Her hand trembled as it brushed through the woman's shoulder. Already the tears were spilling down her cheeks. Every doubt she'd had about Omega fell away.

Omega could defy time. Could defy death. He had proven as much over and over again. How much more proof did she need?

"Sally Longfield, is that you?"

Chapter Forty-Six

Captain Bill Henderson

Bill swore to himself as yet another missile slipped past his best attempt at defense. Predictive tech could only get him so far, and it was frustrating to see the incoming strikes but know that he couldn't work fast enough to disarm them all. Al's involvement had helped, but it wasn't enough.

This is futile.

He exited the sim. His legs had gone numb, and when he tried to stand, he ended up stumbling away from the command chair, as if he'd spent his time drinking rather than fighting for his life.

"What now?" Rupnik demanded.

Bill caught the arm of the chair to steady himself. "Surely you can see we're fighting a losing battle. If we stay in it much longer, we'll be dead. And for what?"

Rupnik bared his teeth in a snarl. "Have I failed to make my orders clear? You will fight. And you will win."

"Brilliant battle strategy," Bill snapped. "Fight. Win. Why didn't I think of that?"

Rupnik grabbed the front of his jacket. There was a new spark in his eyes that looked uncomfortably like madness. "If you exit the sim again without having defeated the Crendelen, I will bring Norder back to the bridge, and I will kill him in front of you."

He would do it, too. What Bill didn't understand was how that threat was supposed to help. He swatted Rupnik's hand away and fell backward into the chair, if only so that he wouldn't have to look at the young man's face anymore. The temptation to punch him in the teeth was too high.

The kid was just like Nonus. Bill had spent years studying battle tactics, both in the modules taught at the Academy and in more...extracurricular manners. His whole life had been preparation for events just like this, and yet that training got thrown out the window when some ignorant upstart decided he wanted to be in charge, regardless of his qualifications. Bill looked around the sim, glaring at the setup. The smart thing would be to withdraw, but Rupnik wasn't letting him be smart.

So he'd need to find another strategy.

The S-590s kept coming, and until the Crendelen ran out, that wouldn't change. Given how many ships there were, Omega's hull would be breached well before the firepower ran out. Defensive tactics weren't working.

So what are my offensive options?

The Hailstorm missiles were good for larger targets and creating shrapnel fields, but whoever was leading the Crendelen charge had made their use mostly ineffectual. Omega's Peregrine missiles were smaller, but they were also faster, and their targeting and tracking were superior. If he was careful with his aim, he could take out a couple of Crendelen ships. Then he'd have fewer S-590s to worry about, which would make it easier to launch another offensive.

He sent a quick message to Al: Trying a new strategy. Roll with me.

There was no time to wait for a response. Hopefully, Al could help with the nav end of things once they got going, but for now, Bill would have to run the whole show.

"Give me my old chair back," he told the simspace. He'd always liked Tennyson's control system, and he knew it like the back of his hand. The simspace obliged, and the holographic array wrapped around him in the familiar gyroscopic layout: a sim within a sim.

The controls were familiar, but Omega's version was even more intuitive, responding to his thoughts with a speed that defied reason. Even in the simspace, he felt Omega reel beneath him as he took the ship on the offensive. Omega was a massive target, and the closer he got to the warships, the easier he would be to hit. That was how it felt in the chair: like he was the ship, hurtling through the void with his targets growing larger by the second.

Changing his position and trajectory so suddenly meant that some of the S-590s that would have otherwise hit him went wide. Bill selected one of the enemy warships, launching half a dozen Peregrines at once from as many launch tubes along Omega's massive length.

Before they hit, he fired off a handful of dumb rounds, to make it more difficult for the Crendelen to neutralize the Peregrines. But the target didn't have time to react, and it burst apart.

The warships were smaller than Omega, but their nav systems weren't up to snuff. Bill knew that from his years studying them while serving in the Ornu's greater vassal military.

He took advantage of the fact and positioned himself to attack another ship. Only half his Peregrines hit this time, but a few of the dumb rounds also landed, and that ship, too, went dark.

His advantage couldn't last, however. The other warships maintained formation as they repositioned themselves. He'd hoped they would cluster up in response to his sudden attack so that he could use Hailstorms effectively. It would have helped him ward off attacks, too. If the missiles were more clustered, he stood a better chance of taking them out.

By the time he'd taken out his third ship, the Crendelen seemed to have sussed out his plan of attack and were maneuvering to surround Omega. There were still seventeen ships in play.

What they needed was some backup.

Or, barring that, a miracle.

Chapter Forty-Seven

Former Signifier Nonus

The day started off like any other. Nonus lay in his bunk, flicking the tip of his tail absently back and forth as he doodled in the journal he'd been permitted. For the most part, he kept his notes and comments benign, since he suspected the guards would happily paw through his possessions at the slightest provocation.

He did, however, allow himself the luxury of a small cartoon—that of an Ornu flipping the kill switch of a human, who was captured mid-collapse, with a lolling tongue and two Xs in place of his eyes. The Imperators could hardly blame him for that, could they? After all, humans were now Defunct, and it had been satisfying to watch Bill Henderson die, even if death hadn't stuck.

He was drawing scales on the Ornu's tail when the door to his cell opened. Nonus lowered the notebook and cast a weary glance. The guards were always tormenting and taunting him, but as long as he ignored them, they were more likely to leave him in peace.

There were multiple guards this time, and one of them looked far more official than his usual jailors. The female in the lead turned cold eyes on Nonus and beckoned with one hand.

"Rise, Nonus, son of Livia."

He set the journal aside and did as she asked. Arguing would only lead to punishment, as he knew all too well. She looked him up and down, then motioned to his journal. "Bring that with you."

Nonus hesitated. "Where are we going?"

"Your trial is today."

Panic thrummed through him. "Nobody told me that," he murmured as he slid his notebook into the lining of his jacket. High suns, what did it mean that Philo hadn't come in person? He must have a plan—he always did. Nonus would have felt a bit better, however, if he'd had the faintest idea what that might be.

What was he supposed to say? What argument could he deploy at court?

He would have to trust that Philo knew best. As always.

* * *

Pertinax had been droning on for what seemed like forever. Per the rules of the Imperial court, Nonus was not allowed to defend himself, so he sat there with his eyes glazing over and his head drooping toward his chest from time to time.

Yes, his reputation and indeed his life were on the line...but the legal process was painfully dull, and Pertinax's smile was so smug that it turned his stomach. Nonus despised him more than he'd ever despised anyone before, but he seemed to have the court eating out of the palms of his hands.

Of course.

He drummed his talons on the tabletop and sulked in silence. Pertinax was the poster child of the fleet. He was an Imperator, after all, and clearly thought himself above the law. He'd get what was coming to him eventually, though. Philo would put him in his place just as soon as he arrived.

He sat up straighter when the First Juror said, "Thank you, Imperator Pertinax. We will now hear from Consul Secundus."

Nonus suppressed a groan. Of course there would be another witness to back up Pertinax. His attorney shot him a sidelong glance—they hadn't exchanged ten words, but Philo had assured Nonus that he'd employed the best attorney money could buy—and Nonus composed himself. This was the Emperor's court, and the charges against him were significant. He should have expected that this would be an ordeal.

His stomach was rumbling audibly when Secundus' interminable monologue finally drew to a close. It was late, and even the most seasoned jurors had begun to fidget. The presiding magistrate, an Imperator schooled in Ornu law, rose upright on his tail to address the packed room.

"We will reconvene tomorrow," she announced. "At that time, we will hear from witnesses to the character of former Signifier Nonus."

Former Signifier. She might as well have slapped him in the face. Was it really necessary to remind the jurors and the audience how far he'd fallen?

But all that had been lost could and would be restored. He believed that with his whole heart. He had to believe it. The alternative was too terrible to contemplate.

"Will I be sent back to my cell tonight?" he asked his attorney.

The attorney shook his head and rose upright. "They have accommodations for you here."

"Here?" he echoed. "In the courthouse?"

The attorney paused. He met Nonus' gaze and grimaced slightly. "You're likely safer here. If they have to transport you through the streets, you may encounter trouble. Many citizens of Lindinis hold you responsible for the war."

"For the...!" He cut himself short. The fraction of his brain that had been paying attention to the trial replayed some of Pertinax's key arguments. He'd blamed Nonus for everything, which was hardly fair. Decisions had to be made in the field, and those decisions could have consequences. But which war, exactly, was to be laid at his doorstep? The ongoing conflict with humanity and their massive Primeval ship? Certainly that was bigger than him. A Henderson plus ancient, mystical tech equalled a recipe for disaster.

As for the Perseids, that war had raged on forever. Yes, he'd escalated things, but the clash had been inevitable. Why would anyone blame him?

Because they needed to blame someone, he realized, especially if things were going wrong. For the first time, the precarious nature of his situation struck him. He wasn't being tried over a tactical decision. He was being offered up as a potential sacrifice. Something the humans would call a scapegoat. He'd seen it done before, but never to an Ornu. Their lives, unlike the lives of vassal species, were sacrosanct.

But he would slip the noose. Tomorrow. Philo would put it right.

Wouldn't he?

* * *

After a sleepless night in a cramped cell, Nonus' nerves were frayed. Perhaps it was his imagination, but the crowd seemed more excited as well. He searched their faces, trying to guess who was on his side, and who sided with the likes of Pertinax. He found very few sympathetic faces in a sea of hostility.

The magistrate ascended to the dais and lifted her hands. Gradually the room fell quiet, although Nonus could still hear harsh whispers amid the audience. He kept his chin up and his eyes forward. He wouldn't let his attention wander anymore. He would listen. Intently.

"Attorney Toxius," she intoned, "you have heard Pertinax and Secundus speak. You have witnesses to call, do you not?"

The attorney, whose name Nonus hadn't bothered to ask, rose upright and glided to the front of the room. "Indeed, honored one. I speak on behalf of Consul Philo, the uncle of the accused."

Nonus cocked his head. That was odd, surely? Philo wasn't the one on trial. His scales began to itch with anticipation. He should have asked more questions yesterday. He should have tried to contact Philo the night before. Where was his uncle, anyway?

"First, I would speak to Minder Esquil." The attorney gestured behind him.

"Esquil?" Nonus whispered. That was a name he knew well, although he was surprised to see how much his old teacher had aged. Esquil had been his minder when he was little more than a hatchling. The venerable Ornu made his way to the center of the theater, alongside Toxius, and folded his hands behind him.

"How do you know Nonus?" Toxius asked.

Esquil's reply reverberated throughout the room. "He was one of my wards when he was young. I never forget a neonate, especially not one like that."

"Like what?" Toxius urged. "How would you describe him?"

Esquil fixed his eyes on Nonus. "To most, I suppose he would have seemed...ordinary. Unremarkable. He was not a bright child, you understand, or so it would seem. But when our backs were turned, he was quick to bully and threaten his fellows."

Nonus leaned forward, his mouth agape. Bullying? Threats? What was Esquil talking about?

"He was, in short, a master manipulator," Esquil said with cold finality.

Nonus turned to the attorney. Surely, he would ask that the old minder's words be stricken from the record. But to his horror, the attorney thanked the witness, then turned back to the magistrate.

"It is my contention, honored one, that Nonus has been engaged in an elaborate ploy to facilitate his own rise to power. He has played the fool with those from whom he stands to gain nothing, while he has abused and manipulated those in his inner circle for years. Only now that Pertinax has brought his crimes to light, followed by his removal from public office and subsequent imprisonment, do they feel safe to come forward and speak against him."

Nonus hunkered down in his seat and cupped his hands to either side of his face. He wished he could make himself so small that he could slither away unnoticed. Or, better yet, disappear entirely.

He'd been right about his position as a scapegoat, but wrong about whose hand held the knife. He'd even admitted the truth to Philo, sharpening the sacrificial blade himself.

A parade of witnesses made their way forward: old classmates whose names Nonus had long since forgotten, fellow trainees, other Signifiers. He had to close his eyes when his half-sister Cispia took the stand to detail her ill-use at his hands. The little traitor's eyes welled with tears as she recounted Nonus' supposed reign of tyranny within their home, and how he'd threatened and belittled his stepfather, Hadrian, at every turn.

Lies upon lies. He no longer hated Pertinax, or at least not with the same fire as before. How could he, when the Imperator's betrayal paled by comparison?

Even Livia came forward to corroborate the story. Unlike Cispia, she did not cry, although she trembled as she spoke. Was that pity he saw in her eyes?

It didn't matter. Nothing mattered anymore.

As she withdrew, she paused beside him and whispered, "I'm sorry, Nonus. It's better this way."

"For who?" he hissed.

"For everyone." She didn't linger, and Nonus wondered what the audience made of their little exchange. Perhaps she should have spat on him to really drive the act home.

Last of all came Philo, who professed his innocence, swearing in the Emperor's name that he had not known the extent of his nephew's moral depravity. "He was my own flesh and blood," Philo sighed. "Any instinct I had, any inkling, was quickly smothered. I did not believe that my kin—indeed, that any member of our species—could be capable of such treason."

All around the room, heads nodded in agreement. Nonus gritted his teeth against their self-satisfied smiles. How many of them were hiding secrets? How many of them thought themselves safe and righteous, little knowing that they, too, could be cast aside without warning?

To cap off his performance, Philo played for the courtroom a recording of their conversation on the day he'd visited Nonus' cell.

Nonus closed his eyes, seething. He hated them. Every last one of them. And someday, they would all pay. He would see to that, somehow.

He wasn't sure how, but he'd find a way to repay their insults...or he'd die trying.

Chapter Forty-Eight

Commander Bina Chakravarti

The being made of light smiled. "I am not Sally Longfield," she said.

Bina jerked her hand away. She studied the figure, trying to make sense of the shape beneath the glow. It was a woman, certainly, but her features were smudged and blurry.

"Then who are you?" she whispered.

"You may call me Judith." The figure folded her hands over her chest. "And as you have surely guessed, I have been sent here by Omega."

"Sent?" Bina frowned. She'd always believed that Omega made the simulations, but after her experience with Hyx, she was no longer sure what to think. Was Val something invented by the ship's core, or was he modeled on someone real, just as the simulated Hyx had been?

"Omega recognizes the urgency of your situation," Judith explained. "I am here to help you and the captain get out of your current predicament."

Bina sucked in a breath. "So you were listening. Or Omega was. You know what's been happening."

"I have been made aware of the ongoing humanitarian disaster aboard the ship," Judith agreed. "I expect that, once you have the chance to reflect on all that has happened, this will make you angry."

Bina nodded tightly. "You could have stopped all of this."

"By what means?" Judith cocked her head. "Should Bill have been forced to follow Omega's directives? Or should those who turned against him have been killed for their actions? Already, many who doubted the captain have made the choice to come to his aid. People make mistakes, Bina. Should everyone who makes a mistake be punished, or eliminated, for noncompliance?"

Bina bit the inside of her cheek and turned away. "But you're here now. Does that mean Omega has decided to get involved?"

"You will recall that Bill Henderson was not our first choice when it came to leadership. But he has proven that his intentions are honorable, and he has seen the outcome of his actions. We did not make this happen, Bina. We did not put Rupnik in power, or start the riots, or kill Sally. Nor have we denied access to the command simulations or the weapons caches. We are not like the Imperium, and Omega believes in free will...inde ed, upholding it is one of his main priorities. Bill wanted to work alone, and he has been given the chance. He has seen the consequences of doing things his way. Now we will help him, and you, put things right."

"I think you'll find that Bill's a little busy right now, though," Bina said. "We're under attack from the Crendelen, in case you hadn't noticed."

"Sarcasm is not necessary." Judith sounded amused. "But yes, we have noticed, and it has been taken into account. Time will be made for what is necessary. In the meantime, haven't you forgotten something?"

Bina shook her head. "Of course. The Nourishers. Did they...are they...?"

Judith held out a hand. "An excellent question, Commander. Why don't you let me show you the answer?"

Chapter Forty-Nine

Captain Bill Henderson

Bill was deep in the sim when, without warning, the simspace went dark. For a moment, his hands hovered over the spot where the controls had been. Was a power outage to blame? Had one of the Crendelen missile strikes finally taken out a fuel cell? Surely, if that had happened, he'd have been kicked out of the sim...unless his consciousness was trapped in the broken system. Was that even possible? With Omega, he never knew.

If the atmo went down because he wasn't fast enough, humanity would be wiped out in a single fell swoop. It was a terrible prospect, not the least because it would mean that he'd fallen to the Crendelen.

A sound behind him made him turn. The chair he'd been sitting in seemed to fall away as he rose to his feet and stumbled toward the sliver of light behind him. As he drew closer, he began to hear strange sounds, muffled and faraway but somehow familiar. The clatter of wheels passing over cobblestones, distant voices, and...rain?

The light was coming from a doorway in the simspace, and even before he reached it to push it ajar, he had a feeling he knew what he'd find on the other side.

Sure enough, he emerged from the artificial darkness into an equally artificial version of 19th century London.

The street was busy, and the nearby Holograph and Pint was packed. The last time he'd visited, it had been win-ter, but in this simulation it was warm, with a crisp wind that suggested an early autumn evening. Above him, a quarter moon was visible, although the stars were hard to make out with the gas lamps and candles of the era blazing bright.

Bill took a deep breath, preparing for his sojourn into the bar, and immediately regretted it. Omega's sims captivated all the senses, and the scent of the old city was...potent.

Three men stumbled out of the bar with their hats askew, and Bill caught the door before it slammed shut in their wake. He nudged and elbowed his way to the bar in search of the only person in the crowd that mattered.

There was Val, sitting and sipping a glass of rye. When he saw Bill, he raised his glass in greeting, though his dour expression remained fixed in place. There was an empty stool beside him, even though the bar was packed. Bill made his way over and claimed the seat. The other patrons paid him no mind, and the barkeep didn't acknowledge his arrival. The whole experience had a dreamlike quality that left Bill shifting back and forth on the stool.

"Nice of you to turn up," Val said.

Bill drummed his fingers on the bartop. "I was in the middle of something, actually."

"So I hear." Val took another sip.

"It was rather...urgent."

Val chuckled grimly. "I am well aware that the situation is life or death, Captain. Don't worry. For all intents and purposes, time has been stopped. Or, if it makes you feel better, consider that this place exists outside of time."

That wasn't hard to imagine, given the feel of the place. But did that mean

Omega was delivering this experience as a single jolt of synaptic input?

He ran one hand over the stubble that had grown on his cheeks over the last few days. "You're back, then?"

"So it would seem. Listen, Bill, because this is important. I understand where you're coming from with your desire to chart your own path and all that, I do. But if you want to get out of this mess and regain your command, you need to start following Omega's rules. Trust me, you will be much, much better off doing that. Even if you don't always understand them. But honestly, I don't understand what the problem is. You've always followed orders in the military, and you were always subject to a command structure. What's the difference now?"

"Sometimes, I don't like the orders given."

"You've commanded AI to do things he doesn't like."

"We respect each other. We've earned each other's trust."

Val cocked his head. "And Omega hasn't?"

Bill raked his hands through his hair. "Well...."

"Bill, Omega has your good in mind, always. Believe it. Along with the good of everyone aboard this ship."

"I don't even know what Omega is. Or why the Primevals created him!"

A bemused smile settled across Val's features. "What makes you think they did?"

Chapter Fifty

Captain Alden Stone

Bill's new tactic seemed to be working, but Al could see the writing on the wall. Already, the advantages of the surprise attack were at an end, and the unexpected charge had brought them within range of the Crendelen warships' laserfire.

Then, unexpectedly, one of the warships exploded in a cloud of debris.

Bill had seemingly abandoned use of the Peregrine missiles in favor of rapid-fire dumb rounds—and the aliens still didn't seem to have accounted properly for just how fast Omega could fire those. Dozens of solid-core projectiles launched from the great ship simultaneously, targeting one of the Crendelen ships. Less than three seconds later, another barrage targeted a new ship. The attacks were perfectly coordinated and unbelievably precise, but they seemed to be targeting the converging vessels at random, rather than working their way down the line.

No, he corrected himself, not at random. Following Omega's charge toward the fleet, the ships had reoriented themselves, but into a much tighter formation than before. The dumb rounds were being strategically fired at specific ships in order to create the biggest debris cloud possible.

Al felt his jaw drop, even as several of the surviving Crendelen ships fired back with S-590s. Multiple missiles collided with the expanding debris cloud and detonated, well out of range of Omega's hull. And Omega's point defenses made short work of the rest.

It was a spectacular display that required perfect calculations and perfect timing. Bill was good, but he wasn't that good. In all his years of combat, Al had only ever seen one comparable event. His heart stutter-stopped in recognition. Was it possible...?

"Al," Bill said. "Are you listening?"

Al hesitated, suddenly fearful Rupnik and his cronies would overhear them. Then, he realized that they could likely talk within the sim without being overheard. "I'm listening," he said.

"That bought us enough time to fill you in, I think. Have you guessed what's happening yet?"

"Val's back. Isn't he?"

"Yes, he is. Which means Omega's back. And he has a plan, so listen close. I only have time to go over this once.

Things on the ship are about to go dark. The lights, the screens, the interfaces, the backups...everything. The ship will still be running, but nobody will be able to see anything, except your folks with their exosuits. Make sure their sensors are set to infrared, and they'll be able to see everything. Even the screens. Do you understand? Everyone aside from your team will be groping in the dark. You'll have the advantage."

Al had a million questions, but this was hardly the time to ask, was it?

Anyway, the explanation didn't matter. It also didn't matter that he wasn't currently wearing an exosuit. Even the knowledge of what was about to happen would put him at an advantage over the Slovenians.

He had a mission. A plan. It felt even better than the hours he'd spent in Miriam's company while they'd treated the sick.

If Val was back—if Omega was back—they might actually have a future.

He could hear the grin in Bill's voice. "Here we go, Al. Three...two...one—"

The simulated view of the battle disappeared, revealing the bridge...but actually, revealing nothing. Complete darkness had already taken hold.

Gunfire echoed behind him, but it stopped when Rupnik started screaming in Slovenian. Al caught the word Henderson in the mix. Presumably, Rupnik was concerned that a stray bullet fired in the dark would accidentally dispatch the only link he had to Omega's mainframe.

The shouting was helpful, as were the retorts of the soldiers. Al could hear them yelling at each other in panicked voices, trying to find each other in the dark.

That, more than anything else, proved their inexperience. If they could find each other in the dark, he could find them, too. He lay with his belly to the deck for the span of three heartbeats, long enough to pinpoint all seven of the militiamen, before launching into action.

The nearest two Slovenians were off to his left, and he went for them first. It wasn't difficult to find them, given the volume of their shouting. He reached the first man and, based on the location of his voice, guessed where his head would be. He grabbed the man by his grown-out hair—a good reminder to trim his own as soon as possible—and yanked him off his feet. He drove his knee between the man's shoulders, seized his head, and twisted. The Slovenian stopped struggling at once.

Their scuffle had been brief, but not so brief that it went unnoticed. Cries went up from the other Slovenians, including the companion of the man he'd just killed. Under other circumstances, that would have been very bad news.

In this instance, it was dark enough to hide his movements—and now, thanks to the dead man slumped beneath him, he was in possession of a weapon.

To Al's surprise, the night vision setting on the rifle was no use at all. Strange phantom images blurred through the bridge, as if it was filled with ghostly specters. On the other hand, Bill had warned him that only infrared would function properly, and now he understood why: the Slovenians had access to night vision, but not infrared. Omega had gone to great lengths to stack the deck against them.

Focus, he scolded himself. Dispatch as many enemies as possible. Bring your team up to speed. And get to your suit.

Firing in the pitch black was a risk, but at least none of his people were on the bridge. He closed his eyes and listened, smiling to himself when he realized that the Slovenians were scrambling toward the exit hatch—much to Rupnik's annoyance. Al took a few shots in the rough direction of the voices, and was rewarded with a cry when one of his bullets found flesh.

The Slovenians appeared to decide that they were better off in the unlit corridor than trapped on the bridge with an unseen killer. Several of their voices faded as they escaped to the passageway, only to rise in pitch when a loud thump reverberated through the deck. Al's first thought was that another of the Crendelen missiles had struck the ship, but the thumping continued, deepening in resonance until Al's ribcage thrummed with the sound.

A huge hand grabbed him by the back of his shirt and hauled him to his feet.

"Are you hurt?" Tull's deep voice asked.

"Tull!" Al grabbed the Roughback's shoulder, partly in greeting, partly to steady himself in the dark. "What are you doing here?"

"Power went out," the Roughback leader grunted. "Wanted to check on you. Humans aren't used to the dark, I think."

Al beamed in his general direction. Of course—the Roughbacks lived underground. He should have guessed they would know how to navigate in the dark.

Chapter Fifty-One

Tull of the Roughbacks

"You haven't been to see us in some time," Tull observed. His crew fanned out behind him, poking around the bridge. They'd encountered a group of humans in the corridor who didn't seem to belong up here, but it was hard to tell...humans were such funny little creatures, with no shells and useless teeth and barely any muscle to speak of. Tull knew better than to say so, but he had a hard time telling them apart by sight alone. Their voices were much more distinct, although they were almost uniformly high-pitched and whiny.

"We haven't," Al agreed.

Tull folded his arms and listened to the Marine captain fumble around on the bridge. He'd long since committed the layout of the ship to memory, a habit common to the Roughbacks.

Al went on, "There was a coup by a group of the survivors we took in. They tried to overthrow the captain and steal our food stores. Bill didn't think you'd be willing to help us even if we alerted you."

Tull ran his tongue over his molars in thought. "No," he said after a little while. "We probably wouldn't. Or, if we had, I would have known better than to recommend an alliance with our leadership. If your species can't handle your internal squabbles, why should we risk our necks to help you?"

Al muttered something under his breath, perhaps to hide his annoyance with Tull's response, perhaps because he'd just slammed his fleshy torso into the corner of a command console. "I'm surprised you didn't approach us about the food stores."

"What about them?"

"Aren't you starving?"

Tull cocked his head in amusement. "Are you? That's very irresponsible. We have reduced our metabolisms significantly."

"You can just decide to do that? Like flipping a switch?"

"You saw the nests we built." Tull flicked a flake of dried mud from his arm as he spoke. "We have recreated the conditions of the lean season and spent more time asleep. We can also hold undigested food in our stomachs and break it down over time for sustained nutrient uptake."

"That's...gross." Al seemed to find the chair he was looking for, and slid into it.

"We also have several non-essential organs that we are able to break down for sustenance in emergencies such as this one. The organs then regrow once we regain regular access to external calories." At the man's answering shudder, he added, "Things have yet to get that dire, though."

"May I have a quiet moment, please?" Al's nimble fingers began pecking away at the console in front of him.

One of Tull's kinsmen, squatting on the deck next to the dead human, uttered a soft, questioning grunt. Tull considered asking Al if he had any plans for the remains—if the humans were anything like his people, they would revere their dead and want to hold elaborate rites over their remains.

Two considerations stilled his tongue. First, they were far from home, and any planet-bound rites would be impossible to complete. Bringing it up might even offend the human, or reopen an old wound. Besides, he had killed this man. His fate could not be considered that important under such circumstances.

Tull grunted an affirmative.

Al finished typing out his message and swiveled back toward Tull. "Now, onto the next consideration. This coup—"

Tull cut him off before the man could waste both of their time. "I am not interested in your internal difficulties. We do not have this sort of trouble among our people. Once or twice in our planet's history we have competed over food, or over water in drought years, but fighting among our people is a grievous ill. We will not be conscripted into your little war." Already, they'd discussed the matter too much. Tull's jaw ached from all the talking; he didn't know how humans put up with it. They relied so much on words and had invented so many of them. Like the humans themselves, their methods of communication were exhausting.

Al sighed. "Fair enough. I didn't realize the Roughbacks were such pacifists."

"Oh, we aren't," one of Tull's kinswomen said. "There were two other intelligent species on our homeworld. We did war with them after they violated an old treaty."

Tull nodded. "They are long extinct."

"Right." Al got to his feet and shuffled carefully back toward them. Tull couldn't see him in the most literal sense, though it wasn't difficult to determine his relative location based on the sounds of his movements, the thump of his accelerated human heartbeat, the rustle of his clothes, and the faintly sour smell of his body so unlike the sweet, earthy richness common to the Roughbacks. It was a lucky thing Tull's people were built to rely on other senses more than their sight. It had served them in the burrows, and it would serve them again now.

"Is there some other way we can help?" Tull asked, much to the disapproval of the soldiers under his command, who emitted low and rumbling utterances of disdain. This was not their fight.

Al took a moment to consider this. "Rupnik, the leader of the coup, made me leave my exosuit in my quarters. Can you get me there?"

"Which quarters are yours?" Tull asked. Before Al could answer, he interjected, "Never mind, we can go by smell." He strode over to the man, who was taking an awfully long time to navigate back toward him, and picked him up without warning. Al yelped as Tull lifted him onto his back. "Come on, let's go."

His crew loped off into the passage with their leader at the fore. He flared his nostrils in search of the room that smelled the most like Alden Stone.

From the corridor, they could make out the echo of faint, distant screams. The voices were human, but Tull had to grit his teeth against the memories of his own people, trapped underground and besieged by the Crendelen.

Even though the humans were bad at making peace, he felt sorry for them. It seemed to him that those at the top of their hierarchies were the ones who waged battle, while those at the bottom paid for it.

Chapter Fifty-Two

Sergeant Shawn 'Funny Bone' Piker

Funny Bone's new friends had led him right to the Slovenians' door when the lights died.

Immediately, people began to scream—or rather, continued screaming, but with new intensity and less coherent intent.

To his relief, no one in his party followed suit. Even the civilians remained calm, though he heard a woman's voice ask, "Are we done for? Was that caused by missiles hitting us?"

Funny Bone paused a beat before answering. "I don't think so. I didn't feel any impacts that would have caused the blackout." He tried switching his helmet to night vision, but something was wrong with the readings.

"What do we do, sir?" Awad whispered.

"Good question." Funny Bone hesitated. "Hold position for now. Marcus, Dorsey...you think we're close to where our guy Norder is being held?"

"Very," Dorsey replied, not bothering with an honorific.

"How far ahead, would you say?" Funny Bone asked.

Trinica spoke up. "A corridor? Maybe? They're being kept in a small chamber used for storage."

Hardly an exact measurement, but she was a civilian, and she and her friends had already risked a lot to find Norder and then reach out to Funny Bone. She'd done her part. He needed to do his.

But how?

As if prompted by the question, a brief message came from Al over the teamwide channel:

"Use infrared."

Funny Bone switched the settings over and whistled long and low when the passage ahead came into focus.

"Wait here," he told the trainees and civilians.

"Where are you going, sir?" Kan asked in clipped, precise English.

The others wouldn't have access to infrared vision, and Funny Bone didn't feel like taking the time to explain that he could see now, or why.

"Just...keep these folks safe. I'll be back when I can."

He ranged ahead until he reached an open hatch. Inside the small chamber beyond, two people were tied to chairs, while four others stood around them, talking to each other in urgent Slovenian.

"Keating and Norder," he breathed. Dorsey and Marcus had been right about the location of the captured crew members. Still, even with all the advantages he had, how was he supposed to free the pair of them? If he started shooting, the Slovenians wouldn't be able to see where he was, and he'd have the protection of his suit...but Norder and Keating had no such advantages.

I have to try.

And so he did.

The first shot sparked chaos, but he was already pulling the trigger by the time the next mark started to move. Number Three took two shots to bring down, and by then the fourth Slovenian had already drawn a long, brutal-looking serrated knife and pounced on the two officers. He made a swing for Norder, but missed by a few inches.

Keating, who had been lying so still against her restraints that Funny Bone had feared she was dead, rocked sideways into Norder. Both of them toppled, still bound to the chairs. Her timing was impeccable—if she hadn't knocked them both aside, the next knife slash would have crossed Norder's throat.

The Slovenian stumbled, unable to make out the new arrangement. Before he could puzzle it out, Funny Bone had planted two rounds in the back of his head.

The militiamen defeated, Funny Bone began helping Norder and Keating while hailing the Marine channel. "Team, I'm going to need a report. I've got our officers back. Where are the rest of you?"

"Taking care of business, sir," Guns replied. "I just made quick work of a pocket of Slovenian bootlickers."

Funny Bone bit back a curse as he untied Norder's hands. "What happened to holding the line?"

"Sorry, Sarge." She didn't sound the least bit sorry.

"The supplies are guarded," Al's voice cut in. "I've got Tull and the Roughbacks on the storage bays. They've made it pretty clear they're not interested in fighting our battles for us, but they do make a solid line of defense."

Splat asked, "Captain, I've got thirty, maybe forty folks here who just laid down their weapons. What am I supposed to do with them?"

"Keep them contained. Restrain them if you can. We're not killing anyone who surrenders, and when the lights are back on, we can sort all this out. There's been enough bloodshed."

A distant impact shuddered through the bulkheads and deck. Keating groaned.

"Sounds like we're still under fire," Funny Bone said.

"We are, but Bill's on it...and Omega's helping him." Al's voice was tense despite the good news. "I don't know the details, but I do know that we've got to find Rupnik. Does anyone have him?"

One by one, the team sounded off in the negative. Despite the unexpected success of his mission, that information sat poorly with Funny Bone. "Any idea how much longer we'll be in the dark?" he asked the captain.

"No idea. In the meantime, hold your position. I don't know what that little rat is up to, but I intend to deal with him."

Chapter Fifty-Three

Maks Rupnik

Every last one of them was going to pay. Alden Stone for the stunt he'd pulled, Bill Henderson for this trick with the lights, and his own men, for being incompetent cowards. Everyone had either disappointed him or tried to make a fool of him, and he could not allow it to continue.

While his people fled, Rupnik tucked himself against the bulkhead, behind a support, and waited. He heard one alien leave the bridge, and a few minutes later, the rest followed. He was too far away to hear what had become of Alden Stone, but he suspected that the Roughbacks had protected him. And they were supposed to be a rational species. Ha! They'd backed the wrong person. They, too, would pay the price.

There was a very real possibility that his next actions would be his last—but his father had been willing to risk his life to see Bill Henderson deposed. If nothing else, Maks couldn't let the man who'd killed his father survive. He would avenge his pride and his father both in a single glorious act, and there was no one left to stop him.

Once the heavy tread of the Rough-backs had faded away, Rupnik began his painstaking journey back the way he had come. He had to take small, shuf-fling steps and feel his way along the bulkheads, but he'd counted his turns when he fled the bridge, knowing that he would have to find his way back with-out the aid of sight. It seemed to take an interminably long time to retrace his steps, especially since he stopped every few paces to listen in case someone returned to stop him.

Nobody did.

At last, he shuffled through the hatch to the bridge. He knew it by sound as much as anything else—all the machines were still running, despite the outage, and there was a faint hum in the air. He could also make out the steady breathing of another person in the chamber with him. Henderson had retained his seat in the command chair.

Not for long. Once Rupnik reached him, humanity's so-called "savior" would meet his end.

His steps quickened as he felt his way along the command consoles. He swore he could hear his quarry's heartbeat, although perhaps it was his own. When the toe of his boot bumped the outer edge of the dais where Henderson sat, his heart leapt. While he was in the sim, the man was lost to the world. Rupnik had observed him several times, taking note of his shallow breathing and the ways his eyes moved behind their lids, like a dreamer deep in REM. Henderson wouldn't see him coming until it was much, much too late.

Rupnik lifted his rifle and held it out, aiming down toward where Bill's chest and shoulders should be. He would be firing point-blank. It was impossible to miss.

Just to be sure, he prodded around with the barrel of the rifle until it touched something solid. Rupnik grinned to himself as he pulled the trigger once, twice, three times...with each shot, he moved the barrel slightly, just to be sure he hit something vital. If he'd had his knives with him, he could have made the man suffer more. Instead, he'd have to settle for being practical.

He pulled the trigger until the magazine was empty and dropped his weapon to the deck. In hindsight, he ought to have saved a few rounds to defend himself with, should the Marines return. Not that it would have made any difference in the dark.

He groped toward the chair. "I want you to know it was me," he rasped. "I'm the one who got you in the end. The untouchable Captain Henderson." He laughed. "Even the Imperium couldn't sink you, but I did."

Rupnik's fingers found the arm of the command chair. He gripped it for dear life and reached out to where the former captain's still-warm chest should have been. He expected to find fabric tacky with spilled blood.

But there was nothing. No matter how far he reached, he felt nothing.

"What?" He waved his arm in wider arcs until it struck the back of the command chair. "What? Surely you didn't leave your post...you coward...."

He flinched when the lights came on, blinding after nearly an hour of pure darkness. He had to blink a few times before his eyes adjusted enough to see the empty chair before him. The thick padding was marred with bullet holes through the back and the seat, but there was no blood, and no sign of the man he'd been so desperate to kill.

"Looking for someone?"

Rupnik dropped to his knees, still gripping one arm of the empty command chair. A few feet away, standing over him with a pistol drawn, stood Henderson. "What?" he rasped. "How?"

"Someone let me know you were on your way." The captain's smile was almost rueful. Even now, he was playing the part of the reluctant hero. It made Rupnik sick. "Do you intend to surrender?"

"To you?" Rupnik's mouth was painfully dry, but he still managed to spit at the captain's feet. "Never. I'm going to have Keating and Norder killed for this. I'm going to be the last thing you ever see."

Bill shook his head. "No," he said. "I'm sorry to tell you, it's going to be the other way around."

"I'm going to find your parents," Rupnik snarled as he turned his back to the captain again, leaning over the command chair as he clawed as covertly as he could for the handgun he kept in a concealed chest holster. "And I'm going to break every bone in their—"

But the captain's pistol roared, and darkness returned for Rupnik.

Chapter Fifty-Four

Captain Bill Henderson

"You do not seem pleased," Val observed after Bill returned to the command sim.

"Why should I be pleased?" Bill's brow wrinkled as he stared down at the controls. "I killed a kid. A terrible kid, whose father told him that power was the only thing that mattered, but still a kid. I'm glad he's not a danger anymore, but I wish there was another way."

"There was."

Bill bit back a curse. "If you're going to tell me that I should have listened to you before—"

Val held up a hand. "You should have, but that's not what I meant. Quite the opposite, actually. What I mean is that Omega will make specific requests, or advise specific actions, only when the alternatives have been exhausted. He is not, for example, going to dictate what you'll do with your Slovenian prisoners. He's also not going to tell you what to do now." Val waved a hand to the battle arrayed before them. "You must use the gifts you've been given to the best of your ability. As ever."

Bill drummed his fingers on the arm of the command chair. "All right, then, what are we dealing with?"

Val stepped forward and maneuvered between the simulated images of the Crendelen fleet. "Right now, six of the twenty vessels remain intact. Three others are too damaged to give chase at full capacity. Also..." He waved a hand to the blackness beyond, and a few dozen more ships appeared in the distance. "More vessels are on the way, and will be within firing range in approximately two hours."

"Then, we're going to do what we should have done when the Crendelen first arrived. We're skipping the system. We've got food stores now. And minerals to trade, thanks to Rupnik's greed. As for a destination…" Bill paused to weigh his options. They needed the SRJ drive, but before they could dock for upgrades, they needed allies. He still planned to petition the Roughbacks, but they wouldn't thank him for leading the Crendelen to their door.

"Just get us out of here," he said at last. "We're going to take the scenic route to the Roughbacks. See if we can lose our tail. Keep us away from any planets that might launch an attack on us, or get us caught in the crossfire if the Crendelen pursue us. I want to take stock of our supplies and get things under control before we make any political overtures."

There was another concern—one he felt reluctant even to voice aloud. If the Ornu found out about the Omega's intended trajectory, they might post a guard to deter them...or lay waste to the planet in question, rather than risk letting humans plunder another world. That would be drastic, but he very much doubted they'd be above doing it.

As Val deftly extricated the Omega from the engagement, Bill felt his tension drain away. He was getting a second chance. A third one, if he counted his resurrection in the ship's medbay.

Omega broke away from Vale and headed off through the quadrant. A few of the Crendelen ships followed, but they didn't seem particularly enthusiastic about giving chase. The Crendelen weren't a particularly bold or clever species. It was a good thing the Ornu hadn't set a fleet of Jackals on them, or they would have been in for a protracted battle. But that would have been expensive. Unless forced to hire the mercenaries at that scale, the Imperium would much rather employ its most servile, most vicious vassal species.

Even with Val taking over navigation for the time being, Bill had his work cut out for him. He was partway through making himself a to-do list—find Bina, find Norder and Keating, determine what to do with the surviving Slovenian insurrectionists—when Val turned to him.

"Captain," he said gravely, "now that we're out of immediate danger, we need to talk."

Chapter Fifty-Five

Commander Bina Chakravarti

Bina had largely avoided the Engineering decks, not out of any particular aversion, but because all the machines and equipment down there were, quite literally, alien tech. Of all the things that had gone wrong abroad Omega, they had never gotten an alert that anything required repair. Lucky thing, too. She could only imagine the type of chaos that would have ensued if something vital had failed. Nevertheless, she recognized the route Judith chose.

They were almost at their destination when the lights went out, and Bina's heart nearly leapt out of her throat.

She bit back a cry and reached for her weapon, remembering too late that she was unarmed. It wasn't as if she could fight off the darkness with bullets, but at least it would be reassuring to have a weapon at hand.

"Be calmed," Judith said in her soft voice. Her glow had dimmed with the sudden darkness, but she was still present, if unseen. "The lights were extinguished by design. It will not last."

Bina pressed her back to a bulkhead and tried to breathe. "Omega planned this?"

"It will help," Judith promised.

She sank to the deck and wrapped her arms around her knees. The darkness reminded her of the Wreck, and all the days she'd spent wandering its dark tunnels. She had done terrible things in those tunnels, things that went against her very nature. She'd been such a coward back then.

Are you any better now? she wondered. Considering what you did to Ridding....

She tipped her head forward to rest on her knees. "Why did Omega speak to me?" she asked. "Why...why fold time so that I could see Hyx?"

"Because Omega cares about you," Judith said. "Very much."

"Yes, but why me? Why not Longfield? Why not someone good? I've made so many mistakes, Judith."

Judith chuckled in the darkness. "It is true. And it helps that you acknowledge it. But if Omega didn't work through broken instruments, then he wouldn't work at all."

Bina paused as that sank in. There seemed to be a lot to unpack in that one statement.

"Reflection is necessary." Bina could no longer see Judith, but it sounded as if she had sunk to the ground at

Bina's side. Did she have a body? Was she…real? Even that seemed like the wrong question. In a place like Omega, where reality bent and folded at surreal angles, what did that word even mean?

"And by admitting that I've done something wrong, I'm reflecting on it?"

Judith hummed. "As he is now, if Bill Henderson was faced with the same challenge a hundred times, he would make the same choice again and again. He would be convinced of the righteousness of it. In some ways, that kind of thinking is an asset. Conviction and confidence are valuable qualities in a leader. But rigid thinking can also be a detriment."

Bina relaxed slightly. "True. But it would be better if I hadn't made my mistakes in the first place. There would be nothing to regret."

"There is always something to regret," Judith said softly.

They sat there in the dark for what seemed a very long time. Bina was thinking about all the things she'd do differently, given a second chance. What Judith was thinking, if anything, remained a mystery.

* * *

When the lights came back on, Bina shook herself out of the dreamlike state into which she'd slipped. She had heard shouts and cries from a distance, but there was nothing she could do to help. With the light, however, came near-silence, and a bone-deep sense of relief.

Judith was once again visible beside her. The two of them got to their feet.

"We are close now," she said. "Come."

"Aren't you going to tell me what happened?" Bina glanced over her shoulder. She should go check on Bill, shouldn't she?

Judith shook her head. "Patience. One thing at a time."

The Nourishers were more important, so Bina did as she was told. She followed the woman made of light into one of the outermost rooms of the Engineering deck.

She didn't remember exactly what had been there before, and the machines Judith led her to hardly looked new. They wouldn't, of course. Her end of the conversation with Hyx had taken place only hours ago, but for him, it had taken place before this ship was even a blueprint.

"These are the Nourishers." Judith pointed to each portion of the system in turn. She began with an enormous chamber, which was connected to each of the outlets by pipes. Chutes ran from the deck up to the top of the chamber, and a series of walkways criss-crossed it to allow for easier access. "Matter is deposited in the chamber to be reconstituted into edible, and more palatable, substances. Nearly any type of matter is permissible, although for obvious reasons, organic matter is best."

Judith directed her to the output tubes. "As far as these go, you have several options. Food items can be requested in bulk and distributed en masse, or individuals can make particular requests. I've taken the liberty of preprogramming some options based on the food people brought aboard during Earth's evacuation. More options can be added to the 'menu,' but I do suggest making sample sizes at first. Chemical compounds, for example, can be replicated more readily than flavor profiles or textures, which can be harder to program correctly."

Bina brushed her fingers over one of the small screens, which immediately came to life, displaying a variety of different meal options. For the moment, all of them were grayed out, pending material to fuel the Nourishers.

"Judith, this is…." Bina's throat closed. It was nothing less than a miracle.

"Of course, one Nourisher will not be sufficient to meet the needs of the whole ship, but the engineers had the foresight to build several of them all around Omega so that they could be more easily accessed and operated." Judith tipped her head down the corridor. "Would you like to see the rest?"

Chapter Fifty-Six

Captain Bill Henderson

Between one blink and the next, Bill found himself standing in the middle of a medieval royal court. The room appeared all at once, but the sounds kicked in more gradually, as did the smells: a mixture of rich food and fragrance from various bouquets sprouting from vases interspersed with the dishes.

Bill held up his hands and examined his sleeves. He hadn't changed, but Val had, from his boots to his hose and tunic. Even his hair was different—now long enough to brush his shoulders, complemented by a beard that reached almost to his chest.

All around them stood courtiers, advisors, nobles, and soldiers, clustered in distinct groups and glancing warily at one another. A musician wandered from group to group strumming a lute, as did a court jester in a jingling hat decorated with brass bells. At the outskirts of the party, a group of young men were defacing the tapestries and using charcoal sticks to draw on statues displayed in the room's alcoves, much in the same way Bill's schoolmates had sometimes drawn in textbooks when their Ornu instructors weren't looking. Lengthy tables ran along multiple walls, laden with food, and the wealthy loaded their plates to overflowing, while the only common folk in evidence thumped their fists against the stained glass windows from the outside, begging for a bite to eat.

Bill wrinkled his nose as he took in the chaotic scene before him. "This isn't how I imagined a royal court," he said.

Val snorted. "Were you hoping for some semblance of order? Because according to my first-hand observations, this is all quite reminiscent of a certain ship I might name."

Bill squinted at the boys who were amusing themselves by pulling at the loose threads of a likely priceless tapestry. A few of them looked familiar. In fact, many of the people who filled the room bore a striking resemblance to certain inhabitants of the ship at his command. The knights and guards looked a bit like his Marines, while the courtiers bore more than passing resemblances to the various heads of state they'd rescued from the Crendelen prison on Titan.

Worst of all were the narrow, dirty faces of the peasants pawing at the windows. He swore he recognized his mother among their pitiful number.

"All right," he murmured, "this is an allegory, but I'm not sure I get the point yet."

Val's eyes wandered to the empty throne at the head of the room. "I warn you, this is an imperfect example, but it's at least one you'll recognize. You are one man, Bill. You can't change the minds and hearts of every person aboard this ship, but you can make choices about what actions will be encouraged…and discouraged. Who is the only political master these people have known?"

"The Ornu," Bill said at once.

Val snapped his fingers, and a likeness of Emperor Albus appeared at the head of the room. Ornu flooded through the doors, flanked by Jackals and Crendelen. They arrested the jester, smashed the musician's lute, and forced the courtiers to their knees. Those who resisted had knives held to their throats. Along the back walls, the raucous youths cheered and laughed. This seemed to amuse the emperor, who gestured to his guards. The guards placed knives in the hands of the youths, and the emboldened young men charged toward the buffet, where they stabbed anyone who got in their way and fell upon the offerings with gusto.

It all happened so fast that Bill had no time to respond, and as the party collapsed into chaos, a sickening instinct—drilled into him by Ornu indoctrination, no doubt—told him that it had always been this way, and always would be.

Val laid a hand on Bill's shoulder. "Under the Ornu, violence and chaos were rewarded. Albus nurtured that which divided you. He appealed to the appetites of people who preferred violence and greed over the interests of the community, because community and unity were the things he feared most. If you spoke to each other and listened to each other's grievances, you would soon discover their source." He nodded toward the throne.

"But before the Ornu...." Bill trailed off. His Imperium-approved textbooks had painted a pretty grim picture of the world before Empowerment. He didn't believe the propaganda, and had sought out texts printed by those few who dared speak against their Ornu masters. Unfortunately, those texts hadn't painted a rosy picture of humanity's past, either. "Before the Ornu was much the same, I'm afraid."

"And yet, there are a lot fewer of you now. A lot fewer. Only a handful of you remain. What politicians are left to you have been neutered by their enslavement." Val gestured toward the compliant courtiers, and to the youths running amok, harming their kin because nobody interceded. The people outside had only grown more desperate in their attempts to break in, although it seemed to Bill there were far fewer than before.

"I'm with you so far," he said.

"A groveling politician has no hope of reining in the sort of chaos seen on your ship lately. He would only declare the mob his master, and ask them how they'd like him to lie as they trample him underfoot."

Bill grimaced. "Graphic, Val."

"But accurate." Val sniffed. "Even worse, you have multiple 'leaders' who are every bit at odds with each other as your nations of old were. Officials with no idea how to act in this current environment. This is not a recipe for order, not to mention effectiveness."

"What's our alternative?" There was no way this cheerful little bedtime story came without a moral.

"What indeed?" Val snapped his fingers again, and the Ornu disappeared. The room did not return to its former state, however. Those who had been killed still lay on the deck, while the politicians wrung their hands and the youths continued their reign of terror. "Or rather… who? It is the king who sets the tone of the kingdom."

"King? Are you saying we need to bring back monarchy? How is that any better?"

"A captain should be king aboard his ship. Should he not? Must he not have the expectation of having his commands followed without question? The difference here is, unlike practically every ship captain throughout history, you have a public aboard your ship. A public that is desperate and without direction. And so you must become a king, in name as well as fact."

"Wait…you're saying I should become king?"

Val climbed the dais and laid a hand on the back of the throne. Beneath his touch, the gilded seat transformed into a familiar command chair. "Why, yes."

Bill followed in Val's footsteps. Even though he knew that nothing in the sim was real, he still took great pains stepping over and around the wide-eyed dead. "On whose authority?"

"On Omega's authority. Humanity has long been enamored of the twin adders of individualism and collectivism—too enamored for a monarchy to be viable. Until now. With Omega's backing, you can be a king, Bill. In fact, Omega requires it. He will not suffer a repeat of these recent transgressions." Val waved a hand toward the chair.

Bill, still hesitating by the bottom step, was lost for words.

Val clicked his tongue at his reticence. "This isn't so different from how you've always operated, Bill. A captain should always be king of his own ship. No military leader can allow his subordinates to vote on a course of action—he must choose one, and execute it decisively. As before, you have your subordinates—it just so happens that for the time being, they include thousands upon thousands of civilians. And you also have your superior. Omega."

Bill gingerly mounted the steps until he reached the command chair. He stared down at it for a long time. Val had even included the bullet holes left by Rupnik in this rendition of the sim. It was tempting to sit, but a sense of unease lingered in his gut. If he was to play the part of king at Omega's command...what did that make Omega?

He ran a palm over the arm of the chair. He'd already promised to follow Omega's commands. And if he refused, what would become of the civilians? Or of his crew?

He turned to face the great chamber. Those still alive had fallen silent, with every eye fixed upon him. Outside the windows, the people had their faces pressed to the glass, apparently anxious to see how he chose.

Warily, he lowered himself into the chair. Val produced a crown from thin air and held it over his head while the crowd below them applauded.

The metal circlet had just brushed Bill's forehead when the great hall of the castle vanished, and he was left on the silent bridge of Omega once more, with Rupnik still lying glassy-eyed at his feet.

Chapter Fifty-Seven

Sergeant Shawn 'Funny Bone' Piker

Funny Bone woke from what felt like the best sleep of his life. After almost forty consecutive hours on duty securing first the Slovenian prisoners and then the new supply of stores brought aboard from Vale, he'd tottered into his rack and collapsed face-first without even bothering to shower. True, he smelled like a wild pig that had rolled in something rancid, but at least he could be fairly certain he wouldn't wake up to another disaster. Omega had it covered.

He rubbed at his eyes as he sat up in his rack. It was already 0800 hours, which meant he'd been asleep for almost twelve hours. No wonder he felt so refreshed, except for his disgustingly dry mouth. His meeting with Stone wasn't for a while yet. He had time to grab a meal and maybe, if he was lucky, a cup of whatever passed for coffee these days. As he stretched his arms above his head, his stomach lurched...he needed a shower before he subjected anyone else to his presence.

By the time he wandered into the mess hall an hour later, the rest of the Marine team was already gathered. Funny Bone looked around in surprise. "If you're all here, who's on duty? Surely not the civilian police."

Guns wrinkled her nose. "Those guys? Uh, no."

"They didn't all defect to Rupnik," Tubes pointed out.

"But we don't know who did," Guns replied, "and we certainly can't trust them to tell us who went behind our backs."

"The Roughbacks are guarding the supplies," Stone cut in. "And I told a few of your trainees to back them up. Bill's up and about, too."

Funny Bone pulled out a chair. There was already an MRE at the one empty seat, just begging to be demolished. "What about everyone else?"

Stone ticked names off on his fingers. "Keating's still in the medbay, and she's already looking better. Norder's back in his quarters, but Bill insisted that he rest until at least tomorrow. I checked in on the Hendersons earlier...they're not great, but they're still alive. And your new friends, the civilians who backed up Bill, are on standby for now. Bill assigned them to the team distributing rations, since they seem to have a better grasp of where that system is breaking down."

Funny Bone tore open the wrapper of his MRE. It was stale, but at least it wasn't spoiled. He started to divide it in half, but Stone shook his head. "Eat the whole thing. We've got a lot of work ahead of us, and just took on some new supplies."

While Funny Bone tucked in, Termite leaned his elbows on the table. "So, Captain, you wanted to talk about the new recruits?"

"I did." Stone's brows pulled together. "I'm worried about Nemec."

Funny Bone chomped on a cracker. "What did she do now?"

That brought the Marine captain up short. "Now? As in, she's done something else?"

"Besides poison herself, you mean?" Guns rolled her eyes.

Every head at the table swiveled toward her.

"Come on." Guns draped an arm over the back of her chair. "We were all thinking it, right?"

"I sure wasn't," Splat muttered.

Stone, too, was frowning, but he didn't deny her implication. "What makes you say it?"

Guns shrugged with one shoulder. "Call it women's intuition, if you want. It would be nice to have another gal on the team, don't get me wrong, but it's the only thing that makes sense. Nobody else we talked to had the opportunity to poison her, but we never thought to check her person for evidence."

"Because she'd ingested lethal amounts of strychnine!" Splat snapped.

"Yeah, but riddle me this." Guns held up one finger and tilted her chin up so that she could look down her nose at all of them. "Strychnine poisoning doesn't result in immediate symptoms, and with so much of it in her system, by the time symptoms set in, she should have been pretty far gone. So either she ingested the strychnine during our exercise routine, or…"

"Or it was in the water, but she decided to get our attention so that she could be treated in time to be saved." Termite's eyes bulged. "That's sociopath-level behavior, Guns. And it would still be a terrible risk. Why would she do it?"

"Maybe to get the second-best candidate disqualified? Maybe just to mess with us?" Guns shrugged again. "I don't know, but the whole thing seems fishy to me. And did you see how fast she flipped for Rupnik? For all we know, he put her up to it. Or maybe she works for some other faction we don't know about yet."

Termite looked thoughtful. "Guns, remember when we were on patrol and that group of civilians tried to cut us off in the corridor? I thought it was suspicious at the time, but what if Nemec tipped them off?"

Stone steepled his fingers. "These are serious accusations. Funny Bone, what do you think?"

Funny Bone took his time chewing, and not just because the dehydrated meal was tacky in his mouth. He wasn't sure exactly what it was supposed to taste like, although the label indicated the contents were supposed to resemble pizza in some cursory way. They didn't. When he finally choked down a mouthful of the stuff, he said, "I think there's a reason you were worried about her, Captain. As to the matter of her being a sociopath, I can't say one way or the other, but she has made some concerning statements in my presence. Even if this is all speculation, we don't trust her, and we need to trust our teammates."

Stone nodded as if he, too, had reached the exact same conclusion. "So she's removed from the pool of candidates, and we'll keep an eye on her to see what she does next. All agreed?"

There were nods all around the table.

"As for the rest, I think we should divide them into teams of three and have them patrol with us. I don't know how we're going to make up for a shortage of exosuits, but the more time we spend with them, the better sense we'll get of their thinking. Does that suit everyone?"

More nodding.

"Good." The captain ran a hand through his hair. "I'll be honest, I don't know what's going to happen now. Removing Rupnik isn't going to be a magic pill that makes everything run smoothly, but I expect our enemies will think twice before making another grab for the captaincy."

Guns smirked. "You mean the throne."

Stone whipped toward her. "I don't want to hear a single one of you making fun of him, especially not where others can hear."

The smile slipped from Guns' face, and she saluted. "Yes, sir. Won't happen again."

"Good." Stone got to his feet. "We've won a battle, but we're a long way from winning the war. I'm glad to have the ship back under our control, but we're still in an extremely tight spot, no matter how you dice it. With any luck, the Perseids attacking the Ornu will buy us the time we need to do what we have to do. But in the meantime, I think we need to be ready for anything."

Chapter Fifty-Eight

Commander Bina Chakravarti

Thanks to the Nourishers, it was possible to create a varied and genuinely enjoyable meal. Their dinner that evening looked and tasted indistinguishable from chicken cutlets, steamed greens, and boiled potatoes. Bina caught herself enjoying the flavor. After months of MREs and the usual swill served on Ornu ships, it was deeply satisfying.

Bill certainly seemed to be enjoying himself. He'd barely spoken since they'd tucked in.

"So," she said. "You're a king now."

He paused momentarily, to look at her over a forkful of greens. "Apparently," he said before stuffing them into his mouth.

"What's that like?"

"It's, uh..." he said through the half-masticated food. "It's nothing, really. I think Val just needs a backstop. Someone to make a final call on important stuff. And to provide an overall direction, without the fear of a politician undermining the plan."

"Uh huh."

"Val gave me, um, a manual. Of sorts. Guidelines, rules...whatever you want to call them. They're lengthy, but they seem reasonable enough. All stuff we'd recognize as moral and fair—at least, stuff we would have recognized as moral before human society went off the rails. A few of them will still probably cause some protest, though."

"Well, we're no strangers to that.'"

"Yeah. I just...I still can't get over the idea that I'm supposed to be a—a king now. It just seems...." He trailed off.

She agreed, but she still found herself slipping into her habitual role of confidant and advisor. "It does seem odd, but is it really that different from what we were living under before?"

"Under the Ornu? I hope it's different." Bill shuddered. "If it's worse, I should be jettisoned into space."

"I meant before the Ornu. Even under a democracy, there were still representatives who made the laws. Don't you think?"

"I suppose." Bill didn't sound convinced. "But a king? It's a bit too close to an emperor for my tastes."

Bina was warming to her topic. "I have a background in medieval studies, and I can tell you that the modern impression of that era is pretty warped. It wasn't nearly as backward as we've been led to believe. Actually, in some ways, we're the backward ones. These days—the days before every major city on Earth was destroyed, anyway—if you got in trouble with the Revenue Service, for example, they could make your life completely miserable, and there'd be no one to stand in the way to stop them from doing that. But if a monarch wanted to target you in the medieval era, he had to navigate several layers protecting you. He'd have to go through the local lord, the landowner, the sheriff, the guild, the Church. Those layers were almost all deemphasized or discarded by our day, which exposed us to whatever the government saw fit to do to any one of us."

Bill hummed. "And then came the Ornu."

She scooped up her plate. "I'll never argue that we were better off under them. All I'm saying is that the government is only ever as good as the people in power. A kingdom where the laws are valued is better than a democracy with despots at the helm."

He gathered his dishes, which they deposited in the cleaning bin near the mess hall hatch.

"We need to work on the infrastructure," Bina said. "Put some failsafes in place. Although, to be honest, I think a lot of that can wait until we can figure out where we're going to settle, and we have no idea when or where—"

Her train of thought was derailed by the tenor of a man's screams. "There she is! Traitor! Get her away from the captain!"

Bina turned to look down the corridor. A cluster of Marines and trainees, alongside the new doctor, Norder, and Keating, were gathered around an emaciated figure who stood in the passage, pointing a skeletal finger directly at her, even though they were still yards apart.

She blinked a few times, certain she was imagining things, but she knew the man on sight. He was all too familiar.

"Ridding?" she asked.

Lieutenant James Ridding stumbled forward on shaky legs, trailing the bewildered group of their friends and colleagues in his wake. "Someone arrest her!" His voice was thin and raw from disuse, but his eyes were as sharp as ever. Hatred burned in their depths, the likes of which she'd only ever seen aimed at the Ornu, but which was now directed at her. "We have to stop her, Captain. She's the one who sold me out to Nonus. She works for the Ornu!"

Chapter Fifty-Nine

Lieutenant Felicia Keating

Keating hadn't said a word since Bill had ordered all of them into the mess hall for a private meeting. Only moments before, she'd been on the verge of tears, so happy to be reunited with her old colleague that she'd literally been shaking with excitement.

Longfield was gone, but Ridding had been almost miraculously restored. She'd believed him dead after his arrest, and seeing him in the medbay hadn't given her much cause for hope. He'd looked so terrible in that pod—small and shrunken like a mummy from some old museum display, preserved behind glass.

Whatever Omega had done to him had gone a long way to restoring his old vitality, though he still looked gaunt and strained. The worst part of being reunited had been looking him in the eye and seeing how he'd been thinned by the whole experience.

But that was before he'd seen Bina and made those accusations. The rage in his eyes had been terrible to behold. He was still glaring at Bina, who sat at Bill's side.

It was a mistake. It had to be. Bina wouldn't betray them, would she?

But we never did determine who the spy was….

Bill spoke clearly, in a placating tone. "Tell me what happened, Ridding."

"I'll tell you exactly." Ridding pointed across the table. "She reported me to the Ornu! After my sister was killed, I talked about attacking Nonus and getting revenge. She went to him and told him everything."

Guns snorted. "And where did you hear that from? Nonus? Come on, think for a second. Divide and conquer is their whole strategy. He obviously lied."

"He had a recording." Ridding folded his arms over his chest. "He played it at my trial...such as it was."

Keating winced. She knew exactly how Ornu trials went.

Guns frowned and sat back in her chair.

"Unless you think they faked that, too," Ridding spat.

The Marine shook her head. "I'm not calling you a liar, Lieutenant. I would expect the Ornu to mess with your head, but...." She lapsed into silence.

Bina had been notably quiet during the whole exchange. She sat with her hands folded in her lap, her head down. In the tense silence that followed Guns' words, she said, "It's true."

"What's true?" Splat asked. He sounded desperate. Keating, too, was holding her breath, hoping fervently for an explanation that would put her mind at ease.

Bina lifted her chin and looked directly across the table at Ridding. "I told Nonus what you'd said."

A beat of silence followed before the shouting started.

"Why would you do that?" Norder demanded.

"Because she's a spy for the Imperium. They told me she was planted from the beginning to keep an eye on the captain—"

"Is it true, Commander? Have you been leaking our position this whole time?" Tubes looked sick to his stomach. "Is that how the Crendelen found us near Vale? Did you tip them off?"

Termite thumped his fist on the table. "Porker thought it was me. Porker died thinking that I was the one who sold out Ridding!"

The new Marine trainees were watching Funny Bone and Stone for guidance. Keating watched them so that she wouldn't have to look at Bina. What she'd done was horrible, but what hurt was the knowledge that Longfield had trusted her. She'd thought they were friends. Had Bina worked with the Slovenians too? Had she passed them information? How deep, exactly, did her treachery go?

Stone motioned for his team to be quiet. Unlike the rest of them, his focus wasn't on Bina. "Bill," he growled, "you're being awfully quiet. You knew about this, didn't you?"

Bill rubbed his forehead. He didn't answer right away, but his silence spoke for him. Keating bent double, feeling as if she'd just been punched in the gut.

"We discussed it," he said at last.

"You condoned her actions?" Ridding's face, already flushed, took on a furious purple tint.

"No!" Bill had the temerity to look shocked. "After you were arrested, she confided in me. She explained her reasoning, and I didn't approve, but I understood. We agreed that she would come clean when the time came."

Stone turned away and pressed a fist to his mouth. "But you never got around to it."

"Other things took precedence," Bill retorted. "The world ended, Al. I knew her reasoning. And so did Omega. We've all made mistakes—"

"Turning me over to the Ornu was a mistake?" Ridding's lip curled back to reveal his canines. He looked feral, like a cornered animal with his hackles up. "I heard her voice in the recording they played, Captain. It didn't sound like a mistake to me."

Bill turned back to him. "If you'd had the opportunity, would you have made good on your threat to attack our Signifier?"

Ridding's nostrils flared. "If I'd had the opportunity."

"And what do you think would have happened then? The Imperium was looking for an excuse to flip our kill switches. I'm not the only one they were watching. We all know why we ended up aboard the Tennyson." He waved around the room. "I was an extremely competent liability. So were the rest of you. They put us together because they knew how effective we would be, working together for the Imperium's ends...and so that if we caused trouble, we could all be erased in one fell swoop."

"Which is why they needed a spy." Ridding glared at Bina. "To help keep us in line."

Bina opened her mouth, but Bill spoke first. "And what would have happened if you'd sought revenge? Our whole crew would almost certainly have been punished. They had no problem flipping my switch, and if you'd gone through with what you were planning, I'm sure they would have made an example of all of us. And then what? Who would have acted to save these people? No one would have stood up to the Ornu when they came for Earth."

"But they wouldn't." Keating hadn't meant to say the words aloud, but every head swiveled toward her. She swallowed and took a deep breath. "If we'd been killed, they wouldn't have risked that level of collective punishment. We'd be dead, but Earth would be un-harmed. They went after Earth to make a point. To us. To you."

Bill had gone very still. He didn't seem to be breathing anymore, and Keating wondered if she'd pushed too far this time.

Stone cleared his throat. "They would still have had Omega," he said. "We can't know how things would have played out in the long run. There are too many factors."

"So you're taking their side now?" Ridding demanded.

Stone and Bill exchanged a long look. "I don't agree with what Bina did, but I understand why she did it," Stone said at last.

"Oh, then I guess all is forgiven!" Ridding shoved his chair away from the table and made to rise.

Stone held out a hand. "It's not up to me to forgive her or not. She harmed you, but she thought she was protecting the rest of us. If I was in a battlefield position, and I had to make a choice between the life of one Marine and the life of my whole unit, I know what I'd choose. What I'd have to choose."

"On top of that, Bina's the one who rekindled our connection with Omega," Bill added. "If she hadn't done that, the Slovenians would still be in charge. We'd either have died on the receiving end of Crendelen missiles, or Rupnik would have had the rest of us killed one by one."

Keating rubbed her arms, fighting off the cold prickle of goosebumps. The others had heard Longfield die, and a few of them had seen the aftermath, but she was the only one who'd been there to see it happen. Bill was right...Rupnik would have killed them all.

Horribly.

"I'm sorry I spoke to Nonus," Bina said. "I know there's nothing I can say to make it right, James. I've been visiting you in the medbay ever since we retrieved you. Watching your progress."

"Ready to pull the plug in case I woke up and ratted you out," he spat.

Bina shook her head. "Hoping that you'd recover. Because that way, we could move forward. If I'd gotten you killed...." She pressed a hand to her mouth.

Were they crocodile tears? Keating wasn't sure. She no longer knew what to believe. The one thing she'd been sure of was the crew, but that old faith had fractured under the weight of this new revelation.

"Bina stays on," Bill announced. "Ridding, if that means you can't work with her, I understand, and I won't hold it against you. But I'd love to have you back on the bridge. I hope we can move forward."

Ridding sucked his teeth. "I need to think." He got to his feet and strode toward the hatch. Nobody tried to stop him. Instead, they followed him, shuffling along in silence, their eyes downcast, their faces lined with exhaustion. Bill went after Stone to speak with him, leaving Bina on her own.

Keating lingered until she was the only one left in the mess hall with the commander. She picked at her thumbnail as she tried to find the right words.

Bina looked at her with a sickeningly hopeful expression. "Did you want something, Lieutenant?"

She nodded. "I want you to stay away from me. The captain might have forgiven you, but I won't. Most of us won't. I can't believe you sided with the asps."

She didn't wait for an answer, but got up and left. There was nothing that scale-licker could have said to change her mind.

Chapter Sixty

Commander Bina Chakravarti

They'd arrived at last in orbit over Kot-bulo, the Roughbacks' homeworld, after taking a roundabout route through the stars to shake off any pursuers.

"Are you certain you want to leave me aboard Omega?" Bina asked. "My reputation's kind of at an all-time low right now."

"Would you rather I leave Ridding to spread rumors in your absence instead?" Bill asked.

Well, he certainly had a point there, and one that Bina was in no great rush to challenge. Ridding wasn't the only one who'd been frosty with her, though.

Norder had been civil. The Marines hadn't spoken to her, but they nodded when they passed her in the corridors, their expressions carefully neutral. Nobody but Bill was willing to speak with her for any length of time.

At least the Roughbacks didn't care. Then again, they didn't know.

"If someone spreads a rumor that I'm a liability, it could compromise the mission."

"Who would be spreading rumors if I only take a few men with me?" Bill stabbed his fork into his largely untouched meal, a passable imitation of chicken piccata and grilled zucchini. "I'm thinking I should take Splat and Funny Bone. Leave Al and the rest with Mom, here. And Tull will be coming with me, obviously."

"Won't all the Roughbacks want to go with you?"

"That's up to Tull. If they want to go back, I won't stop them. I don't want it to seem like we're holding them hostage."

Bina nodded. "Fair enough. Finish your meal, then, and we'll make preparations."

* * *

Rarely had Bina seen a homeworld that was so...brown.

"Ah, Kotbulo." Tull sighed longingly, like a man who had lived in lengthy exile and was finally allowed to return home. He pressed one hand over his heart. "I have missed her."

"It doesn't look very..." Bina groped for the right word.

"Habitable," Norder suggested.

"It has not been. Not on the surface, not since the Imperium began their barrage. Their orbital bombardment was relentless. Our world was stripped bare." Tull shook his head, then turned his back on the screen to address their little crew directly. "We moved fully underground. We have found ways to persevere despite the cruelty and greed of the Ornu."

"Speaking of which, where are the Ornu?" Bina leaned forward and craned her neck to look at Norder, who was on nav. "Kotbulo was the most recent planet to fall to the Imperium. Why isn't there a fleet here?"

Norder kept his face turned toward the screen, but at least he answered her. "I suppose they've recalled everything they had here to defend against the Perseids' invasion. But maybe the Roughback government can tell us more."

"I'm hoping said government is less complicated to engage with than that of the Awn," Bill muttered.

Tull cocked his head. "I don't know what you mean by complicated."

"The Awn were broken down into hyperlocal regional enclaves led by co-senators," Bill explained. "We had to talk to more than a hundred of them just to get a consensus."

"Huh." Tull scratched his chin. "We don't have that. We have the Confluence."

"Which consists of what, exactly?" Bina asked, suspecting she wouldn't like the answer.

"All of us get together. Whoever can attend."

Bill's eye twitched. Bina was starting to fully appreciate the fact that she'd be able to sit this mission out. She tried to imagine meeting with thousands of civilians as disorganized as humanity currently was, but with the whole quorum being as literal and block-headed as Tull. That wasn't her idea of a fun trip planetside.

"Marvelous," Bill said. "And I take it we'll be meeting them in their new quarters, belowground?"

"Of course. I will guide you. You are lacking a translator, but it is a role I'm more than willing to fulfill." Tull puffed up his chest. "I cannot promise you will get the outcome you want, Captain, but I swear that I will do everything in my power to ensure that you acquit yourself honorably before the Confluence." There was a cadence to his words, a weight and a significance that made it seem as if he was repeating the words of a ritual. He bowed slightly.

"Thank you, Tull." Bill mirrored the gesture.

He and Tull left together. Bina remained on the bridge, bound to the ship by duty but reluctant to face her detractors, who so freely roamed the crew's quarters. She folded her hands behind her and sucked in a deep breath, staring at the screen.

"Shame about the planet," she said to Norder.

He let out a little huff of what might have been laughter. "Seems appropriate to me."

"What does?"

He snuck her a sidelong glance, then cut his eyes away, as if looking at her for too long turned his stomach. "In Roughtongue, Kotbulo means mudball."

Chapter Sixty-One

Sergeant Shawn 'Funny Bone' Piker

"Usually," Tull said, as the Can approached Kotbulo's barren surface, "those who wish to approach the Confluence must travel there on foot. It is not good to rush things for the sake of convenience." His beady eyes were fixed on Bill's face.

The captain's smile was thin. "One might argue that this is an unusual circumstance. I can hardly traverse the space between Omega and your world on foot, even if I wanted to."

Tull snorted. "Well. Even the Confluence can make an exception for a king. Time is short. We will take the trains."

Kotbulo was even bleaker when seen from eye level. From a distance, it was possible to imagine there were valleys and riverbeds and plateaus, gulleys and shallow seas. Perhaps the landscape had once been populated by those things, but that time had long since come and gone, with the planet's face blasted into featurelessness by the Ornu bombardment.

The cavern mouths were little more than holes in the planet's surface—craters into which scree and rubble had collapsed. Splat landed the Can as close to one of them as he could without risking collapsing the hole.

Tull had assured them that their Marine exosuits would be more hindrance than help, and that weapons of any kind would be frowned upon by the Confluence. All the same, when Funny Bone first emerged from the Can, he wished he could have worn some sort of protective layer. The heat was excruciating, and the breeze, which should have offered some relief, but was instead hot and acrid, and forced grit into his eyes.

"It's better below the surface," Tull assured them. "This way."

The handful of accompanying Roughbacks made their way into the cavern one after the other, following Tull's lead. Bill walked in their midst, but Splat held back, eyeing the hole warily.

"Worried about leaving the Can behind?" Funny Bone asked.

The pilot looked upward, as if in search of Omega. The sky was a bruised twilight purple, and a few stars shone brightly enough to be seen through Kotbulo's dusty atmosphere. It was entirely possible that one might be Omega itself, visible from even this vast distance.

Splat grunted. "It's not the Can I'm worried about. It's…being underground. Being on the ground is a rare enough treat. Stepping into the hollow of a new world? I'm less enthused about that."

"If the Roughbacks can do it, so can we," Funny Bone said.

Splat grimaced at him. "That doesn't stand to reason, I'm afraid. You go first."

Most of the time, during planetside deployments, Funny Bone wore his exosuit. The Marine team's primary purpose was combat, not diplomacy. The captain might not find it strange to be engaged in this sort of mission, but Funny Bone wasn't sure what to expect.

He was even less sure how to feel about being so exposed. As he descended into the mouth of the tunnel, his boots skidded on loose rubble. The passageway was too wide for him to catch himself on the bulkheads, so he had to take small, shuffling steps, with his arms outstretched to aid his balance. He kept looking around, expecting something to pop out of the darkness. Surely the Roughbacks didn't leave their caverns open to invasion? But there was no sign of any other living thing in that place, only rough-hewn stone and detritus in places where the stone had crumbled away.

At least they'd thought to bring lamps and flashlights. Funny Bone was relieved when, up ahead, Bill swept a yellow beam of light through the cavern. He felt it doubly so when Splat's lit up behind him. The Roughbacks, of course, didn't need the illumination. Their black eyes turned silver-green when the light reflected off them, which was even eerier than their usual flatness.

The beams were no match for the wider part of the tunnels, but they soon narrowed. After a hundred yards or so, the passage widened again.

"A bottleneck," Tull explained. "When Jackals or Crendelen try to come through, we can pick them off more easily in these places."

It soon became apparent why they'd encountered no resistance. When Tull had described the Roughbacks' living situation, Funny Bone had pictured a mine. He'd never encountered a mine of this depth and complexity, though. The tunnels seemed to go on forever, sometimes flat, sometimes sloping abruptly downward. He estimated that they must have walked half a mile before they reached the trains.

They were winding and serpentine, waiting in a row at the apertures of another set of tunnels. Several of the tracks were empty, presumably because their carriages waited at the other end of the line.

Tull led them aboard one of the cars, while one of the other Roughbacks went to the front of the train and engaged the controls. Funny Bone was hardly seated before they plunged into the tunnel, moving almost silently and at tremendous speed.

"So." Bill spread out on one of the seats and studied Tull. "I mean no offense by this, but Confluence seems like an august sort of word for this event."

"It is a major event," Tull countered. "Any species-wide decision is not to be made lightly."

"Does that mean Confluences are a rarity?"

Tull wagged his head back and forth. "It depends what you mean. Smaller Confluences can be called on behalf of a single burrow. Not everyone can attend, being busy with other affairs such as burrow construction. Young-rearing. Mineral gathering. Food production...."

"If they're too busy to attend, why hold a Confluence and not leave some decisions up to leaders?" Bill asked.

"Like kings?" Tull asked, somehow even more drily than usual.

Bill cleared his throat and sat back against the curved seat. "Maybe."

"If the matter under discussion is a priority to the individual, they come. Besides, whoever ends up attending is considered a product of fate, and we are content with trusting in fate to guide the future."

The Roughbacks under Tull's command nodded. One of them added, "If someone doesn't get a chance to speak, or doesn't like the outcome, they can simply move to another burrow."

"But you can't do that for matters of war," Funny Bone countered.

Again, the Roughbacks nodded.

"That is why so many of us will be there," Tull said. "This Confluence will likely be the largest since our surrender."

"Since our Empowerment," another added. A series of disapproving grunts reverberated through the space.

Funny Bone had lost all track of the outside world. In the quiet bubble of the train car, it was impossible to tell how much ground they'd covered, or even their angle of descent. He was startled when the train stopped and disgorged them onto another platform. They must have been deeper than before, as the air was thick and close, and not quite humid—it wasn't warm enough for that—but oppressively damp.

Within a few breaths, his lungs were burning. There was much less oxygen in the air than he was used to. Once again, he missed the climate control of his exosuit.

"Come," Tull said. "We're more than halfway there. This is the exciting part."

"Great," Funny Bone mumbled under his breath. "Just what we need. More excitement."

Splat let out a strangled chuckle as they plunged into the maze.

* * *

Funny Bone missed the relatively open tunnels of the upper levels. The deeper passageways were so much worse. At times, their group was forced to walk sideways to squeeze through tall openings so narrow that he had to suck in his belly and contort his spine to avoid getting stuck. At others, they dropped to all fours, or even onto their bellies, to crawl through low tunnels that raked at Funny Bone's knees.

"You all right back there?" he called to Splat after a particularly grueling crawl.

"Why wouldn't I be?" Splat wheezed. He didn't sound all right at all.

Funny Bone wasn't prone to claustrophobia, but the Roughback tunnels tested that. It was bad enough for a human, although the aliens had it worse. Their bulky shells and thick limbs scraped continuously against the rock walls. Funny Bone flinched at the sound of what was surely an uncomfortable experience, but they didn't complain.

"Do you ever get cave-ins?" Bill's voice sounded distant, but Funny Bone couldn't quite pinpoint how far ahead he was.

Splat groaned. "Why would you ask that?"

"We do," Tull said, ignoring Splat's complaint, if indeed he heard it at all. "We deal with them using a mix of technology and instinct. We are generally able to avoid the most dangerous routes."

"Generally," Splat repeated. "Instinct."

"We always knew this was going to be a rocky road," Funny Bone said.

There was a long silence before Splat said, "With all due respect, Sarge? Shut up."

Funny Bone measured the passage of time by his hunger and weariness, though by that count, three days might have passed. He stopped to drink water once or twice, though he was reluctant to drink too much.

Even so, his lungs ached, his bladder throbbed, and sweat was pouring down his grimy face in rivers when, without warning, the passage expanded into a large, cool room. He sucked in a grateful breath as he clambered to his feet, marveling at the complete change in the atmosphere.

Even the air was clearer, although there was a notably warm, earthy smell not unlike the scent of the Roughbacks themselves. A cool, blue-green glow illuminated the space, but Funny Bone couldn't see much. He turned off his flashlight anyway to preserve the battery for the return trip.

Behind him, Splat groaned in relief as he, too, stood upright and flicked off his light. "Finally. I thought for sure one of us was going to get wedged in there and stuck forever."

"Where are we?" Funny Bone asked, since he'd rather not think about how close they'd come to being buried alive.

"This is a Cluster," Tull said. "My Cluster. Come, we're not far out now." He led them onward, with more enthusiasm than usual. That was understandable. It must be good to be home.

Funny Bone's vision adjusted swiftly to the odd light, which grew brighter as they walked. There was something weird about the way it illuminated things, picking out light colors and making them glow in turn. Soon, he could see quite clearly, even though what he saw had a notably bluish cast to it.

"Where's that coming from?" he asked, craning his neck to get a better look at the light source. They were erratic shapes, set at random intervals along the cavern wall.

"Bioluminescent moss," Tull grunted. "Gives off light and filters the air. We learned to cultivate it early on."

Funny Bone was so entranced by the mossy growths that he didn't immediately register when the first buildings appeared. In his defense, he wouldn't have thought to call them that when he first saw them. Some of them were constructed from mud, some from stone, some built into the walls themselves. What he'd taken for stalagmites were residences, a handful of which climbed so far toward the cavern roof he couldn't see their peaks.

"It's a city," he said softly, awed by the strangeness of the sight before him. "A Roughback city." All around him, Roughbacks were emerging, from small pups the size of toddlers to thickset adults. It was nothing like what he'd expected, but there was beauty in it.

Life could thrive, even under duress. All was not lost. The Roughbacks were proof of that.

Chapter Sixty-Two

Captain Bill Henderson

The Confluence began to gather as soon as they arrived. The largest room in the Cluster was, to Bill's immense confusion, also called the Confluence. Whether this was because it was the only space large enough to house the communal event, or whether the Roughbacks were simply disinterested in expending the effort to come up with a new name, no one told him.

While they waited, Bill, Splat, and Funny Bone were offered food and some sort of earthy tea.

"Why haven't we seen any Ornu yet?" he whispered to Tull as they waited for the Confluence to began.

"Remember," Tull said, "we became a vassal species only recently. I have heard that the Ornu have not appointed Monitors to oversee our planet. They are planning to do so soon, as I hear it, but I suppose they're having trouble finding volunteers to live among us. Soon, they will conscript Monitors to send here. I am sure of it."

The Confluence was a dome-like cave, almost perfectly rounded in the interior. Not only did the walls bristle with the spongy fronds of bioluminescent moss, but clumps of the stuff were brought in by each new Roughback arrival. Although the quality of the blue-green light still played tricks on his eyes, it was the best-lit room in the whole Cluster.

One of Tull's elders, a deep-voiced female named Mora, led them to the center of the room. The floor was slightly sloped, so that they sat in the center of an immense bowl, which made it easier for the others to see and hear all that was said.

"Brother Tull," she boomed, crossing her legs and bending toward him, backlit by the glowing moss, "explain why you have brought these strangers here."

Tull answered, not directly to her, but to the room at large. "After we surrendered to the Ornu, I was pressed into service, along with my crew. We served the interests of the Imperium and did as they commanded."

As Tull spoke, the others began to hum, quietly at first, and louder. "For a time, we did as we were told, until our paths crossed with that of the humans. Though their people have served as vassals for generations, Captain Alden Stone and Captain Bill Henderson decided to fight back. They gained control of a Primeval ship, one the Ornu badly coveted." Tull began to sway back and forth, his words falling into a rhythm. Once again, Bill was surprised by his eloquence—not because he thought Roughbacks incapable of lengthy speeches, but because they'd never struck him as so inclined. All around them, the other Roughbacks swayed too. Hints of harmonies began to emerge in their humming.

"And you joined them?" Mora asked.

"The captains swore we would be as brothers to them," Tull replied. "If we would help them, they would help us. To make them bleed would be the same as to make us bleed; to harm them would be the same as to harm ourselves."

"You risked our species being deemed Defunct," Mora said, without a hint of anger or accusation.

"I did," Tull agreed. "And I risked my own life, and the lives of my crew. I believed the bargain worthwhile."

"And why do you come to us now?"

"To lay the deal before you." Tull swiveled his head. "To see if we will make the same promise I did. So far, they have acted honorably. I have done the same. Now, all that remains of their species is above." He gestured to the domed roof of the cavern, and the skies beyond. "All that remains of our kind is below. We are not the same, but our battle is the same."

Mora spread her arms. "We hear you, Tull. Let us consider."

What with all the pointed questions, Bill had expected some pushback. Tull had taken a monumental risk, and yet no one had challenged him for doing so. Clearly, after holding out against the Ornu for so long, they resented the yoke that the Imperium had placed on them, and were eager to buck it as quickly as possible.

Mora turned her eyes on Bill. They shone strangely in the light of the moss, giving the impression that a hundred irregular stars shimmered in their depths. "Tull has spoken for you, human. Are his words true?"

Bill inclined his head. "They are. We've bound our fate to his."

"And what do we stand to gain by helping you? How do you plan to honor your part of our oath?"

He held his tongue while he considered this. If the Roughbacks backed them up while they acquired the surge drive, he couldn't very well flee the quadrant as soon as they were done, even if that was his original plan. "I'm not sure," he said at last. "It depends how far we get. What I can tell you is that I've respected the Roughbacks for their resistance against the Imperium, and that I hold no love for our mutual enemy. I will do whatever damage to them that I can. You have my word on that."

Mora sat back. Her expression was inscrutable, doubly so on account of her inhuman features.

The humming was growing louder. Funny Bone looked anxiously at the ceiling a few times, and Splat was sweating. Every few seconds, he wiped his hand across his gleaming face. Bill tried to guess what the aliens were thinking, but as with the Awn, he found himself at the mercy of a species whose customs and speech he did not understand.

The melody that had begun during Tull's story fractured and broke apart. Different sounds threaded through, trying to pull the song one way, then another. The notes threaded and converged, braiding together, until they became one again. Mora clapped her hands twice, and the sound abruptly died.

"We have come to an agreement," she announced. "Perhaps our brother has come to trust you enough to make this offer, but to the rest of us, you are an unknown quantity. In order to comfortably enter into this agreement, you need to prove your commitment to our survival. To do so, you need to lay down your life for us."

Bill tugged at the collar of his uniform. The air was cool, and it was easier to breathe in the Confluence than it had been in the tunnels, but he felt as if Tull was sitting on his chest. "What does that mean, exactly?"

Tull turned to him. "It means what it sounds like it means, Captain. To persuade my brethren of your allegiance, you have to sacrifice yourself."

Chapter Sixty-Three

Commander Bina Chakravarti

"What became of Hyx after he built the ship?" Bina asked. "And who are the 'soulless?' The signal that originally led us to Omega warned us of them."

Her watch in Miriam's company had ended for the day, and by rights she should have been resting, but sleep had been elusive lately. She found more respite in the company of Omega's avatar than she did alone in her cabin.

The glowing woman hummed. "Interesting questions," she said. "Come with me."

Bina closed her eyes and slipped seamlessly into the nothingness of simspace. The darkness quickly resolved into a new scene: a garden, as wild as a jungle but threaded through with walkways and terraces that commingled with the wilderness itself. It did not resemble the carefully maintained gardens the Ornu kept on Earth, or the vast monocropped fields where food was grown in the ag districts. This garden reminded her of Earth's ancient ruins—once-tamed spaces that the wilderness had reclaimed. The walkways were maintained, though, meandering between plants both familiar and alien.

"This way." Judith waved her along, and they walked for a while. Bina marveled at the gardens, at the strange plants with boughs weighed down by unfamiliar fruit in unlikely colors. One such plant resembled a giant fern, but in between its spiral fronds stood bruised-purple mouths like man-sized pitcher plants.

Squat succulents played host to stalks brimming with what appeared to be miniature scarlet bananas. A willow-like tree was ribbed with climbing vines that flung out sprays of white berries.

"This is beautiful," Bina said eventually. "But it doesn't answer my question."

Judith paused at the top of a flight of stone steps carved into the bedrock. "Where do you think we are?"

"One of the Kanami's settlements?" Bina guessed.

"Don't you think it's odd that you refer to worlds by the names of their conquerors? And only one of their conquerors? The Kanami have been dead for a long time. They were not the first. They will not be the last."

Bina breathed deep, relishing the world's oxygen-rich atmosphere and the acidic bite of the air. "You're saying each world has a history I don't know?"

Judith nodded. "And a future beyond your estimation."

Goosebumps prickled up the back of her neck. Omega had been able to fold time so that she and Hyx could speak directly and impact the present. Her present. But Hyx had been living in the present, too, hadn't he? Omega's action hadn't just altered the past, it had altered the future, depending on which side of history you counted.

It was in her nature, perhaps in the nature of all humans, to think of herself as the endpoint, the culmination of the universe's efforts, even if she knew that she was just one point on an unending line—or in the curve of a circle, given time's cyclical nature. But if Omega could change what had been and what would be, that changed her fundamental understanding of reality, didn't it? It expanded the map of time along new axes.

Judith descended the steps. "I can't tell you what happened to Hyx. Or the identity of the soulless. Not yet. When the time comes, I will explain what I can, but to tell you now would be useless at best, harmful at worst. Everything must happen at the appointed time."

"In Omega's time," Bina guessed.

Judith chuckled. "Exactly."

Bina followed her down the incline. "How does Omega feel about this meeting with the Roughbacks?"

Judith's tone soured. "Like you never should have made this deal with them. Omega was always sufficient for humanity, and the aliens will get much more from this arrangement than the humans. It could prove harmful for humanity, having to shepherd another species while fighting for the survival of your own. But now that you have entered into this agreement, you must honor it. Omega recognizes this as well."

Bina nodded. "Interesting. I see."

Judith paused beneath the spreading limbs of a massive tree. She folded her hands behind her back and turned her face upward, to the sunlight that scattered through the leaves. "Do you see these flowers?" she asked.

It was such an abrupt change of topic that at first Bina wondered if she'd misheard. She looked upward in search of blossoms and found none.

"Where?" she asked.

"Look more closely."

Gradually her vision resolved, and she made out a pale green bloom among the leaves. Once she spotted the first one, she became aware of more, and then more still. They were almost the same color as the leaves, but they were a different shape, like the star-shaped blooms of dogwood trees. Silver stamens and pistols erupted from their centers.

"These trees are interdependent with a particular species of bee," Judith said. "They are drawn by smell, but indifferent to color. It is the only species that can currently pollinate the tree. Eventually, the bees will go extinct."

"Then the trees will die, too," Bina said. She could see where this was going: by becoming too dependent on a fallible ally, they'd risk their futures.

Judith shook her head, and her luminous hair waved around her shoulders. "No. It will be a close thing, and the population will dwindle, but these trees are long-lived. Before they die out, the bees will be replaced by a pollinating moth that will move into the area, drawn by the shape of the blooms, and the trees will begin to adapt. Eventually, their blossoms will change color, variegating between strains. They will survive."

"But it hasn't happened yet," Bina said. "So how can you know that?"

"Because it will happen," Judith said.

"But how do you know?"

Judith swiveled to face her. "Because it must. Don't fret, Commander. This deal with the Roughbacks may have been a mistake, but Omega has a way of drawing good out of bad. In the meantime, you must leave the Archive and head to the bridge, to reap the fruits of the agreement you have made. The Crendelen are here now, and unexpected allies come with them. They've come because they know the Roughbacks have been working with humanity, and they've decided to render them Defunct. With the king below, it is you who must defend this ship and everyone on it."

"The Crendelen?" Bina stumbled backward. "Allies? What are you talking about?"

"I am talking about the future." Judith cocked her head. "You are not the woman you were when you surrendered Ridding to the Ornu. You cannot be. Remember that."

Bina was disgorged back into the Archive with Judith's words still ringing in her ears.

Chapter Sixty-Four

Corporal Bob 'Splat' Oriel

Splat dabbed at the trickle of sweat that trickled down his forehead. His anxiety was reflected in Bill's expression, which made his skin crawl—not because Bill was afraid, since he had every right to be, but because he showed it. He'd seen the captain come through all kinds of scrapes before, and the man usually had a somewhat manic, defiant air about him—hardened under pressure, like diamond.

"Sacrifice myself," Bill repeated. The whites of his eyes glowed in the cavern's phosphorescent illumination.

"We're speaking metaphorically, I assume?"

"What sort of metaphorical sacrifice would make your point?" Mora asked. She was not smiling, but there was something like amusement in her delivery. "A metaphorical sacrifice might warrant a metaphorical alliance."

Bill swallowed hard. He turned to Tull, averting his face so that Splat could only see him in profile. "Sorry, Tull, but I'm going to need you to break this down for me. You're saying that in order to have an alliance with you, I'm going to need to offer up my life. But if I do that, you won't have anyone left to be allies with."

Tull rumbled. "We'd have your officers, Bina and Al. They seem competent, and they are both favored by Omega."

Bill stiffened, rolling his shoulders back and lifting his chin. "Is that what this is really about? Getting access to Omega?

Because I happen to be the one Omega has chosen to command his ship."

Tull laughed. The sound was low, like boulders rumbling down a mountainside. Splat looked around, just to reassure himself that no boulders were on a collision course with their party. "Omega chose Al," the alien said. "Omega chose Bina. If you are truly their leader, sacrifice should not be so unthinkable."

"It's one thing to risk my life, and another to throw it away," Bill snapped.

Splat flicked his eyes sideways to where Funny Bone sat. It was hard to tell by mosslight, but the sergeant looked paler than usual. Splat knew what he was thinking: that they were a mile or more underground, without weapons or exosuits or even a way to call for backup. If the Roughbacks turned on them, they would stand no chance of self-defense.

Tull got to his feet, moving in the ungainly way of his people. If Splat hadn't seen them fight, he'd have believed that they were too slow to be much of a threat.

Alas, he knew better. Tull, alone and unarmed, could kill the three of them in a matter of moments if he so chose. Never mind the fact there were more than a hundred of his people watching their conversation unfold.

"Why don't you come with me, Captain? I have something to show you that should make things clearer."

Bill licked his lips. "Is this little trip going to end with me dead?"

It was Mora who answered by slapping her knee and letting out her own basso laugh. "Only you can sacrifice yourself, Captain. We can't do it for you. And if we were going to try, wouldn't we have done it by now?"

As reassurances went, the sentiment wasn't as comforting as she seemed to think it would be. Still, Bill got to his feet, and the two Marines followed suit. Tull led them out of the cavern, through the crowd. The rest of the Confluence watched their departure without comment or movement. Still, Splat felt the weight of their eyes on him.

Rather than leading them back out of the room the way they'd come, Tull led them to what seemed to be another exit. Instead of returning to the Cluster, however, he showed them to a fissure in the rock face. It was slick with runnels of what smelled like freshwater, though it was hard to tell in the dark. A film of algae clung to Splat's skin and clothes when he wriggled through.

The fissure opened into a long, low passage, although it wasn't as claustrophobia-inducing as the worst parts of the way in had been. Still, he had to keep his head ducked low to avoid scraping his scalp on the irregular ceiling, where the beginnings of stalactites stuck out like calcified fingers. Tull walked ahead, followed by Bill and then Splat, who was unaccountably grateful when Funny Bone fell into line behind him. He wouldn't have wanted to bring up the rear.

A few dozen yards into the tunnel, Tull began to speak. "We Roughbacks have a reputation for being laid-back and grounded, yes?" The stone warped his voice, so that it seemed to come from behind them as well as ahead.

"You do," Bill agreed. "Which makes what you're asking of me a little surprising. Not to mention bizarre."

Tull snorted. "It makes perfect sense. But I think you're missing an important piece of the puzzle. The reason Roughbacks are so calm is that we accept whatever fate dispenses for us, trusting that whatever happens, be it good or bad, is ultimately for our benefit. Even suffering can be counted on to teach us something we had to learn, or to make us stronger, or correct for a past injustice, or prevent something even worse from happening. But when I told you we trust in fate, I wasn't giving you the full picture—and that's because we Roughbacks know that humans don't take anything seriously that they can't measure, or that doesn't operate within the universe's physical laws as they understand them."

Splat wrinkled his nose. Great. Now that we've gotten him talking, he's never going to shut up. Since when are Roughbacks interested in philosophy?

"You're starting to lose me," Bill said.

Another of Tull's rumbling hums saturated the air around them. "In short, it isn't in a personless, ill-defined 'fate' that we trust, but the All-sire. It is he who ensures that everything that befalls is ultimately to our benefit. And it is trust in him that saw Roughbacks to victory over the other sentient species who once shared Kotbulo with us, and who sought to kill us."

"How does this factor into me sacrificing myself, exactly?"

"We could not forge an alliance that the All-sire did not smile on, Bill. Sacrificing yourself doesn't only prove your resolve, but it also represents a profound gesture to the All-sire. You must cast your life onto the pyre, so to speak. If it happens that somehow the flames spare you, then we shall know our alliance is desirable indeed."

"And how do you suggest I sacrifice myself, exactly?"

"There are a number of ways. You could descend into the lower pits, where the shadow dogs dwell, and bring us a pack-leader's head. Their numbers and viciousness are such that only two Roughbacks have ever returned from such a mission. You could face our

Mighty Five singlehandedly in bladed combat. These are both crucibles all but certain to kill you."

Splat tripped over an outcropping of sandstone. Why had he come along, again? He should have stuck it out back with the Can. He'd had it with Rough-backs and caverns and underground streams.

The passage ended abruptly, opening into a much smaller chamber than the Confluence. This room, too, was well-lit, although the only thing inside was a medieval-looking instrument. It most re-sembled a guillotine, though its blade was a lot broader than those Splat re-membered seeing in pictures and muse-ums. Something dark was crusted along both the blade and panel beneath. His already watery guts churned at the sight of it.

Tull leaned one arm against the frame of the device and slapped it affectionately.

"But all those options take time. If you want to expedite things, you could simply lie beneath the Disseverer and wait as one of us lets loose the blade."

Chapter Sixty-Five

Captain Bill Henderson

The Disseverer.

A gruesome name for a gruesome instrument. Bill crossed his arms over his chest and studied it with what he hoped could pass as a thoughtful expression.

Several things occurred to him at once. Among them was the realization that his analysis of why the Roughbacks had managed to hold out against the Ornu for so long was incomplete. Their success wasn't only about dwelling so far underground, beyond the reach of orbital bombardment. It was also about an inexorable single-mindedness that he could never have guessed at from the Roughbacks' generally unassuming demeanors.

Beneath Tull's unpretentious veneer was a mind like a boulder crashing down a hillside, one as beholden to its grim logic as that careening boulder would be to gravity. Of course the Ornu had such a hard time enslaving the Roughbacks...they were astonishingly fierce and implacable in their simplicity.

Another thing that occurred to him was what a bad idea this whole venture had been.

"Just to make sure I understand this," he said slowly. "You want me to lie down, stick my neck out, drop the blade, and...what? See if the All-sire decides to temporarily reverse gravity to save my neck?"

"That is an ungenerously sarcastic assessment," Tull said. "But yes, in essence."

"If I ask you to take me back to the surface, would you take me?"

Tull didn't hesitate. "Of course. If you think we mean you harm, Captain, you have misunderstood. I will guide you back to the train the moment you ask, and it will return you to your shuttle. I take it you have decided against an alliance with the Roughbacks. Although, I would find that unfortunate, since you did make a promise."

Funny that you left out this element of our agreement, he thought. Tull's blunt, casual description of his options made it clear that this was nothing out of the ordinary. If he'd clarified that their alliance would end in a damp room at the foot of a device designed exclusively for the chopping of voluntary necks, would Bill have made the same deal?

If he was being honest with himself, he probably would have. At the time, they'd been desperate, and he'd probably have reasoned that he could come up with a suitable alternative before the time came. But in this room, watching mosslight spill silver across the blade, it was hard to muster his usual foolhardy confidence.

"I wasn't exactly fully informed about what that promise entailed, was I, Tull?"

The Roughback ran his fingers along the sharp edge of the instrument. "I don't know what humans do in such situations. How was I to know that this would come as a surprise? This is our way."

"I understand that," Bill said. "Either way, I'm not saying no. I'm saying I need to think about it, and to consult my officers." Although, he was so close to a 'no' that the distinction felt almost meaningless. "This is...quite a departure from our original plan."

Tull nodded slowly. "Very well. I will accompany you to the surface. Let me inform Mora and make arrangements." He lumbered back to the passage through which they'd arrived.

Bill lingered for a moment, reconsidering the machine. He'd laid down his life once before, and Omega had saved him… but a flipped kill switch was one thing, and a severed head was quite another.

"Captain?" Funny Bone tapped his arm. "You're not seriously considering it, are you?"

Tull wasn't out of earshot, and who knew how good Roughback hearing was? The stone might carry his words all the way back to the Confluence. He'd do well to choose them carefully.

Bill forced a smile. "Like I said, I need time to strategize."

He wasn't going to throw away the possibility of a Roughback alliance without serious consideration. The blade, though, was out. There must be another way—one that didn't involve shallow dogs or the Mighty Five or the Disseverer. He just needed to work out what it was.

Quickly.

Time was running short. The Imperium would come after them eventually, and Bill would prefer not to be a severed head when they caught up.

* * *

True to Tull's word, the Roughbacks made no attempt to stop them. Tull alone led the three men back through the winding tunnels to the trains. Bill's body was exhausted, but his mind whirred with the possibilities. Surely there must be an alternative to the Disseverer. He'd survived Rupnik, he'd survived the Imperium, he'd survived death itself. Didn't that count for anything?

It's always something, he thought wearily.

He flopped onto one of the train seats, and Funny Bone collapsed across from him. They both looked like they'd survived a war zone. Splat looked as though he'd barely survived; he was bleeding from filthy scrapes along his cheek and temple, where he must have grazed his face against the wall or the floor during their journey back to the platform.

Funny Bone wiped his sleeve across his forehead, leaving a flaky black stain behind. Guano, perhaps, or half-dried cave algae. "All due respect, Captain, but if you come back for the Disseverer, you're gonna have to bring AI. I'm never going down there again."

Bill snuck a sidelong glance at Tull. The Roughback was fiddling with the train's controls. "I hear you," he said. "And maybe it would be best for AI to come along, if—"

His com chirped. Bill checked the screen; he hadn't gotten connectivity of any kind underground, but now it clicked on, revealing all the messages from Bina that he'd missed. He felt the blood drain from his face.

"Captain?" Splat asked.

The train was coming to a halt, but Bill made no move to rise. Instead, he cursed.

"Well, that sounds like it'll be great news," Funny Bone muttered.

"Looks like the Crendelen caught up with Omega. They're engaged in long-range combat as we speak." Bill looked up. "And they were off gathering supplies, so...."

"So we're stuck on Kotbulo with only the Can for transport," Splat finished.

There was no way the little ship could navigate a firefight, which meant there was no reason to rush back to the surface. For all intents and purposes, they were stranded on an alien world.

One whose inhabitants would only agree to help Bill if he faced the Disseverer.

Chapter Sixty-Six

Tull of the Roughbacks

The Roughback fleet was modest, with only two warships present in the system.

Back in the time before their war with the Imperium, there had been a great many more Roughback fighters, but they had never been a true military power—certainly not one that could compete in galactic power games.

There had been no need. At one of the Confluences long before Tull's birth, the Roughbacks had agreed that, since they had no designs on interstellar conquest, they would prefer to devote their time and resources to defense rather than offense.

Less than three solar cycles ago, they had been one of the best-defended planets in the quadrant. Alas, the Ornu had worn away at those defenses bit by bit until nothing much was left. They had little to rebuild, and few resources with which to work. The Ornu hadn't wanted to give them a chance to fight back.

Which was exactly what Tull would have done, given half the chance.

Bill stared down at his com unit. His pink face had gone even pinker, while the other two were as pale as dead moons. Tull was constantly fascinated by the way human skin changed according to their emotions. They were like stunted marlgroppers, a now-extinct fish that had once populated Kotbulo's lakes, whose flesh changed color and even texture based on their satisfaction with their environment.

The captain's enhanced pinkness suggested extreme discomfort.

"How many ships?" Tull asked.

Bill shook himself. "What?"

Tull repeated the words more slowly and precisely. "How. Many. Ships?"

"No idea." Bill tapped a button on his com's screen. A few seconds later, Bina's voice crackled through the speakers.

"We're in trouble, Captain. I don't suppose—any chance—Roughbacks are going to help us?"

Bill winced in Tull's general direction. "Ah, about that...."

Tull's patience was worn thin. He reached over and pried the com from Bill's hands. "Commander, how many Crendelen warships are you up against?"

"Not sure—more than Vale, but—ty-seven?"

"Twenty-seven?" Bill squawked.

"Thir—seven on scan—so far."

Tull sucked in a breath and closed his eyes. He was not prone to flashbacks or reliving difficult memories, but he'd been on the lower train platform when Kotbulo fell. To be in the same place, knowing that the Crendelen had re-turned, rekindled that long-dulled sen-sation of hopeless acceptance.

"Are they above Kotbulo?" he demand-ed.

"Nearby—asteroid. We went—harvest minerals...."

"Keep them occupied," Tull said. "We're coming." He cut the communique short and rose to his feet. When he held the device out toward Bill, the other man stared at him open-mouthed.

"Come," he said.

"But..." Bill groped for the com. "We haven't decided..."

Tull sighed. "This is not only about you, Captain. We may not be confirmed allies yet, but the Crendelen have the power to render my species Defunct. My people may not be ready to defend you, but we will defend ourselves. I assume that if I can get you back to Omega, we will work toward the common cause of fighting our enemies. Correct?"

"Of course." Bill rose at last. "But the Can won't be able to carry us all the way to Omega now."

"It doesn't have to." Tull loped toward the door of the train car. "It just has to get us to a nearby asteroid."

* * *

The two Roughback warships would never have been sanctioned by the Imperium...if the Ornu had figured out what they were. Fortunately for the Roughback forces, the Ornu weren't as smart as they thought they were. Two massive asteroids were locked on the same orbital track as Kotbulo, far enough out of range that the Imperium had never bothered with them. They were, by all outward appearances, nothing more than debris.

Tull laid the course for Orbital Unit 1 and leaned against the back of Splat's chair as the Marine navigated toward the asteroid.

"What are we hoping to find?" Splat asked warily.

Tull watched the Marine from the corner of his eye. "You will see."

When they were within range of the asteroid, he held out one hand to Bill. "Give me your com."

"Why?"

"So that we don't get blasted out of the void."

Bill acquiesced. Fortunately, all the tech used by the humans that wasn't part of Omega had been taken from the Imperium, which meant Tull was at least passingly familiar with the controls. He dialed in the channel for the warships' coms. "This is a pebble from the Deep River speaking. Requesting contact with the High Peak. Please respond."

Splat pursed his lips, but he stayed the course. The com stayed silent.

"High Peak?" Funny Bone scratched his cheek. "That a code name or something?"

"Or something," Tull agreed. He tried again, repeating his message three times in the span of as many minutes. He didn't want the humans to see how much the lack of response bothered him. He'd been away for a while. It was possible the Imperium had discovered the asteroids' true purpose after all. Perhaps they had just been targeted by the Crendelen, along with Omega.

Perhaps they were already lost.

He was finishing his fifth repetition when an answer came in.

"Deep River, this is High Peak. How can we help?"

Relief spilled through him like water through the underground gulleys after a spring flood. "Requesting permission to land."

Whoever he was speaking to hummed. Tull immediately matched the melody. This was another layer of authentication...if Tull had been making his request under duress, he would have chosen another tune, and Orbital Unit 1 would have reduced the Can to shrapnel.

"Permission granted," the voice said, and the call cut out.

Tull returned Bill's comms unit. "When we land, don't mention Mora. She won't have been able to communicate with OU1, and there's no point in overcomplicating things."

Bill squinted at him. "How about we just let you do the talking?"

"Very wise," Tull agreed. "Splat, take us there." He indicated the coordinates he'd selected on the asteroid's surface. "You should be able to find the corridor from there."

Splat must have known better than to ask, because he followed Tull's instructions without comment. By the time they were close enough for the asteroid's gravitation field to exert its pull, the corridor entrance had opened in the ragged stone face.

It was a tight fit—the Can wasn't large, but the Roughbacks had taken care to make those dead hunks of rock appear as innocuous as possible. Splat took it slow, plunging them into darkness and clearly following the sensors rather than his eyesight.

The airlock at the end of the entry corridor opened, and the lights came on. Bill let out a little yelp of surprise.

Tull, not a natural showman by any means, couldn't contain his grin as he waved to the asteroid's interior. "Well? What do you think?"

OU1, like its twin, had begun life as a simple asteroid, mined for its rare mineral deposits. The material was ultra-dense and required specialized equipment to drill into. Once some cavities had been made, however, the Roughbacks had repurposed the great rock. It had been outfitted with life support systems, control systems, and thrusters.

Their offensive capabilities mostly consisted of breaking off chunks of asteroid with controlled detonations, quickly fitting a thruster and a few sensors to them, and accelerating them at enemy ships or artillery—the thrusters were designed to home in on their target. The asteroid-chunk missiles, or prekbulos, were fairly hard to neutralize with point defense systems, being so big.

Admittedly, the warship's arsenal was somewhat limited—break off enough of an asteroid-ship, and the Roughback forces would need a new asteroid. But they'd made the chambers in the asteroid ejectable so that, should the asteroid be compromised, there was still some hope of the crew's survival. They were also equipped with thrusters and drills so that the crews could locate a new asteroid and drill down into it to seed a new warship.

Surely the humans could not glean all that from their first view of the interior. They gawked like children when Splat brought them in to land, navigating deftly onto the embarkation platform.

"Remember," Tull told them, "I'll do the talking."

The humans seemed incapable of stringing so much as a single reply together. Probably for the best. In general, they were a far too talkative bunch.

Tull took the lead. He adjusted his gait to a swagger, one that would have been disrespectful in Elder Mora's presence, but which suited his greeting with the ground crew just fine. He barked a laugh when he saw who he'd been speaking to on the coms: Rork, one of his old sparring partners. They'd pelted each other with pebbleguns back when the surface of Kotbulo was still lush and habitable.

Rork pulled him into a crushing, back-slapping, casual sort of hug that was only appropriate among agemates on informal terms.

"Tull! Thought you'd been reduced to pulp by now. What are you doing here?"

Rork peered over his shoulder and frowned. "With Ornu vassals?"

"They're not vassals anymore," Tull said. "They're revolting."

"I can tell that just by looking," Rork said. A rumble of laughter passed through their group, much to the humans' obvious dismay.

"I mean," Tull clarified, "that they're here to fight with us. There's a Crendelen fleet nearby. The humans have a Primeval ship, but they can't fight back alone. Nearly forty Crendelen ships are in the system. Less, maybe, by now...but too many."

Rork punched a fist into his open palm. "I should have known you'd bring trouble, Tull." His mouth widened into a familiar blunt-toothed smile. "Let's show those feathery kakbule how the Roughbacks play."

Chapter Sixty-Seven

Commander Bina Chakravarti

Thankfully, Norder seemed willing to take orders from Bina, and Keating had even come to the bridge, although she made a point of ignoring her even when addressed directly. Nevertheless, they had a skeleton crew to keep the ship going, which was better than nothing.

Even in their time of need, there was no sign of Ridding. She'd let herself be irritated about that later, when she wasn't facing down a whole fleet of Crendelen.

"How are there so many of them?" she snarled, as Val assisted her strategizing efforts in simspace. When Judith first alerted her to the attack, she'd expedited what little material they'd managed to mine directly into munitions manufacturing.

"The Crendelen have always been numerous, haven't they?" Val asked mildly.

Bina directed another round of missile-fire before answering. "The Imperium is still at war with the Perseid Confederation. If they can spare this many units to attack us, how are they going to be able to continue their other war?"

"They are allocating their resources toward the greatest threat."

She paused long enough to wrinkle her nose. "We're one ship on the run. We haven't even attacked them."

"Not yet," Val agreed. "But surely you see the danger you represent to the Imperium's core values? A vassal species who has defied them, and fled? The Ornu empire only functions if the vassal species follow their commands. If you escape, or if you rouse the other Enlightened species to action...." He trailed off meaningfully.

"Of course," Bina growled.

"It is an honor to be a symbol of resistance, against such a power," Val told her.

She'd have been more honored if being a symbol didn't put them at the center of the Imperium's scope, but whatever. She directed the next few rounds of defensive missile-fire.

The Crendelen ships were attacking in formation, in a pattern that made them easy to predict but difficult to counteract. Too many of their missiles had gotten through, and while she'd managed to avoid many concentrated hits, weakening the ship's hull at multiple points wasn't ideal.

She was planning her next move when a raw hunk of rock spun toward them, gleaming red on the scanners. Its path brought it on a collision course with one of the Crendelen warships, which burst apart as it plowed through it.

"What is that?" she cried.

Val brightened. "Allies," he said. "Don't target them, Commander. Watch closely."

The asteroid's trajectory was set to bring it close to Omega without actually making contact. Bina watched in wonder as the Crendelen ships scattered, offering a temporary relief from their former relentless bombardment.

The asteroid passed close to Omega and looped behind it. At the deepest point of its arc, when it passed around the far side of the ship where it was most defended from the Crendelen, a small ship emerged from the stone.

"The Can!" Bina whirled to Val. "Is that thing a ship? I need to talk to Bill. Now. Can I...?"

"I will guide Norder and Keating for the moment," Val said, dipping his head in a genteel fashion worthy of a gentleman.

Her last glimpse of simspace showed the asteroid looping back to scatter the re-grouping warships, and absorbing the next missile assault with no sign of being any worse for wear.

Then Bina was stumbling across the bridge, her legs prickling with pins and needles after so much time spent in the chair.

She raced to the landing bay, pausing each time Omega rolled so that she could brace herself against the bulk-heads. Seeing the XO tumbling through the corridors head over heels probably wouldn't do much for morale aboard the ship—or for her personal reputation.

She met Bill in a corridor halfway between the bridge and the landing bay. "What happened on Kotbulo?" she asked, at the same time he asked her, "What's our status?"

"You first," she insisted.

Bill glanced over his shoulder to where Tull, Splat, and Funny Bone followed. He lowered his voice. "The Roughbacks are insane," he whispered. "We...didn't make a deal."

As they made their way back to the bridge, Bill offered a truncated explanation of his time in the caves.

"There's no way I can agree to that," he concluded. "We can't win this battle, anyway."

"Whoa." Bina stopped short and grabbed his arm. "You mean we're going to withdraw? Bill, Omega didn't agree with Tull's offer of an alliance to begin with—but now that we've made the request, we can't just back out."

"You want me to lose my head?" he asked.

She lifted her hands helplessly and looked from one to the other, although her eyes were unfocused. The conversation with Judith in the gardens, her time with Hyx...she was beginning to see the shape of Omega's thought process, even though she didn't always understand it.

"Remember what happened the last time we defied Omega?" she said at last. "He left us, the Slovenians took over, and we lost Sally. If we leave, the Crendelen are going to turn on the Roughbacks. That won't be a good thing for them, certainly, and probably not for us either. We led the Crendelen here. We involved the Roughbacks. It might be time to trust Omega, Bill. Even if we can't see the way through this ourselves. I don't want to lose him again, and I don't want to lose any more of our crew."

Bill groaned and scrubbed his hands over his face. "This is a terrible idea."

She smiled at that. "Between the two of us? We've had worse."

He uttered a few oaths, swaying on the spot as if being pulled in two directions. "Fine," he said at last. "You're right. We need to stay and pull out a victory here somehow. At least that way, even if we don't seal the alliance with the Rough-backs, we can leave on good terms."

And without their blood on our hands, Bina added silently.

She had broken enough promises in the course of her life. No more.

Judith was right: she had changed.

Chapter Sixty-Eight

Captain Bill Henderson

By the time he and Bina returned to simspace, the second Roughback asteroid ship had joined the fray.

"These are quite remarkable ships," Val observed, studying a hologram of OU1. "I admit, I may have underestimated the resourcefulness of this species."

"Can we communicate with them?" Bill asked. "I want to take advantage of this chaos."

"Of course. I'll open lines with OU1 now."

There were no physical settings to change, but Bill could hear the change in audio settings when the ship linked in with the Roughback channel.

"Do I have to say the bit about the High Peak?" he asked wryly.

Bina frowned and mouthed, What?

On the other end of the channel, Rork snorted. "Don't waste my time, human. What's the plan?"

Bill rubbed the back of his neck. "Depends what you're up for. I don't know your strengths."

"Right now, we can absorb fire more easily than we can launch it. Although this is quite fun—brace for impact, boys!" A chorus of whoops sounded through the channel as the OU demolished another Crendelen ship by crashing into it headlong.

The orbital units were exactly what Bill should have expected from Roughback battle tactics, he decided: blunt, messy, and direct. It wasn't a sustainable tactic, but their reckless strategy seemed to have put fear in the Imperium forces. The ships hung back, splitting their missiles between the Roughback ships and Omega.

Bill nodded. "In that case, I'd like the two of you to act as shields. Draw the Crendelen fire while we withdraw from their range. If you can take their shots, we'll return fire."

"Acceptable, human."

Bina waved her flattened hand across her throat, signaling for Val to end the conversation. Given his recent run-in with the Disseverer, Bill found the gesture to be a bit too on the nose for comfort. He waited until the channel cut out; whatever Bina had to say wasn't meant for Roughback ears.

"We're running low on Hailstorm missiles," she said.

Bill sighed. "Of course...how low are our supplies?"

Bina waved to Val, who announced, "We're down to twenty percent of our Hailstorm capacity, and at the moment, Omega is unable to produce more in any meaningful quantity within a useful timeframe. We are, however, up to forty percent capacity on our Peregrines."

"We'll withdraw as we planned," Bill said. "For now, we'll use the Peregrines...and save the Hailstorm missiles for the endgame."

"Excellent." Val folded his hands behind his back and watched the battle play out before them.

Firing from a distance presented certain difficulties—namely, that the Crendelen had more time to adjust their movement patterns. If they'd been fighting alone, they would have risked taking more damage in turn.

The Roughback orbital units helped on both fronts. In addition to drawing the Crendelen's fire, they also drew their attention. While several ships were able to avoid Bill's staggered Peregrine bombardment, most of them were so preoccupied with the rogue asteroids that they didn't alter their courses in time.

As the Crendelen regrouped, they were forced to reopen their channel with OU1 to coordinate their movements.

"Let me know before you adjust your course," Bill said. "I don't want to waste rounds hitting your ship."

"Are you running low on rounds, human?" Rork asked. "You should have said something."

The significance of this reply was lost on Bill until almost a minute later, when a sizable chunk broke off from the Roughback ship. He spotted drones zipping around the chunk's surface, rapidly installing a few instruments and a thruster assembly—and then the chunk began accelerating toward the nearest Crendelen ship, which turned to flee, taking some of its fellows with it. The combination of the fast Peregrines and inexorable asteroid chunk seemed to throw a wrench into the enemy's fleet posture, and their formation crumbled further as more of their ships went down.

"They're down to thirty-one ships," Val announced. "And there's a debris storm in their midst. Their scanners will have trouble distinguishing between types of debris."

"Perfect. Let's fire Hailstorms…just a few, and we'll choose the targets carefully."

One by one, they whittled down the Crendelen fleet, until the wreckage filled the battlespace.

Chapter Sixty-Nine

Commander Rork

When his old friend Tull first brought the humans aboard OU1, Rork had been taken aback by how...squishy they were. They looked eminently breakable, with slender limbs that spoke to the brittleness of the bones within.

But having seen what their ship was capable of, he was quickly gaining a new-found respect for them.

"Mountain Pass, this is High Peak requesting a tandem flight," he said into the com.

He didn't recognize the female voice that replied in the affirmative, but that was no surprise. Ever since their people had surrendered to the Imperium—a decision reached in a Confluence that Rork himself had been unable to attend—the forces working against the Ornu had remained purposefully anonymous. It was easier to avoid giving up your comrades under torture if you didn't know their names to begin with.

"Flight request granted. What pattern do you have in mind?"

Rork considered the flight patterns they'd studied under their old mentors. Most of them were defensive maneuvers, given the political and military history of their forces. They were also designed for more ships than this, but the patterns had been drilled into their memories over years of training and observation.

"We'll be on a Modified AO-3," he decided. "Can you mirror me?"

It was an unorthodox request, and OU2's captain would have been well within her rights to deny him. After a beat, she grunted. "We'll mirror you, with a two-phase delay."

It was a diplomatic way of telling him, You first.

The flight path he'd suggested was a thirty-three-phase maneuver. Leaving his fellow captain two phases in his wake meant that, if the enemy recognized their pattern, her ship would be in danger. On the other hand, if she didn't mirror him exactly, the Crendelen might not realize that their flight paths were predetermined. The Crendelen weren't very smart. Either way, they were gambling their lives by working with an alien species who didn't seem to understand their ways.

"Beginning now," Rork said.. He turned his attention to the Roughback soldier operating OU1's targeting system. "Fire on the arc," he said. "No need to time it perfectly. Keep them guessing."

The goal of drawing the enemy fire was to keep the Crendelen on their toes. Even if Rork and his people couldn't take their ships out, they could at least draw the fleet's attention away from their real target. Every warship the humans destroyed meant one less threat to Kotbulo, and their Clusters beneath the planet's surface.

Rork's hands traced out the necessary movements easily, flicking across the porous digitized pad that allowed him to navigate across multiple axes. He appreciated the tactile quality of the system—the reluctance of the material to give beneath his touch. It was so much easier to manipulate than the impersonal, digitized systems of the Ornu and their vassal species. Who wanted to control their ships with a screen? How could they properly pilot at all when they couldn't feel the movement of their ship through the empty places?

The Crendelen adapted quickly to the Roughbacks' new tactic as the two orbital vessels fell into the steps of their deadly dance. The enemy fanned out in a loose ring around the three ships. Rork laughed at their efforts—as always, the Crendelen were relying on their numbers, rather than on skillful maneuvers.

He adjusted one angle of his position to draw fire from an Imperium warship, then looped away. As the enemy's shots went wide, Rork's engineer managed a direct hit with a chunk taken from their own ship.

"That's right, waste your resources!" He pumped his fist in the air, then reached for the mic. "Let's see you pull a move like that!"

The female captain grunted her approval. "Not bad, pup. I'm almost impressed."

"I don't suppose you can share your flight patterns with me?" Bill asked. Rork had forgotten the human was still on the com. If he was dismayed to be left out of the conversation in Roughtongue, he made no comment.

"Nav coordinates incoming," Rork agreed.

Afterward, he would wonder if his message had been intercepted, or if the fact that OU2 was two positions behind had given the Crendelen enough data that they could predict the other ship's trajectory.

All he knew for sure was that, less than a minute after Rork conveyed their flight pattern to the human captain, six Crendelen ships fired on his dance partner, OU2, in almost perfect unison. Under ordinary circumstances, the modified asteroid could have weathered the barrage, but with the strikes coming from so many angles—after the ship was already weakened by chunks of rock that had been knocked free to create makeshift missiles—the impact was too great.

"Get out!" Rork screamed into the mic, his hands stalling in their pattern.

It was a silly thing to scream, of course; anyone who wasn't already protected by the escape chambers was already dead. As the ship collapsed, he did make out a few of the pods spinning away from the wreckage, guided by automated systems.

They didn't get far. They were too small, and the battle raged too hard. And the Crendelen numbers were too vast.

"Captain?" one of Rork's crewmen asked.

He shook himself back into action, hardening his heart against the fate of his kinsmen lest he lose his focus and perish, just as they had.

Chapter Seventy

Captain Bill Henderson

"Val?" Bill said, turning to his liaison. "I don't suppose Omega has a plan for this?"

"Give me five minutes." With that, he vanished."

Bill frowned, then refocused on the battle. Their store of missiles was low, and dropping by the second.

He couldn't abandon the Roughbacks...but he saw no other way to keep the ship intact and its two million passengers alive.

In the meantime, he was operating by muscle memory, choosing targets by instinct as much as anything else.

Val materialized at his elbow. "Omega has a plan."

"Great." Bill swung toward him. "Which is?"

"We need to retreat."

Bill's eye twitched. He rubbed his forehead. "Retreat? As in, turn tail and run?"

Val nodded. "Toward the closest point in the asteroid belt."

Bill looked out into simspace. The distant curve of the asteroid belt hadn't registered in the simulation before, but it was there now, almost impossibly far away. Some of the asteroids glinted with mineral deposits, refracting light from the Roughbacks' sun.

"I thought Omega wanted us to stay and honor our agreement with the Rough-backs."

"You've decided to trust Omega, right?"

Bill narrowed his eyes at him. "You were monitoring my conversation with Bina?"

"Or, I deduced as much from the fact you're asking Omega's advice. Either way, it's clear you are trusting him now."

"Yeah," Bill murmured, wondering if he had any secrets left. "I guess I am."

"Then I'd suggest you continue doing that."

Bill hesitated. "What about the Rough-backs?"

Val cocked his head to one side. "What about them?"

"Are we just going to leave them on their own?"

A slow smile worked its way across Val's features. "You and I are, yes. But before we go, I have one more suggestion for you."

"What is it?"

"Talk to Captain Stone." With that, Val vanished once more.

Chapter Seventy-One

Captain Alden Stone

The worst part about fighting a battle in deep space, especially with a ship like Omega, was that there was nothing Al could do about it. Back on the Tennyson, he'd been able to jump into action at any time. But that ship had been much smaller—Omega's hull was too vast for there to be much chance he'd be able to contribute to the battle, no matter what section he popped out of.

More importantly, the stakes had been lower. He had the crew to worry about, yes, but if their ship was ravaged by enemy fire, they would be the only ones who suffered.

He was pacing the corridors around the bridge, waiting for some opportunity to leap to the rescue, when Bill contacted him on his com.

"Al, we're in a tight spot here. I don't see a path to victory—and when I asked for Val's advice, he went to Omega. The advice was to flee."

Al rocked back on his heels. "Wait—but the Roughbacks. We had a deal."

"Not exactly."

"We were in the process of making a deal!"

"I understand that!"

Al began to pace again, striding in a tight line as he tried to marshal his thoughts. "I don't believe this."

"Well, I'm telling you, that's Val's plan—"

"I understand that. But I don't believe it. There's more to this than meets the eye."

Bill sighed. "How do you mean?"

"The Crendelen are here to render the Roughbacks Defunct, right?"

"That's my understanding. And actually, they've already started deploying shuttles. Looks like they're headed for the planet's surface. I suppose the only way to render the Roughbacks Defunct is to bring a huge terrestrial army along for the ride. Though how they're doing this while at war with the Perseus Confederation, I still have no idea."

Al would worry about Ornu tactics later. He'd already decided what to do. "Send me and my Marines to the surface."

"What? Are you crazy? We're leaving, Al. I just told you that."

"There's no way Omega is having us go back on our agreement while abandoning the Roughbacks to their fate. He has a plan, and I want to do my part in it. Bill, give me authorization to take the Can with my Marines down to Kotbulo."

Bill fell silent. He knew his friend well enough to guess what the other captain was thinking. If he denied Al's request, Al would argue, but he wouldn't break ranks. They'd played this game before, and sometimes Bill's harebrained schemes worked out. Even when they didn't, Al had never openly defied him. They'd both tested the limits of their friendship and their working relationship time and time again, and knew exactly how much stress it could withstand.

"Listen," Al blurted, desperate to convince Bill that he was right, "the Marines and I are no help up here. Let me fight the troops on the surface. We'll keep a line of communication open with the Roughbacks and prove that we're willing to fight beside them for their freedom, if nothing else. Put us to work. Let me lead this mission."

"You know," Bill said, "it's funny... Val told me to contact you and tell you we're fleeing. I wonder if he suspected you'd have this reaction."

"You're letting us go?"

"I'm letting you go. Godspeed, Al. And don't be stupid down there. I want all my Marines back on board alive when all this is through."

"Yes, sir. And, Bill?"

"Yes, Captain?"

"Thank you."

* * *

It was the oddest mission Al had led in his professional career, with only a handful of armed and trained Marines. At first, he thought they would set out alone, but Funny Bone's new recruits quickly disabused him of that notion.

"I can still fight, even without a suit," Angelo Christiano insisted. "And it's not as if we're safe here. If we're going to die, at least let my death be worth something."

That was a sentiment Al could hardly begrudge, so he nodded to Funny Bone. "Round up your strongest recruits. Anyone who'll come. If they bow out of this mission, it'll tell me everything I need to know…but be quick."

Funny Bone bolted for the trainees' quarters, shouting as he went, while the rest of them suited up. Tull, who had been waiting with the rest of the Marines, seemed perplexed by the flurry of action.

"What's happening?" he asked. "What are you preparing for?"

"A mission to the surface. You're coming with us, I hope?"

The alien frowned at the Marines and trainees running last-minute checks on their equipment. "I suppose. Although, what use it will be, I don't know. Is the king coming?" Al wondered if there was a note of sarcasm in Tull's use of the title, although the Roughbacks weren't known for their snide remarks.

"He'll be along later," Al said, daring destiny to prove his words a lie. He didn't know what precisely had happened on Kotbulo, but he had the sense the alliance was far from cemented. At the very least, Bill wouldn't abandon the Can and its crew.

They were about to move out when Funny Bone returned, looking wary and uncertain.

"I've wrangled almost nine recruits so far," he said, "but there's a problem—"

"It is not a problem." The woman behind Funny Bone glared at his back.

"Jana Nemec," Al said mildly. "What a pleasant surprise."

"I want to volunteer for this mission," she said. Her proud stance made it clear that any reticence on Al's part would end in a fight. "I want to help."

"As do I."

Al didn't recognize the Frenchman who'd spoken. When he looked to Funny Bone for confirmation, the sergeant sighed. "His name is Hugo Garnier. We had...issues with him, but nothing we could prove."

"Same for Nemec," Al said. "Any word on...?"

Funny Bone shook his head. He turned his attention to his console, and a few seconds later, a message popped up on the team chat: We've been monitoring her, but she hasn't done anything unusual since. I don't fully trust her, but she is an excellent marksman.

Al read the message twice. He hated the idea of fighting shoulder to shoulder with someone he barely trusted, but that's what they'd asked the Roughbacks to do, wasn't it? He'd be a fool to turn away any help they could get.

He turned to Nemec and Garnier. "Welcome to the team," he said. "Grab a weapon. We're leaving in two minutes."

Chapter Seventy-Two

Tull of the Roughbacks

Tull was starting to think that he might as well live in the shuttle.

The loss of Orbital Unit 2 weighed heavily upon him. He regretted the loss of the ship, though not out of guilt—after all, the Crendelen would have targeted it eventually, given the apparent nature of their mission. Whether they helped the humans or not, there were costs.

He was not much concerned about Mora's response to his decisions, either. She was no more in charge than any of them, and had less knowledge of these particular enemies than he did.

What saddened him was that, after everything else that had occurred, Bill had not changed his mind. Tull had promised him brotherhood, and even the death of his kinsman had not moved the captain.

It seemed the Crendelen were here to render the Roughbacks Defunct. If his actions had brought further scrutiny to Kotbulo, he was sorry for it. If the Imperium had decided that the Rough-backs weren't worth the trouble...well, so be it, but Tull would have preferred not to witness it with his own eyes.

"Are we going to meet with your crew?" Al asked.

Tull lifted his head. "Everyone is be-low the surface now. They should re-main there, in hiding. We've survived before."

Al took a moment to respond, looking to Funny Bone for inspiration. "The last time the Crendelen were here, the Ornu wanted to subjugate you," he said slowly. "They wanted you cowed, but alive."

Tull rubbed his knuckles against his temple and frowned. For some reason, humans liked to say everything but what they meant. "And?"

"And if they've decided you're not worth the trouble, they'll...eradicate the trouble." Al leaned forward and braced his elbows on his knees. "You lot live underground, right? What's to stop them from blocking the surface exits and pumping poison, or flammable gas, into the tunnels?"

"They wouldn't find every tunnel."

"They wouldn't have to. Whoever they didn't kill would need to find other quarters. The population would become too condensed. Use up the available food supply. Or they could poison your water, drive you to the surface."

Tull rocked back and forth in his seat on the shuttle, so subtly that he hoped the Marines would interpret it as the rocking of the ship. He couldn't seem to swallow properly, and when he blinked, he remembered.

Crendelen spilling through the train tunnels.

The cries of the pups.

So many friends, lost to battle.

At least when they'd fought, he'd felt powerful. He'd had agency. There was no glory in bunkering down in the tunnels and watching his people die slowly and in pain.

"It is possible," he rumbled at last.

"We're going to help you," Al promised.

The Marine captain looked around at the paltry group: a handful of armed fighters and half a dozen new recruits.

Against how many Crendelen? The math didn't bear out.

"Thank you for making the effort," Tull said. "But the captain does realize that this still won't constitute a partnership between our species, does he not? Such a partnership would still require that he sacrifice himself."

Al blinked. "I, uh...assume he realizes that."

"I'll tell you about the Disseverer later," Funny Bone said in a stage whisper.

So Bill hadn't explained the terms of the alliance. Ironic, given that he'd accused Tull of keeping secrets. So much for going back to Omega to discuss the terms with his officers. Bill had made his decision after all.

How disappointing.

Tull considered the humans before him and tried to put his reservations aside.

"How exactly do you intend to help?" he asked.

"If the Crendelen want to cut off your escape routes and block you in, they'll need to come in person," Al said. "We can be boots on the ground...and they won't see us coming."

At Tull's frown, Al made some adjustment to his suit. Within seconds, he appeared to vanish, as his exosuit took on the colors and textures of the wall behind him.

"A clever trick," Tull conceded. "But not all of your team has suits."

"We'll improvise," one of the trainees said. "Roll around in the dust, if we have to."

Tull nodded slowly. "There are a few dozen routes we could take...but your exosuits are even bulkier than we are." He considered the tunnels he knew, and decided he could safely eliminate as many as half the routes. "How large will your teams be?"

Al considered this, counting on his fingers. "We'll split the core team into three groups of two, with three or four recruits as backup, since we have eleven altogether."

"Very well." Three exits...he'd have to spread them out. "I may be able to request backup, but it will take some time. And you'll forgive my people if we're less inclined to trust you now, after the captain-king's display of ambivalence."

"Fair enough."

"Uh, Captain?" Splat twisted in his seat to look over his shoulder. "So, there's a problem."

"What now?"

They were close to Kotbulo, and Tull could see the lay of the land through the glass. Already, Crendelen forces were amassing on the surface; either a warship had broken off from the fleet at some point, or they'd somehow deployed shuttles during the fight.

"Stay high," Tull warned. "We'll keep going, find another entrance where we can land and deploy without being shot down."

Guns cursed, craning her neck to look out the window at an angle. "Are those Jackals?"

A scramble ensued, causing Splat to protest as the Can listed sideways.

"Son of a—" Al shook his head. "What are Jackals doing here? The Ornu normally don't bother with hiring them. They usually send their vassal species to fight for them. Save the cash."

"It's especially odd," Tubes added, "since the last time we saw them, they were working against the Imperium."

Termite dabbed at his forehead. The young man's skin was a much more appropriate Roughback-like color, but he still possessed the human tendency to change to a pinker pigment when stressed. "Anyone else getting a creepy-crawly feeling about all this?"

"Nah," Jana Nemec said with a smirk. "That's just what happens when you don't wash your cammies."

Chapter Seventy-Three

Captain Bill Henderson

The Crendelen chased them across the system, dogging Omega and the Roughback vessel as they went.

"I didn't plan to abandon my people," Rork complained. Both ships had been taking fire, and the Roughback ship in particular was in hard shape. "There had better be a plan at the end of all this..."

"There is," Bill assured him, with more confidence than he felt. Val has a plan, or at least Omega does.

They were approaching the asteroid belt that Val had designated as their endpoint. Val had not reappeared after Al's deployment, although the sim continued to operate in accordance with Bill's commands. All the sensors were red; their munitions had dwindled to a distressingly low stock, and they'd taken far too many hits for comfort.

He muted the com connection with Rork before saying, "Hey, Val? A little help?"

Val appeared, wearing what looked like an 18th-century military uniform, though what country it might have belonged to, Bill wasn't qualified to guess. Val tugged on the hem of his coat, so that the gold fringe of his epaulets aligned correctly on his shoulders. "What can I do for you?"

"You can tell me what I'm supposed to do now that I'm where you said to go. We've reached the edge of the asteroid field, at the coordinates you gave." Bill waved to the sim.

Val considered their position before saying, "Go deeper."

Bill stared at him as though he'd grown a second head. "The ship's maneuverability will be severely curtailed deeper in. The smaller Crendelen ships will eat us alive."

"They will. Unless something else happens."

"Something else? Like what?"

But Val only smiled.

"Can you tell me why, at least?"

"It'll make no difference. You'll either do as Omega commands or you won't, just as you defied Omega when you were over Earth."

Bill pressed his lips together. "Fine. I'm sailing deeper into the asteroid belt. Hopefully I'm not consigning the remainder of humanity to its doom."

"Yes, hopefully not," Val said mildly. Before Bill could utter another word, he disappeared again.

Chapter Seventy-Four

Captain Alden Stone

Rather than split up the team on the planet's surface, Tull brought them belowground to a set of what looked like hovertrain platforms, not so different from the public transport Al had grown up with back on Earth. Two of the platforms were empty, while the rest were blocked by cars.

"Engineer," Tull barked, pointing to Tubes, "come with me. I'll show you the easiest way to take the train out of commission."

"Why would we want them out of commission?" Angelo Christiano asked.

"To block the tunnels," Al said. "We'll take a third train down. The rest of the tunnels will be inaccessible, at least at first...rather than waste time repairing the trains, the first wave of soldiers will go on foot."

"Since we'll be taking the train," Tull called, "we'll beat them there. Have time to set up so that we're ready to confront them once they arrive."

The petty officer and Tull worked their way down the line of trains. Even as they did, the sounds of the approaching Crendelen reached them from the upper tunnels—hissing and clicking accompanied by the tromp of their boots.

They must have seen us come in.

"Captain?" Tubes called. "We're ready."

They boarded the train, which lurched into motion as soon as they were all on, plunging them into deeper darkness.

"Here's the plan," Al told the group. "Those of us with suits can rely on our helmets to tell us where to shoot. We'll also have a better chance of blending in with the surroundings. Trainees, we'll need to scope out a place for you to post up and draw Crendelen fire without making you into sitting ducks."

"I can show you the layout," Tull said. "We fought down here before. It's the perfect place for a last stand. The Crendelen are unlikely to risk the tunnels...if they were going to try to gas or smoke us out, this would be their base of operations."

Al nodded, even though he didn't like the sound of a last stand. "What about the Roughback forces?"

"I don't know how they've responded," Tull said. "I need to contact Mora and find out what's going on. The enemy forces have Jackals among them. I didn't know that until we flew in, which means the Clusters don't know it either. They need to be forewarned."

The train came to a stop on the lower platform, and they disembarked. Tull took them on a cursory tour, then showed them the tunnels beyond.

"What are we supposed to do?" Garnier demanded. He fumbled in the near-dark, swinging his flashlight around the open space. "With your helmets, you can see just like you did during Rupnik's blackout, but we'll be fighting blind."

Tull grunted and circled back to the group of volunteer cadets. "You are not the only ones. The Crendelen need light in order to fight. The Jackals are more dangerous, it's true, but they will also be fewer in number. When their troops approach, they will bring lights with them. I advise you to turn yours off. Aim toward the lights when they arrive; you can pick them off in the dark. Let those with enhanced vision fight the Jackals, and hold the line."

Al nodded along as Tull spoke. "You've done this before."

"I have," Tull agreed dully. "And I hope your battle goes better than mine did. I will go to my people and see what troops I can muster." He thumped his fist against his chest. "All-sire smile upon you." He turned with surprising speed and agility, given his usual lumbering movements, and disappeared into the lower tunnels.

They didn't have long to wait before the Crendelen forces began to arrive. In fact, Al was surprised it took them as long as it did—either they'd spent longer marshaling their forces than he'd anticipated, or they'd struggled to find the entrance to the train tunnels.

Al broke his core team off into pairs: Splat and Termite, Funny Bone and Tubes, himself and Guns.

"That way, if we have to retreat, we've got two teams who have some familiarity with the tunnels," he explained.

"Not that it matters," Funny Bone griped. "You didn't see those passages, Captain, but I'm telling you right now, we'd never get through with our suits. Quarters are too cramped."

"If it comes to that, abandon your suits," Al ordered.

"Sir?" He couldn't see Funny Bone's pallor, but the tremble in his voice was obvious. The exosuits were their most valuable asset, and now that they were cut off from any supply chain they knew, they were irreplaceable.

Each suit was attuned to its particular Marine, activated by retinal scan, so that they couldn't be stolen and repurposed by theoretical human rebels. If one of the Marines went rogue, the Imperium would have been able to recognize the suit's ID and neutralize its wearer by use of the kill switches embedded in their flesh.

The Ornu had valued the suits more highly than human life. For all their many uses, AI didn't feel the same.

"If it's a choice between your life and the suit, leave the suit. That's an order. As for those of you without suits, I'll post you in three locations where you can't catch each other in the crossfire. Your goal is to sow chaos and fire as many rounds as you can, pure and simple. We'll be switching to our radio feed when the Crendelen arrive so that we can coordinate without being heard. If you need to know something, one of us will relay that information. Got it?"

The recruits agreed, and AI relied on Funny Bone to divide them up, since he knew their temperaments better than Al, from their training sessions. Al didn't even know all their names, although he recognized Kan, Awad, and Christiano among their number.

When the time came to decide their positions, Funny Bone sent two units to the outer corners, on raised rock piles guarded by thick walls that came to waist height. Nemec, Garnier, and some recruit Al didn't recognize were placed front and center overlooking the platforms, where a hastily constructed stone barrier would guard them from Crendelen fire.

Al directed the other two Marine pairs to post up near the two teams in the back. "I want Funny Bone and Splat closer to the tunnels."

"Oh, sure," Guns griped, "so you and I can go up front and take the highest risk. Wonderful. It's my lucky day."

"I would have thought you'd be happy to be right in the heart of the action."

She rolled her shoulders a few times, a maneuver that took more effort than it was worth when they wore the suits. "When you put it like that, I guess I don't mind. Let's bust some Crendelen heads. I wouldn't mind taking a swing at a Jackal or two, either. I owe 'em one."

"Careful what you wish for," Splat warned.

A clattering sound from the tunnel made them all turn. The first lights were coming into view, signaling the arrival of the Imperium forces.

"Get ready to fire!" Al called through his speakers. "We're about to go silent. Remember, recruits, quantity over quality. Don't wait for a perfect shot. Fire into the group's mass, and you're bound to hit something."

Moments later, the first soldiers breached the tunnels, and the platform devolved into chaos.

Chapter Seventy-Five

Lance Corporal Rhonda 'Guns' Penney

The recruits were taking Al's call for maximum mayhem seriously. Guns was impressed.

She crouched low, with her back to the stone wall that guarded Nemec and her comrades, keeping her helmeted head out of the line of fire. Her time would come.

The Marines' strategy of blocking off some of the tunnels had worked, at least for the time being. Each of the units fired at a different opening, reducing the first wave of Crendelen soldiers to so much blood and feathers.

They were lucky that the other vassal species were ill-suited to protective suits like the ones she and the rest of the team wore. The bird-boned Crendelen were too slender and brittle to use such heavy equipment, especially with their weak joints. They had to rely on their numbers...and their viciousness.

As far as the Imperium was concerned, human lives were cheap, but Crendelen were even cheaper. At least, they had been before the humans were Defunct.

Guns held her fire, watching the tunnels—for what, she didn't know.

She started when the first Jackal emerged from the tunnel: not on the ground as the rest of the Imperium forces had, but shimmying across the ceiling like an oversized and heavily armed gecko.

"Guns?" Al said.

She saw her next move and barked a laugh. "On it, sir."

The three Roughback trains had already taken a beating from the recruits' erratic fire, which left holes and dents in the metal bodies of the cars. Guns lumbered toward one and grabbed a rung of the ladder at the back. She hoped the construction would be strong enough to bear her weight as she hauled herself up the side.

The train car groaned under the heft of her suit. With each step up, the metal groaned and protested, and the bars that passed for steps sagged beneath her boots, but the rivets held fast. Those deadpan turtle-creatures sure knew how to build things to last.

The Jackal was halfway across the cavern by the time Guns climbed to her feet atop the train car. She fired off two shots at the alien's back. The first fell short, since she'd failed to account for its zig-zagging path, but the second struck true. The Jackal fell from the ceiling and hit the stone floor below with a definitive thump, audible even through the gunfire, and accompanied by a puff of dust. She let out a whoop that crackled through the mics, making her crewmembers groan.

"Think you can hold the fort down, sir?" she asked Al. "I've got an idea."

"Feel free to get creative," Al told her.

From her position above the fray, Guns could see a little way into the tunnel, though it was difficult to tell exactly what she was looking at: the Crendelen hoard was a writhing mass of bodies, some of whom must have been hit, but had no space to fall to the floor. Others were being trampled between the splay-toed feet of their fellows.

She made her way along the top of the sleek train cars. The metal buckled beneath her boots, leaving shallow footprints in the steel as she walked. When she reached the front of the car, she aimed deeper into the central tunnel and opened fire. A scream went up from the Crendelen, who'd apparently thought themselves momentarily safe.

Getting the jump on Imperium soldiers should have made her feel better about the whole thing, but when she saw how far down the tunnel the Crendelen forces extended, it was hard to remain optimistic.

The second Jackal must have come from one of the side tunnels, because Guns didn't see it arrive. Her first hint that anything was amiss came when the train shifted beneath her in a movement she hadn't initiated.

The Jackal leapt over the top of the train car and lunged at her. Bullets didn't have much effect on the suits, but there were weak points in their construction. The

Jackal had come prepared with a punching knife that slotted over its fist.

Guns' first instinct was to protect her face, so she lifted one arm of the suit to block its path to the glass. That wasn't its first target, however. Its blow caused her arm to jerk, and the Jackal fell back a few paces into a crouch, its tail held out as it balanced on the curved metal roof. It leered at her. She could tell, even with her modified sight, because all of its teeth glowed white.

"Eat lead!" she bellowed, and fired into its open mouth. Or rather, the head of her M234 was aimed at the alien's mouth. No matter how hard she squeezed, no rounds emerged.

The Jackal had sabotaged her weapon.

It lunged again, but this time, Guns was ready. She swung the heavy head of the M234 like a pair of brass knuckles and hit the lizard before it could reach her again. The Jackal staggered, and Guns flung her bodyweight forward and tackled the alien over the edge of the car. When they hit the ground, she was on top—her, and all five hundred pounds of exosuit and ammo.

And that's the end of you. Guns lurched to her feet. "Bad news, Captain. I'm unarmed."

"Get back to me," he said. "We'll make a new plan—"

He was cut short by a shudder in the ground. Guns froze and held her arms out, waiting for whatever came next. "What was that?" she demanded. "An earthquake?"

"A cave-in," Splat said.

"No," Tubes told them, "it's the trains."

"The what?" Guns asked.

She was still standing below the platform next to the car from which she'd jumped. With a terrible sense of foreboding, she turned to look over her shoulder. There was nothing to see in the dark, but she felt it coming like one of those old explorers in pre-Empowerment movies, outrunning unlikely booby traps in ancient ruins.

The trains.

She hadn't fully processed what the rumbling meant when she started to run.

"Running" in the exosuits was perhaps an overstatement. It was more like falling in slow motion, hoping your feet would catch you before you wiped out in the dirt. Guns' right knee hydraulic wasn't working right—it must have gotten damaged in her topple from the top of the train car.

The ground was shaking by the time she reached the end of the track and tried to shimmy up the wall. Her knee joint was locked up. She mewled and swore as she tried to pull herself up.

At the last moment, Al grabbed her arm and yanked her up, wrenching her shoulder as he did so. The pair of them fell back just as the first train rushed out of the tunnel, hit the end of the track, and disintegrated, showering them with shrapnel.

Guns clung to the captain as a series of staggered booms! shook the floor as one train after another came rushing through. The Crendelen hadn't managed to turn them back on, but they must have realized that they could get the trains going simply by pushing or blasting them off the upper platform. After that, the deeply sloped tunnels did the rest.

The train would have crushed her if she hadn't moved.

"Guns?" Al wheezed. "You good?"

"Not sure," she grunted back. "Feel awful…"

Al wriggled free from the wreckage, pulling her after him. Guns sobbed when he dragged her by the arm. Her shoulder was, at the very least, dislocated.

Getting free of the train car's wreckage did little to relieve her pain, but she managed to find her footing when Al hauled her upright. She looked around, trying to assess their situation. Her stomach heaved when she caught sight of Jana Nemec.

Without an exosuit to protect her from the crash, she'd been pinned in place by a section of train that had flipped over the stone wall.

Guns hoped she'd died instantly. She averted her eyes.

"Retreat," Al barked. "We'll regroup near the tunnels."

"Captain—" someone protested.

One of the train cars exploded.

Guns dropped to her good knee. The explosions were so loud, especially in the confined cavern, that they left her momentarily deaf. She only heard the first two. By the third, all she heard was a thrumming ring.

We're going to die down here, she thought. The Crendelen forces had pulled back for now, probably because they'd known what was going to happen, but she'd seen how many of them there were. When they returned, she'd be as good as useless.

"—explosives! On the traincars!" Tubes was losing his mind over the Marine channel.

"The tunnels!" Al cried.

The blasts had stopped for the moment, but Guns barely knew which way was up, much less how they were going to re-group. She must have knocked her tem-ple against the inside of her helmet dur-ing the train crash. It happened sometimes. Nothing in her head was working right.

Another blast left her reeling.

Al dragged on her arm, and she went with him. At the back of the cavern, near the tunnel mouths, he took a quick survey of their group. Both other teams looked rattled, but they were alive. Of the three recruits that had backed up Al and Guns, only Hugo Garnier had survived.

"Hold the line," Al said. "Tull might still be coming. Let's wait and draw their fire for the moment and see—"

Boom.

Guns cradled one arm in the other. The rest of her team was fixed on the platform and the repeated, destructive blasts. Her eyes were fixed on the tunnels that led down to the Cluster.

She was, therefore, the only one who saw Hugo Garnier step into their depths in defiance of Al's very clear order.

"Come back," she rasped, although her voice was so hoarse he couldn't possibly have heard her.

Despite her inaudible plea, Garnier did turn. He drew a deep breath as he lifted the head of his grenade launcher. When he saw Guns looking, he shrugged.

"Captain!" She slammed her shoulder against Al's to get his attention, even if he couldn't hear her words. He turned, and she pointed into the tunnels just as Garnier stepped deeper and fired the first grenade.

The inner tunnels were small compared to the ones that housed the trains, much less the cavern that held the platforms. The first grenade brought a shower of shale flakes cascading from the ceiling.

The second brought down a stalagmite.

And with the third, the tunnel came down, blocking what would have been Tull's path back to them.

They were trapped.

Chapter Seventy-Six

Captain Bill Henderson

The Crendelen warships navigated the asteroid belt with minimal trouble, just as Bill had feared they would. Their smaller size meant that a single direct strike from an asteroid would do a great deal of damage, but their smaller size and shorter response times meant that they were able to slip between the hunks of rock.

Omega was much too large for such a delicate dance. Bill grimaced each time an asteroid struck the hull...which left him wincing almost constantly.

"What are you doing, Captain?" Rork cried.

Bill replied through gritted teeth. "Following the plan." The plan that seemed terrible and ill-considered to him. The plan that seemed almost guaranteed to get them killed.

He was doing as he was told. Val had said he needed to trust, and he was trying his best to do that. But he couldn't help feeling just as doubtful as Rork sounded.

Not only did the Crendelen have the advantage in the narrow space—it was also nigh impossible for Bill to open fire against them. The Hailstorm missiles were almost gone, and the Peregrines would be lucky to strike a ship rather than an asteroid.

The Crendelen still employed most of their missiles effectively, however. They fired infrequently, but still managed to do a fair bit of damage.

Bill willed himself back to the bridge. He sat forward and placed his head in his hands. Bina sat at Keating's old position, not far from Norder. Both of them turned to look at him.

"Captain?" Bina's voice was soft and wary. "What's the plan?"

He nodded to the screens before them. "This. This is the whole scheme. Omega wanted us to show our trust, so here we are."

Norder had gone ghostly pale. He stumbled to his feet, nearly falling when the ship was hit with another bombardment. Asteroid or missile, it hardly mattered. Soon enough, even the ship's thick and massive hull would fail, and they would be lost. Bill would go down in galactic history as the man who'd single-handedly destroyed humanity's only hope of survival.

There would be no humans left to remember him and spit on his memory. The only annals that would record him were those in the Emperor's library.

"Captain," Norder wheezed, "there must be something we can do..."

"Omega wouldn't lead us here to kill us," Bina insisted.

"Funny," he snapped, "because it sure looks that way from here."

"He wouldn't." Bina narrowed her eyes. "You didn't say anything to drive him off this time, did you?"

"No!" Bill lifted his hands in the air. "I agreed to Val's plan! Not enthusiastically, I suppose, but I still did it."

She turned back to the screens. "Then we must be missing something."

Her patient faith nearly set him off. Since when was she so compliant? Once upon a time, she'd questioned everything. She'd been sharp and calculating...and desperately unhappy, of course, but so were the rest of them. He hardly recognized her anymore.

"I don't know what you think we could have missed," Bill muttered, well aware he was speaking from a place of churlish jealousy, although whether he was jealous of Omega for having won Bina's trust, or of Bina for extending that trust in the first place, it was hard to say.

She ignored him. Her eyes were fixed on the view beyond the screens, her brow furrowed, her mouth pursed into a small frown. "Did you see that?"

Norder braced his arms on the control panel. "Where?"

"Two o'clock, maybe...thirty degrees from center?" Bina pointed.

All that Bill saw was a shifting mass of asteroids moving at slightly different rates, the same as on the rest of the screen. Just rocks. Debris. Nothing special.

The com pinged. Bina linked in without taking her eyes off the screen, although she missed the button on her first two tries. Her eyes were narrowed, making the old X-shaped scar between her eyebrows pucker and flex.

"We've taken too much damage," Rork said. "We're done for."

Bina shook her head. A curl of black hair fell free from her bun. Bill had rarely seen her so focused. "No," she said, "you aren't. Hold your course."

"We need to evacuate. One more hit—"

"Hold your course, Captain," she said. "And check your scanners."

"For what?" the Roughback asked. His momentary pause was followed by an awed oath in Roughtongue.

"You see that?" she asked.

Bill still didn't know what she was talking about.

"Will of the All-sire. How is that possible?"

And then, at last, he saw it. Bina was indeed looking at asteroids, but Bill had made one critical miscalculation...the asteroids were not all moving in their usual pattern. Several of them were on an entirely different path altogether. They weren't following the same orbital patterns as the stones around them.

"How?" Bill asked.

Even as he spoke, one of the asteroids careened toward a nearby Crendelen ship and struck it head-on. At first, it left only a hole behind, but the ship had lost its ability to maneuver out of the way. More asteroids struck it—ordinary asteroids this time, which hammered it until it was completely laid open, and it exploded.

The rogue asteroids weren't alone. One by one, the Crendelen ships were picked off. When the others tried to flee, they were chased down or barred from their exit routes, so that they were forced to choose between being crushed by a rogue hunk of rock or flying right into a cloud of shrapnel and debris left by their defeated allies.

"Did Omega do that?" Norder choked.

"All-sire be praised," Rork grunted.

Bill glanced at Bina, who stood straight-backed and proud. There was wonder in her features, bright and hopeful, as if she'd known it would end this way.

All around them, the Crendelen ships burst apart. They had pursued Omega too deeply into the belt to escape. Soon, only Rork's ship and Omega remained. Everything else had been utterly destroyed.

Chapter Seventy-Seven

Private Jorge 'Termite' Gonzalez

If Termite ever saw Hugo Garnier again, he was going to break off the man's foot and feed it to him. Then he'd stuff him into one of Omega's medbay pods, wait till the foot regrew, and do it all over again.

It wouldn't work that way, of course, but imagining how he'd get revenge made him feel marginally better about his own impending death.

The Crendelen hadn't returned to their underground battlefield, but they still found ways to make their presence known...namely via the seemingly infinite supply of explosives they kept launching into the cavern.

"Garnier!" Funny Bone screamed, clawing at the rockfall that blocked their egress. "Are you kidding me? All this time?"

"Why would he do that?" Christiano looked genuinely perplexed. "Why strand us here?"

"To save his own skin," Tubes spat. "He's probably one of those asp-worshipers who thinks he can worm his way back into their good graces. Think about it: what do you suppose the reward would be for turning Omega over to the Imperium?"

Termite did, indeed, think about it. He couldn't imagine the exact value Albus would place on Bill's head, but if someone aboard Omega managed to weasel his way into a position of control and sell out the whole ship....

He cursed.

Tubes pointed at him and nodded. "Exactly."

"Forget Garnier for now," Splat moaned. "How are we getting out of here?"

No one answered.

"Come on." The pilot looked around at them, though surely he couldn't make out much detail in the dark. "We're not just giving up, are we?"

"Can your suits withstand an explosion like that?" Awad asked.

Another blast shook the cavern. Fragments of stalactites showered down on their heads.

"...No," Splat admitted.

"Well, I'm not going to try to catch them in my hands and hurl them back up the tunnel." Awad sat down with his back to the wall. "So I guess we do what the captain said, and we wait."

Kan did the same. "Does anyone have a cigarette?"

"Are you serious?" Termite demanded. Their complacency made him almost as angry as Garnier's betrayal. "What are you thinking?"

Awad's laugh was incongruous with their dire straits. Termite was almost glad that another explosion cut him off. "You've never fought an impossible battle, have you?" The Egyptian fighter bent one leg to his chest and rested his elbow on his knee. The other leg stuck out ahead of him. He might as well have been sitting under a tree on his lunch break for all his casual manner. "You Marines, your lives were different under the Ornu. The rest of us know that it's only a matter of time."

"This is why we never revolted!" Termite snarled. "People like you ate your synth-starch and played games that let them own the world."

Awad snorted. "And how did you fight back?" he asked.

The words died on Termite's tongue. He'd always wanted to defy the Imperium. He'd snubbed Nonus along with the rest of them. But what had he ever actually done?

"Back home, I worked with a ring of resisters," Awad said. Another blast. Another deafening silence. He went on. "We monitored Ornu records. Kept track of people who came under the Imperium's scrutiny. Sometimes, I made those records disappear. For small infractions, that was enough...the Ornu were careless with that sort of thing. Other people? We made them disappear."

Kan was nodding. "How many people did you help?"

"Me, personally?" Awad was quiet for a moment. "Twenty-six. I never worked alone, though."

"That's not so many," Christiano said.

"Enough," Awad countered. "More than you."

"Is that so? Are you sure?"

"You have a story, too?" Kan asked.

"Ever heard of Operation: False Bottom?"

"No!" Kan sat up sharply. "That was you?"

"Really?" Even Tubes sounded awed.

"What is he talking about?" Al asked.

"Remember that Ornu embassy that collapsed in Istanbul a few years back? Killed five Consuls who'd been central in oppressing the people there? I'd heard rumors it was intentional, but it was ruled an accident. Apparently, the bottom floor collapsed unexpectedly."

"Some of us were expecting it," Christiano said smugly. "But they couldn't prove anything, because we didn't blast it out. We built it that way."

"Brilliant," Kan said. "Wish I'd thought of that. Only thing I ever did was 'accidentally' mistime a shuttle launch order."

Christiano sucked in a breath. "No way. That was you?"

"That was me." To the Marines he said, "Three Imperators got vaporized on the landing pad. All vocal advocates for killing more humans to make them into examples. I was let go the next day, but they never managed to prove I'd done it on purpose."

Awad said, "That's what I mean. You know how it is when you get raided. When you're caught between the rock and the hard place, you accept that there's nothing more you can do but wait and hope."

Termite had begun to tremble as he took in their stories. How come I've never heard of any of this? Maybe the recruits were lying.

Or maybe they were telling the truth. Maybe the whole time he'd been chafing under Ornu rule, convinced he was powerless to fight back against the asps, there had been hundreds of tiny acts of resistance taking place right under his nose.

Of course the Ornu would never report such things. Of course the approved channels never admitted that their overlords could be bested in any way.

Why had he never thought to question that?

"Listen," Tubes said. Termite rose to his feet and looked back at the train platform. There was nothing to see but smoldering debris.

When was the last time something had exploded? During the start of Awad's confession? Had there been another one after that?

Then came the rasp of stone on stone. The rock pile Garnier had brought down behind him shivered and bulged, gradually splitting open to reveal the tip of an immense metal drill. The humans scattered out of the way until the drill pulled back to reveal the little chamber behind it. Tull sat in a protected chair behind the slowly revolving drill head.

"You made it!" he cried. He reached beneath his seat and removed something as big as a briefcase. When he flicked the switch on, it began to glow. The light was off-white, but so bright that Termite found it painful to look at. It took his eyes a long time to adjust.

"We're alive for now," Al said in a strained voice. "But one of our men betrayed us, and the Crendelen have us blocked in."

Tull looked almost cheerful as he disembarked from his riding drill. "Well, I have three pieces of good news for you. One, we caught your traitor. We're holding him just down the tunnel a ways."

"We?" Al echoed.

Tull held up the light. From the tunnel behind him, dozens of pairs of beady black eyes reflected it. "We, as in the Roughbacks. Fifty of them came with me. The rest found other exits and came in from the rear to flank the Imperium lackeys. Our plan was to surround them and launch a two-pronged attack. We were going to get you out of here, let them in, and collapse the whole platform on them. Obviously the plan has changed."

"Because of the explosives?" Al asked.

Tull's leathery face split into a huge grin, revealing thick, blunt teeth. "Forgive me, Captain, your com equipment doesn't work down here. I should have started with the best news of all: Omega defeated the warships. The Crendelen have surrendered."

"All of them?" Splat asked. "How?"

"I don't know yet," Tull said. "I'll let Captain Henderson tell that story. All I know is, the Crendelen laid down their arms when they found out they were beaten. The Confluence is deciding their fate even as we speak."

Awad braced himself against the wall as he rose to his feet. "You see? What did I tell you? You do what you can, when you can. And when there is nothing more you can do, you wait. And you hope."

Chapter Seventy-Eight

Former Signifier Nonus

Imperator Pertinax stared across the table at Nonus, his eyes glinting in the bare bulbs of the interrogation chamber.

Nonus had long since lost track of time as the days ran into one another. He was convinced that this was intentional on the part of his jailers—that they turned the lights on and off at erratic hours just to make him think he was going mad. Time was slippery, and the dull, featureless rooms of the prison gave him nothing to hold onto. Had it been a week since he was sentenced? A month?

How long had it been since his uncle betrayed him?

Nonus stared at Pertinax because the alternative—staring at his uncle—was worse. He couldn't bring himself to acknowledge Philo's presence in the room. If he did, he might scream, which would be bad enough.

Or he might cry, which would be much, much worse.

"Why are you here?" he asked Pertinax.

The Imperator smiled and looked Nonus over, clearly delighting in his misery. Nobody had given him a mirror in which to see his own reflection, but he knew he was skinnier than he'd ever been in his adult life, and that his once-bright scales were tarnished and dull. He preferred not to imagine what his face looked like.

"We're here to ask you a few questions," Pertinax purred.

Nonus jerked his head toward his uncle. "Ask him. He's the authority here, isn't he? He knows all about my crimes, both real and fabricated."

Pertinax's arm whipped out with such force, when his palm struck Nonus' face, he tasted blood. The Imperator's smile remained.

He enjoyed hitting me, Nonus thought. He delights in this.

"No more treason," Pertinax said. "You've been found guilty by a revered magistrate and a jury of your peers. To imply that their findings are flawed is to question the very nature of our justice system, and Emperor Albus' place at its head."

Nonus rubbed his stinging cheek and thought, There is no justice here.

"Please, nephew." Philo's voice was so familiar, especially after his prolonged confinement, that Nonus had to force back tears. "We are not here to antagonize you. We are here to offer you a way to redeem yourself."

Nonus swallowed a few times until he was certain his voice was under control. "Are you saying I can overturn my sentence? How?"

Pertinax laughed cruelly. "Always looking out for himself, isn't he?"

Why not? No one else is.

The only thing Nonus had learned, the one lesson he could glean from his ill-use at his family's hands, was that some thoughts were best kept to himself. In a strange twist of fate, he found himself longing for his days on the Tennyson: not only because the times had been simpler, but because he could have punished the insolence of humans in a way he could never punish the insolence of his own kind.

He missed being powerful.

He missed having a place in which he was master.

"You have been deemed a traitor," Philo said, not unkindly. "But the Imperium needs your help. It might behoove you to improve your standing in their eyes."

"By doing what?" He finally let himself look at his uncle, and immediately regretted it. Philo's sympathetic expression was almost believable.

But Nonus knew better. His uncle had betrayed him, and convinced the rest of his family to do the same. They were no longer kin in any way that mattered.

"We want to know everything you learned about Bill Henderson," Pertinax said.

Bill Henderson. Of course. It always came back to him, didn't it?

"What do you need to know?" Nonus asked.

"Whatever you can tell us."

Pertinax rolled his shoulders. "He has challenged us and beaten us time and time again. Do you have any idea how many resources he's cost us? How many troops we've thrown at him?"

Nonus probed at the cut on the inside of his cheek, where Pertinax's blow had driven his teeth into the tender flesh of his mouth. "Too bad they didn't send you," he whispered.

Pertinax narrowed his eyes. "I beg your pardon?"

"If they're going to throw lives away, they could choose more wisely." For a few seconds, Nonus was fearless. He could still be a little powerful, he realized. Pertinax had no actual power over him. Because he had nothing left that could be taken away.

Pertinax lunged at him so suddenly that he overturned the table between them.

They went down in a mass of flailing limbs and table legs. The Imperator held him by the collar with one hand and rained down blows on his face and chest with the other three.

Nonus tried to fight back at first, then curled into a ball in an attempt to ward off the blows. Neither effort was particularly helpful, given that all four of his hands were manacled and bracketed to the table, which now lay on its side. He could not contort himself in a way that would spare him, much less make anything more than a feeble effort to return Pertinax's violence in kind.

"Oh, dear." Philo was unperturbed. "What an aggressive display, Pertinax. How unbecoming."

"Get him off me!" Nonus begged.

Philo took a sip from the bottle of water he'd brought with him and made no move to rise from his resting bench.

"He'll stop when you tell him what he wants to know."

Nonus whimpered and curled even tighter, until his tail was a tight spiral against his back. "There's nothing to tell!" he wailed. "He was an upstart. He deserved to be punished, so I punished him. He's a trickster! A sneak!"

Blood trickled into his eyes. Pertinax stopped beating him, only to yank him half-upright by his collar. "I want to know his weaknesses."

"What weaknesses?" Nonus panted. "He has a Primeval ship. He's a soft, pink-skinned little monkey with a powerful toy. And he won't. Stay. Dead." His throat betrayed him, and he let out a strangled sob. "Believe me, I tried."

Pertinax curled his lip back in disgust. "Pathetic. Someone your age should know how to take a beating." He shoved Nonus back to the ground and withdrew.

Nonus shuddered, but he had the presence of mind to press his tongue to the roof of his mouth to keep from whimpering. He hurt everywhere, and he already knew his open cuts would not be treated. The guards didn't care what happened to him. No one did. If he died from his injuries, they would throw him into the swamps, and let the glassbacks feast on his flesh. No one would mourn.

But at least he wouldn't give them the satisfaction of begging.

Philo flicked the end of his tail. "So we need to separate the monkey from his ship," he mused.

"Or destroy the ship," Pertinax said.

Philo hummed. "A Primeval ship would be a valuable asset...but I agree, if we can find a way to destroy it, we should take the opportunity." He rose and stretched, almost languidly, and looked down at Nonus. "I'm disappointed, nephew. I thought you would have lunged at the chance to make up for your past transgressions. Once again, you fall short."

Nonus turned his face to the floor and closed his eyes. He let a single tear roll free, not out of weakness, but to hide his true thoughts behind a less dangerous facade.

Someday, I will get the chance to change my fate, he thought. And when I do, you will be the ones who pay.

Chapter Seventy-Nine

Commander Bina Chakravarti

"Did Val tell you how Omega did it?" Bina asked.

Bill shook his head. For a man who had just won an impossible battle, he looked more haunted than relieved. There was something behind his eyes that made her uneasy, a sort of dissociative listlessness that Bina had never seen in his expression before. He was like a stray dog who'd been kicked one too many times to be able to tell friend from foe anymore.

They sat on the bridge, with Bina in what should have been Keating's seat, and Bill in what used to be Sally Longfield's.

Norder had charted their course back to Kotbulo, with the battered Roughback vessel trailing in their wake.

"Bill." She reached out, but stopped short of touching him in case he spooked. "This is a good thing. You know that, don't you?"

"Maybe," he said.

"It turns out, listening to your superiors can bring good results," she said wryly.

"Is that what Omega is now? My superior?" Bill shuddered and shifted so that his back was partway to her.

"Unquestionably, I would say."

He shot her a wounded glance.

"Does it matter?" Norder asked. He'd been quiet ever since the asteroids ambushed the Crendelen ships, but he'd been sneaking furtive looks at the pair of them as they spoke. "No offense, Captain, but your ego isn't the most important thing in this situation."

"This isn't about my ego," Bill insisted.

"Isn't it?" Norder nodded to Bina. "We've all made mistakes. We've all made choices that we'd take back if we could."

Bina nodded her agreement.

"I know you're used to having all of this weight on your shoulders, sir. You're the king, apparently. But I don't think it matters much when compared to the ship's survival...and the survival of its cargo."

Bill looked down at his threadbare trousers and began picking absently at a small hole in the material. His face was perfectly neutral. Bina had no idea what he was thinking.

Why was he being so stubborn? Omega had done everything for them. The thought made something itch at the back of her mind, a nagging discomfort that told her she should never rely too much on anyone or anything. But if they couldn't trust Omega, what did they have left?

Omega had to be good, because the alternative was unthinkable.

"I know you want to be master of your own fate," she told Bill quietly, "but this is bigger than you are. Than any of us is. Until we learn to value the collective good before our individual comfort, we'll never be able to do this right."

"Of course." Bill passed his hand across his forehead. "Of course you're right."

They sat in silence for a while, watching as the featureless outline of Kotbulo grew on the screens, until they were approaching its orbit.

Eventually, Bill used the com to hail Al. The first thing he said into the speaker was, "You better not be dead."

"No, although we did have an incident," Al replied. Bina exhaled a sigh of relief at the sound of his voice.

"Get back to the ship, and you can tell me all about it," Bill said wearily. "We need to figure out how to infiltrate Ornu space and secure the giant shipyard without the Roughbacks' help." He lowered his voice to add, "Unless Omega already has a plan and simply hasn't shared it yet."

Bina lowered her head to hide her smile. Clearly, it would take him a while to get used to yielding to Omega's oversight.

"Actually, Bill, the Roughbacks want to talk to you," Al said.

"I'm sure they do. But I don't plan to sacrifice myself. They'll have to settle for being grateful that we took out the Crendelen warships and let the matter of the Disseverer go."

"The what?" Al asked. "C'mon, Bill. Listen, I don't know anything about the weird conversations you've been having with these aliens. All I know is, Tull says they're ready to lend us their full support."

Bill frowned and scratched his jaw in thought. A little spark of curiosity flared in his eyes.

That was good—it meant he hadn't given up entirely. "All right, then. I'll be right down, I guess."

Chapter Eighty

Sergeant Shawn 'Funny Bone' Piker

There was no way any of them was going to wriggle through the tunnels into the Roughback Cluster. Splat had made it perfectly clear that once was enough.

"I don't think you should go, either," Funny Bone told Al while they waited for Bill to arrive on Kotbulo. "They were nice enough, I suppose, but if they turn on you, they'll either kill you on the spot or leave you stranded in a cave system you don't know how to navigate. Either way, you won't make it out alive."

"If they turn on us. Which they won't."

"You say that now, but you didn't see their death machine."

Al narrowed his eyes. "Are you talking about this 'severer' thing again?"

"It's called the Disseverer."

Al raised both hands in surrender. "Forget I asked. Either way, I'm going with Bill. In the meantime, I'm leaving Garnier in your hands. When we get back, I want an explanation."

* * *

The Can was still in working order, much to Splat's relief. He crooned to it as the Marine team returned to Omega. "Who's a good girl? Yes, it's you. You're a good ship. You never fail me, do you, baby?"

Guns was still looking worse for wear, but she managed to roll her eyes at the back of his seat. "He's such a freak. I don't know why we keep him around."

Termite nodded. "I mean, pick a lane. If he treated the ship like his girlfriend, that would be weird enough, but then he acts like he's talking to a puppy or something, and it just gets weird."

On the deck, the trussed and bound form of Hugo Garnier lay ignored. His bulging eyes rolled back and forth like those of a frightened animal, but he didn't speak. Mostly because of the rag Funny Bone had stuffed in his mouth earlier.

They'd left Jana Nemec's remains behind on Kotbulo: not out of intentional disrespect, but because by the time they'd gotten to her, there was nothing left to reclaim. Funny Bone still didn't know her true intentions, but he was profoundly aware of the fact that he'd failed her twice over.

The Crendelen were already being dealt with. And Garnier wasn't going to get away with what he'd done.

When they reached Omega, Funny Bone grabbed the man under his armpits, while Termite took his ankles. Together, they carried him to the upper decks.

When they reached the mess hall, Funny Bone tried to send Guns to the medbay.

She set to work peeling off her exosuit instead. "Nah, I'm okay. Nothing a little sleep can't cure, and the doc's busy anyway. Besides, I don't want to miss this little chat."

The others seemed to feel the same way. Funny Bone turned a skeptical eye on the recruits. "You should go, at least."

Christiano pulled out a chair and hovered behind it. "Why? He tried to kill one of us. You almost blamed me for what he did."

"He tried to kill all of us," Awad clarified.

Well, they had him there. There was no point arguing, so he stopped trying. Let them stay. They all deserved to know the truth.

He took his time getting out of his exo-suit, then sent one of the recruits to get a pot of coffee from the Nourishers.

When they were all ready, he knelt beside the whimpering traitor. "I admit, I'm curious," he said. "Why'd you do it?"

Garnier blubbered something into the rag.

"Sorry," Funny Bone drawled, "I didn't catch that." He yanked the rag free.

Garnier rolled onto his side. "Just kill me," he said.

Funny Bone gripped the rag in a fist. "Why? What have you done to deserve that?"

Tubes snorted and tipped his chair back on two legs. "He's done plenty, don't you think?"

Funny Bone hunched over Garnier. "Yeah, but I want to hear his explanation."

"They were going to kill us!" Garnier bawled. "I thought...if I joined the team, I could...." He squeezed his eyes shut. "The Ornu didn't want us. They wanted him. Henderson! Everything they did, they did to get at him!"

"And you wanted to hand him over to them on a silver platter," Funny Bone guessed.

"How did Nemec factor into it?" Christiano asked.

Perhaps Funny Bone should have told the man off for speaking out of turn—he wasn't really part of the team, after all—but since they'd spoken in the cavern, the lines between their positions had blurred. They'd fought together. Bled together.

And they had just as much reason to despise Garnier as he did.

"Wanted her spot," Garnier panted.

"How did you do it?"

"In her bottle. The night before. I thought no one could trace it back to me."

Funny Bone cursed and lurched to his feet. Garnier flinched, anticipating a kick to the rib, but the sergeant began to pace instead. "Who are you working with?"

"Just me," Garnier said. "It was only me."

It was possible he was telling the truth, though Funny Bone wasn't inclined to believe him. Even if he'd concocted the scheme on his own, he must have believed that someone would back him up. A man couldn't sell out all of humanity by himself.

Although...Rupnik had tried to take the ship, thinking he could control Omega on his own. The kid had been wild, but his father might have had a grander plan. If one of them approached the Imperium with total control of Omega, what would Emperor Albus have done for him? Would he reward the traitor for his efforts? And would he kill all the survivors, or simply deem them Defunct?

What Funny Bone believed was less important than what other people assumed. If there were people aboard who thought they could overthrow Bill and take control of the ship, either for selfish reasons or for stupid but noble ones, they would always be in danger of insurrection.

"Sarge?" Termite asked.

Funny Bone shook off his musings. "We'll take him to the brig for now. Let him think about what he's done. The captain will question him later."

Termite stepped forward, but when he tried to lift Garnier to his feet, the man shuddered so violently he couldn't stand. Thick, viscous saliva dribbled from his lips, and his eyes rolled back in his head.

Termite recoiled. "What the—?"

Funny Bone dropped back to the man's side, cursing.

Garnier's body stiffened as his muscles spasmed. He let out a strangled sound as his cheeks darkened and the veins in his neck bulged.

How long ago had the Roughbacks caught him? How long since he'd swallowed the poison? Funny Bone cursed himself for his own stupidity—of course Garnier hadn't brought just a single dose of poison aboard with him. He'd had enough for Nemec and himself, and probably more besides.

Assuming that Garnier had brought the poison in the first place. Funny Bone had planned to let him stew and interrogate him later, but it seemed he wouldn't get the chance.

He started dragging the man toward the medbay, in the hopes of saving him in time…but time was against them. Hugo Garnier's secrets died with him.

Chapter Eighty-One

Captain Bill Henderson

If Bill never visited the Confluence again, it would be too soon. He wanted to be in his rack, blissfully comatose after the abysmal day, not squatting in a stuffy hole miles below the surface of a dying world.

At least Norder was off-duty now. By the time he got back to Omega, they'd be ready to chart a course away from Kotbulo to...well, to wherever they decided to go next.

The chamber was more crowded than it had been the last time. Al sat beside him, somehow managing to look perfectly at ease despite the strangeness of their surroundings.

"How many more are coming?" Bill asked. The Confluence was packed from wall to wall, bristling with occupants, though there was no sign of Mora among their number.

"Hard to say," Tull mused. "We put out a call for aid to the other Clusters when we thought we were going to war."

Bill rubbed his temples. He still couldn't rationalize what Omega had managed. Having seen what the Roughbacks could do with hollowed-out rocks, it had oc-curred to him that Omega might have simply manipulated Roughback ships that had been abandoned in the area.

To replenish their munitions, Val had un-leashed a fleet of drones from Omega to go mining from some of the asteroids that hadn't moved of their own accord. They would return before Omega left the system, to convert the materials into the weapons they'd need for whatever was to come.

Tull sat up a little straighter. "Here they are," he murmured.

Mora and several other elders strode into the Confluence, marching in a straight line. They approached the low center of the room, where Bill and the others sat. His instinct said to rise and greet them in some formal manner, perhaps by bowing, but when he made to rise, Tull gripped his shoulder and guided him back to the floor. He shook his head without taking his eyes off of the elders.

Bill sat.

At the center of the room, Mora raised her arms, and the murmurs of hundreds of voices stilled. She let her head roll back.

"The human, Bill Henderson, called upon us for aid," she boomed. "He asked us to fight side-by-side as if we were kin. In response, we told him that he must prove his worth. He must complete an impossible task, to prove not only his sincerity, but also that the All-sire smiles upon him."

"Impossible task?" Al whispered.

Bill waved him off. He didn't like the direction this conversation was taking. If they tried to drag him back to the Dis-severer, he was going to pitch a fit.

"We gave him choices," Mora went on. "Tasks that our greatest heroes have accomplished. The human, Bill Henderson, refused."

Bill made awkward eye contact with a surly-looking Roughback elder and offered a weak smile. Did they really have to make such a spectacle over denying his request?

"Instead, he did something none of us have ever done. Something truly impossible." Mora swept one hand toward him. "He risked his life to defeat the Crendelen invasion, against impossible odds. He fought alongside our warriors. His people shed their blood in the same halls where we have shed ours. From today forth, they are to be treated as Roughbacks, and they will treat us as human. Our two species are bound in accordance with the old laws. There is to be no difference between us."

Tull elbowed Bill in the ribs, and he let out a wheeze.

What just happened, exactly?

"The Confluence has spoken." More of the aliens bowed. The Roughbacks rumbled their approval and began to rise. The meeting was over.

He'd won. Somehow, without intending to, he'd won. He was going to owe Val a pint of bitter after this.

"Congratulations," Tull told them.

"Did you know they were going to do that?" Al asked over the hubbub of shifting Roughbacks.

"I had a hunch."

"A little warning would have been nice!" Bill rubbed his palm against his chest and tried to catch his breath. He was grateful, of course, but the heart attack they'd almost given him was less than desirable.

"I spoke for you, as did Rork. He was quite…effusive."

Bill tried to envision a Roughback being effusive, and failed. "How many other species have enjoyed an alliance like this one?"

Tull waved a hand back and forth. "It depends what you mean. Plenty of individuals have forged alliances with groups or factions. No species has ever earned an alliance with our people as a whole before, though."

A nagging suspicion made Bill glare at his new ally. "How many have tried, via the Disseverer?"

Tull scratched his chest. "Oh, lots."

"How many survived?"

"Depends who you ask."

He considered pressing the issue, but since there was a possibility that one of the answers might be none, he'd prefer to leave the topic behind altogether. "Guess I got lucky," he said instead. "Or, uh, the All-sire smiled on me?"

Tull shook his head. "There is no need to be disingenuous...brother."

But Bill didn't know for sure if he was being disingenuous.

Either way, their conversation was cut short by the arrival of Mora and the other elders, who approached and stood over them. For all that they'd just announced their acceptance of him, Bill still found them intimidating, and none moreso than Mora.

"Come," she said. "We have matters to discuss, and time is rolling away from us. The ore will not dig itself." She walked toward the exit, with the clear expectation that they would follow.

"A figure of speech, I assume?" Al asked Tull as they rose to their feet.

Tull's browridge wrinkled. "Does the ore dig itself on your world?"

Leave it to the Roughbacks to be literal with their aphorisms. If they were going to be kindred species now, Bill supposed he would have to get used to it.

They ate by mosslight in a private home in the Cluster, helping themselves to the five dishes served in large crocks and platters laid out in the center of the table, family-style. The textures and flavors were unfamiliar, but as before, the food was palatable, and featured a few aromatic herbs that were almost pleasant. Bill helped himself to a second serving of a chewy plant that tasted pleasantly of nuts and had a meaty texture not dissimilar to pork. The liquid served in their cups was less pleasant. He thought it might be alcoholic, and it tasted nice enough, but smelled of steamed shellfish.

"Captain Rork is in the process of seeding a new ship," Mora announced. "He will begin tomorrow. By the time he is finished, the rest of our fleet will have arrived."

"There are more ships?" Al asked. "How far are they?"

"None are within this system. There are five altogether, none more than three systems away. In the coming days, they will return to us. Rork and his crew will stay here." She paused and gave Tull a quelling look. "His job is to protect this planet, not to go off starting wars."

"He did not start it," Tull replied. "The Crendelen came to render us Defunct. He did exactly as he ought."

"Mm." Mora pursed her lips into a thin line. "I suppose you're right."

Al finished chewing a bite of his meal and swallowed. "If we have a few days, we should be able to completely replenish our missile reserves."

And get some rest, Bill added silently. Kotbulo wasn't the ideal planet for an R&R break, but they could all use rest. Besides, there were plenty of problems left for Omega to deal with in the meantime. He'd have a chance to sort things out properly before launching another mission.

It was as if Mora could read his mind and didn't want him to have nice things. "Once you're ready, I suggest you return to Vale and try to secure the Awn's help in the coming fight against the Ornu. We will send Tull and several of our people with you as ambassadors."

Bill forced a chuckle. "We're not exactly ready to fight the Ornu."

"I don't think the Ornu will wait for you to arm yourself," Mora rejoined. "Besides, we have a history with the Awn. Like us, they are attuned to the harmonies."

"The harmonies?" Al repeated, bewildered.

Mora began to hum, and the other Roughbacks at the table immediately joined in. Bill had forgotten that the Awn had a similar means of communication. The two species looked so unalike—one squat, colorful, and amphibious, the other built like humor-impaired boulders—that he hadn't taken much notice of their similarities.

"Do the Awn do much fighting?" Bill asked. "Until we get the surge drive installed, I don't think we're equipped to do much more than keep a low profile."

"It is not up to you," Mora said. "We have been speaking to the Crendelen prisoners. Did it not strike you as strange that the Jackals fought beside them?"

Al nodded. "We did. Last time we saw them, they were working for the Perseids."

"They still are. The Perseids and the Ornu have never been friends, but the Emperor has convinced them that they have a common enemy...the man who opened fire on Armon." She nodded to Bill.

The room spun, and Bill had to grab the edge of the table to keep from pitching sideways like a new recruit who didn't yet have his space legs. "What?"

"I do not entirely understand what Albus offered them, but he seems to have placed the blame for what happened to the Perseid homeworld squarely on your shoulders. Several of the Ornu have attested to the fact that you acted outside your orders. The Emperor has promised the Perseids that he will punish you for your transgressions, if they help him bring you in."

An alliance between the Perseids and the Ornu should never have come to pass. A species bent on galactic conquest, and an alliance dedicated to their collective liberation? There were no two more natural enemies.

Mora had undersold him: it seemed Bill had managed to bring more than one impossible task to fruition. Decades of threats and skirmishes had failed to offer what he'd managed in a matter of weeks. He'd provided the two factions with common ground: their hatred of his person.

The Roughback elder was right about one thing...he needed all the help he could get.

Chapter Eighty-Two

Commander Bina Chakravarti

On their way to the Awn home system, Bina showed Bill her findings.

She and Norder had done a bit of digging, and Tull and Rork had volunteered some of the Roughbacks' records at her request. Usually, she would have asked Judith for help, or even Keating, but the former had been notably absent of late, and the latter still insisted on pretending Bina didn't exist.

"So, I was looking into those asteroids. The ones that helped us against the Crendelen by smashing into their ships?" She slid her notes across the table. Al had joined them for breakfast, and he craned his neck to see what she'd written. She shifted the angle of the paper so that they could all have a look. "All of those asteroids were outfitted with thrusters."

"Like the Roughback ships," Al noted.

"Sort of. See, according to Tull's records, some asteroids had these thrusters installed as part of an ice-mining operation that they started shortly before their war with the Ornu began. The work was never completed, but the thrusters are of Roughback design."

Bill bobbed his head and reached for his cup of coffee. "I figured it was something like that. Makes sense."

"It does," she said slowly. "Except that there's no record of almost thirty percent of those asteroids ever having been outfitted with thrusters. Some of them didn't even have a significant amount of ice, meaning there was no reason to give them thrusters in the first place."

All three of them pondered this for a moment. "Maybe the records they gave you are inaccurate," Al suggested. "To be honest, the Roughbacks don't seem like they'd be meticulous record keepers."

"Most people aren't great at meticulous recordkeeping," Bina replied. "And yet our species managed it. Mostly because at least a few of us end up having a talent for it."

"Yeah, well...maybe it's different with the Roughbacks?"

"Maybe." Bina rested her chin on her fist and reviewed her notes.

"Tull said something about automatic seeding," Bill pointed out. "Remember when OU2 was destroyed? Parts of it broke off and went off to seed another asteroid—or tried to, anyway."

She nodded again, although that math didn't track, either. If one of the asteroids with equipment had been destroyed, those thrusters might have redirected themselves to a new one, but it wouldn't make them multiply. The discrepancy didn't add up.

Maybe she wasn't giving Omega enough credit. If he could fold time so that she could alter the past, why couldn't he manipulate reality in other improbable ways?

She scooped up her notes. "Thanks for talking it over with me. I don't know why this sticks out to me, given everything else that's happened."

Bill licked his lips, like he wanted to say something, then looked down into his coffee cup. "Whatever happened, it is what it is, and it certainly doesn't seem like a reason to complain. In the meantime, we have more pressing things to focus on."

She took his advice at face value and asked no further questions. Omega had saved them; that was what mattered.

Anything else was a distraction, a thorn-bush along the path Omega had laid for them. She would simply have to stay the course.

Chapter Eighty-Three

Consul Philo

Consul Philo was in his quarters when he received the summons from the Emperor. His first impulse was to strip everything off and dress again, this time in his finest attire...but would such a display impress Albus, or draw attention to the fact that Philo had time to concern himself with appearances, even though he'd still failed to gather the information the Emperor desired?

Better to leave right away, he decided, and show submission. Albus generally responded well to that.

He was not entirely surprised when he met Imperator Pertinax on the walkway over. Like him, the Imperator had answered the summons right away. Pertinax was doubly glad he hadn't dawdled in his room. If he'd arrived late, he might be accused of indifference toward their ruler.

"Imperator." Philo inclined his head and clasped his lower hands behind his back as they walked. He used his upper pair of arms to gesture while he spoke. "It's a pleasure to see you again."

"I don't suppose you've gone to see your nephew lately, Consul?" Pertinax asked.

Philo let out a hollow laugh. "I'm not fool enough to speak to him alone. One can only imagine the rumors that might be spread were I to do so, especially since he remains noncompliant. One might reach the conclusion that I was up to something nefarious."

"And it would be a shame, wouldn't it, to find yourself on trial, pitting your word against that of someone more well-regarded?" Pertinax laughed and flashed a grin that suggested they were in on the joke together.

Philo chuckled, but his heart wasn't in it. He didn't feel guilty about what he'd done to his nephew, which, after all, had been an act of necessity. Still, there was something dirty and tasteless about the whole affair. Nonus had trusted him. Yes, the boy was a fool for trusting anyone, but Philo had turned on his own flesh and blood.

"You know what he's going to ask us," Pertinax said.

"I do. Or at least, I have an idea." In many regards, the Emperor was predictable. Philo's primary concern at that juncture was how to evade his wrath.

And yet, even before they reached the Emperor's presence, he surprised them. When they reached their escort, they were not led to the skybound shuttle, but one of the halls within the fortress.

Even Pertinax, who usually managed to hide his emotions behind a smirking veneer, was visibly taken aback.

They were taken into the Emperor's presence in a heavily fortified hall belowground. Albus was reading from a tablet when they arrived, but he set it aside as soon as they approached.

"It is an honor to be invited, Emperor," he said, before Pertinax could beat him to a greeting. "I did not realize you set scale upon Lindinis herself anymore."

Albus' scaled brow twitched. "My advisors thought it unwise to remain on high, given the...situation with Omega."

Of course that was why he had gone to ground. Philo should have guessed. It was a tactic wisely borrowed from the Roughbacks, although he knew better than to suggest so aloud.

"It is our honor to be here," Pertinax simpered. "What can we do for you, Your Majesty?"

Albus' slitted nostrils flared. "I wanted to give you two a chance to redeem yourselves. You're aware, of course, of the new alliance with the Perseids?"

Both of them inclined their heads.

"That was accomplished thanks in no small part to your efforts. For that reason, I have overlooked your past failures." The Emperor leaned forward. "But you have not extracted the information I need from the traitor, so I am forced to test your loyalty again."

Philo understood exactly what forced Albus' hands. On Earth, it had been his business to be suspicious of any officer rising too quickly through the ranks. So long as Albus kept his subordinates humble, they would be less likely to attempt usurpation.

Philo had questioned many people over the years, and thus already knew the right answers...and the wrong ones. He would have to make himself valuable, but not invaluable, as the latter would draw too much attention. Suspicion would be sure to follow, and he knew better than most that evidence of guilt, if it could not be found, could be easily fabricated.

"My humblest apologies, Emperor, but I do not believe it is possible to extract the information you desire. My nephew is—" He was about to say, My nephew is a fool, but caught himself just in time. To do so would be to incriminate himself by suggesting he'd been outsmarted by a dimwitted child. That would hardly be a recommendation of his own intellect. For his lies about Nonus' character to hold strong, he must reinforce them at every turn. "—a narcissist of the highest order. I do not believe that he credited Bill Henderson's intellect."

"A grosssss oversight," Albus hissed.

"None of us foresaw the depths of Henderson's treachery." Philo was playing with fire, but he soldiered on. "Otherwise, he would not have been assigned to this mission, or allowed any fate save that of the Defunct."

The implication being, You let this happen, too, Emperor. He would not speak the words aloud. He was not as brazen as all that.

"I...underestimated him," Albus said. The words had the tone of a challenge.

"I believe that we all underestimated the capabilities of a Primeval vessel," Philo corrected. "Henderson is no outlier. He is a primitive with a weapon that allows him to overstep. Without the weapon, he would still be nothing more than a rube with complex speech patterns and opposable thumbs."

Albus' smile was fleeting. "Of course. But how do we reclaim this ship?"

Philo demurred to Pertinax, who lifted his chin and rolled his shoulders back. "Emperor Albus, allow me to take command of the armada. With the force of the Imperial fleet, we can crush—"

"No." Albus waved one dismissive hand between them, already averting his attention from Pertinax. "We have lost too many ships in misguided displays of force. The armada will remain in defensive formation around Lindinis. We were already bruised in the conflict with the Perseus Confederation, and our latest loss was too great. I do not wish to risk sending our planet's defenses against a colossus of a ship like Omega, which has unknown capabilities."

"Then allow me full use of the Crendelen fleet, as well as the budget to hire every Jackal throughout the empire and in any adjacent neutral territories, along with every Jackal gunship. We don't yet know where Omega will strike, but with those numbers we can patrol likely systems."

Pertinax flashed Philo a look that said, clear as speaking, Back me up here.

"With respect, Emperor," Philo said, "Nonus cannot tell us more than we already know of Bill Henderson's character. However, we can learn what a man might do based on what he has done. If you recall, his grandfather once headed a significant rebellion. Humans are not terribly creative creatures, nor are they prone to subtlety. It is possible Henderson believes he has a legacy to fulfill."

"And he would do so by attacking Lindinis." Albus' voice was cold.

"We would be wise to assume that is his end goal," Philo said.

Albus considered this. He lifted his upper arms and picked at his claws, his movements precise but his gaze far away. When it came to moving game pieces around a board, Ornu thinking was often dispassionate—or at least, it ought to be. A threat to Lindinis, however, meant more than a threat to Albus' power. Everything and everyone that mattered was housed there. The planet was the sacred ancestral world of the beings who had made the empire possible. To colonize the worlds around them was their right. To be colonized by a lesser species was unthinkable.

"Take the warships," Albus said. He lifted his burning eyes to Pertinax's face without moving his head. "I don't have to tell you to come back with the Primeval ship or not at all, do I?"

"You do not. My mission is to capture Omega if I can...and destroy it if I cannot. If I fail, it is because there is no life left in me."

The words were bold, but Philo heard the crack in the Imperator's voice when he spoke the ship's name. For all his bravado, there was real fear there. Of Henderson? Surely not. But of the ship itself? Or of what it could accomplish?

Pertinax knew something that he had not shared. This came as no surprise. Philo had secrets of his own, ones that he would not admit, even under threat of torture.

The Ornu were always scheming. And he'd been playing this game for a long, long time.

Chapter Eighty-Four

Commander Bina Chakravarti

Judith was still absent on Bina's next visit to the Archive, but when she slid into her usual seat—the one designed for Kanami proportions, rather than for humans—she was immediately carried away to another time and place.

She didn't know much about Kanami biology, but when she opened her eyes and saw Hyx walking through a construction site, she could tell he was older than he'd been the last time she laid eyes on him. They were still on Azure, judging by the landscape, but the archaeological site when he'd first found Omega was transformed.

A vast grid had been laid out on the ground, which Hyx walked with a group of what appeared to be young engineers. He was pointing to part of the grid, then up toward the sky, gesturing his arms in sweeping motions as if to encompass something so enormous, the engineers could not comprehend its scope.

"But why not assemble it here?" one of them asked.

"Haven't you been listening?" Hyx asked. "If we built it here, we'd be fighting gravity the whole way, and the amount of fuel it would need to break through the atmosphere would be astronomical. Never mind the damage such a liftoff would do to the terrain! No, the only way to see this through would be to build the pieces here, and then assemble them onto the frame..." He pointed to the sky again.

The engineers exchanged a look. "It'll be costly," one of them said.

Hyx's enthusiasm sharpened to bitter humor. "I am in a position to pay."

"It's an ambitious project." The shortest of the engineers scratched her chin and squinted toward the heavens. "And I'm not sure we can go about it in the way you describe... assembling it from the inside out, I mean. However, if we plan the interior carefully, then start by constructing the hull..."

"And life support systems!" one of her peers chimed in.

"Precisely. We would essentially be constructing our own workstation."

"If we draw resources from the asteroid belt, rather than mining the planet itself, we could save a great deal of effort..."

"And we'd be able to test the design firsthand, modifying flaws as we go!"

Hyx watched with evident amusement as the engineers began to talk amongst themselves, discussing the possibilities. As their excitement mounted, the shortest of them held up her hands.

"Very well. Hyx, as you can see, we'd be more than happy to work on this. If you can obtain the funding and the necessary permits, we'll see that the work is completed to your satisfaction. Although, given what you're asking for, this work will likely span years—"

"Decades," one of the others murmured, seemingly delighted by the prospect.

"Tell me what you need from me, and I will secure it," Hyx promised. "I have connections that will aid our work, one way or another. I intend to be involved in every step of the process, but I will not hamper your vision, so long as it does not conflict with mine. If anything, I value your insight."

"Hyx?" Bina and the Kanami both turned to see Kalykk, the archaeologist he'd first met on Azure, jogging toward them. "You have a visitor."

"Please excuse me." Hyx bowed to the engineers. "I look forward to this partnership." With that, he turned and strolled off toward Kalykk, with Bina dogging his footsteps. She was never quite sure how her movements in simspace corresponded to her movements in the Archive.

Assuming this was simspace. Hyx didn't acknowledge her presence the way he had during that one conversation, but Bina suspected this was more than a reel played back, eons later, for her amusement. Omega had mastered the impossible, and so long as she was here, she was resolved to take nothing for granted.

"Who should I expect?" Hyx asked as the two of them made their way down the hill to an expanded cluster of buildings.

Kalykk's usually sunny expression was less enthusiastic than Bina remembered. She wrung her hands and hunched her shoulders when she spoke. "Are you familiar with Teraphim?" she asked.

Hyx stopped so abruptly Bina nearly walked through him. "The Teraphim? Is he here?"

Kalykk nodded. "I read that he's the oldest of our kind. The first one to afford life extensions."

"I don't know if he was the first, but he's certainly the most infamous," Hyx muttered. "We have a...history. For some reason, he's taken issue with my stance that our people have no business extending their lives centuries beyond their natural scope. I can't think why."

Kalykk shuddered. "I understand your position, Hyx, but he's a powerful enemy."

"He can't stop what I'm doing here," Hyx said firmly.

"But he could shut down the dig."

Hyx reached out to squeeze her shoulder. "Ah, I see the trouble. Don't worry, I'll handle him. Alone."

Kalykk wilted with relief. "Thank you. He's waiting at the site. And before you ask, yes, I secured the locks on the storage rooms earlier, so he can't take anything without us at least noticing what he's done."

Hyx's lips twitched into a smile. "Good work."

Bina recognized his tension all too well. He moved the same way Bill did when going off to handle a meeting he dreaded: with defiant purpose, his chin held high, his stride long and precise. Bina loped after him, grateful she wouldn't have to be visible for whatever conversation lay ahead.

A single Kanami stood by himself near the storage buildings, flanked by two of the creatures Bina remembered were called voidlings, or voidservants. Even standing still, the diminutive beings, no more than two feet in stature, were in constant motion—the colors of their unbroken skin swirling endlessly.

The Kanami they accompanied appeared to be studying what little he could see of Kalykk's work from where he stood. A few new finds were laid out on a covered table, ready for processing, and he alternated between examining them and surveying the excavation. A handful of students were hard at work beneath a protective dome that shimmered silver in the sunlight. A shield, Bina realized—one that preserved the site from the elements while they worked.

"Come to admire your old stomping grounds, Teraphim?" Hyx called as he approached.

The newcomer chuckled. "I'm not that old, as you well know." Despite Kalykk's rumors, he didn't look much older than Hyx.

Hyx came to a stop a few paces away. His expression was almost bored, but his eyes gave him away. He was as wary as a kicked dog in the other Kanami's presence. "Would you please send your voidservants away? I don't have important conversations in front of them, as a rule."

Teraphim inclined his head. "I'm flattered you think this will be an important conversation. But I don't understand your issue with voidlings. The universe gave us an incredible gift, with their discovery. Beings willing to do our bidding unquestioningly. Beings that don't even need to be fed. What scruples could you possibly have about such low-cost servants?"

"Slaves, you mean," Hyx said. "And I'm not convinced they eat nothing. It seems quite possible they're simply eating something we can't see."

Teraphim chuckled. "That sounds like very...unstructured thinking, if I may say so, Hyx. But I'll respect your wishes." He flicked a hand, and the void servants scurried away.

"May I ask what brings you here?" Hyx said. "There's no shopping, little tech. No fine dining. I doubt someone such as yourself, with so much varied experience, will find much here to amuse him."

"You couldn't be more wrong." Teraphim returned his focus to the dig site. "You offer something I have not experienced in a long time. Novelty."

"A dig site is hardly novel."

"Ah, but what about your new project? Word has spread of your grand design." Teraphim nodded toward the hill. "When I first heard of it, I thought perhaps you'd come around. You were always a tech-hater. What changed your mind?"

"I opposed nothing more than excess, and continue to do so." Hyx straightened his back further still.

"A noble sentiment, I'm sure. Although, one might argue that your proposed project is an indulgence in excess."

Bina couldn't work out what to make of Teraphim. He wasn't friendly, but he didn't exude the malice she'd come to expect from the likes of the Ornu. She circled him, trying to find evidence of all the things Hyx despised about their flawed society, and found nothing. His jumpsuit was quite ordinary, so similar to the one Kalykk wore that they might have been assembled by the same hand. It was newer, true, but it was hardly ostentatious.

"I have plans," Hyx said. "What business is it of yours?"

Teraphim chuckled and wagged a finger at him. "Because I recognize the game you're playing, Hyx. You're trying to build something that will outlast Kanami society, because you expect it to collapse. And maybe it will collapse...but isn't that part of the fun?"

Hyx bristled at the implication. "It's no laughing matter. If the rest of us die, you will not survive on your own. You're not above us."

"Oh, believe me, I know." Teraphim waved the thought away. "Everything dies. Even me. That's not remarkable. But I think you and I have come to the same conclusion. If we build something that is meant to last, we will outlive our mortal forms. We will outlive even our species. To that end, I've come to make you an offer."

Hyx had clearly been preparing an argument, his lips already forming around the words, but Teraphim's statement stopped him short. "An... offer?"

"I want to pay for your project. Exclusively."

"I already have donors."

"Do you have enough to support a project like this? One that may drag on for decades? Consider how much time you'll spend asking for support, when that time could be better spent bringing our vision to life."

"Our vision," Hyx repeated coldly.

Teraphim took a step toward him, his glittering blue eyes fixed on Hyx's face. The light within them grew brighter, until Bina's guide was bathed in their glow. There was an air of the fanatic about Teraphim now.

"I love the universe, and I love living in it. I want to leave my mark on it. Let us work together, and you will never want for anything—"

"No." Hyx stood his ground. "I am already making plans, and they do not involve you. Thank you for your offer."

"Is that the game you want to play?" Teraphim's smile was manic. In someone else, such determination might be tantamount to madness, but given what Teraphim had supposedly accomplished, Bina was convinced that whatever the man set his mind to would come to pass, one way or another. He wasn't as reckless as the Rupniks had been. His mind was a cold and calculating thing, and with enough power and wealth, such calculations could change the course of the universe—and not necessarily for the better.

"It's no game," Hyx said. For the first time since she'd met him, his voice faltered.

"Everything is a game," Teraphim corrected. "When you live as long as I have, that becomes apparent. I respect your mettle, Hyx, but make no mistake: I will not allow you to win. I am the oldest of our kind, and my endeavors will outlast yours. I, too, will build something that lasts. And if we are not to build a monument to our people together, so be it... but I will ensure my efforts supersede yours. Whatever you build, rest assured, I will tear it down eventually."

He spun away from them and set off toward the shuttle that had brought him to Azure's surface. Hyx's gaze followed him until he disappeared through its doors. Bina wished she could ask him what he was thinking. Hyx was clever, after all, and he had Omega on his side. Perhaps he'd defeated Teraphim during their lifetimes.

But if that were the case, why would Omega show her this memory? And if

Teraphim had succeeded, what did that mean for their future?

Chapter Eighty-Five

Captain Bill Henderson

Bina was already in the sim when Bill joined, and Al appeared soon after. Both of them linked in near the round table, but Bill appeared on the throne.

"Ha, ha," he said aloud. "You know, this courtly imagery isn't as subtle as you seem to think it is. Are we doing a twist on King Arthur now? Do I have to pull a sword from a stone?"

Tobias, seated between Val and Judith, raised an eyebrow. "Interesting. I'm surprised Arthurian legend survived the Ornu purge of your libraries."

Bill left the throne to pull out a chair around the table, though he didn't yet sit. "Nice to see you again, by the way, Tobias. It's been a minute."

Tobias inclined his head in agreement. "Much has happened between now and then. And much remains to be done. But our table has empty seats that must be filled in the meantime, so...." He waved a hand.

Three more figures appeared, one at each of the remaining chairs. Keating rubbed her knuckles against her eyes and looked around. Norder's jaw dropped. Ridding stumbled and had to support himself on the back of a chair.

"Where are we?" Keating rasped. "Am I still asleep?"

"You are still resting," Val said. "But this is not a dream. Time is short. so we're multitasking."

"Captain?" Norder looked around, taking in the detail of the sim. Bill was so used to Omega whisking him through a variety of realities that he'd forgotten how disorienting the first experience with simspace could be. "Is this...real?"

"I wish I knew how to answer that, Commander. What I can tell you is that Omega brought us here. You've heard about Val, of course. And this is Tobias, and Judith."

Keating and Norder stared in bewilderment at their hosts. Ridding, however, took the information in stride.

"I see they've brought Bina here, too." He folded his arms. "Which means that she's either managed to bamboozle Omega along with everyone else, or that the ship is willing to let traitors through."

Bina wilted in her seat. Bill opened his mouth to call Ridding to task, and to inform him that if he couldn't let go of his grudge, he was no longer part of the crew. Before he could speak, Judith rose to her feet and circled the table.

"James," she said. "Enough. I understand your anger, but the world is not what it was. Many things could have come to pass, but have not. Many things have happened that were most unfortunate. I know you are angry, and you have every right to be. But I also know you have doubts."

He shied away from her touch. The wood of the chair back creaked under Bill's white-knuckle grip, and he forced his hands to relax.

"You can't know what I think," Ridding snapped.

"I know what I'm permitted to know. But what is in your heart is not so difficult to intuit. People change, James." Judith laid a hand on his arm. "You know it to be true, because you have lived it. Nothing is as it once was. While you cling to this anger, you are holding onto a past that no longer exists."

"So you want me to forget what she did?"

It was Bina who answered. "If you hate me so much, drag me to the nearest airlock and throw me into the void. I won't fight you. Or find some other way to kill me. You're right: I've made mistakes. Even if you let yourself forget, I won't. I have to remember, because I can't go back to the way things were. But if the only way to make amends is to perish, so be it. I'll accept your judgment."

"Bina, stop." Bill's voice was harsher than he meant it to be.

She held up a hand. "Ridding seeks redress. And you're the king. Crimes such as the ones I've committed deserve to be punished. Ridding is owed the same justice as any other person aboard this ship. I'm not above the law."

Ridding's mouth opened, but no sound emerged. He looked from Bina to Judith, then to Bill, as if waiting for someone to challenge Bina's words.

Val was watching the conversation with open interest, while Tobias' expression remained neutral.

"No." Ridding cleared his throat. "No, that won't be necessary. If anything like this happens again, I'll put a stop to it, but for now…let's just put it behind us." He sat in the chair that had been provided for him and scooted close to the table, not looking at any of them.

"I am glad to hear the matter is settled," Tobias intoned. "Now, if the rest of you will sit, there is another matter to discuss."

Bill, Keating, and Norder did as they were told. Keating was still side-eyeing Bina, but she seemed to have accepted that Ridding was satisfied, and that the subject, at least for the time being, was closed.

"Excellent." Tobias sat back in his chair and looked around at them. "Now, as to the matter at hand. The upgrading of Omega, with the SRJ drive."

Al leaned in. "What worries me is, I'm not sure how to convince the crews at the scrapyard to install the surge drive. What's to stop them from dawdling and giving the Ornu a heads-up while we're stranded and incapacitated?"

"I can address part of that concern," Val offered. "You will not need the crews to complete the installation. Our drone units will be reassigned from missile manufacturing to drive installation. With their assistance, the short-range jump drive should take approximately five hours to install."

"Five hours?" Bill repeated. "If we can get into the shipyard without being noticed, that's not too bad."

"But it's deep in Ornu-controlled space," Al said. "We can't count on the element of surprise here. We need a solid strategy going in."

Ridding had listened to the plan in silence, but at Al's words, he slapped his palms on the table. "Wait, wait, let me get this straight. We're going to invade the imperial space of the species that until recently enslaved most of humanity. We're going to take their largest shipyard, and we're going to hold it until we've completed extensive upgrades to the Omega, helped by just six ships piloted by our new overgrown rhino-turtle allies. Do I have that about right?"

Norder aimed finger-guns at him. "Bingo."

"And that's the full extent of the plan?" Ridding asked.

"That's why we're here," Val informed him. "To improve the plan."

Ridding rolled his eyes. "Why bother? This is off to a great start already."

His tone was hardly becoming of an officer, and Bill didn't appreciate it. The man was clearly fishing for a reaction, and while his demeanor was incredibly unprofessional—not to mention irresponsible, given the thousands and thousands of lives that hung in the balance—Bill let it slide for the moment. They'd have words later.

Rather than taking the bait, Bill turned to Al. "I'm expecting Jackals to attempt to board the shipyard while the upgrade is happening."

Al nodded. "So am I. The Roughback vessels can guard us from any warships that get sent our way, but we're going to need to guard the drones. If the Jackals, or anyone else, start picking them off, we'll be stranded for a lot longer than five hours. The trouble is, we've only got six exosuits."

"So have Omega make more of them," Ridding said.

Bill blinked at him. "I'm sorry, what?"

Ridding shook his head. His expression of surprise was the mirror of Bill's own. "Omega has enough drones and minerals to build an arsenal of high-tech missiles. Can't it just make enough more exosuits to arm whoever Al wants to bring onto the Marine team?"

"I don't know." Bill pivoted toward Val. "Can it?"

Val raised his eyebrows, tilting his head to one side. "Well, I'm not sure we can build exact replicas. But since you ask, I'm sure we can come up with a suitable alternative." He chuckled at his own pun.

"Well, good, then. Al, please provide Val with a list of people you'd like on your team so that Omega has time to outfit them appropriately."

They talked for another hour, spitballing ideas and fleshing out the promising ones.

Once they were finished, Bill sensed that morale was improving among his officers, for the first time in what felt like an eternity.

They had a direction, and they had a plan. Success was far from guaranteed...but they had new allies, and they had Omega. If they could successfully install the surge drive, who knew what vistas might open to them?

Chapter Eighty-Six

Intern Drusa

When Drusa first joined the lab, she had actually enjoyed her job. It had been academic, unexciting, with each day moving in a comfortably familiar pattern. Mornings were spent poring over artifacts, afternoons in heated discussions with her peers, and evenings were reserved for the library. Several of her more enterprising colleagues enjoyed the occasional night on the town, but Drusa didn't see the appeal. Why drink with strangers or waste her energy on feasts and parties when she had access to the most extensive library on Lindinis, with books just waiting to be devoured?

Alas, her dream job had taken a frustrating if thrilling turn with the discovery of Omega. The ordeal with the humans had sparked a mad scramble among Ornu labs to procure more Primeval tech for analysis. Her cushy academic job had been co-opted by military interests.

Wasn't that always the way of it?

"Have you had a chance to study that probe?" Signifier Rufus asked as he slid past her workstation.

Drusa's forked tongue darted between her teeth. The one I'm looking at right now? she wanted to ask. Her patience had been tested many times in the past weeks, and her frayed nerves would no doubt get her in trouble sooner or later.

She took a deep breath. "My notes are nearly finished, sir."

"Anything unusual to report?"

How would you know what's unusual, if you never read the reports? Drusa merely shook her head.

"I was afraid not." Rufus sighed. He spared her current project a cursory but unschooled glance. He was not an academic, and he had no business in the labs, but she had no choice but to endure his ignorance.

Or quit, perhaps, but that was unthinkable. If she did, she would be barred from the field she had spent her whole life striving toward.

"Well, when you're done, there's another piece that requires inspection."

"Another probe?" she asked, hoping it would be something marginally more scintillating.

"A pod," he said, waving vaguely toward the door of the research facility. "It's on the bay floor."

A pod was only slightly more interesting than a probe, in Drusa's estimation. They came through the lab all the time. For the most part, they were nothing more than cargo storage, although most of them were empty by the time they were picked up.

"Can't Paulus manage it?" she asked, barely keeping the whine from her voice.

"Paulus has his hands full."

She closed her eyes and took a deep breath. Paulus always had some excuse. Nobody seemed to notice that she did twice the amount of work that he got through, all without complaining, but that was a battle she was unprepared to wage at the moment. "I'll see to it after I'm finished here."

"Excellent." Rufus was already moving on. "I'll see you tomorrow, then."

So he was leaving? Why was she even surprised? The military feigned urgency, then wasted her time on busywork. She would run the standard tests and jot down a few rudimentary notes, all of which could go into a file on a server that no one would ever review.

I hope they kill the human rebels soon so that things can go back to normal, Drusa thought sullenly as Rufus disappeared into the hall.

From what she'd witnessed with regard to their efficiency, she wasn't holding her breath.

* * *

The pod, as Rufus had called it, was about the size of a private shuttle, large enough to seat three or four occupants, though she thought its original purpose must have been rather different. Drusa fired up a drone assistant to record her notes and take measurements.

"It looks like a cargo pod," she said, circling the unit. "From what we know of

Primeval society, their settlements were widely dispersed. I would posit that this device was designed to carry perishable cargo long distances." Her enthusiasm rose slightly as she perused the external controls. "Interesting...it locks from the outside. Definitely not meant for personal transport, then. And the panel isn't damaged. There's a very real possibility that whatever was placed in here is still intact." Even if it had degraded, there would still be something to study. She hoped it would be an interesting delivery—perhaps a seed bank sent to help establish a productive biome on a colonized world.

The drone dinged with a text prompt, a reminder to secure the seal on the research dock before activating the panel, to avoid unleashing bacteria that might harm the population of Lindinis.

She nudged the screen. "Yes, yes, I've already done that. And of course I'm wearing my biohazard suit. Who needs that reminder?" Probably interns like Paulus, with the brains of a wibble. She clicked through the standard reminders. "You know, I wonder if we're seeing more of these pods because Omega was activated, or because that original probe somehow interfaced with other existing Primeval tech? If so, the range is remarkable."

The drone dutifully noted her questions, although it offered her no response.

"That would explain the uptick in Primeval tech we're seeing," she mused. "Maybe I should bring it up with the research lead." It might win her some recognition, if she could prove the theory. Such research might even benefit the Ornu military. If they could use Primeval tech to hack Omega's systems, they could sabotage the humans from afar. Blow out their airlock, for example. The problem would solve itself as all their hairless little bodies were sucked into the vacuum of space.

Drusa smiled at the mental image. If she could pull that off, maybe the Emperor would recognize her personally. He might even grant her a research lab of her own.

"Open it," she told the drone.

The device hovered over the controls and began to input random strings of code in an attempt to activate the controls and spring the latch. The Perseids had developed that handy bit of tech. They were a strange, backwards collection of peoples, but at least a few of them had enough brains to problem solve and reverse-engineer old inventions. When she had her own lab, she'd hire a few of them. It would give her workshop a cutting edge.

The drone beeped again and spun its digital face toward hers to reveal the next prompt. She activated it with the press of a finger, and the hatch on the Primeval pod sprung free.

A high-pitched keening noise emerged through the gap. Drusa tried to cover her ears to block the shrill sound, but her biohazard helmet barred the way. With each passing second, the sound increased in volume and intensity, making her head ring and her eyes water. She tried to speak to the drone to issue a verbal command, but she couldn't hear her own voice over the alarm.

Her lower pair of arms whipped out and tried to press the hatch closed again. It shifted under her weight, but something blocked the way.

Drusa let out a strangled sob and fell back. How could a noise be so painful? It was as if someone was digging their talons through her ear holes into the tender flesh of her canals, spearing the delicate organs as it went. Something warm trickled down the side of her head, and she could not tell if it was inside of her or outside. Her vision swam.

She yanked the biohazard helmet away and tossed it aside. Even with her palms fitting snugly against her earholes, the sound penetrated into the very meat of her.

The hatch opened wider. A tall, bipedal, organic-looking lifeform stepped through. It was impossible that a living being could have survived within the pod for so long, and yet the creature moved toward her. It stopped to snatch the drone out of the air and flung it to the ground with such force that the metal casing crumpled.

"Help me!" Drusa cried. "Make it stop!" Her words were lost in the shrill noise.

The figure advanced anyway, catching her by the throat and pressing her lower to the ground. Some dim, dissociated corner of her brain reminded her that the Ornu did not meet the eyes of lesser beings. It was unbecoming.

That was Drusa's last thought before the creature lifted its other hand. The blade of the slim knife it held caught the light.

Then it caught her throat, slicing keenly through scale and muscle and ligament. Straight to the bone.

Chapter Eighty-Seven

Captain Alden Stone

"You mean to tell me Omega could have made us new exosuits anytime it felt like it?" Funny Bone's eye twitched. "But it didn't, because we didn't ask nicely?"

"That's an oversimplification," Al said. "When we first brought the Awn's supply of minerals aboard, Rupnik had effective control of the ship, and then we were deployed to the surface of Kotbulo, where Omega couldn't help us."

"I suppose," Funny Bone grumbled, as he followed the captain through the lower decks, "but I wish we'd discovered that little tidbit earlier. Jana Nemec might still be alive."

"And Hugo Garnier would have had an exosuit to his name."

The sergeant shuddered. "True."

"At any rate, we're getting them now, which is good enough. So if you'll give me a list of the recruits we should be requesting suits for, we'll be in much better shape for the next fight."

Their walk had taken them through civilian corridors, and as they pro-gressed through the section, someone called out to him.

"Hey, boss!" Danny trotted up beside them, who Al recognized from his time helping Miriam. He was a nurse in one of the new makeshift medical wards that had been popping up to provide greater care to the population aboard Omega.

Danny pulled down his mask and grinned. "I was hoping to talk to you, if you've got a minute?"

"Of course."

"Hold that thought. Don't leave!" Danny gestured for him to stay put as he jogged away.

"Are we taking orders from civilians, now?" Funny Bone muttered.

"At ease, Sergeant. Danny's one of the good ones." Friendships were small matters in the grand scheme of things, given that their everyday revolved around clashes with empires. Even so, they were irreplaceable.

Danny returned a few minutes later with a stocky man in tow. "I thought you should meet Blaise. We got to talking about you the other day, and I thought you ought to get acquainted."

Al sized the newcomer up. "What can I do for you?"

"I have some intel you might want." Blaise ran one hand over his bald head. "See, there's this group forming down here. Multinational, no affiliation. Mostly ex-military personnel, working together."

Al tensed, and Funny Bone sucked in a breath. After everything they'd been through with the Slovenians, he had no intention of letting another group get the jump on them—especially not now, with the SRJ drive so close at hand. "You did well to bring this to me. Let's find somewhere more private to talk. I want numbers and names. Who's in their hierarchy? What are they planning?" When Blaise opened his mouth, Al held up a hand to stay him. "Don't answer yet. Just follow me, and try to look casual."

"It's not like that, Captain Stone." Blaise's bemused smile revealed a dimple in one cheek. "I'm part of this group. We're not looking to start anything. We want to help."

"Help? How?"

Blaise shrugged. "I'd have thought that would be obvious. We want to fight the aliens with you. We know about the shipyard, and your plans to take and defend it."

Al narrowed his eyes and took a step closer. "How do you know that?" Another mole was the last thing they needed.

But Blaise stood firm. "I can't tell you. Can't give up our source. But it's a good thing that we know. Because you need the help, and we have the skills to give it."

Al considered him. They'd fostered too many traitors in their midst for him to take this man at face value. On the other hand, they'd need all the help they could get in securing the SRJ drive. Perhaps Blaise and his crew could play a role in defending the ship, even if he wasn't ready to trust them with suits just yet.

"I'll bring it to the captain," he said at last. "But I can't make any promises."

Blaise broke into a grin, like Al had just offered him a Porsche and a ranch in Texas. "That's all I'm asking, Captain Stone."

Chapter Eighty-Eight

Captain Bill Henderson

Bill's crew was smaller than it had once been, but it was still a pleasure to sit on the bridge with all of them in their rightful places. Keating and Norder were seated shoulder to shoulder, Ridding had taken Longfield's old spot, and Bina stood by his side, ready to relay information through the sim to the crew.

Shipyard 83 orbited the heavily populated Imperial planet of Terraco. Unlike Earth, the population of Terraco was non-native. It was an industrial hub of the empire, built on a resource-rich but supposedly unpopulated planet. Some of the texts Bill had read in the academy indicated there may have been an endemic sentient species, but no mention was made of what had become of them.

At present, Terraco was populated by a mixture of allied and vassal species, though they weren't ruled with the same iron fist as the vassal homeworlds.

"You'd think such a valuable planet would warrant more ships guarding the quadrant," Ridding mused.

Norder snorted without looking up from the readings. "Why? Who would be crazy enough to fly a warship into Ornu airspace?" He shot a sidelong glance at the captain. "No offense intended, sir."

"None taken," Bill said, with all the sarcasm he could squeeze into two words. "What defenses are we facing?"

"Four ships," Keating announced. "And some stationary defenses, but they'll have a hard time targeting us once we're docked—unless they want to destroy the shipyard, too."

"I wouldn't put it past them to sacrifice the shipyard if it meant compromising us." Bill tapped one knuckle against his lips while he thought. They'd formulated a plan, but seeing the lay of the land in person always presented new concerns.

He saw that they'd have to dock carefully, and even then, they'd still be a sizable target.

He reached for the com unit on the arm of his command chair. "Tull, are your people in position?"

"We're ready," Tull replied. "Lead the way, Your Highness."

Bill grimaced up at Bina. "See you when we land," he told her, and tumbled into simspace.

Val was waiting for him, the array of weapons and the map of the Terraco defenses at the ready.

"Welcome back, Captain. I await your commands."

Bill snapped his fingers and pointed at the hologram of Shipyard 83. The shipyard was staggering in its size—the biggest any known species had ever built. And the only one in existence large enough to accommodate the Omega.

"I need a map of the shipyard's weapon emplacements, he told Val, "and I want you to map our docking options and transmit them to Norder. While you're at it, mobilize the drones. I want them ready to go as soon as we touch down."

"So demanding," Val teased. Six points of pulsing red light appeared on the simulation of the shipyard. "According to everything I've been able to access in the Ornu schematics, these are the locations of their mounted laser cannons."

Bill stuttered over his next command. "Hold on. You can access Ornu data?"

Val nodded. "Most of it is just waiting to be mined. Their security protocols are lackadaisical at best."

"Can you alter data?"

"That's a bit trickier. If I did, it would likely be noticed, and perhaps flagged by their programmers."

Bill filed that bit of information away. It annoyed him that Val so rarely volunteered relevant information, but at least he seemed to answer truthfully when asked. "Right. Good to know. In the meantime, we're going to target one of the four defense ships. Hit it with dead rounds...no need to waste Hailstorms on this first salvo. Aim for..." He considered the positions of the four ships, then pointed to the closest one. "Here. If they think they have a chance to escape, they may take it. We won't be giving chase. I just want them gone."

"Very good, Captain. I'll convey targeting data and let Keating determine the timing."

Bill would have fired immediately, but Keating waited, probably under the belief that they should bide their time until the last possible moment. A wise choice, when he considered it. The less time the crew of the shipyard had to prepare, the less resistance Al and his crew would face.

Her tactic seemed to pay off. It only took three staggered hits to reduce the vessel to a cloud of debris. The other ships withdrew even as the first was under fire, falling into formation around the planet. They must have assumed Omega had arrived with the intent of striking a blow to the empire's resources.

Good. They hadn't yet guessed Bill's true purpose, which would help buy time.

"Have you figured out how to dock?" Bill asked.

"Norder has determined our course based on the data I provided." Val waved a hand, and a faint outline of Omega drifted across the simulation and into position alongside the shipyard.

Bill studied the positioning, eyes narrowed. "Perfect. Take out the three turrets on our side of the shipyard. But I don't want to risk damaging anything we'll need to install the surge drive."

"Shall I use dumb rounds?" Val asked.

"No. Laserfire. I want the shipyard intact."

One by one, the pulsing dots on the map went dark. Val nodded when only four remained. "There you are. What next?"

"Bring us in." He cocked his head. "Are there any other ships in-system?"

"Eleven Crendelen warships, although three are headed away from Terraco."

Bill quietly cursed. He'd hoped to go a little longer without having to deal with reinforcements. Eight enemy warships shouldn't be a huge concern, but Omega's weapons would be offline during the skirmish while the upgrade was in progress.

"Open the com system. I want us all on the same channel for the moment."

Val dipped his head and the channel opened, flooding the simspace with background chatter.

"Al, can you hear me?" Bill barked.

"Loud and clear," Al replied. "Are we ready?"

"Val will send you a countdown 'til docking time. I want boots on the ground the second the bay opens. We're giving you a sixty-second head start before we deploy the drones to begin installing the upgrade. You've got four turrets to worry about."

"And some incoming warships," Al observed.

Tull cut in. "Leave the Crendelen to us, brothers."

"I trust that you'll handle it, Tull. Al, stay safe and stay frosty." He signaled for Val to disconnect the com. "Looks like we're golden for now. I'm going to pop out and have a quick word with Bina."

Val nodded, and Bill lurched back into the bridge. The same scenario that Val had played out for him in the sim was unfolding before them on the scanners. The mammoth shipyard was almost in range.

"If the warships get past Tull, they're going to fire on us," Bina observed. "Our shields will be down." Her lips were pressed into a thin, tight line, and a muscle jumped in her jaw. "I know this was the plan, Bill, but I hate the thought of being defenseless. Especially here, over an imperial world."

"You're thinking about what we did over Armon?" he asked.

She nodded once. He'd been picturing the same thing: the way they'd filled the atmosphere with shrapnel by blowing apart the Perseids' orbital defense systems. Only this time, they'd be the shrapnel darkening the skies of Terraco.

"It would be a big loss for them," she said. "Not just the cost of the shipyard, but the chaos that would follow. They saw the fallout of what we did to Armon. The people of Terraco wouldn't risk such a thing happening to them."

"Maybe not. But I suspect the Emperor would risk the political backlash of sacrificing Terraco if it meant destroying us."

The worry lines around Bina's mouth deepened, and the scar between her eyebrows puckered. She seemed to have no response to that.

Chapter Eighty-Nine

Captain Alden Stone

The countdown displayed on the inside of Al's helmet ticked down as Omega pulled closer to the docking point. His whole body vibrated with the adrenaline rush of having so many people under his command. After limping along with a shorthanded crew, he had more than tripled the number of fully-equipped Marines in his team, and he had backup to boot.

He and Blaise's corps of volunteers had compromised—Omega had built them modified suits that weren't as high-tech as the model his team used, but that would still allow them to traverse the shipyard and offer some protection from enemy fire. His console included a remote deactivation option for each of the suits, which was also available to Funny Bone.

"I don't like the fact that we've built kill switches into their armor," Funny Bone whispered.

"We can lock them up remotely," Al said. "But it's not like we're going to cut their air. Besides, they agreed to this. We didn't plant a detonator under their skin, for crying out loud." He understood Funny Bone's sentiment, though.

The rest of their core team held no such reservations. Guns was spoiling for a fight, and took every opportunity to whip the new crew into a frenzy. "We're having drumsticks for dinner, kids. Any Crendelen gets in our way, we fry 'em!" She pumped one arm over her head, and the rest of the team, along with

Blaise's volunteer corps, roared their approval.

"Eat the Crendelen?" Tubes asked from the edge of the crowd. "Is that the motto we're going with?"

Al kicked the volume on his external speaker up to max. "One minute, folks! Remember, Marines in the front—we're better equipped to take heavy fire. We'll need to make our way to the other side of the shipyard in order to take the turrets."

The cloud of drones whirred above them as excitement boiled among those about to deploy. Al focused on his breathing to keep from being caught up in the rising fever of their excitement, grounding himself in those last remaining seconds before the adrenaline took over.

The countdown ticked toward zero. The bay doors opened.

Al was the first Marine off the ship.

The new volunteers had been warned about the gravitational shifts, but were clearly unprepared for the reality of leaping out of Omega and into a reduced-grav zone. Shipyard 83 was built to accommodate humongous ships, as well as the resources needed to service them. Setting the workstations to full-grav would have been a waste of power and would have made the work itself more difficult. Why expend resources to weigh down behemoths, only to expend even more dragging metal sheets and struts through the field?

The volunteers, in their lightweight suits, tumbled and bumped through the bay like ungainly versions of the drones that were soon to follow. Those with exosuits moved more gracefully, guided by their onboard AIs.

Al's boots hit the deck of Shipyard 83. He was used to the calculations skimming along the inside of his visor, and he ignored the majority of the readings as he took in his surroundings. This portion of the shipyard was open to space, but there was a large station located along the platform to house the shipyard crew and their equipment. The platform beneath his feet was flat, but the readings indicated there was a second docking point on its other face, which would likely be occupied as well.

He didn't wait for the volunteers to get their bearings as he charged across the platform. Better that they should experiment with their capabilities in the shadow of Omega than in mid-combat.

Besides, the fight was already on its way.

The Crendelen warships hadn't reached the shipyard yet, but the crews weren't going to surrender quietly. He expected a fight.

Although, he didn't expect the form it came in.

He was halfway to the first crew station when gravity kicked up a notch. The tumbling swarm of volunteers hit the deck with grunts that echoed through the open com channel. Al would have fallen, too, if it weren't for his exosuit, whose reinforced joints steadied him even as they became almost impossible to move.

The gravitational field impacted more than just the humans. The platform shuddered beneath their feet as the updated shipyard settings warred with Omega's thrusters.

Omega's systems had the capacity to deal with this new development; the drones did not. Al switched channels to his team's private chat, where he wouldn't have to shout to be heard over the moans of the volunteers.

"Tubes, I need you with me," he said. "We need to take the shipyard's systems."

"Coming, boss." Tubes grunted and began slogging his way in Al's direction.

"As for the rest of you—" Al looked back to see that Splat and Guns were positioned within a cluster of downed volunteer troops. Given the extra strain on their suits, they likely wouldn't be able to step over their newfound allies without crushing them underfoot. "Splat, Guns, stay where you are. Offer cover fire. Christiano, Jennings"—he really hoped that recruit's name was Jennings, or he was going to look like he didn't know his crew, which was truer than he'd like it to be— "back them up. The rest of you, with me. We're taking the station."

Even with his exosuit's hydraulics, traversing the platform was like slogging through molasses. He'd have set it to autorun, which would have spared him the effort of initiating the movements himself, but switching back to manual would cost precious seconds if they came under fire.

He flipped channels again, this time to the officers' coms. "Bill, you're going to have to hold those drones. We have a problem."

"All right, but—"

"I know." Every second the drones weren't deployed meant a delay with Omega's upgrade. "We're working on it. I'll let you know when we're good to go."

At least the shipyard crews were in no hurry to make a stand. The station airlock remained closed when Al reached it. He took a moment to catch his breath while Tubes arranged a handful of small explosives to blow the entrance open.

"Cross your fingers," the petty officer panted, "and hope they haven't upgraded from Plasmodium IVs."

"When the empire improves their systems, you'll have to retire," Al replied.

Tubes snorted. "I wish they would. But I'm not holding my breath." There was a slight pause before he added, "Brace."

Al locked the joints of his suit in place just in time for the blast. The airlock sprang open.

The shipyard's crew had used their time wisely. Construction equipment had been used to form a barricade between the hatch and the crew's last stand. Most of the crew were Kyndega, the diminutive vassal species. Their four legs ended in surprisingly dexterous hands, while their saucer-like eyes stared out from their torsos. Like the Marines, they wore exosuits, although theirs were designed to aid in construction rather than to resist gunfire. Al took aim at the nearest crewman and pulled the trigger of his autocannon.

He'd forgotten to account for the enhanced gravitational field. His shell arced sharply through the air and plunged to the deck in the midst of the construction equipment.

"Nice shooting, boss," Tubes observed.

"Aim high," Al told the group, ignoring the taunt.

His next shot struck a Kyndega worker in the shoulder, punching down and through its suit's bulky paneling. The others scattered, leaving the Marines to fight their way through the equipment.

Under normal circumstances, Al's suit would have allowed him to shove the loaders and transports aside, but with the upped gravity, they might as well have been welded in place.

"Al?" Bill's voice prompted through the com.

"I'm working on it." Al kicked a digi-dolly aside. "Tubes, where are we likely to find the shipyard controls?"

"To our left." Tubes made a painfully slow gesture to their destination. "But it won't mean much if the crew can just switch 'em back."

"We'll worry about the crew. You get the grav field back to normal. Without the drones, the mission's stalled out, and I'd like to get this show on the road. Termite, go with him."

"Roger that." Both men set out for the control room, while Al motioned for the rest of the crew to follow him. The Kyndega had fled to their workshop to make a last stand, but they weren't trained for combat, and Al felt almost guilty facing down a crowd of laborers armed with spanners and hammers.

"Take prisoners, if you can," he told his team. "They might know something we need to—"

"Oh, wow," Tubes' voice cut in.

Al's stomach dropped. "What?"

"They're running the shipyard on Plasmodium III. I swear, it's like they want to be hacked. Seriously, they might as well have printed out an open invitation to steal their stuff. One second…"

Al breathed a sigh of relief as gravity's pull eased back to its former low-grade intensity. The adjustments left him more agile, even in the exosuit. He pushed off with one foot and leapt toward the Kyndega. He had no way to lock into their com channel to demand their surrender, but as the volunteer fighters began to arrive, the Kyndega were quick to lay their weapons aside. They allowed themselves to be restrained and subdued.

"Tubes, Jennings," Al called, "I want you to stay here in case anything happens. We can't let the Imperium retake the shipyard." He directed a few of the new recruits and volunteers to stand guard over their prisoners. Only when the station was secured did he radio Bill. "We're in, Captain. Let the drones do their thing."

As he strode back out of the station, a wave of drones emerged from Omega's bay doors and set to work, moving with all the efficiency of an ant colony. Al admired them for a few heartbeats before sweeping one arm above his head.

"Marines, with me," he ordered. "I won't be happy until we secure those turrets."

Chapter Ninety

Tull of the Roughbacks

"**M**ore gunships incoming," Rula observed. She had agreed to let Tull ride along in her ship, not only as acting co-captain, but also as the unofficial advisor of the overall mission. His relationship to the human forces gave him added insight into their actions and motivations, and earned him respect among the other captains.

He hadn't explained that the humans had more or less blundered into their alliance. They were a fickle and exhausting people, but they were his kin now, according to the will of the All-sire...who, according to the scanners, had also seen fit to pit them against at least a dozen more enemy vessels, including several Jackal gunships.

"Are you seeing this, Henderson?" Tull asked.

"Unfortunately..." He could picture Bill wringing his hands on Omega's bridge. "But we have no reason to assume they know what we're here to do, or how fast we can do it."

"We'll keep them off your back for now," Tull promised. "You focus on your drones and getting the drive installed."

The first eight warships were approaching. Tull changed channels and slipped into the easy familiarity of Roughtongue as he issued commands to the rest of the Roughback ships.

"Stay close, and circle up," he said. "We want to keep as many of them at bay as possible. Use your ammunition wisely—we'll need to keep this bombardment up for five standard hours, at least. If we pick them off in waves, we should be able to watch each others' backs."

"Formation eighteen," Rula advised. "Keep it moving, people!"

There was elegance to Roughback tactics, even if none of the other species could see it properly. Their ships danced around Omega like a flight of motherbirds protecting their communal nests—at least, the way they had before the Ornu razed the surface of Kotbulo and the motherbird population along with it.

Every beautiful image that Tull held deeply in his heart belonged to a world that the empire had scourged. He carried those memories with him as he fought, keeping them alive. The Ornu wouldn't destroy his people's past until they eradicated their future, and try as they might, the asps had yet to succeed with that.

The Roughback ships drew Crendelen fire until the warships were within range before launching the first hunks of rock. The humans had been bewildered by the way Roughbacks cannibalized their own ships to create their artillery, but that only proved the smallness of their mindsets. What was war if not the sacrifice of one's own body in the service of one's belief?

The first chunk of rock tore a hole right through the heart of a Crendelen ship, piercing its hull and collapsing its Engineering deck inward. It careened off-course as its metal framework buckled. The blunt prow scraped along the hull of its neighbor at an acute angle, ripping a gash in the hull.

At Rula's command, they fired another rock right into the second ship's lacerated interior. The resulting tangle of metal and ultralight carbon fiber was glorious to behold.

The other Roughback ships weren't having as much luck. One of the asteroid ships had broken free of their agreed-upon formation. Tull bit back a curse when he realized it had taken a critical hit. The crew had opted to abandon it, and their escape pods skittered away through the night, bright as shooting stars in the light of Terraco's sun. Very likely, they would be caught in orbit for a while until they were picked up, shot down, or their automated systems managed to break free and carry them off to safety.

"One down already?" Rula huffed. "Not good."

"Means we'll have to pick up the slack, is all." Tull fixed his launcher's sights on a third Crendelen warship. The Roughback guidance systems were of the latest design, and their ammo was almost unstoppable at this range.

His shot fired off at the same time two of the other Roughback ships targeted the same vessel. The ship spun erratically with each hit.

"There," Tull said smugly. "Five against five. I think we can handle that, Rula, don't you?"

His co-captain, however, had gone rigid in her seat. "What have we gotten ourselves into?" she murmured.

"What?" Tull turned his attention to the long-range scanners. More ships were coming, but they already knew that. Their number hadn't increased.

"I know that ship." Rula pointed a trembling finger at the screen. "It's not an ordinary craft."

"The Jackal gunships, you mean?"

"Not them. Look." She tapped her finger on the screen. "That ship at the front is an Ornu flagship."

Tull uttered a curse and flipped the mic back on. "I've got some bad news, Captain Henderson."

"The Ornu flagship?" Unlike Rula, Bill Henderson sounded resigned. "Yeah, I see it. It likely has an entirely Ornu crew. The Imperium's not messing around this time."

"You know whose ship it is, don't you?" Tull asked dully.

The human captain hesitated for a prolonged moment. "Please tell me it's not who I think it is."

"I am happy to oblige, unless you think it belongs to Imperator Pertinax, in which case I will not lie to you."

The five surviving Crendelen warships had retreated to the edge of the Roughbacks' optimal firing range. If Tull chose to give chase, he would be leaving Omega open to a flank attack. If they waited here, they'd be facing twenty

ships at once, just begging to be surrounded.

With those odds, Tull wouldn't be able
to protect Omega from being hit—and
with the ship's systems offline, any hit
it took now could cause immeasurable
damage.

And now, on top of all that, they were
fighting an Imperator.

"Well," Bill said, "on the bright side, at
least we know they're taking us seriously."

Chapter Ninety-One

Imperator Pertinax

It would have been a pleasure to lead the Imperial Fleet against Omega, but Pertinax was content with the might of the Crendelen ships. They'd been ravaged by the dozen in other skirmishes, but the Crendelen had brains the size of walnuts, and no sense of style. No cunning. No tactics. With an Ornu flagship at the forefront of this firefight, victory was assured.

"Anything noteworthy on the scanners, Secundus?" he asked. From the top of the command dais, he could see all the consoles where his Ornu bridge crew were stationed.

"In addition to Omega, there are five Roughback ships." Secundus glanced over his shoulder. "There were six, but our reinforcements already destroyed one."

"The humans and the Roughbacks," Pertinax intoned, his voice laden with disgust. "What a fine alliance. The weakest of our vassal species paired with the dullest. They deserve each other."

"Duller than the Kyndega?" Secundus asked.

Pertinax lifted his chin. "At least they know their place." The Roughbacks and the humans thought so highly of themselves. Their delusions of grandeur knew no bounds. They truly thought themselves a threat to the Imperium's order, even though their worlds had been rendered barren and Defunct.

They disgusted him. It would be his pleasure to render the final verdict on their fate.

As for Omega…beneath his scales, Pertinax's skin itched. He had tried his best to forget the visions he'd experienced on the Primeval ship, but he still woke in the dead of night, sometimes convinced that he was covered in blood, or that a wibble had crawled into bed with him to pluck out his eyes or crawl between his lips and tear at the soft flesh of his tongue. The mere thought was enough to make him lift his hand to his throat and shudder.

Aware that Secundus was watching him, and unwilling to let one of his subordinates witness his weakness, he cleared his throat. "We'll make a run at the Roughback vessels. Put the Jackals out front. Their ships should be able to dodge whatever those animals throw at us." Jackal gunships were smaller and more maneuverable, designed exclusively for combat, while the Mark VIs were also meant to transport soldiers and equipment. "Have them draw

Roughback fire and disorient the vessels. The Everwell has her orders, and I want a backup with her to ensure that the mission succeeds. Everyone else will keep the Roughbacks engaged."

"What about Omega?" one of the junior officers asked.

Pertinax slithered down from the dais and clasped his hands behind his back. He kept his eyes fixed on the screens, even as he offered his reply. "Omega appears to be offline. Given their choice to dock at a shipyard, I can only assume the ship is compromised in some way. We will never have a better opportunity than this." Like the wibbles in his nightmares, they would seek out the tender, vulnerable parts of the ship and mutilate it from within. Omega would perish in the skies over Terraco… or else, Pertinax would be sent to an early grave. There was no alternative.

Secundus relayed his orders, and the Jackal gunships broke away from the fleet, weaving between their larger counterparts. There were six of them altogether, along with a dozen Crendelen-crewed vessels, Pertinax's own flagship, and the five that had survived the Roughbacks' first onslaught.

The might of the Roughback warships was soon on full display. Their synchronized flight formations were effective, and their timed barrages were brutal and controlled enough that even the infamous Jackals couldn't outrun them. As he watched, one of the hired gunships was obliterated by a chunk of glittering rock.

The two specially outfitted Crendelen vessels broke apart from the others. They went dark on the screens, coasting toward their destination on the shipyard with only critical life support systems engaged. It made them harder to pick up on the scanners, although they were hardly invisible. Luckily, the Roughbacks had their hands full, and failed to notice the enemy ships creeping toward Shipyard 83. At least, they failed to engage them, anyway.

Pertinax spared a sliver of his attention for each stage of the plan, but he was also watching the readings coming off of Omega. Like the pair of Crendelen warships, the behemoth had gone dark, diverting all of its remaining power to life support.

If it was part of a scheme on Henderson's part, Pertinax couldn't divine the play. They had come a long way into hostile space, which suggested true desperation. His heartbeat quickened, keeping pace with his certainty that this, at last, was his chance to redeem himself.

He had lost Omega to the humans.

He would also be the one to win it back.

"Send the other ships closer," he ordered. "Tell them to prepare their shuttles. If the Everwell fails, we'll deploy every soldier we've got. In the meantime, crowd the Roughback ships. If their goal is to defend Omega, they won't risk firing on the ship...or each other."

His orders came to life in real time as the ships responded. Pertinax crossed his lower set of arms over his chest and used his upper pair to adjust the collar of his uniform absentmindedly. The fleet matched the Roughback formation with a tactical arrangement of their own, spreading out to avoid catching blowback from their damaged allies, while gradually separating the modified asteroids ships from the behemoth they had hoped to defend.

"The Everwell is docking," Secundus announced. Pertinax couldn't see the far side of the platform on visual, but he trusted the intel. Even better, despite their creeping approach, Omega still hadn't responded with defensive fire.

"Shuttles are loaded," the junior officer announced.

Pertinax chuckled in anticipation. "Let's see what Everwell can manage." The ship's crew had been offered up as a sacrifice. If all went well, Omega would soon be dead in the water.

And Pertinax would finally have his revenge.

Chapter Ninety-Two

Sergeant Shawn 'Funny Bone' Piker

Funny Bone was only a few steps behind his captain when they reached the edge of the platform. A transition point was built onto the edge of the deck, allowing people and equipment to navigate from one side of the shipyard to the one perpendicular to it with minimal difficulty.

His stomach still flipped with the perspective change, and several of their new teammates and members of the volunteer militia came to a halt, disoriented by the first ninety-degree shift. They lingered on the twenty-foot span of ribbed metal while the more experienced crew pressed on.

When they had emerged from Omega's cargo bay, Terraco had lain below their feet. That side of the platform faced open space, and had been designed to accommodate megafreighters and new construction. The transition point placed Omega at their backs and had them facing down toward the planet's surface. Terraco's gravity was neutralized by the shipyard's onboard gravity field, but even after months, if not years, spent shipboard, there was still something instinctive that told most people, Running sideways down a wall will get you killed.

A dozen strides later, Funny Bone met the next transition point, and his perspective flipped again. Terraco was now overhead, with Omega's outline looming large below.

Three relatively smaller bays lay before them, large enough to accommodate warships like the Mark XIs favored by the Ornu military. Only one of the bays was occupied. Unfortunately, the enemy warship was still online.

"Turret at ten o'clock!" AI boomed, indicating their first target. The tower was designed to defend against enemy airships, not shipboard rebellions, and judging by the erratic laser fire from the mounted gun, it also wasn't built to fire on itself.

The engineers who'd installed it must not have foreseen a circumstance in which they'd need to fire on their own. The Kyndega were notoriously loyal to the Imperium, after all, and point-blank laser fire could cause real damage to the shipyard's structural integrity.

The warship had no such limitations. Funny Bone had barely passed the transition point when it opened fire on them.

The exosuits were built to take a beating, but a direct hit from shipboard laser fire could roast him like a Thanksgiving turkey. At least the reduced gravity meant his response times were more manageable. He pivoted away from the turret and returned fire. He managed to blow one of the warship's turrets off its base before drawing fire. As the enemy set their sights on him specifically, Funny Bone dove behind a stack of metal sheets intended for hull repairs.

He looked around to reassess, surveying the stacks of materials to get a better lay of the land. Crendelen were swarming out of the warship, but they seemed disinclined to engage, even when Funny Bone shot one in the back.

"Not very sporting," Splat said wryly as he skidded to a stop at Funny Bone's side. "Are we taking her?"

"No. Just covering ourselves until Al secures the shipyard turret," Funny Bone said.

"Too bad. I wouldn't mind turning the Ornu's weapons back on them." Splat shot him a sidelong glance. "They wouldn't see that coming."

A slow grin spread across his face. "When you put it like that..." Funny Bone looked over his shoulder. "Kan! Awad! New orders!"

The two new recruits doubled back to their side, while the rest swarmed the turret. They'd have it captured in a matter of minutes, judging by numbers alone. The Crendelen were launching little forays along the edge of the battle, but they must have decided to defend the other two defense turrets, given that the first was so clearly lost to the human assault.

"We're making for the Mark XI," Funny Bone said. "Shoot to kill."

Kan and Awad nodded in unison and slipped away between the shipyard supplies. Funny Bone and Splat went the other way, sneaking along between the supplies to flank the cargo bay door from each side.

A handful of Crendelen remained to guard the warship, but it was fewer than Funny Bone would have anticipated. Awareness of their unusual strategy continued to ping in the back of his brain, warning him that something was off. The Crendelen weren't usually this sloppy.

We surprised them, he told himself. They're still getting their bearings. It wasn't like they were known for being brilliant tacticians, after all.

They caught the handful of Crendelen soldiers off-guard and blasted through their cheap, lightweight suits, sending plumes of feathers spewing through the rips in their armor. Above them—below them?—a handful of ships passed between their heads and the face of Terra-co.

"Why aren't they firing on us?" Kan asked. He was right: their laser cannons were trained on the Omega, but they weren't firing at this side of the shipyard.

"Dunno," Funny Bone admitted. Perhaps he'd missed something—maybe there was a plan after all.

Bright bolts of laser fire issued from the turret that Al and the rest of the crew had targeted first. Funny Bone let out a whoop of joy when it scorched a series of holes in the side of the nearest enemy vessel. His exclamation was echoed across the channel by other voices. They'd taken the defense turret.

Splat had already ducked through the bay of the warship when the platform beneath their feet bucked alarmingly. His first thought was that the new group of attacking vessels had finally opened fire, but when he looked around, he saw that one of the other turrets had gone up in smoke.

The second exploded about ten seconds later. He was watching for it, and could tell that it hadn't been fired on. Funny Bone could have kicked himself for being so dense.

"Al!" he yelped. "The Crendelen are laying explosives. They're going to take out our surface defenses!"

Al's response was unintelligible.

Kan and Awad followed Splat onto the ship. Funny Bone hesitated on the shipyard platform, caught between loyalties. Al hadn't authorized this maneuver, and if the Crendelen were targeting turrets, they'd be converging on the spot where the human forces had gathered.

"Al?" he tried again, this time on the closed team channel. All he got was static "Guns? Termite?"

Nothing.

They're jamming our channels, he realized. They wouldn't be able to coordinate a retreat or organize their defensive positions if they couldn't rely on their coms.

Indecision was still pulling him in two when the approaching warship opened fire on the last turret.

The audio abruptly cut back in, flooding his helmet's speakers with screams. Funny Bone's throat closed up and his esophagus stung with a sudden surge of bile. The shipyard's defenses were down, and the ground crew needed control of the stolen warship now more than ever.

"Sergeant!" Splat called.

"Coming," Funny Bone rasped. He bolted through the Mark XI bay doors.

Right into a circle of hired Jackal mercenaries.

Chapter Ninety-Three

Commander Bina Chakravarti

"The platform is damaged," Bina announced. "All three of the turrets are down, and I have no communication with AI or the Marine team."

Bill hissed a curse and turned to Keating. "What have you got for me, Lieutenant?"

Keating's hands flew across the controls. "We're down to thirteen enemy ships."

The Roughback bombardment had been astonishing to watch. The theoretically simple thruster-powered, asteroid-chunk volley had allowed them to inflict a staggering amount of damage in an incredibly short time. Unfortunately, they were in a marathon rather than a sprint, and the incoming intel from the Roughback ships made it clear they were quickly exhausting their resources. Their firepower, as well as their corresponding defenses, were down.

Bill punched his fist into the opposing palm. "Please tell me they at least hit the flagship?"

Keating merely shook her head.

Bill rubbed a hand over his face.

"—aptain?"

Bina jumped as a voice crackled through her coms. "Al?" she asked.

"Not Al—kkssh—lost the connection—kkssh—jammed our channels, but—" The voice gradually became clearer. "I think I've hacked it. Can you hear me now?"

With the improved communications quality, she was able to identify his voice. "Tubes, what's going on down there?"

"A whole crew of Crendelen laid explosives along the platform. And they found a back way through the workstations. I don't know why we didn't think of that—of course there's a way to go between the workstations without stepping out into the void."

Bina exchanged a worried look with Bill. "Are you okay, Tubes?"

"We're fine...scared some Crendelen silly, but I don't think they were expecting us. This face of the shipyard is secure for now, but it sounded like they roughed up the other side pretty good with explosives. Have you heard from Captain Stone?"

Bina shook her head, knowing full well Tubes couldn't see her, but her voice had gotten lodged in her throat. They'd known this would be a tough battle, and that they would be at their most defenseless during the upgrade, but she hated the thought of leaving their people undefended even though they were so close.

Assuming they were still alive.

"No," she managed at last. "No, we're...we're in the dark, too."

On the scanners, the Roughback ships were hemmed in by the encroaching fleet. A wave of shuttles was descending on the shipyard. Did that mean the first ships' mission had failed, or that they'd managed to take out the rest of the Marine team?

Bina leaned forward, cupping both hands over her mouth and doing her best to catch her breath. They're dead. They're all dead...

And if that were true, what chance did Omega stand?

It was too late to simply disengage from the shipyard and flee. This deep in the system, they were already surrounded. They'd need the SRJ drive in order to make an escape, but the installation was hours away from being completed.

Norder let out a soft cry and pointed to the screens. A second Roughback ship broke apart, scattering rocky debris in every direction. She couldn't tell the ships apart from this distance, and had no idea if the destroyed ship was the one on which Tull had been co-captain.

Another sound chimed through the bridge, and Ridding swiveled his chair toward them. "We've got an incoming message," he said in a hollow voice.

Bill spun one hand through the air in a silent injunction to play it.

Ridding nudged the controls, and three of the bridge's primary screens lit up with a video of a smug-looking Ornu Imperator. Bina had never seen him without his goggles before, but she recognized Pertinax at once. Her skin prickled at the sight of those strange, slanted pupils. Vassal species never looked an Ornu in the eye and lived.

The implication was clear: regardless of what they did, they would not be permitted to leave Terraco alive.

Pertinax smirked down at them through the cameras. "You're in a very bad situation, aren't you, Captain?"

Bill sighed. "Imperator—"

"It's just a recording," Ridding interjected. "He can't see us. We received the message as a drop. Looks like they're not interested in having a conversation."

"Right." Bill rubbed the wrinkle between his eyes. He dropped into the command chair. "My mistake. I should have expected that."

Pertinax was still speaking, so Ridding had to roll the message back a few seconds to make sure they caught it all. "—aren't you, Captain? Twenty more warships just entered the system, all under my command. I have limitless resources at my disposal. You have a cargo ship bogged down with refugees. The only hope for your species is your immediate surrender. If you do that, I will petition Emperor Albus to show your species some level of mercy. Of course, this will only apply if you surrender at once. And don't you owe that to the last survivors of your species? Don't they deserve a chance?" Pertinax leered at the screen. "I will accept your surrender, or carry out your extermination. It matters very little to me."

The message blinked out, and the screens resumed their display of the battle. A cold sweat had broken out all over Bina's body. Fear was nothing new to her. She had faced death before, but she had never wanted to live so badly. She felt as if she'd spent her whole life sleepwalking, barely clinging to her will to survive. Omega had given her purpose and direction. It had made her feel that there might be something more out there.

It had made her feel.

She wasn't ready to give that up.

"You aren't seriously considering surrender?" Ridding asked. His hawklike eyes were fixed on Bill, his lips pursed in a disapproving frown.

"They'd have me executed," Bill said, but distantly, as if he was discussing a mathematical equation rather than his own demise at the hands of a tyrannical empire. Perhaps his perspective was different from the rest of theirs, having already been executed once and survived.

Or perhaps he, like Bina, couldn't see how they would escape their predicament alive.

"Captain," she snapped. "Bill. You can't be serious."

He lifted his head to meet her gaze. She saw the pain there, and the uncertainty. "Let no person value their comfort over the lives of their neighbors. That's what Omega preaches, isn't it? I'm sure I heard Val say that, once."

Bina narrowed her eyes. "If you surrender to Pertinax, you won't have saved anyone, even if you get to play the martyr."

Ridding tilted his head to one side and let his eyes sweep over her.

"Do you disagree?" she asked.

"No," Ridding said slowly. "Even if Pertinax was true to his word, which I highly doubt, the Emperor's mercy would likely resemble my imprisonment. There's no Earth to go back to. The only way out is through, and if we die, we die together."

Bina nodded. It seemed they were confronted by a narrow pathway, filled with brambles. But if they were willing to bleed and press forward together, there might just be easier and more welcoming trails ahead.

"Together," she agreed. To Bill she added, "You promised people freedom. The only thing Pertinax can offer them is torment. They put their trust in you."

"We all did," Keating added softly.

Bill took a deep breath and sat back in the command chair. "In that case, the only thing to do is hold on. And to hope."

Chapter Ninety-Four

Corporal Bob 'Splat' Oriel

Jackals tended to come in groups of nine. Splat was used to fighting two-to-one odds, or worse, but Jackals were a whole different ballgame. Four humans against nine giant lizards?

No thanks.

For the moment, he could only see four of them, which meant the other five were either somewhere on the ship-yard, or waiting for them inside the warship.

Either way, not great.

The nearest Jackal hissed at him and dropped back into a defensive stance.

Splat responded by firing right into the creature's face.

At point-blank range, it should have been a guaranteed hit, but the Jackal leapt into the air before the round left the head of the autocannon. Splat ducked, only to have a Jackal hit him from behind and drive him chest-first into the deck.

The weight was only on his back for a moment before the Jackal was hit by another shot. A hand closed around the back of Splat's exosuit and hauled him upright, revealing his rescuer to be Funny Bone. The sergeant gave him a once-over before shouting something.

The coms were dead in Splat's ears, and he couldn't lipread his superior's commands. Funny Bone must have realized this, because he shoved Splat toward the bay doors, hard enough to make him stumble.

Right. The mission. They didn't have to fight a pack of Jackals; they just had to figure out a way to beat them.

Splat lumbered toward the interior airlock that separated the bay from the inner corridors. He had the disorienting sensation of being back on the Tennyson, having just returned from one of countless missions. How could he be nostalgic for the old days, when the old days had been so terrible?

His sentimental musings were cut short by three sharp blows to his back that knocked the breath from his lungs. He staggered, but managed to keep his footing. The percussive blasts were surely gunfire, and while he was rattled like a sardine in a tin, the exosuit's protective material did its job. He pressed on.

He'd just activated the interior airlock, prompting the hatch to open, when he was hit again. The resulting pain was instantaneous and blinding—the sensation started at the base of his neck, slightly above and directly between his shoulder blades. The shell didn't pierce his armor, but the blow rolled his shoulders forward while his neck snapped back, resulting in the closest thing to whiplash one could experience inside the metal reinforcements of the exosuit.

He staggered forward and caught himself on the edge of the hatch. "Funny Bone, can you hear me?" he called.

Nothing. Splat might as well have been alone, and if he understood the plan correctly, he needed to get to the bridge.

Alone.

The Jackal that had shot him was right on his heels. Splat used the edge of the airlock hatch to push off with both feet, swinging himself through the hatchway in an arc. The move would never have worked with the platform's gravity at full power, and he dented the interior bulkhead when his back hit the metal paneling, but the move brought him out of the Jackal's way just in time. The alien slammed into the bulkhead, rather than tackling him.

He let go of the airlock frame and pushed off again, this time landing in a graceless heap on top of the Jackal. The alien squirmed and thrashed beneath him, and even managed to get in a blow with its tail that nearly sent him sprawling. Inspired by the still-throbbing pain in his upper back, he palmed the back of the Jackal's helmet and pulled back sharply. The alien's back bowed, arching away from the deck at what must have been a painful angle.

Splat pressed the head of the auto-cannon between the Jackal's shoulder blades and fired point-blank. Twice.

The alien went limp in his grip.

"That's why you shouldn't let the Imperium sign your paychecks," he panted. "Those snakes are gonna get you killed."

He kicked the body as he struggled back to his feet. Funny Bone, Kan, and Awad were still holding their own in the cargo bay. The rest of the Jackal squad had appeared, and Splat hoped the Mark XI was otherwise unmanned.

"Sorry, guys," he murmured. "I'm coming back for you."

One of the Jackals turned to look at him. Its shoulders rolled forward, in obvious preparation to tackle him.

He engaged the airlock just as the beast charged, head lowered like a running back, with its long tail whipping back and forth behind it. Splat didn't lift his gun. Instead, he pressed his thumb to the emergency override button.

It reached the airlock just as the hatch closed. Usually the sensors would have stopped it from mangling a body, but Splat's thumb was still firmly in place.

The Jackal's exosuit held shape for almost three seconds. It thrashed, trying to free itself from the hatch, but it held it in place.

Then the suit buckled, and the hatch closed. The Jackal stopped moving.

Good thing this is a Mark XI. He knew this ship like the back of his hand, and he knew all its operational quirks. The Ornu had long thought that conformity would be their path to conquest, but—like with Tubes and those stupid Plasmodium controls—that very conformity made it easier to hack from the inside.

He activated the secondary airlock, waited for the green light, then limped off down the corridor toward the bridge. Rather than fading, the pain in his neck and back seemed to amplify with each movement. He stretched his neck, hoping for some relief, and felt something in the suit give way with the motion. An alert popped up on the inside of his visor, telling him his suit's envelope was compromised. If he tried to leave now, he'd suffocate in the thin air of the shipyard's platform.

So he'd have to complete the mission successfully in order to survive. What else was new? The threat of death had been hanging over his head his entire life, and had lost much of its potency. Now, there was something more than base survival to fight for, a future in which he could be...free.

They all could be.

He kept up his internal pep-talk even as the fingers of his left hand tingled and started to go numb. At one of the corridor intersections, he stumbled across a pair of Crendelen, and fired wildly. Both of them went down before they had the chance to fire off a single shot.

They were the only resistance he encountered before the bridge. There, in the hatchway, he came to a halt.

Splat had somehow forgotten that all Mark XIs had an Ornu Signifier stationed aboard. Humanity had always required extra supervision, but the Crendelen were considered more compliant.

Then again, who would be compliant about being sent on a suicide mission for their overlords? Of course an Ornu had been stationed on the ship. He should have expected it.

The asp lifted his head as Splat entered the chamber. Its forked tongue flicked between its teeth.

A lifetime of pain and punishment had taught Splat to fear the wrath of his betters. His body locked up of its own accord.

The Ornu Signifier reared up to his full height. Perhaps he sensed Splat's decision paralysis. Perhaps they both responded according to their training, with the mutual understanding that one was inherently superior to the other.

Splat stared at the Ornu's face, mesmerized by the subtle swivel of its head, the lithe movements of its body, the sheer unrelenting size of it. For generations, these creatures had tormented the people of Earth.

No more, Splat decided. I refuse to be afraid.

In a move that would have spelled his certain death only months before, he swung the autocannon head onto his shoulder and fired, point blank, into the asp's face.

Then he limped over to the nav station. Sure enough, one of the crew had implemented a signal-jammer, which was still blocking their coms. Splat powered it down, then lowered himself into the nav chair.

"Funny Bone, can you hear me?" he asked as he fired up the engines. He knew the controls by heart.

"Splat!" The sergeant's voice was hoarse. "Are you on the bridge?"

"Sure am, Sarge. I need you to hold onto something. Are Kan and Awad with you?"

"We're here." Kan's voice was clipped. "But the sergeant is hit. We're surrounded."

Splat didn't ask how bad the hit was. There was nothing he could do from this distance. "Make sure he's secure, and lock your boots to the deck. You see the setting?"

"I do, but—"

"Don't try to hold onto anything!" Splat warned. He lifted off from the shipyard, steering mostly one-handed thanks to the numbness that was spreading down his left arm. "And let me know when the Jackals are gone."

The shipyard's gravitational field only extended a few thousand yards from its surface. Splat felt the minute when they punched through the envelope, prompting a strangled cry from the men on the other end of his com. The ship's warnings flashed to inform him that the bay doors had been left open. The three hundred and sixty degree sensors showed that several flailing figures and a fair bit of cargo were disgorged into the vacuum.

"Jackals are gone!" Awad yelped. "We're sliding, though, one of Kan's boots is malfunctioning..."

Given that they were both wearing newly-minted exosuits, Splat figured it was more likely user error than technical issues, but that didn't stop him from activating the bay doors.

"Everyone okay?" he asked.

"The Jackals sure aren't," Funny Bone chuckled grimly. At least he was alive. Quite possibly, they were the only two survivors of their original team.

"Ha ha," Splat deadpanned. "Get up to the bridge, Sarge. We need to figure out our next move."

Seen from ground level on the shipyard, things had looked bad. From on high, they were revealed to be worse. The shipyard was pockmarked with blackened scars from where the other Mark XI had taken out the mounted turrets with laserfire. Dozens of shuttles the size of the Can filled the surrounding airspace, bearing more soldiers. Even if Al and the others had survived the destruction of the turrets, they would soon be overrun.

If the enemy managed to breach Omega's hull in its defenseless state....

Best not to think about that.

Splat banked to one side. A com alert popped up at the neighboring station, but he ignored it. As soon as the Crendelen discovered that they'd managed to take a ship, they'd become a new target. He wanted to see the drones, to get a sense of how much work remained on the drive installation. Time lost all meaning while in combat.

What he saw instead was an explosion of rock. Small chunks of condensed minerals bounced off the Mark XI's hull. Two of the Roughback ships had collided, sandwiching a Jackal gunship between them. All three were destroyed on impact.

Hurry up, Omega, Splat thought, turning his attention to the Primeval behemoth so that he wouldn't have to watch the enemy ships pick off the Roughback escape pods one by one. We can't hold out much longer.

Chapter Ninety-Five

Tull of the Roughbacks

Rula uttered a haunting refrain even as she chose their next target. Tull couldn't bring himself to join in, even though the melody was the same one that sang in his blood. His brothers and sisters had chosen to sacrifice themselves to further a mission he had brokered.

He could not shoulder the whole of the blame, for the All-sire had spoken in favor of humanity. If this was his will, so be it. Tull had chosen to remain neutral during the humans' internal conflict, and Bill Henderson had come out on top again and again. How could one man have survived such impossible odds without divine approval?

Even so, Tull had taken action at a key moment...and now his people, his kinsmen, were dying.

Mora had foreseen this. She had known what was at stake, but that knowledge did little to assuage Tull's guilt.

"What now?" he asked Rula.

She flinched. "Structural integrity is at thirty-seven percent—" Another light flashed on her screen. "Make that thirty-six."

He inhaled through his mouth. Out through his nostrils. "How much longer can we hold out?"

"If we don't get hit, perhaps...one Imperial hour?"

He could have reached out to Bill to ask for an update, but what was the use? Calculations wouldn't save them.

The work would be done when it was done, and not a moment before, or it would never be done at all.

"Shall we go on the offensive?" Rula asked.

Tull considered their only other surviving ship. If they launched an attack now, they would do so knowing that they would not survive. Short of crashing into one of the Crendelen ships the way their kinsmen had done, they wouldn't be able to inflict much more damage before their ship gave way of its own accord.

"No," he said. "We hold the line here. Protect Omega from this angle. They're already diverting their forces to the platform—Al and his people will hold them off, if they can. If we go down, Omega will be destroyed. We target the incoming firepower, and that's all." He didn't have to articulate the fact that, one way or another, this would be the fleet's final attack. "We'll draw this out as long as we can."

Which wouldn't be much longer, but it was the only viable option available. If the All-sire smiled on them, they would pull off another miracle.

If he did not...

Then Tull might as well have exposed his throat beneath the tarnished steel blade of the Disseverer.

Chapter Ninety-Six

Private Jorge 'Termite' Gonzalez

P rivate Jorge Gonzales was not sure how long he'd lain beneath the rubble of the pulverized turret. He'd cried out for help more than once, even as he tried to punch his way free of the wreckage. The suit had kept him from being crushed, but he could barely bend his limbs, and was finding it impossible to build up enough momentum to do more than stir the debris that pinned him in place.

"Help," he panted. "Someone, please…"

The channel was dead. Or, maybe it was working just fine, and he was the only person left alive on the shipyard. He wriggled again and paddled his feet as much as he could.

Quite suddenly, his perspective shifted. The detritus blocking his line of sight was lifted away, and a gloved hand closed over his own.

Guns' suit looked as if it had been fed through a trash compactor, and Al's face was so pale he might have been mistaken for a corpse. Guns tapped the side of her helmet and shook her head, indicating that their coms were down, too.

"What happened?" Termite asked, gesturing with his hands to drive his point home. He looked around at the wreckage of what had been Shipyard 83's defensive turret.

Mixed in with the debris were dozens of bodies. Termite's gorge rose as he took in the carnage. Those who had been farther away from the turret, like him, were still trying to drag themselves free. Those who had been hit directly...

He turned his head away from the dead, only to find more blank-eyed corpses staring up at him through the visors of their helmets. Closing his eyes didn't help, since images of Porker and Newbie danced inside his eyelids.

Guns waved her arms frantically, trying to get their attention, then pointed to the sky. Termite had been so taken aback by what lay around them that he'd forgotten to look up.

A swarm of shuttles was converging overhead, bringing more Imperium soldiers with them. Termite looked around frantically for his M234, but there was no sign of it anywhere. The metal clips that secured the heavy ammo can to his suit were mangled and broken.

He was unarmed.

Al was already getting the attention of the surviving militia members and the new Marine recruits, miming a complicated series of orders that the terrified volunteers couldn't possibly comprehend. Termite waved to Guns, then indicated the broken clips and mimed looking around for his weapon before shrugging. Her answering grimace was accompanied by a movement of her lips as she cursed.

Al moved away, still miming orders. The first of the enemy shuttles had already touched down. Two warships circled overhead, although one appeared to be moving away, perhaps to make room for the shuttles.

Guns waved and motioned for him to follow. She made a strange gesture with her hands, like two objects fitting together. He shook his head, and she sighed. She repeated the gesture again, this time mouthing a word.

"Cubes?" he asked. Hearing it aloud made it click. "Tubes!" Of course. The petty officer was still waiting in the shipyard station with a bunch of untested volunteers. He could be in danger—and if the Imperium's soldiers retook the shipyard, they were screwed.

Guns nodded and took off, not to the edge of the platform as he'd expected, but to a small building in between the three bays. There was a dead Jackal outside the hatch. Termite stopped to look it over.

Guns tapped his shoulder and flipped one hand toward the hatch. Come on.

He held up one hand and motioned, Wait, before retrieving the dead alien's weapons. There was a massive blade at its side, with a hook on the tip meant for rending, as well as a lightweight rifle. When she saw what he was doing, Guns nodded her approval.

The shuttles were already touching down. Others had opted to stay airborne and pick off the human forces from a distance. Termite wasn't sure what was worse: not being able to hear anything and being forced to imagine their situation, or being able to hear what would surely be the screams of the dying.

Guns led him to an airlock, much like the one Tubes had blown open on the other side of the platform. She jabbed at the controls a few times before Termite nudged her aside. The blade he'd taken from the Jackal was thin and deadly sharp, and once he figured out how to wedge the hooked end into the seal around the hatch, he was able to pry it open. He destroyed the blade, and probably the airlock, in the process. So be it. Even a big knife wouldn't do him much good in a gunfight anyway, and if the Jackals could open the airlock that easily, the hatch wouldn't have held them off in the first place.

He tossed the blade aside when the airlock swung open. Guns gestured for him to retrieve it and pointed to the second airlock, but he shook his head. He placed his back to the hatch and pulled the outer airlock partway shut behind them, leaving a large enough gap that they could easily shoot through, but making it difficult for their enemies to target them. It would be the perfect way to hold the tunnel, while Al and the others focused their attention on the transition points at the lip of the platform.

Above them, one of the warships opened fire, although for some reason it hit a few of the shuttles, as well as the closest Mark XI to it. Termite frowned in confusion, but any curiosity he felt was quickly dampened by the sudden return of the coms.

Well, that answered one question: hearing the battle was worse than ignorance by far.

With the screams of injured and dying men and women ringing in his ears, the battle resumed for him in earnest. A shuttle's worth of Crendelen rushed at them, presumably in hopes of using the tunnel to access the shipyard's control center. He and Guns returned their fire. There was no way to miss, but the sheer number of their enemies was staggering.

In short order, the ground around them was littered with the bodies of dead Crendelen, and more than a few Jackals. But more were coming. With his back to the airlock, Termite had nowhere to go. No choice but to hold his position.

The Crendelen kept coming, and his ammo soon ran out, making whatever was left in Guns' can all that remained between them and being overrun.

If they fell, Tubes would fall.

And if the shipyard was taken before the SRJ drive was installed, there would be no survivors.

Chapter Ninety-Seven

Captain Bill Henderson

Bill watched the two surviving Roughback ships hollow out their cores with volley after volley, defending Omega from harm. He pressed both hands to his face and breathed into his palms. Was it his imagination, or was the air in the bridge getting thinner?

Certainly, the ship was quieter than usual, despite the display taking place outside. With all of its systems on their lowest settings, and the massive engines powered down, the bridge was preternaturally quiet. He could hear the ragged breathing of his crew.

"Pertinax is going to destroy the station," Keating said. Her tone was flat and unaffected, almost disinterested.

Ridding hummed. "Even with all the Jackals aboard? If he sacrifices them, they'll never work for the Imperium again. They're not like the vassal species. They'll resent being used as cannon fodder."

Norder scoffed. "You haven't met Pertinax. He's ruthless, and I'm not sure he's smart enough to think that far ahead."

Ruthless and reckless. It seemed to Bill that he'd been facing down a lot of enemies that fell into both those categories lately.

What worried him was that both qualities might just as readily describe himself, too.

Bina choked on a cry, and Bill's eyes refocused in time to watch the next-to-last Roughback ship shatter into sand and pebbles. Time was running out, and with the ship's systems focused on the upgrade, he couldn't even ask Val for advice.

He couldn't talk to the ship. He couldn't trust his impulses, which had been honed in years of Ornu "reeducation." All Bill had left was his subconscious. He closed his eyes, pressed his fingertips to his eyelids until he saw stars, and breathed deep.

I'm in the wrong place, he thought. I don't want to die on the bridge of this ship. I don't want my last thoughts to be about the number of missiles in our arsenal, or the whims of the Ornu, or of doubt. I want to be somewhere else.

I want to say goodbye to my family.

Sentimentality was among the first things the Ornu had drilled out of him. Don't think about family: think about your career. Don't think about love: occupy yourself with duty. Don't give into weakness: you are obligated to be strong. For the empire. For the system. Vassals are nothing more than fodder for the machine.

If he was meant to die, then at the very least, his last act could be the ultimate form of defiance. It would be his reeducation. The Ornu could take his liberty and even his life, but they could never own him. Never again.

He lurched to his feet. "Let me know if something changes," he barked.

Bina's eyebrows rose. "Bill?" she asked. "Where are you going?"

"Where I'm needed," he said. He strode to the hatch, turning his back on the screens, on Pertinax, on the whole bloody war that had chased them across sectors.

He was only a few corridors away when he ran, quite literally, into his mother. Miriam had her arm looped through

Gordon's. Her face was pale and pan-icked, but Bill's eyes were drawn to his father. Gordon stood upright, his chin lifted, his narrow frame reinforced with defiance.

"I'm not going to let them take you, Billy," he announced. "They won't do to you what they did to me. I told Miri she needs to hide you..."

"I'm sorry," Miriam said. "I've been trying to explain to him that you're busy, and that you're not a boy anymore. I don't know how much he understands, but he insisted on coming to find you."

"I understand plenty," Gordon insisted. He turned back to Bill. His eyes, usu-ally unfocused and empty, blazed with clarity. "Every day. Every single day, I thought of you both. While they tortured us. While they starved us. While they de-nied us water and interrupted our sleep. Always, I thought of you. Both of you." Gordon's jaw tensed and relaxed. His throat bobbed. "The only thing that got me through was...this. Seeing you again. I missed you."

Bill took a step forward and threw both arms around his father. He was so frail that Bill was afraid the old man would fall apart under his hands if he wasn't careful.

"I missed you, too, Dad," he whispered.

Gordon went slack in his grip. He patted Bill's back with a weak hand. When they pulled apart, his eyes had clouded over again. "Billy?" he asked.

"It's me, Dad." He managed a smile even though he had to fight the trembling in his lips to make them curve upward. "It's me."

"You got big, Billy." Gordon pulled away. "Sorry to bother you. You've got better things to do, Miriam always says..."

"I don't." Bill took his arm. "I really don't. Come on, let's go back to the bridge."

He stepped between them, looping one arm through Miriam's and the other through Gordon's, and led them both back onto the bridge. Ridding and Norder exchanged a surprised glance at the sight of civilians, but Keating waved to Miriam, and Bina nodded in greeting.

Gordon almost tripped over his own feet when he saw the battle unfolding outside. He pointed a shaking finger at the images. "Is this...real?"

"Sure is." Bill sat in the command chair and waved for his parents to sit as well. Miriam helped Gordon lower himself onto the lip of the dais, then sat beside him, arm in arm. "We've taken the war to the Imperium, just like you taught me. Just like gramps taught both of us."

Gordon nodded his approval, his eyes fixed on the screens. "Good work. Very good work, Billy."

Bill licked his lips before he added, "I'm...not sure we're going to win."

Gordon exhaled sharply. "Better to fight and lose than to accept defeat from the outset. I'm proud of you, Billy."

Pertinax's ship loomed large on the screens. The Ornu would try to board and retake the ship. Even if Val and the other avatars refused to cooperate with them, it would be too late for humanity.

We had a good run, Bill thought. If nothing else, I'm proud we made it this far.

The bridge went perfectly still. The images on the screens froze. Bill frowned at them and scrubbed his hand over his eyes, trying to make sense of what he was seeing. Had the displays glitched out thanks to some new damage to the ship?

When he lowered his hand, he was sitting in the Holograph and Pint.

Val sat at his usual spot along the bar. Apart from that, the room was empty. The lights were dim, as if they had wandered into the bar after hours. The street beyond the mullioned windows was still—empty except for a few flakes of falling snow.

"Please tell me this isn't the afterlife," he groaned.

Val cocked his head. "Would that be so bad?"

Bill lifted one shoulder. "How long are we going to sit here?"

"We just have another, oh, let me see." Val fished a pocket watch out of the vest of his coat and flipped it open to examine the face. "One fourteenth of a second to kill."

"And then what?"

"The mission ends," Val said simply.

Bill wasn't as distraught as he thought he'd be. Maybe it was like taking a bullet, in those liminal seconds before pain set in—before the body fully registered the extent of the damage. You failed every-one, he thought, but what more could he have done? He'd given everything he had. He'd held nothing back.

Gordon was right. There was no shame in that.

"I know how to pass the time," Val said, tucking his pocket watch away. "There's something you might like to know." He looked Bill up and down, resting one arm casually against the bar as he did, his features softened by the dim light. "The SRJ drive is almost installed. It'll be operational in..." He reached for the pocket watch again.

Bill whipped out a hand to catch the other man's wrist. "Wait, what? It...worked?"

"Oh, yes." Val fluttered his eyelashes dramatically. "Yes, it did."

Bill's lassitude evaporated. All the emotions he hadn't felt when Val implied their imminent demise coursed through him and set his heart racing. We're going to live. We're going to live.

They'd made it.

"You did that on purpose," he croaked.

Val chuckled. "It's possible. So, would you like to plan our next moves? We've only got one twenty-sixth of a second left, and this is going to take some coordination."

* * *

No time at all had passed for the bridge crew when Bill sat up in the command chair. His time in the sim had taken less than the span of a breath, but the whole plan had been laid out in detail. Val had agreed to run the weapons displays while Bill issued commands in real time and made sure that the rest of his crew, along with the last surviving Roughback ship, knew what was expected of them.

The officers jumped when Bill whipped out his arm, apparently without provocation, switched on the coms, and began shouting orders.

"Ridding," he said, pointing to the lieutenant. "Hail one of the Crendelen ships. Channel 224." He pointed to the screen as he spoke, indicating the one warship that had broken off from the rest. Its name was painted on the hull in Ornu lettering, but he'd spent enough years in the reeducation programs to know that it was called the Everwell.

"O…kay?" Ridding's face pinched in confusion.

Bill didn't stop to explain himself. There was no time. "Al," he barked into the com. "You there?"

"I hear you, Captain." Al sounded like he'd been through a lot. "We can't hold them back much longer—"

"You don't have to. Tell your people to hold onto something or lock their boots in. Now." He flipped channels. "Tubes, do you hear me?"

"Yes, sir."

"When I give the signal, cut the gravity fields and flush the atmo from the shipyard."

"Yes, sir...?"

There was no time to explain the full scope of the plan. Flip. "Tull, are you still with me?"

"Yes, Captain." Like the rest of them, Tull sounded defeated.

"Pull back to dock with one of the warships. It's called the Everwell. You can hold your fire, but I need you to stay close to the shipyard." He must be almost out of time; Val had ordered the drones to fall back to the ship's interior. As soon as they were safely aboard, it would be time to test their new drive.

"You want me to dock with an enemy ship?" the Roughback asked in that slow, deliberate way.

"It's not the enemy anymore," he said. "But Pertinax won't know that. Just trust me, okay…brother?"

There was a pause that felt eternal, given the urgency of the situation. "As you say, brother," Tull said at last.

Ridding looked up from the com controls. One of his eyes was twitching. "Captain, I've hailed the Everwell. Splat answered."

"Perfect," Bill said. "Patch him through."

"How did you know that?" Ridding muttered, even as Splat's face popped up on the screen.

Bill did a double-take. "Is that a dead Ornu behind you, Lamprey?"

Splat twisted around to look over his shoulder. A frisson of pain crossed his

features. "Guess so," he said indifferent-
ly.

Bill nodded. "Listen, I need you to stick close to the shipyard. Al and whoever's still alive there are going to need a lift, and Tull's bringing his asteroid to you. Gather them up as soon as Tubes finish-es flushing the trash off the shipyard."

Splat licked his lips. "If Tull's coming to us, who's going to cover our backs? Per-haps you haven't noticed, but we have just a few enemies out there."

On the arm of the command chair, a small light burned green: Val's sign that the drones were restored. "We are," Bill said.

He wasn't sure what to expect from the SRJ drive. He'd imagined that it would feel like the old carnival ride he'd ex-perienced only once, when he and a few classmates had been granted leave to visit an amusement park. He expect-ed his stomach to churn as the Omega jumped, and for his head to bobble on his neck when it stopped.

Instead, the ride was unbelievably smooth. One minute, they were bellied up to Shipyard 83. The next, they were on the far side of the fleet.

"What on Earth was that?" Norder leapt to his feet. A disbelieving smile illuminated his usually grim features.

"The surge drive," Bill said conversationally. He caught Bina's eye and grinned. "If you'll excuse me, I'll be with Val. You know how to reach me." He closed his eyes and slid into simspace as naturally as breathing.

"Down to twelve enemy ships," Val announced. "I'm going to lead them on a merry chase for a bit. Get them away from Al and the others."

Bill ran the pad of his thumb over his lips and smiled to himself. "Save Pertinax for last. Would it be awfully petty of me to send him a cheeky communique? Tell him to surrender immediately, or I'll kill him?"

Val wrinkled his nose. "Bill, I think you know better than to make promises you have no intention of keeping. If he did surrender, would you accept?"

Bill waved the thought away. "Nah, good point. Let's use him to send a message to the Emperor instead. Can you imagine how irritated he'll be when he finds out we've killed a whole shipload of his supposedly untouchable subjects?"

"It will send a message," Val intoned. "One that will reverberate through every corner of the empire."

"And one that'll make him angry enough to hunt us to the ends of the universe."

"That was always inevitable, Bill. This is not a fight you can outrun forever." Val paused for a moment, the embodiment of intense concentration. On the virtual display, Omega jumped again and changed angles, targeting more of the warships, including the last of the Jackal gunships.

"Pretty impressive," Bill said. "You can't even feel it."

"You can't," Val corrected. "The jump puts intense strain on the ship's superstructure. On top of that, the drive was not designed for a ship this size. We cannot jump indefinitely, and these short-range jumps require complicated calculations to ensure that we don't smash into anything in our path." He rubbed his temples. "Put quite simply, it hurts."

Bill grimaced. "Sorry, I didn't realize."

"It's bearable," Val assured him. "And I expect the calculations will become easier with practice. In the meantime, we should hurry. The third wave of enemy warships is on the way, and our forces are depleted."

They jumped once more. Bill breathed a sigh of relief as Pertinax's warship was blasted into oblivion by an overly vigorous barrage of Hailstorm-fire.

"Someone was holding a grudge," he teased.

Val looked amused. "If you're referring to your grudge, I'm sorry to inform you that we identified small ship traffic fleeing that warship. It's almost certain that Pertinax was no longer aboard."

"He ran away," Bill choked out. "That slippery little—we have to get—"

"No," Val said firmly. "We do not have time. And as you yourself said, the destruction of the warship itself will be enough to send a message."

Omega moved back toward Shipyard 83 under its own power this time. Small bits of debris pinged off the shields as they went.

The shipyard's atmo was flushed, and the surviving Marines and militia were already bundled into the Everwell, along with Tull and his little crew of Roughback soldiers. Val held their position until the Everwell slid into Omega's vast cargo bay.

And then, just as the third wave of the Imperium's warships entered their sector, they made one final jump.

Chapter Ninety-Eight

Lieutenant James Ridding

What Ridding really wanted was sleep. In light of their recent battle, he settled for instant coffee.

Tull and Rula sat side by side at one end of the table, representing the sole surviving Roughback crew. Funny Bone, Splat, and Termite were still in the medbay, leaving only Tubes, Guns, and Al to represent the much-expanded Marine team.

Bina was directly across from Ridding, and kept casting him fretful glances. He mostly ignored her. Whatever else he thought of her, they were on the same side. Besides, he wanted to trust her. Paranoia was exhausting.

Bill, Norder, and Keating rounded out their quorum. Miriam had been invited, but had gracefully declined. She and Gordon were back in their new quarters near the bridge; Bill had insisted on keeping them close.

"So." Bill steepled his fingers. "It seems clear the Ornu will attack Kotbulo. They know the Confluence sent ships with us to Terraco, and they were already planning to render the species Defunct. We owe it to our allies to defend—"

"No," Tull grunted.

Bill paused, obviously bewildered by the response. "No? Wasn't that the whole point of this alliance?"

Tull shook his head. The other captain, Rula, kept her eyes downcast. She had hardly spoken a word since she arrived on Omega. The rest of her crew had done the same.

"We already discussed this," Tull said. "The Confluence agreed to fend for themselves in the belly of Kotbulo. Your offer of aid is both appreciated and anticipated, but we have survived before. They want humanity to be free to find its new home...and to make a stand against the Imperium, when the time comes."

Bill shook his head. "When did you even discuss this?"

"I told you. In the Confluence." Tull breathed deeply and closed his eyes. "We also agreed to send our surviving warships with you on this mission, but the All-sire had other plans."

Bina leaned forward. "But the Roughbacks could be facing a fate similar to humanity's. Maybe even worse, without Omega to rescue anyone."

"And what would you have us do?" Tull asked. "Crowd onto Omega?"

"We could at least—" Bina began.

Rula looked up. "It is done. Your species put their lives on the line for us. It is only fitting that we return the favor."

An uncomfortable silence descended over their group. Bina fidgeted in her seat, clearly disturbed by this turn of events.

I forgive her, Ridding realized. She really has changed, and I forgive her. He felt the relief in every muscle of his body, as if a poison had been drawn out of him.

Bill slapped his palm on the table. "If that's what you've decided, I accept it. We'll do our best to honor the gift you've given us. Now, all we have to do is figure out where we're going next."

"Another habitable world, obviously," Guns said.

"But with enough resources that we can build a life for ourselves," Keating said.

Bill nodded. "I believe Omega has a suitable candidate in mind."

"Oh." Bina placed both palms on the table and sat up straight. Her dark eyes were wide with understanding. "Oh. Of course he does. And I bet I know exactly where he has in mind."

Epilogue

Former Signifier Nonus

News of the humans' triumph had reached him through the guards. Nonus was reluctant to gloat too much, although he would have been happy to spit in his uncle's eye when he heard the first of the rumors.

See? That's what you get when you tangle with Bill Henderson. He ruined me, and now, he's ruined you. Let's see what Emperor Albus thinks of you, now that all your advice has failed him...

He'd had days in which to compose a lengthy speech taunting his uncle's downfall. Much to his chagrin, however, Philo had not arrived. The speech went wasted, despite its many artful and poignant turns of phrase. Nonus eventually jotted it down in the margins of one of the few books he was still permitted.

His most recent revision had kept him distracted long past the usual dinner hour. The angle of the sun slanting through the tiny window, set high on the otherwise featureless wall, was his first hint that something was amiss.

"Hello!" He abandoned his scribblings and went to rattle the bars of his cell. "Have you forgotten me? Prisoners still need to be fed, you know...I've memorized my rights."

If he had to press the issue, he doubted there was a single magistrate on Lindinis who would hear him out, but he might very well go mad if he considered the terms of his confinement too closely. He shook himself against the bars again. "Hello!"

The rattle of metal echoed down the hall and died away to silence.

The stillness was so absolute, it made his scales itch. It wasn't unusual for him to taunt the guards, but they always answered eventually. Sometimes with mockery, sometimes with a beating, but never with total indifference.

The skin beneath his scales itched. Surely they wouldn't just abandon him. But then again, why not? What more could he offer them if Bill Henderson had slipped away once again? Pertinax and Philo had been unwelcome visitors, but at least they cared enough to despise him. If they had been imprisoned or executed, who was left to consider what became of him? His mother? She'd cut all family ties, that much was clear.

"Hello? Can you hear me?" Nonus pressed his face between the bars. "Listen, ah...I've been thinking, I might know something useful. Something that Emperor Albus will really want to hear."

The longer he went without being answered, the harder his heart struck against his ribs.

"I have insight into Bill Henderson," he called. "I just remembered it, and it's terribly important. See, when he was first talking to Omega—"

"Omega?"

Nonus jerked away from the bars and slithered back. "Th-that's what I said."

"You know of Omega?" The voice was unfamiliar, and it was accented enough to indicate that it didn't belong to a native speaker. Nonus shuddered and tried to get his breathing under control.

He did his best to channel his uncle's easy confidence. "Of course I do. I was there when it was discovered, after all."

"When it was reclaimed, you mean. You were not the first to find it." Steps sounded in the corridor: not the whisper of scales over metal, but the strike of booted feet. What in the name of the Emperor was a biped doing on Lindinis?

If it was Bill Henderson, Nonus was going to lose his mind. He was very close to doing so regardless.

The figure stepped into his line of sight. He was tall and lean, built rather like a human but with much more elegant lines. His eyes were blue all the way through: no white, no pupil. He leaned against the bars of Nonus' cell and peered in at him, the way people stared at caged beasts in a zoo.

"You must be Nonus."

"I am." The former Signifier drew himself upright. "Although I can't begin to guess who you are."

"No, I suppose you wouldn't. But it seems we have a common enemy." The man examined his hands, which Nonus hadn't realized were stained with blue-green blood. Ornu blood. "I am unfamiliar with Bill Henderson, but I know Omega...oh, very well."

His instincts warned him away, but the predatory note in the stranger's voice drew Nonus forward. "You do?"

"Intimately. Furthermore, I know where it is going. Perhaps you and I could help one another." Those blue eyes flicked upward to fix on Nonus' face. There was a brighter circle of blue at their center where the pupils should have been. They were not ordinary eyes, and Nonus found himself wondering whether they saw more than the normally visible wavelengths—whether they could perceive something more personal that he was unprepared to reveal.

"Because you don't know the captain?" Nonus guessed.

"We have not yet crossed paths, but I am most eager to meet him."

"I can help," Nonus wheedled. "Captain Henderson served under me for years. Together, we can—" He stopped short, uncertain of the stranger's goal. Whatever it was, Nonus would help him achieve it, if it meant getting a chance at revenge.

"We can destroy Omega," the stranger finished.

"Yessss," Nonus breathed. His sibilant note of anticipation slipped through.

"Let us shake on it." The being reached through the bars. "Is this common among your people?"

Nonus eyed the blood-stained nails. "It is." He extended one of his own arms. "But if we are to make a pact, I must know your name."

The being smiled. "Of course. You may call me Teraphim."

Acknowledgments

S cott Bartlett and Joshua James would like to thank the following readers for helping make this project a reality by backing it on Kickstarter:

First of all, we want to thank Chris Evans, who showed amazing support for Eternity's Battleship by pledging at the tier, "Pick Our Brains." In our gratitude, we confer on him the honorary rank and title of Lieutenant Commander, Logistics and Mission Support - a title he himself came up with!

Next, we want to thank these readers, listed in alphabetical order by first name, for backing the Kickstarter at any level. Whether you backed for the eBook or the limited edition hardcover (which was only available through the Kickstarter), we are so very grateful for your support:

Adam Bradley, Adam Roeth, Adel R, Adrian Gibbons, Alan Alsemgeest, Alen D., Alex Grade, Alex Harlequin, Alex K., Alex Kilnear, Alexander J. Hale, Allen G., Alli Flowers, Amos Farrington, Andrew Brough, Andrew Drenner, Andy Anderson, Andy F, Andy Tinkham, Angie Allen, Anonymous Reader, Antti Paavonperä, Arend van 't Oever, Arne Keller, Arthur Payne, asakunotomohiro, Ayron Taylor, B. Klein, Barry Conroy, Bill Ince, Bill Mercer, Bill Paradis, Bill Spicer, Bonnie Kolton, Brad, Bradley Baker, Brandon Hight, Brandon L'Amoureux, Brendan Moylan, Brian Dechant, Brian Demming, Brian F, Brian Griffin, Brian Potter II, Brian T, Britmick, Bruce C. Lunde, Bryce, Brynjulf, C. Dennis Slepak, C. T. Ellis, CallMeBruce, Callum McCa, Carl Floyd, Carl Harris, Carl Spitzer, Cathleen Ann Mairead, Cathy Parsons, Cathy

Valdez, Chad Abbs, Chad Boyer, Chad Walter, Charles E. Chambers, Chase R. R., chesscommands, Chief Hal Day, Chip Orlikowski, Chris Belham, Chris Christoforou, Chris Evans, Chris Glatte, Chris Nicholson, Christian "Mecki" Hejl, Christian K., Christian Meyer, Christine Robinson, Clayton Smith, Cliff Stoltzfoos, Cody A. Jones, Colin Blair, Con, Corey Olney, Corrigan Nyberg, Cyril Dennis, D Schumacher, Dale Thompson, Damon Morton, Dan Abott, Dan Andrews, Dan Balkwill, Dan Crews, Dan Early, Dan Vatamaniuck, Daniel E. Hermany Jr., Daniel R Mabry, Danielle Anderson, Danielle Zeibig, danne77sthlm, David Hamelin, David Holzborn, David Hurley, David Koren, David Landry, David Perry, David Schwartz, David Scoggins, David Smith, David Stainton, David W Handler, Dead Fish Books, Debbie Hayward, Dee Noblett, Dennis McCollum, Dirk Schlobinski, DL James, Doe Bathory, Don Curtis, Donald Wheeler, DonDCajun, Dongyi

Zhuyan, Doug "Kosh" Williamson, Doug Lake, Dr. Albert Franke III, Duncan Dunning, Duncan Wilcox, DVO A fan in Maine, Dylan McFadyen, E.M. Hanzel, Eben, Ellen Sullivan, Elway Scholes, Emily Drake, Eric Ballard, Eric Haegele, Ernie Ridley, Eron Lindsey, Eugene Maher, Evan Ferris, Ewelina Korbal, Fallenzap, Franchesca Caram, Frank Christensen, Frank McKinney, Frank Rosellen, Frank Tesser, Frank Warren, Franziska Tinner, Fred Eugene Linard, Fred Westfall, G. Smith, Gail Powell, Gary D Brackett, Gary Kluepfel, Gary Olsen, Gary Spence, Gene D., Geoff Parker, Gerard D'Orival, GhostCat, Gil Madsen, Glen mat, Glenn Evans, Glenn Shotton, Graeme Nicholson, Graham Dauncey, Graham Mackie, Greg Marbach, GrumpySr, Guy Galluzzo, Guy M. Snodgrass, hackebeilchen, Harold E. Roberts, II, Duke of Sealand, Harry, Heiko Koenig, Herlander Simões, HeyItsDoug, Homer Haulman, Howard Smiley, HwrdStamp, Ian

Carmen, Ian Marsh, Ian McCrowe, In loving memory of Basil Martin, In memory of Millie Walsh, Ingo Lembcke, Hamburg, Ira Baker, Ira Tabankin, Isabella Boudoin, J M Feathers, J R Woolley, J. Barlowe, J. W. Mue, Jörgen Bartosz, Jack Lehman, Jacqueline Rose Seatter, Jacques Levesque, Jaime Zamudio, James A Turner, James Connolly, James Fisher, James McGuire, James Packard, James S Skala Jr, James W. Hazel, Jamie Morrison, Jarrod and Lori Alleman, Jason Bradley, Javier Vega, Javoli, Jay Bee, Jay Roye, Jeff D Maynor, Jeff Murri, Jeff Neely, Jeff Stone, Jeffrey Allen Randorf, Jeffrey L Price, Jem Palmer, Jen Pharo, Jennifer Lin, Jeramy Staub, Jeremy Baucom, Jeroen Klaassen, Jerry Koehr, Jerry Snedeker, Jim Fitzwilliam, Jim H. Holzrichter, Jim Meinen, Joe Ficalora, Joe Loftus, Joel Singer, Joey Tan, John C. Jeffries, John Cindi Delugach, John Coverdale, John 'Doc' Strange, John E Rastorfer Jr, John Kern, John O, John Perreau, John Pope, Jon Mark Hancock, Jordan Silver, Jordan W. H. Aggen, Joseph Jacobi, Joseph Matus, Joseph R. Oxendine, Josh Fry, JT Muraski, JTMHyers, Juan O.M., Juan Paulo Po Panganiban, Judith Anway, Julian Delgado, Julian White, K Shaw, K Stoker, K.R.S., Kaia Kallen Grayson, Kar Kau Cheung, Karen A. Jarman, Karen Heys, Karl & Margaret Kerchief, Katherine McKamey, Kelly McMahon, Ken Checinski, Ken Smalewich, Kenneth Hutchins PhD, Kenneth Lerwick, Kenyon Wensing, Keric, Kevin Miraglia, Kirk Cooper, Kurt Adam, L. Alexander, L. Haymjnd, Landon Bentley, Larry McConville, Laurence G, Lee Grenter, Len Riseley, Leo H Engele, Leonard Therrien, Lewis Greaves, Lewis M Brande, Lia Lahi Trapp, Liam Mulvey, Linda S. Adams, Lola Miller, Lonnie Bristol, Lord Gregory Morris of Kerry, Lorenzo, Lorien Herman, Lt Croome, Luke Lofgren, M.A. Franklin, Machiel van Dijk, Madge Watson, Максим Стоялов DENAMAX, Malcolm Pedel (EarthForever), Maria-Vittoria Telo, Mark Oakley, Mark Zygmond, Marque, Matt Chmura, Matt Rowley, Matthew Halligan, Maximilian Corona, MDB, Meenaz Lodhi, Megan N. Quinn, Melissa T, Michael E. Brunk, Michael Gillon, Michael J Locke, Michael Slobbe, Michael the Horologist, Michal Frackowski Michelle LaCrosse, Mick Barry, Mike, Mike Cody, Mike DeCarlo, Mike Galligan, Mike J Grantham, Mike Miller, Mike Strong, Mike Vance, Mike W. Welch, Milo Ander, Misterdj, MJP, MJP, Morten Vestergaard Pedersen, Mr. Natbar, Mr.Bill, Mr.Kerry.Osborne, N Shepard, N. Scott Pearson, Nathan Blackham, Neil P., Neil Phillips, Neill Silva, Nerino J. Petro, Jr., Nicholas Morine, Nicholas Stephenson, Nicholas Whittington, Nick Niemi, Niki Coppola, Nikkii Thompson, Norma, Norman Byers, oldbikerpete, Page Clark, Paolo Louis Geidt, Pascale, Patrick B, Patrick Fowler, Patrick Hay, Patrick Palm, Patrick Starremans, Paul Grubbs, Paul

M Harmon, Paul Monaghan, Paul Ogle, Paul Petach, Paul S., Paul Smith, Peo Zetterdahl, Per M. Jensen, Peter Hull, Peter Kongstvedt, Peter MacDougall, Peter W. Ortner, Phil "HK" Houseknecht, Phil Shepherd, Philip Stanley, Pierre Menard, pizza lover 2, Positronic Solar, Rónán Kavanagh, Rachel Asbury, Rachel D Golem, Rachel W, Rebecca Andreasen, Regina Garowen, Remington Cloutier, René Nobelen, Rex Bain, Richard E. Lally, Richard Earl, Richard Hakala, Rick, Rik Geuze, Riordon Treylourne, Rob, Rob Kolosky, Rob Rex, Robert "Bob" Hobbs, Robert D. Stewart, Robert M. Burns, Robert Simms, Rodney Haydon, Roger Baune, Roger Clancy, Roger J Collado, Roger Lammey, Rohan Kapoor, Roni Poulsen, Ross Hamilton Pitman, Russell Cheezo, Ryan Hanson, Ryan Mitchell, S. E. Willis, S. G. Campbell, S. Kozawa, Sam Bertolami, Samuel A Rhodes, Scott Auld-Hill, Scott Casey, Scott J. Stringfellow, Scott Licoscos, Scott MacFarlane, Scott Morgan, Scott Stewart, Sean Arredondo, Sean Patrick alexander, Sean Timon, Senthil Kumaran Rajasekaran, Shanon M. Brown, Sharrell R Taylor, Shaun Trewern, Shaun Watson, Shawn Marshall, Sheila Myers Beitler, Sid Doyle, Simon Anthony, Skoogs, Spencer hunts6, Stan Suan, Stephen Tyndall, Steve Barnett, Steve Franklin, Steve Gold, Steve 'Graywolfy' Scott, Steve Simmonds-Townend, Steve Tucker, Steven Lunetta, Steven Michelsen, Stijn Soethout, Stoney, Susan Gallagher, Tania, Tanya C. Forde, MSc, Tanya Yo, Taru Ross, Ted Paxinos, Thlaylie, Thomas and Annie's Dad, Thomas Kimsky, Tim C, Tim G., Tim J., Tim Scott, Timothy C. Linusson, Tina L Hutchins, Tina Scribner, Todd Creitz, Tom "mototom" Külaots, Tom Butcher, Tony Croft, Tony Jackowski, Tony Ripley, Travis Siegel, Trevor Roelfs, Tristram Oliver, Troy Frette, V, Valerie Bartlett, Vance Neff, Velvet Knights, Vic Johnson, Vicente Sobrevilla, Vickie Hall,

W Michael Love, Wade Leibeck, Warren Van Houten, Wayne "Fester" Warren, Wayne E. Merkey, Wayne Heaslip, Wayne Viney, Wes Kullhem, Will Lum Brogdon, Wolfgang Atzl, Wouter Kok, and XO Daniel Burt.

And last but not least, thank you to Tom Edwards for creating such stunning cover art!